Everything I grew up learning was a lie.
The woman who raised me murdered my mother.
Both friend and foe have tried to kill me.
But I won't give up.

Twisting around, Maya toggled her wave gun to sonic levitation mode, pointed it down, and shrieked as the stone floor flew up to greet her. She depressed the trigger a second before slamming into the ground.

The cushion of air produced by the gun slowed her descent. As she landed, her forehead banged against the floor, shooting needle-like pain through her brain. The gun jabbed her in the abdomen.

She lay there, fading in and out, woozy and retching.

A gut feeling compelled her to roll toward and beneath what remained of the terrace. Each time she flipped over, her shoulder throbbed, her neck ached, and she almost passed out.

Stones big and small thudded against the floor space she had vacated. Particle beams rained down, blasting the stones into thousands of tiny pieces.

Too terrified to scream, Maya flung her arms up as debris buried her.

Books in the Beyond Saga

Beyond Cloud Nine
Beyond the Horizon
Beyond Yesterday
Beyond Existence

Other books by Greg Spry

Destalis

Short stories by Greg Spry

Bears in Space
Goodbye, Mars

BEYOND THE HORIZON

THE SECOND BOOK OF THE BEYOND SAGA

GREG SPRY

www.beyondthehorizonbook.com

www.beyondsaga.com

U.S. Copyright Office © 2016 Greg Spry

ISBN-10: 0-9908224-3-5
ISBN-13: 978-0-9908224-3-1

Written by Greg Spry
www.gregspry.com

Published by Beyond Innovation Books
www.beyondinnovationbooks.com

Edited by Sunny Moraine, www.sunnymoraine.com
Proofread by Sophie Logan of Sharper Editing, www.sharperediting.com
Proofread by Richard Lawhern, www.lawhern.org
Overall book cover design by Tobias Roetsch, www.gtgraphics.de
Character designs by Aaron Page, aaronpage.deviantart.com

Printed by CreateSpace, an Amazon Company
Printed in the United States of America
First Paperback Edition Published May 2016
First Edition Updated February 2017, March 2017
Second Paperback Edition Published July 2017

One—Circuitous
Auckland, Earth, May 2265 CE

Maya Davis's eyelids fluttered and opened partway.

Centimeters above her nose, the bedroom clock floated in midair, twirling and doing backflips. Antique ringing exacerbated her pounding headache as the bells atop the clock vibrated. By the time her vision focused, the clock face read 08:01 Solar Standard Time.

"Time to get up and at 'em, Maya," the clock's cheerful voice touted. "The *New Horizons* launch ceremony starts in three hours, fifty-nine minutes."

Still half-asleep, she swatted at the hologram, but her hand passed through it. "Turn off," she mumbled while burying her head under a pillow. Curling up in the fetal position, she hugged a tattered Bio Bear, the stuffed animal her aunt had bought her when she was a kid.

Foggy thoughts of Aunt Brooke both warmed and tensed her body. Brooke had raised Maya following the death of her mother, but a recent spat hadn't left them on the best of terms.

"Disabling alarm." The clock blinked away into nothingness.

She drifted back to slumber.

Maya awoke to pitch blackness. Shivers of panic coursed through her limbs. To this day, she had yet to conquer her childhood fear of the dark.

"Blinds," she called out.

The pixels dimming the windows blinked transparent in rapid

succession. Sunlight pierced the panes, warming her face and calming her nerves. The bright light forced her to squint.

"What time is it?" she mumbled.

Maya activated the displays in her i-cite. The chronometer in the bottom corner of her vision read 10:59.

"Eleven?" Gasping, she sprung upright in bed and regretted it at once. Pain stabbed her temples. She hissed when she touched her clammy forehead.

With a thought, she ran a health scan. A simulation of her body appeared in her i-cite. Animated blood coursed through a lifelike diagram of her circulatory system.

She magnified her brain. Virtual text explained the cause of her headache. *Acetaldehyde penetration of nerve cell membranes?* She sighed. *A hangover? I must've forgotten to flush my system before I went to bed.* With another mental command, she accessed her bioware and instructed the nanotech embedded throughout her body to break down the alcohol in her bloodstream.

"Clock, where are you?"

The hologram materialized in front of her nose.

"Why didn't you wake me?" she asked it.

"You turned me off at eight-oh-one," it said.

"I told you to snooze."

"Nope." Its face showed a vidsim of Maya retreating beneath a pillow. A moan escaped her drooling mouth. "Turn off," it quoted her muttering.

She whipped the blankets aside and slid out of bed. Her head pounded as she stood. "That's not what I meant."

"I'm a clock, not a mind reader."

"Turn off," she snapped. "And this time I mean it."

Projecting big eyes crying oversized tears and a frown, the clock shriveled away into nothingness.

Maya rushed over to the windows, tripping over a pair of mag-skates, and gazed outside.

Stratoscrapers jutted up from the city of Auckland. Mount Eden towered above the bustling metropolis in the background. Two hundred stories below, autocars and rovers zoomed along the streets. A tangled web of sonic tubes stretched every-which-way above the roads, catapulting transport spheres filled with commuters between buildings. Boats and hovercraft skimmed across channels connecting glistening bays.

The thin clouds in the sky twisted and wavered, displaced by a hyperspace vortex. A squadron of Pulsars emerged from the wormhole and rocketed off into the distance. The star fighters burst into shooting stars as air molecules scraped against their force fields.

She felt like a queen up in a tower, surveying her fairy tale domain. Often she daydreamed about the kinds of cities that civilizations on other worlds might build, worlds she intended to visit someday.

But she hadn't time for such indulgences at the moment.

The ceremony starts in an hour. I'll never make it to Triton in time. She plopped down on the edge of her bed, stunned by her uncharacteristic lapse in judgment. *How did I let this happen on the most important day of my life?*

Last night, she had allowed her best friend, Jo, to talk her into seeing a neurosynth band perform at a club on Callisto. Jo hadn't needed to twist her arm very hard, though. The concert had been their last outing in the solar system for the next three years.

I've never been late for anything, and I don't intend to start now.

Maya bit her lip and shot to her feet, determined to make it to the ceremony on time.

Rushing into the bathroom, she splashed cold water on her face. As she lasered her teeth, she hummed one of the songs the band had played and summoned a display cube. The three-dimensional projection materialized near the mirror, tuned to the IntraSolar News channel.

"—is the scene from the Interstellar Expeditionary Force shipyards near the Lassell colony on Triton," an ISN anchorwoman reported live from the scene, "the site of the launch ceremony for *New Horizons.*"

Hundreds of IEF graduates, ISC Defense soldiers, politicians, benefactors, and reporters filtered into the outdoor auditorium behind the reporter. Lake Flammarion sprawled across Triton's landscape, with Neptune hanging above the steep horizon.

"Everyone in the solar system eagerly awaits the launch of humankind's first interstellar starship," the woman continued. "*New Horizons* will travel twenty light years to the Gliese 581 system, where it will make contact with the Penphins, the race of intelligent exobeings whose plea for help SETI detected four years ago. Afterwards, *Horizons* will seek out a habitable exoplanet on which to settle its colonists, the ship's original mission prior to the discovery of the Penphins."

Maya bolted out of the bathroom and threw on her IEF graduate uniform. Ignoring her gurgling stomach, she scampered out the door of her apartment into the hall. As she waited for the next sonic tube sphere, she said a silent goodbye to her apartment. She wouldn't see it again for years.

When the transport sphere arrived on the 187th floor, she boarded it and strapped into one of the chairs. "Phase port," she said.

<Destination: Auckland Intrasolar Phase Port,> the AI said. <Initiating transit. Your well-being is our top priority. Please remain seated with your safety belt fastened at all times. This transport will cease motion if it detects an unfastened belt.>

The sphere slid through a horizontal tube, picking up speed and pressing Maya back into her seat. After dropping straight down a hundred stories, it emerged from inside the apartment complex and entered into another vertical descent along the outside wall of the building.

An energetic shimmering obscured the rumbling clouds out over the ocean. Magnetic fields imposed by weather control satellites in low Earth orbit worked to dissipate the storm and redirect it away from New Zealand.

The sphere slid to a halt at the thirtieth floor and shot off along a tube parallel to the ground. The change in direction jerked her body, bringing the throbbing back to her temples. She instructed her implants to increase production of biocites. The little nanites had her feeling better but far from perfect.

Parks, people, and streets raced past below the sphere's clear exterior at hundreds of kilometers per hour. Fewer vehicles congested the roadways than this time last year. The ease with which the phase portals had allowed people to migrate across the solar system continued to thin the population of planet Earth.

The sphere decelerated and stopped at the phase port. The building resembled an arena-sized spoked wheel. She often imagined a giant man grabbing and spinning it.

Maya checked the time in her i-cite. The mental digits read 11:10 SST. *Fifty minutes to go. I can make it if I hurry.*

As she hopped out of the sphere, a blast of ocean air pummeled her in the face. Her eyes watered, and she sneezed three times. A man and woman near her on the sidewalk turned and raised their eyebrows as if she were a disease-ridden invalid.

Accessing her bioware, she pumped medites carrying antihistamines and other allergy suppressants into her system. The meds would relieve most but not all of her symptoms. Despite the wonders of twenty-third-century medicine, prenatal gene therapy provided the only cure for allergies. Maya cherished the memory of her late mother, but she wished the woman had let the doctors code them out of her genome before birth like a normal parent. Pollen, mold, dust, dogs, cats—the list had no end. Anything that could afflict her sinuses worked them into a tizzy, which was why she had grown up with robots and other gadgets as pets instead of animals.

With the irritation in her nostrils and eyes subsiding, she jogged into the terminal, dodging the throngs of people scurrying toward their destinations. As she ran, she accessed the phase port's SolNet app, which calculated the fastest route to Triton. Her itinerary included connecting stops at Luna, Venus, Vesta, and Callisto. The more direct Earth–Mars–Callisto route wouldn't align for another few weeks. Her ancient ancestors had once believed the position of the planets affected a person's fate. *They might be right today.*

She reached the entrance to one of the spokes, which stretched out from the central hub. This particular corridor led to the phase portal to Luna. A line of over one hundred people stood at the security checkpoint to the gate.

A stocky attendant paced up and down the economy line, bellowing instructions. "Step into the DNA scanner one at a time, please. While you wait, please turn your attention to the cubes on your left. The short, instructional vidsim will explain the differences you'll encounter during your time on Luna."

Maya thanked the stars she didn't have to wait in the economy line and rushed over to the guard at the commuter fast-track checkpoint. The woman glanced at the *New Horizons* mission patch on Maya's uniform. Raising an eyebrow questioning what she was still doing on the planet, the guard waved her into the scanner arch.

Purple beams leapt from the arch, caressing her from boots to scalp.

<IntraSolar Commonality citizen identity confirmed,> the port AI said. <Enjoy your trip to Luna, Ensign Maya Davis.>

The moment the attendant on the opposite side of the arch waved her through, Maya broke into a sprint down the corridor. A four-meter-diameter wormhole with a surface like a distorted mirror hovered up ahead. The salmon-pink hue of hyperspace loomed inside the vortex. For some reason, it looked like an overgrown fishbowl to her. Scientists and engineers had done wonders to suppress the debilitating effects of hyperspace, but her eyes still crossed when looking straight at the strange shapes and distortions.

<Please keep moving.> The AI's instructions echoed from speakers embedded in the walls. <Don't stop except in an emergency. Prepare for momentary reduced visibility and a significant reduction in weight. Luna possesses one sixth of the Earth's gravity, which affects mobility.>

She dashed through the portal and emerged on the other side a second later. Crossing the 385,000 kilometers to Earth's moon was as easy as stepping through a doorway. Only a mild bout of disorientation resulted from the trip, which she quickly shook off.

The strain on her muscles and bones lifted. She had plenty of experience in low-gravity environments due to her IEF training, but anyone unfamiliar with walking on Luna might have panicked, stumbled, or fallen. Travelers in the economy line had to remain seated in a sonic tube sphere during their crossing.

Reaching the end of the corridor, she emerged into the hub of the phase port in Armstrong City. Panoramic windows hung meters over the heads of the lumbering businessmen, children, and tourists in the courtyard. A half-crescent Earth reflected sunlight beyond the panes. Stars twinkled against the backdrop of space overhead.

She slowed her pace for fear of bumping into the people hurrying through the terminal. They focused their attention on the readouts in their net specs and i-cites rather than on their surroundings. Few seemed to appreciate the fact that they had passed through a gateway in the heavens that had whisked them to another realm faster than the speed of light.

The mere thought of traveling to other worlds gave Maya goosebumps. As a kid, she had built toy starships out of metablocks and constructed model civilizations for them to visit. One particular colony inhabited by talking turtles had sprouted up on Aunt Brooke's bed. Her aunt had gyrated with fury when a race of evil bug creatures had attacked the colony and launched a powerful doomsday weapon into the core of the bed-planet, ripping apart the mattress.

After passing through the next portal, the pull on Maya's body increased to ninety percent standard gravity. Yellow-tinted white sunlight pierced the dome encasing the phase port on Landis, the floating city within Venus's atmosphere. Puffy yellow clouds of carbon dioxide and sulfuric acid drifted along outside the dome. The clouds buoyed up the inflatable platform on which the city rested.

She loved the idea of the veritable castle in the sky, one which hovered at the right altitude to provide one atmosphere of pressure. She imagined herself kicking back, lounging on one of the puffy clouds, and relaxing, even though the idea was silly.

The city's architects and engineers had fashioned the terminal floor out of clear nanoplastic, giving her the sense of walking on air. Every now and then, she stepped over a break in the clouds and caught a glimpse of Venus's scorching surface. A girl she passed knelt and swiped her fingers over a section of the see-through flooring, magnifying a pair of steaming rocks on the ground.

Maya darted through the farmer's market at the center of the terminal. Booths with piles of mangos, avocados, and every imaginable fruit and vegetable lined her path. The produce hyper-grown on Landis was the city's chief export. Pumps siphoned the surrounding carbon dioxide into hydroponic greenhouses, allowing plants to flourish far more than they ever could have on Earth.

Pangs of hunger stabbed her, courtesy of the smells of the market. The aroma of onions, garlic, and ginger teased her senses. She wiggled her nose to keep from sneezing.

She slowed to a jog and reached for the top pear on a cart overflowing with them. The timing of her grab proved impeccable, but removing the top pear disturbed those below it.

A landslide ensued.

The nostrils belonging to the owner of the cart flared.

Maya skidded to a halt, pivoted, and dove back toward the pile. Landing on one shoulder with a thud, she reached out to catch the falling pears. The avalanche ended with her lying on her back, holding eleven pieces of fruit. Not one struck the ground. *Whew. No casualties.*

Hopping to her feet, she accessed the credit immersive in her i-cite and paid the owner's virtual cash register for all eleven. After grabbing two for the road, she donned an apologetic smile and backpedaled toward her destination.

The owner shook his head and mouthed the words, "Good luck out there."

Maya slurped her fruit and reached the next portal without further incident.

Her chronometer read 11:36 SST during her sonic tube ride through the hollowed-out core of the second largest planetoid within the asteroid belt, Vesta. Engineers had situated Vesta's phase portals at different locations on the asteroid rather than in a centralized port, forcing her to cross from one side to the other. Maya marveled at the mining operation. Drilling rigs the size of mansions bored into the interior walls of the cavern. Smaller bots zoomed to and from the rigs, delivering fuel and carrying away chunks of ore.

The transport sphere passed the central refinery and colony complex, which resembled a gargantuan metal bee hive. Mammoth support beams jutted out from the hive and connected to the walls. The hive's diameter had increased by tens of meters since the last time she had taken this route. Maya did a quick SolNet search. At the present rate of construction, the hive would consume Vesta in fifty years.

At 11:43 SST, she set foot on Callisto.

The attendant at the end of the portal from Vesta handed her a respirator.

Donning the breather, Maya sucked in concentrated oxygen and bounded out into the open-air terminal within New Galilei.

Skyscrapers towered above the previously-domed city, reaching for a Jupiter five times as big as Luna in Earth's sky. A thin layer of breathable air shrouded the moon thanks to the hyper-terraforming effort. The atmosphere had reached the minimum pressure levels needed to support a human body without a space suit, but the air density had a ways to go before it could provide comfortable breathing levels for visitors. Every now and then, she lunged past an acclimated resident not wearing a breather.

Jupiter blocked the sun at the moment, shrouding New Galilei in darkness. The lack of illumination raised the hairs on Maya's neck. Fortunately, the lights of the bustling colony kept things from getting too dark. Music reached her ears from the bar and casino district beyond the terminal. The neurosynth band she had seen with Jo had played in one of the clubs in the district. She had vague recollections of stumbling out of the place only hours ago.

Out of the corner of her eye, she saw someone racing toward her.

She twisted her hips in time to stare down a teen skating at her on a pair of mag-blades.

Unable to stop, the boy drilled her in the midsection and drove her into the pavement. The impact might've dislocated one of her vertebra on Earth, but Callisto's thirteen-percent gravity saved her spine from anything more than discomfort.

His left mag-blade flew off his foot. It skidded across the pavement and struck a roving vending machine with a clank.

Wincing, Maya sat up and pulled the boy up with her. "Are you okay?" she asked, adjusting her breather.

The boy needed a minute to catch his breath. He wasn't wearing a mask, meaning he likely called one of the colonies home. "I think so." He raised his net specs, checked his body for injury, and bounded to his feet. "Gosh, I'm so sorry, lady, but—whoa, aren't you . . . ?"

She rose to her feet.

The animation on the front of his T-shirt depicted a man raising two fingers in a gesture of peace. An artist's rendition of a Penphin stood next to the man, waving eight-fingered hands beneath its flipper-wings, or flings. Its smiling snout bobbed up and down.

The boy had no doubt received the shirt from community service workers at a local revitalization center. The ISC couldn't hand out *New Horizons* merchandise fast enough.

"That's right." She smiled. "I'm IEF."

The boy fidgeted, unable to stand still. "You guys are so fused. Is it true you have scientifically-enhanced superpowers?"

"Well . . ." She bit her lip and tapped a finger against her cheek. "I do have cybernetic implants driven by the latest nanotech. They allow me to interface with SolNet, control my physiology, react faster, and live longer. I suppose you could call those superpowers."

"Too fused . . ."

A reminder blinked within her i-cite. *Ten minutes left. Crap! I'll never get to the Triton portal before noon, unless . . .* "Hey, I'll make you a deal. If you let me borrow your blades, I'll bring you back a souvenir from the mission."

The boy nodded like a bobblehead doll.

"Great," she said. "What's your name?"

"It's Caden. Caden Fisher."

She mind-linked with his specs and sent him her virtual address.

"Wow, thanks, Maya." Caden pulled the mag-blade off his right foot and handed it to her.

"Don't mention it." She rushed over to the left blade. Picking it up, she took a seat on a bench near a fountain.

As she stuffed her feet into each boot, they conformed to the contours of her feet. Childhood memories of Aunt Brooke taking her mag-skating flooded her mind. Her aunt had flashed one of her rare smiles when Maya had first learned to keep her balance.

The memory warmed her heart.

When she thought of the "C" her aunt had given her in her flight simulation class, the warmth ignited and burned in her chest. Maya tensed in anger. The grade had bumped her down to IEF salutatorian.

She shoved thoughts of the unfair transgression aside and focused on getting to the ceremony on time.

In one fluid motion, Maya hopped to her feet while interfacing with the blades. Hyper-conducting magnets pushed against the pavement, keeping her centimeters above it. Her knees wobbled, but years of experience helped her keep her balance.

She pushed off and zipped along through the phase port. The crowds limited her speed, but she made much better time than she would have on foot.

"Hey, watch where you're going," a woman shouted.

A man pointed at a floating PEDESTRIANS ONLY sign. "They don't allow blading in the terminal."

Ten meters from the checkpoint to the Triton portal, a disgruntled mass of travelers stood huddled together, elbow to elbow.

I should've realized the gate would be backed up with people trying to get to the ceremony. Still, most everyone should be there by now. It shouldn't be this bad.

<The Phase Port Association apologizes for the inconvenience caused by the malfunction.> The port AI's voice echoed throughout the concourse. <We anticipate the technical difficulties will be corrected momentarily. Please be patient.>

"Excuse me," she said, pushing through the crowd. "IEF coming through." She shoved her way to the guard at the fast-track gate. "What's the problem?"

"There's a glitch in the hyperspace navigation software." The man yawned. "They installed longer range generators last week, new-fangled models capable of reaching all the way to Earth. Apparently, Einstein has yet to work out all the bugs."

Maya bit her lip at the reference to her uncle, Professor Kevin Sommerfield. Uncle Kevin had invented the faster-than-light phase drive almost two decades ago, a feat that had earned him the nickname "Modern Einstein." Now, as director of the Solar Science Society, final responsibility for the vast network of intrasolar phase portals fell to him.

"Let me through," she said.

"There's nowhere to go until it's fixed."

She noticed a man entering an open service hatch in the corridor beyond the scanner arch. "I might be able to help the repair technicians."

The guard scratched his hairless dome. "What can you do?"

Pointing to a patch on her uniform, she said, "I have an engineering degree in starship operations. I know a thing or two about wormhole theory and phase drives."

"I'm not supposed to let unauthorized personnel enter the generator control room."

Her mental clock read 11:55 SST. *Five minutes to go. So close!*

She played her trump card, the one she loathed using. "You know who my uncle is, right?" Mind-linking with the guard's earpiece, she transmitted her ISC citizen profile. The profile proved her relation to her aunt's husband, Director Sommerfield. "I'd hate to tell him one of his port officials—badge number 80352—was responsible for delaying the launch of humankind's first interstellar starship."

The guard swallowed. "I guess it couldn't hurt to let you lend a hand."

"I appreciate it." Pulse racing, Maya leapt into the scanner arch, submitted to the violet light, and rushed into the control room.

A technician sat at a control station, swiping her fingers through one of a dozen angry red cubes. A second tech stood behind the first with his arms folded. Both of their brows remained creased.

"Have you tried reinstalling the OS?" Maya blurted out.

Both techs flinched at her intrusion.

The first tech stared at her. "Who the hell are you?"

"IEF engineer." She left out the recent-graduate-with-little-to-no-practical-experience disclaimer, a trivial distinction. "I thought I'd see if I could lend a hand."

After glancing at her colleague, the first tech answered her question. "An OS restore would take hours. We're trying to pinpoint the issue, resolve it, and get the system back online sooner rather than later."

"It could take a long time to manually track down the problem. Performing a non-destructive restore of the OS should bring the system back up in thirty seconds, tops."

"True," the second tech said, "but when the system comes back up, it'll spend a couple hours running the preliminary startup sequence."

"Right, so bypass startup and jump straight into operational mode."

The first tech shook her head. "I wouldn't advise skipping the safety and endpoint calibration checks."

Maya tapped her foot. Three minutes remained. "Yes, but if you skip the standard startup protocol and bring the system back online, the main AI becomes available. It can retroactively identify the issue and perform the startup checks in a matter of seconds." *That's how I aced my academy training sim, at least.*

Sticking out his lower lip, the second tech said, "I think she's right."

The first tech swayed her head back and forth in contemplation. "You may be on to something, but if we skip endpoint calibration, we'll need to run diagnostics to verify the expected destination. Otherwise, people could end up walking into solid rock or adrift in space."

Maya's knees bounced as if she needed to use the restroom—and now that she thought about it, she did. "No need. The Lassell colony phase port should be programmed as the default endpoint, and a restart will default to the default endpoint."

The techs blinked at one another and nodded.

"Bypass startup calibration and restore the OS," the first tech ordered the auxiliary AI.

<That procedure is not recommended,> the backup AI said. <Are you certain you wish to proceed?>

The techs looked at Maya.

"Yes!" she yelled.

"Do it," the first tech said.

<Restoring operating system,> the backup AI said.

Every display cube fizzled into nothingness. The plasma strips on the ceiling dimmed. Thirty excruciating seconds passed.

Green cubes popped into existence. The distant whir of the portal generator shook the room with mild vibrations.

Maya popped her head out into the corridor. The wormhole had returned. *Yes!* Her chronometer showed less than a minute to go.

Propelled by pride and giddiness, she sprinted toward the portal. *Another impossible feat accomplished!*

Behind her, she heard one of the techs yell, "Hey, wait—"

Hyperspace consumed her.

Lunging out of the portal, she bolted through the corridor and out onto the phase port concourse.

She collided with a startled woman.

The woman fell backwards. Maya recoiled but kept her balance. Cold liquid splashed her in the face and chest, soaking her uniform and chilling her.

The woman dropped her soda cup, which hit the ground at the same instant as her. The animated label on the cup read L&P, short for Lemon and Paeroa, the national soft drink of New Zealand.

Twirling around, Maya saw the wormhole in the corridor behind her shrink and disappear.

Her knees buckled. Both her shoulders drooped.

She collapsed onto her butt and stared at the overturned cup, not knowing whether to laugh at the irony, weep in defeat, or kick and scream at the stars.

Picking up the cup, she refastened the lid and handed it to the disheveled woman on the ground next to her.

Maya lay back on the floor of the Auckland phase port and tuned out the commuters gathering around her.

Two—Malcontent
Mars, May 2265 CE

Frowning, Brooke Davis-Sommerfield studied a simulated construct of the planet Uranus within her fighter's augmented reality. The gas giant's aquamarine clouds of methane, split down the middle by a vertical ring system, gave the celestial sphere the look of polished marble. She couldn't distinguish the virtual setting from reality, a fact that both impressed and depressed her. As lifelike as the sim appeared, she yearned for the actual experience.

Seventeen years ago, UN Secretary-General Danuwa Ajunwa, now the ISC chancellor, had revoked her commission and pilot's license for taking the phase fighter prototype to save her niece. Brooke hadn't flown a real spacecraft since crash-landing on Europa, and the loss of her dream continued to gnaw away at her.

With a sigh, she resigned herself to another day as a civilian flight instructor.

Brooke ordered her support AI to open a channel to the squadron of Pulsars holding formation behind her. "On the first day of each semester, I observe the same time-honored tradition. I want each of you to attack me, all at once."

"She's not serious," Mackenzie stammered. Every class Brooke taught seemed to have a student who stammered. "Is she?"

"You got me," Owen said, his voice cracking.

Declan snorted. "It's ten against one. We'll blank her, no problem."

Brooke cracked a hint of a smile at her pupils' reactions.

With a mental command, she engaged the afterburners on her PF-5C Pulsar and dove toward Uranus. Signals sent from her headset to her nervous system tricked her body into experiencing the acceleration. Holographic gravgel immersed her virtual flight armor in the rendered cockpit, offering only aesthetic protection against the artificial g-force. Most people couldn't distinguish the state-of-the-art sim from reality, but it insulted Brooke's senses and only heightened her nostalgia for the old days. "Any pilot who blanks me gets an automatic 'A' for the course."

"Have you ever given an automatic 'A,' Instructor Davis?" Mackenzie asked.

Brooke chuckled. The imitation environment may not have compared to the real thing, but it would suffice for her latest massacre.

Three Pulsars rocketed toward her craft from behind. They entered into a pincer formation, surrounding her fighter. Violet particle beams leapt from each assailant. She dodged the blasts with minimal zigzagging and yawned, maintaining her course toward the gas giant.

"She's so damn fast," Owen said. "I'm having trouble tracking her movements." He slowed his fighter and altered course away from Uranus.

Right before the icy clouds of the troposphere swallowed Brooke's Pulsar, she upshifted her craft to hyperspace. The space in front of her fighter tore away and a spherical vortex no bigger than her Pulsar opened, allowing it to slip out of normal space-time. Her phase drive's sensory suppression systems reduced the incomprehensible higher dimension to perceptible but still mind-bending kaleidoscopic distortions. Nebulae, stars, and the planet stretched and twisted as if seen in an array of shattered funhouse mirrors.

She tracked the positions of her prey back in reality. With the help of her support AI, she calculated their trajectories and her point of egress.

Her Pulsar emerged back in real space on the tail of Declan's fighter.

She launched a relativistic seeker at the flare of his craft's exhaust. In the time it took her to blink, the student's fighter exploded and de-pixilated into nothingness.

Launching her Pulsar away from the planet, she chased after Mackenzie and Owen as their craft fled into the rings. She weaved through rocks of water ice, each meters in diameter.

Both fleeing Pulsars disappeared off her mental scope, having upshifted to hyperspace. Rocks flew away from the points at which the spacecraft had exited reality.

Brooke shook her head and checked her phase drive's charge timer.

The ten-second recharge time had elapsed, meaning she could execute another shift at any time.

Reducing speed, she fired her particle cannons, blasting the ice boulders all around her into smaller chunks. Then she reversed course and waited outside the rocky debris field she had created, weapons ready.

Owen's phase fighter reentered normal space in the six o'clock position behind her craft but failed to avoid the shards of ice littering local space. His Pulsar's force field glowed purple and flickered red, overloading on its way to a fiery demise.

Mackenzie's craft materialized in front of Brooke's fighter, clear of the debris field.

More than ready for her, Brooke fired her cannons and launched a pair of seekers. Her ordnance struck the trainee's Pulsar before the girl could react—and passed right through it.

After recalibrating her remote sensors, Brooke identified the Pulsar she had failed to destroy as a false image. *A classic decoy maneuver.* She grinned, knowing Mackenzie could only remain in hyperspace for a matter of seconds or risk draining her craft's antimatter supply.

Her student's Pulsar reappeared in real space on her six.

Squeezing her auxiliary control grips out of habit, Brooke flipped her fighter backwards and barreled straight toward the student fighter at max thrust.

Mackenzie launched an r-seeker at her fighter.

Brooke disabled her craft's wake-limiter and upshifted. Massive gravitational distortions propagated out from the point where she had entered hyperspace.

Mackenzie's r-seeker detonated against the gravimetric wake. The swelling blast consumed her Pulsar and destroyed it.

The trainee shrieked as she met her virtual maker.

Brooke dispatched the other seven students with similar ease.

The combat sim terminated with the explosion of the tenth fighter. The gravgel, cockpit, and stars surrounding her faded away, leaving her sitting at the front of a virtual classroom. The flickering personas of her disheveled pupils sat facing her, each one attending from elsewhere in the solar system.

Standing up from her desk at the front of the room, Brooke paced the aisles between the seats. "I hope each of you learned something from your first flirt with modern space warfare. I throw you into the fire on the first day to give you a sense of reality. It's not all guts and glory. During wartime, combat pilots have an average life expectancy measured in months." She locked stares with Owen. "The lucky ones, anyway."

The skinny eighteen-year-old sank in his seat. If a shell had grown on his back, he would have surely retreated inside it.

They get younger every year.

The whites and blues of Owen's IEF candidate uniform differed from the black and navy outfits of the ISC Defense officers, attire she had worn once upon a time. The class consisted of an even mix of IEF and ISC students—exploratory and military, new and old blood. Supposedly, the lighter colors in the IEF apparel represented the greater purity the human race had achieved in its unification.

Brooke swallowed a disgusted gag at the thought of how the IntraSolar Commonality had formed. She dared not let slip that subversive elements had duped the human race into their blissful but ignorant utopia.

"I'll be blunt," she said. "I'm a tough instructor, and not all of you are cut out to be fighter pilots. It's my job to determine who can operate a Pulsar without killing themselves and destroying trillions' worth of government property."

Returning to the front of the classroom, she whirled on Declan, the first newbie she had killed. "Tell me one thing you did wrong."

"Um . . ." Declan's virtual Adam's Apple gulped. "I guess if I knew, I might not have gotten blanked."

"Well, at least you're honest. And being honest with yourself is critical to staying alive. If you let your ego get in the way—if you believe you're invincible—you're as good as dead."

Wide eyes and twisted frowns met her gaze.

How many times have I ignored my own advice? She kept the thought to herself and plopped down in the seat behind her desk. "Tomorrow, we'll hold an after-action review to analyze what happened, why it happened, and how we can improve. I want each of you to go over today's sim and note three tactical errors you made before next session. Class dismissed."

One by one, her students blinked away into nothingness.

After the last one disappeared, she reached up with her real finger and tapped her headset. The classroom faded from sight, replaced by the extravagant bedroom within the overindulgent mansion she shared with her husband, Kevin Sommerfield, on the outskirts of Red Rock City on Mars. The early morning glare of the sun bathed the room in crimson light.

Brooke whipped off the headset and sank beneath the covers in bed.

Just when she had achieved a semblance of comfort, a sharp pain undulated through one arm, and her body convulsed. She gritted her teeth and fumbled for the auto-syringe on the nightstand. Grabbing hold of it, she stuck her arm and fell back onto the bed. Medicinal nanites raced through her bloodstream, patching the damage to her nervous system caused by former narcotics use—sparking, the junkie gamers had called it back in her day. The injected medites quelled the spasms and hot flashes, and she breathed a sigh of relief.

Charged with raising Maya and barred from flying, she had given up the sparks seventeen years ago. Modern medicine had advanced considerably thanks to the technology the so-called Greys had left behind on Triton and their Kuiper Belt colonies. The meds she now injected prevented the relapses from occurring very often. Most of the time, she didn't experience symptoms. But as she grew older, she knew the meds would stop suppressing the pain. Someday, she would pay the price for the choices she had made in her youth.

All she could do for now was shrug and live her life. She couldn't change the past. If she had to do it all over again, she would do it the same. *For Maya.*

An icon blinked in her i-cite, signaling an incoming comm from her ever-attentive husband. She loved Kevin dearly. He was the only non-blood relative she had ever cared about. He had helped her rescue and raise Maya. He had stuck with her through good times and bad. He was a great man, having invented faster-than-light comm and space travel.

Still, sometimes a woman needed her alone time.

She answered his comm.

"How was class today?" Kevin asked from a screen in her eyesight. No matter how often he shaved, the stubble never seemed to leave his face.

"Same as always," she droned. "Any hope for humanity diminishes with each passing semester."

Her husband ran a hand through brown hair with flecks of gray. "Give it up already, grumpy girl. We both know it's an act."

"But being grumpy gives me such great pleasure." Despite her best efforts, she cracked a slight smile.

"Well, not all of us are like that." He sounded forlorn.

For once, she gave up brooding about her own problems. It wasn't like Kevin to get down—introspective or contemplative, yes, but not depressed. She had the patent on that emotional state.

"What's the matter?" she asked.

"Oh, it's nothing." He scratched his head. "Actually, how I'm feeling is pretty stupid considering what she did to me."

"What who did?"

An icon for a news feed from him popped up in her i-cite. She accessed the feed, which contained an obituary. "Dr. Christine Yeager, co-inventor of phase technology and convicted of treason in 2248, dies in prison stabbing," she read. "Your former colleague."

"I know she sided with Collins and tried to sabotage and steal my work, but . . ."

"But you cared about her."

"Up until I met you, I was certain I'd end up with her. Maybe I'm too big of a softie, but she deserved better."

Brooke shuddered when she thought of how badly—and repeatedly—one individual had to stab another to kill them in an age where medicine could reconstruct someone from no more than a brain and spinal column.

After a moment of silence, she decided to change the subject. "I suppose I should start getting ready, huh? The launch ceremony starts in a few hours, and Maya will disown me if I don't show up to see her off."

"She's still not speaking to you?" Kevin asked.

"Not since our last fight. Ever since she took my class, things haven't been the same." She pounded the mattress. "Our relationship improved when she left for the IEF academy. A little space between us went a long way. Why'd I have to go and ruin a good thing?"

"Did our little prodigy really deserve an average grade?"

"I tell you." Brooke closed her eyes and pictured star fighters locked in combat. The imagery quickened her pulse. "That girl can watch from a distance and tell you what's going to happen ten moves ahead. But when she jumps into a cockpit, she's lost. She understands orbital mechanics better than anyone, but she doesn't have the intuitive feel for maneuvers. A pilot doesn't have time to think—let alone overthink—which is all she does."

"You didn't have an ulterior motive for keeping her out of a fighter?"

"What's that supposed to mean?" When Brooke saw Kevin's raised eyebrows, she disarmed her snarl. "I won't deny wanting to keep my niece out of harm's way, but average pilots shouldn't be fighter pilots."

"It sounds like your conscience should be clear."

"So why do I feel like garbage?" She rolled onto her stomach. "And now she's leaving to explore interstellar space for three years. Not only will I miss her, but I'm jealous as hell. I don't know what to do with myself."

"You'll have to live vicariously—like most parents."

"I guess so." A message icon blinked in her i-cite. "Anyway, I'd better get going if I want to make it to Triton on time. I'll see you there?"

"We've got two front row seats together. Maya reserved them weeks ago and sent you—"

"Yeah, I've got my ticket somewhere in memory. Okay, I'm signing off. Love you."

"Always and forever."

Brooke grinned. "Barf." She terminated the channel.

With her beloved solitude restored, she retreated back underneath the covers and viewed the annoying message. "Again?" she murmured, rolling her eyes. "The imbecile never gives up."

The persistent author had sent her fifty messages in the last few months. She had dismissed the first few as spam, but the individual had dropped enough subtle hints about things few people knew—details regarding the true history of the quaint little farce known as the IntraSolar Commonality—to keep Brooke from outright ignoring them. Still, it didn't matter what the idiot had to say. As much as the burden of truth suffocated her on a daily basis, she knew she could never mess with the status quo. To do so would turn her niece's world upside-down, not to mention throw the human race into anarchy. Brooke refused to be that selfish.

The message read, I'VE BEEN PATIENT, BUT I CAN'T WAIT ANY LONGER. IT'S IMPERATIVE WE SPEAK BEFORE THE CEREMONY. YOU THINK YOU KNOW WHAT THEY'VE DONE— OR WHAT THEY'RE PLANNING? IF YOU WON'T COME TO ME, I'LL COME TO YOU.

"Whatever." *And . . . delete.*

Following a much-needed stretch, she buried her face in a pillow and decided to rest for five more minutes. She faded in and out but didn't allow herself to fall sleep.

A whirring noise accompanied by a rush of air perked her up.

She reached into a hidden compartment in the headboard and pulled out a particle handgun. She kept the weapon around in case members of the Vril or any of Ajunwa's henchmen decided to pay her a visit.

Springing up on her knees, she twirled and aimed the gun at the sound.

A man knelt at the foot of the bed, placing a device the size of a sugar cube on the floor.

"Who the hell are you and what're you doing in my home?" she yelled.

The intruder took his time rising to his feet. "Unless you plan to torch your room, I suggest you put that away."

Keeping her gun sighted between his eyes, she hopped down off the bed and scrutinized him. He didn't appear to be armed, although one could never tell for certain in an age of embedded bioweapons and micro-explosives. A half-head taller than her, the thirtyish young man of Asian descent sported a tweed flat cap, collared shirt under a sweater vest, and jeans.

She pulled the strap of her tank top back up over her shoulder and straightened her boxer shorts, suddenly self-conscious. "I'm late for one of the most important moments in my niece's life, so you'd better have a damn good reason for barging in here."

He tipped back his cap and folded his arms. "You refused to respond to any of my messages. That forced me to resort to more drastic measures."

"Sometimes, no communication is a form of communication, too."

"This is bigger than your selfish need to withdraw. I need your help."

"Then out with it already." She gripped the gun with both hands. "You've got ten seconds to convince me not to blow your head off."

He swung his gaze around the room. Shaking his head, he mouthed the words, "They're listening."

"I've had this place checked and rechecked for bugs. There's nothing to worry about."

The trespasser pointed at the tiny cube on the floor.

She narrowed her eyes. "If you think I'm going to trust you to activate that thing, forget it. For all I know, it's some sort of explosive."

He raised his brow and mouthed, "If I wanted to kill you, there're easier ways to do it."

I'm such a sucker. Grumbling, she said, "Okay, do it slowly. But the moment I suspect the slightest hint of deception, you're dead. Got it?"

Nodding, he knelt and touched a finger to the cube. The device flashed.

Squinting, she wrapped her index finger around the trigger.

The man threw a palm up in a stopping motion.

The flickering ceased. Brooke relaxed her finger.

Standing up again, he spoke without holding back. "The Vril aren't careless enough to plant a physical device you could find. They don't need to resort to anything so crude. You can thank your husband for that."

"What do you mean?"

"Let me ask you this. How do you communicate with people elsewhere in the solar system—in real time?"

Before she could say, "I'm not in the mood to play guessing games," Brooke had realized the answer. "Wormhole surveillance." The implications twisted into her gut.

"That's right." The man formed a circle with his thumb and forefinger. "They're able to spy through tiny, unseen windows in space-time, from anywhere to anywhere and on anyone. The very notion of privacy is extinct—at least, not without one of these bad boys." He directed the toe of a loafer at the cube. "This device distorts space-time in a localized area, enough to prevent the formation of wormholes."

"I see."

"Will you please put the gun down now?"

Brooke scrunched her nose in thought. "It's an interesting story, but so far all you've done is put on a half-assed light show. You've still got a lot more convincing to do."

"But now, at least, you're listening." He bowed. "My name is Shin, Shin Saito. It's an honor to meet the greatest pilot who ever—"

"If you want a hole blown through your chest, keep up the hero worship."

He held up his hands in surrender. "Sorry. I should've known how you'd react, given how closely I've studied your profile, and—"

"What profile? My ISC citizen account?"

"No, the Vril have an extensive identity matrix on each and every human being—all forty billion, not counting the deceased. Yours is so detailed, they could simulate another you."

"And you know this how?"

"I used to be a Vril agent—well, I still am, but that requires a bit more explanation."

"More explanation starts now." Brooke checked the time in her i-cite. "I've got places to be, so make it quick."

"Here's the abridged version. There's disagreement amongst the Vril about how to direct the future of the human race. I'm the head of an anonymous splinter group that's rejected the way in which the leadership plans to usher in a better tomorrow."

"An anonymous splinter group? You mean, a secret group within a secret group." She shook her head at the irony. For some reason, her mind pictured Russian nesting dolls.

"My father and grandmother were members of the Vril. They taught me that drastic measures needed to be taken to save mankind from the threat lurking out there. I stand by the invasion we staged to unite the solar system seventeen years ago, but what we're doing now goes beyond a simple ruse."

"A simple ruse?" She snorted. "That's what you call tricking people into a war against a fake extrasolar threat and killing thousands of people in the process?"

Shin frowned. "I'll admit to a poor choice of words, but I'm serious. The point is that the methods the Vril are using to maintain the human race's unity and accelerate their master agenda cross a line which an increasing number of members aren't willing to step over."

"So now all of a sudden there's a line?"

"Did you ever stop to wonder how the ISC has managed to eliminate poverty, hunger, and crime in just seventeen years?" he asked with a stomp of his foot. "Some of the progress is due to our newfound cohesion after defeating a common foe, but there's no way the disappearance of hate, greed, and differences of opinion in such a short timeframe has come about naturally. Behind the scenes, the Vril have manipulated the media, reprogrammed the neural structures of thousands of people, staged disasters by Mother Nature, and rooted out dissenters with assassinations—and that's not the half of it."

Keeping her gun trained on Shin, Brooke shuffled over to the picture windows overlooking Valles Marineris, one of the largest canyons in the solar system. With the terraforming of Mars in its final stages, olive green grass and tall trees grew beneath an azure sky. Flocks of birds flew over the chasm. On the other side of the canyon, construction bots worked to tear down the transparent domes that had once enclosed the metropolis of Red Rock City.

"I've had my suspicions," she said, "but it's not like I can do anything about them."

"What if I told you there was a way to expose the Vril without bringing civilization crashing down around us? And by the end, you'd be reinstated into the military and get back the pilot's license Ajunwa revoked."

Brooke flared her nostrils. "If you think you can waltz in here, tell me what I want to hear, and expect me to believe you, you're dumber than all the people you've ever conned. This is what the Vril do. Lies on top of lies on top of more lies. How naïve do you think I am?"

"I don't expect you to believe my story without proof, which is why I've arranged to show it to you. There's something you need to see at the bottom of the Martian south polar ocean. The Vril plan to bury it when the solar system's attention is focused on the launch ceremony, so we need to go right away."

Shaking her head in disbelief, Brooke yelled, "Right away? As in now? Forget it. I won't miss saying goodbye to my niece based on this load of crap."

He opened his mouth to protest, but she cut him off. "Besides, I'm just a washed up fighter pilot. What can I do?"

"If my plan is going to succeed, I need the best pilot in the solar system. Plus, you already know the truth, so you're the logical choice. There are one or two places I need to blast my way inside. With you doing the flying, they won't be able to keep us out."

"One pilot can't fight a war for you. The only way to take down the Vril is to out-con the con artists—but good luck with that. I'm out."

"Have it your way." Shin turned and stepped toward the bedroom door. "I hope when you say goodbye to Maya, it isn't the last time you ever see her."

Brooke sprinted over to him, leveling her gun at the back of his head. "What the hell does that mean? Is something going to happen to her or *New Horizons*?"

He turned around and shifted his stare between her and the gun.

"Answer the question," she shouted.

Pulling down his cap, he said, "Let's just say if the Vril have their way, humankind's first interstellar mission won't end well for the crew or the race they plan to visit." He took a step toward her, his face tensed. "You still don't get it. The Vril's agenda goes way beyond you, me, or the human race—beyond the past, present, and future."

"Care to be a little less cryptic?"

"South polar ocean. One hour. I'll be waiting." Shin whirled and headed for the door.

"Stop!" She fired at his leg. The low-yield particle burst passed through him like he wasn't there, scorching the hardwood floor.

His body wavered. The pixels comprising it destabilized and disintegrated. All that remained of his persona was the cube—the holographic emitter—on the floor.

Growling, Brooke shot and vaporized the cube.

She kicked the side of the bed, stubbed her toe on the frame, and cursed in pain.

The mattress knocked into her dresser. One of the vidpics sitting on top of it—the one playing a scene with Brooke and Maya embracing at the girl's high school graduation—toppled over the side of the dresser and struck the floor, shattering.

Brooke picked up the vidpic, wondering whether she should contact Maya or Kevin.

After weighing the consequences, she decided against it. She refused to tell her niece about the Vril but didn't know how else to justify her absence from the ceremony. As for her husband, he would try to talk her out of doing anything rash.

I'm so sorry, Maya, she said to the vidpic, *but if there's even the slimmest chance Shin is telling the truth . . .*

Three—Epitome
Triton, May 2265 CE

High above Lake Flammarion, Second Lieutenant Erik Maxwell rocketed through Triton's periwinkle sky in his Pulsar. Another star fighter came straight at him from the south, piloted by Ankur Suresh, first-ever IEF valedictorian. As top academy pilots, they executed a series of stunts in an acrobatic display choreographed for the start of the *New Horizons* launch ceremony.

A third and fourth Pulsar shot toward each other from the east and west, halfway between Erik's and Ankur's crafts. As the third star fighter dipped, the fourth rose, tracing a series of figure eight patterns.

Erik held his fighter's flight path steady toward Ankur's Pulsar. The upcoming stunt required them to pass between the two looping fighters above the auditorium and trade places going in opposite directions. The feat qualified as dangerous but not to the degree that the casual observer might assume, given the precision of AI support. Still, the trick presented enough perils to unnerve an experienced pilot, let alone a recent IEF Aerospace graduate with only a hundred hours of flight time.

But one of the things that made Erik such a good pilot was his ability to keep calm under pressure. Sometimes, he wondered if his body never produced adrenaline. Compared to his parents' violent spats during his upbringing in Toronto—fights that had often escalated to physical violence—the prospect of dying in a star fighter didn't faze him.

As he neared position above the auditorium, he rolled his Pulsar while maintaining course. A few hundred meters before passing between the looping fighters, he saw flame and smoke spew from Ankur's craft in front of him.

The Pulsar piloted by Ankur veered off course, heading straight for one of the looping fighters. Unable to avoid the impact, the two spacecraft crashed into one another. With its force field having failed, Ankur's Pulsar bounced off the shielding of the looping fighter. Explosions erupted all around the fuselage of his mangled craft, which strayed into the path of Erik's Pulsar.

Erik blew out an even breath. His heartbeat remained at its resting rate. With a thought, he upshifted to hyperspace a fraction of a second before smashing into the crippled spacecraft.

He checked his rear camera views after downshifting clear of the incident. Ankur's burning Pulsar splashed down into Lake Flammarion, displacing enough water to spray the auditorium.

Over an open comm channel, Erik registered the gasps rising up from the crowd below.

◆

"Excuse me," Maya said as she worked her way to her seat, avoiding puddles of water. *Why's everything wet?*

She stepped over and around the outstretched legs of seated ISC Defense officers. The men and women of the old service made no great effort to move for an IEF brat whose kind threatened to render them obsolete. The Interstellar Expeditionary Force was a new type of institution created in the spirit of ancient space agencies like NASA and the ESA. Scientific exploration came first, but Maya had the same basic training as any soldier. If Chancellor Ajunwa had her way, the IEF would someday replace the military, which explained the vindictive attitude of the members of the current armed forces. The merit of the IEF replacing ISC Defense loomed as a hot political topic.

Strangely, everyone in the crowd sat on the edges of their seats. She could feel the tension radiating from hundreds of side conversions.

The ceremony should've started two hours ago.

After ending up back in Auckland, Maya had picked herself up off the floor of the phase port and rushed to Triton as fast as she could get there. The trip had taken twice as long the second time around.

"Maya!" her best friend, Josephine Ryder, called out from a few seats down the aisle. "Where the hell have you been?"

Maya reached the empty seat next to her fellow IEF graduate and plopped down. "What's going on? The ceremony should be over, but it doesn't look like it's started yet."

"You haven't heard?" Jo gawked at her with enhanced pink irises. "The ceremony began with the air show as planned, but Ankur's Pulsar exploded right over our heads."

A vidsim of the incident recorded by Jo appeared in Maya's i-cite. Her pulse raced as she watched Erik shift his Pulsar to avoid Ankur's damaged craft, which crashed into the lake. Jo's recording ended with her getting sprayed in the face by water.

Maya shuddered from a mix of relief and anger. Thanks to her aunt, she had failed to qualify as a pilot for the show. *That could've—and probably should've—been me.* She berated herself for such self-centered thinking. Right now, only her classmate's well-being mattered. "Is Ankur okay?"

"They're saying the explosion disintegrated most of his body," Jo said, "but the doctors think there's enough of his nervous system left to reconstruct him."

"Thank the stars. Do they know what caused his fighter to malfunction?"

"They're still investigating, but the working theory is a manufacturing defect in his Pulsar's phase drive casing."

"If that's the case, we're lucky the Pulsar didn't explode and take the auditorium with it." Maya replayed the footage. Erik's quick reflexes had saved him. She envied the quiet, mild-mannered pilot's abilities. He had scored at the top of their class in flight sims. Her aunt had called him "refreshingly adequate;" a glowing endorsement coming from her.

"At least no one was killed," Maya said.

"That's a definite positive." Jo scrutinized the stain on Maya's chest. "And you missed it—why—to redecorate your uniform?"

"I got doused while doing laps around the solar system."

"Why hasn't your coat fixed itself?"

"The soda must've fried the nanofibers."

Jo snorted. "A smart garment that gets ruined by the mess it's supposed to clean. Hilarious."

"And it's all no thanks to you."

"Me?" Jo lifted her brow. "What did I do?"

Slouching, Maya explained how she had nearly set a new Earth-to-Triton record only to end up back in New Zealand. "I bumped into a woman who spilled her drink on me." She sighed. "I never should've let you drag me out to that club last night."

"'If you could kick the person in the pants who was responsible for most of your trouble, you wouldn't sit for a month.'"

Maya bit her lip at Jo's penchant for quoting historical sayings. "Point taken. It was my choice to go out." Her friend had graduated with a double specialty in—no, an obsession with—history and archaeology. Jo knew more than most Ivy League professors. "Plato?"

"Geez, girl. They wore tunics, not pants, in ancient Greece. Theodore Roosevelt."

"And he was . . . ?"

"The twenty-sixth president of the American Colonies—well, technically, they called the country the United States of America back then."

"I prefer to look to the future rather than the past."

"Ah, but 'study the past if you would divine the future.'"

"I've no choice but to concede to . . . Confucius, right?"

"Damn right. But back on topic, your arm wasn't hard to twist. We all needed one final hurrah before leaving for three years. Not going out wasn't an option." Jo adjusted the very blonde and pink strands within her pigtails. "At any rate, that stylish stain on your shirt and Ankur's accident leave you in a somewhat precarious predicament."

"What do you mean . . . ?" Maya let her words trail off as the realization shook her. "Oh no." Her stomach cramped as the warring factions of butterflies within it tussled. She sprung up from her seat and sat back down again.

As valedictorian, Ankur was supposed to speak on behalf of their class. If, for whatever reason, he couldn't give his speech, responsibility fell to the salutatorian.

"You did prepare something just in case, right?" Jo asked.

"I was about to last night but we went out." Maya bit deeper into her lower lip. "Ankur's the most consistent and reliable person I know. The guy pees at the same exact times every day. I never thought he wouldn't be able to speak." She touched the crusty, dried fabric of her uniform. "Billions of people will be watching."

"I'd swap tops with you, but I'm going on stage, too."

"You're a big help."

"I'm always here for you."

Erik settled into the empty seat on the other side of Maya. Intertwining his fingers in his lap, he stared straight ahead, pale-faced, as if the life had gone out of him.

Jo leaned over Maya and asked him, "What the hell happened up there?"

Erik took his time responding. "I don't know. I'm just glad Ankur's going to survive."

"That's what happens when you send scientists to do the work of real soldiers," a voice behind Maya chastised them.

Looking over her shoulder, Maya found Ensign Trevor Young sitting in the row behind them. The top graduate of the ISC Defense Academy had his arms folded. His expression appeared as robotic and disapproving as ever.

"Interstellar Expeditionary Force," the soldier sitting next to him said. "More like Idiotic Excuses for Failures."

"Hey." Trevor glowered at his classmate. "Let's keep it civil."

"You're just jealous because Ajunwa left Defense out of the ceremony proceedings," Jo fired back.

Maya held her friend's upper arm in case she decided to crawl over the back of her seat and pounce.

"No more war means there's no more need for soldiers," Jo said. "I don't know why you Philistines still exist."

"When the Greys or another exospecies attack the expedition," Trevor said, "which, incidentally, is a waste of time, we'll be the only thing standing between you and them."

"If you're so good at fighting, why did Erik kick the piss out of you in flight sims?"

"I'm more of a tactician than a pilot, a big picture kind of guy." Trevor flexed his fingers.

"Oh, that's right." Jo smirked. "A big picture that includes finishing second to Maya in every training exercise and—"

"Enough, all right?" Maya interrupted, trying to disarm the situation. She had held back in sims and let Trevor win a couple times to appease his ego, but the goodwill gesture had backfired. He had despised her ever since he had found out she had gone easy on him. Enraged by his lack of gratitude, she had destroyed him in command immersives by almost doubling his score. The virtual beat-down had turned him into her bitter rival. *There's no pleasing some people.* "We're going to be stuck together for three years, so let's all try to get along."

"Of course." The edginess in Trevor's tone suggested he hadn't forgiven her. "'Let's all get along,' the enlightened IEF philosophy. Here's a brilliant idea. Let's travel to an inhabited exoplanet with arms wide open without knowing anything about the inhabitants."

"Remote observations suggest the Penphins are friendly, and we know they need help from their message."

"Unless that's how they lure unsuspecting species to their demise."

"The idea is to reach out to others and make peace before they come to Earth. This is an excellent opportunity to do just that."

He shook his head in disgust. "Tell me something. What did we get when optimists broadcasted the human race's existence centuries ago? An extrasolar attack, that's what. We're better off fortifying our defenses at home to give visitors a proper welcome."

"You can always stay here," Jo said.

"And let you roam the galaxy defenseless? Don't worry. We'll be there to fight your battles when things go wrong."

"Attention, ladies and gentleman." The head of the ISC public relations committee stood behind the podium on stage, prompting Maya and her fellow graduates to pay attention. "We apologize for the delay. Please know that the aerial incident resulted in no fatalities. With everyone's safety ensured, the ceremony will now resume."

Top government officials and officers filed onto the stage, taking their seats at the long table behind the podium. High above, the satellite mirrors that provided Triton with warmth and light dimmed, simulating dusk. Lake Flammarion shimmered in the background.

Chancellor Danuwa Ajunwa, leader of the human race, arrived last. Despite having hit the century mark, she walked with only a slight limp thanks to the latest muscle and bone regeneration therapy. The whites, blues, and grays of her head tie and pantsuit matched the color scheme of Maya's IEF uniform.

In grade school, Maya had learned how Ajunwa had lobbied to unite the human race against the Greys, a deed that had helped the woman win every election and remain as chancellor since the inaugural year of the ISC. Ajunwa was an unwavering visionary, a role model Maya admired. She couldn't comprehend why Aunt Brooke loathed the woman.

Then again, Maya had never understood much about her secretive aunt or her abrasive personality. She acted like the Big Crunch would destroy the multiverse if she opened up.

An hour of speeches by VIPs with vested interests in the mission passed, including an inspirational monologue by Alastair Hamilton. The aging benefactor had undergone a procedure to graft his neural structure onto a cybernetic brain and replace his body with a state-of-the-art android model to improve his health so he could join the mission. The story of how his dream of exploration had helped him endure the pain of becoming one of the first humans to go full prosthetic mesmerized her.

As Director of the Solar Science Society, Uncle Kevin took the podium and cited the interstellar mission as being the culmination of his life's work. This moment, he declared, was why he and his team had invented the faster-than-light phase drive.

The head of the SETI division of the Solar Science Society stood next to him along with a man and a woman. Partially for the benefit of the viewers at home—but mostly because Uncle Kevin lived for giving science lectures—he recapped how SETI had detected the transmission from the Penphins four years ago. Astronomer Luke Hartmann and exolinguist Chloe Shoemaker, the two scientists standing next to the head of SETI, had received the amplitude-modulated radio signal while stationed on the New Allen Telescope Array in the Oort Cloud.

Hartmann and Shoemaker waved, prompting cheers from the audience.

As the applause waned, Uncle Kevin discussed the message carried by the signal. From the longwinded content of the message, the SETI outpost's linguistic AIs had translated the language. The words "hello" and "help" had appeared over and over again in the friendly greeting. The Penphins had wanted to see if anyone else was out there, much like humans had done with early transmissions and probes. Whether the Penphins needed help or were offering it hadn't been clear.

Centuries ago, her uncle explained, scientists had ruled out the possibility of intelligent life in the Gliese 581 system, although it had taken them some time to agree on the number of planets around the star.

He waved his hand, summoning a sim of the planetary system that expanded like a spherical canopy above the stage. A raging ball of fire, the red dwarf star known as Gliese 581 floated in the center of the sim. Six orbiting planets of varying sizes and a cometary debris disk ringing the edge of the system surrounded the orange-red sun.

A small seventh world—a white, pink, and mud brown globe—circled the star in an orbit far from the orbits of the other planets. The world had gone undetected for so long, her uncle revealed, because of this unique orbit. In more archaic times, scientists had needed a planet to pass in front of its sun, thereby blocking a tiny fraction of its light, in order to detect it. But this world never passed between Sol and Gliese 581.

Uncle Kevin listed off a number of other fun science facts about the Penphins' home world and the mission before returning to his seat in the front row.

Chancellor Ajunwa replaced him at the podium and spoke about togetherness and the peaceful coexistence she hoped the IEF would achieve with all other intelligent life.

At the conclusion of her speech, she said, "And now, I'd like to introduce the man of the hour, David Reed, the captain of *New Horizons*."

Captain Reed shook hands with Ajunwa and took the podium to the tune of fervent applause. Display cubes the size of billboards hovered on either side of the stage, showing his headshot.

As the applause faded, he said, "Thank you, everyone." His voice projected calm and confidence, the consummate skipper. "I haven't done much to deserve such a reception, but I'll accept your appreciation on behalf of everyone who's labored to make humankind's first interstellar journey possible."

Maya tried not to drool. From a physical standpoint, the captain looked like an average middle-aged man—hardly male model material—but she found him intoxicating. She had studied his service record so closely she figured she might know it better than him. The man embodied the spirit of exploration she held dear. Anyone who inspired others and held the position she intended to earn someday deserved her envy.

Reed had taken a particle blast to the chest meant for a subordinate in a separatist raid in 2246. In 2248, after soaring up the ranks, he had commanded Defense carriers against the Greys near Jupiter and Earth, fighting in the same battles as her aunt. When the war ended, he had led expeditions into the Kuiper Belt to find the Grey's hidden colonies and, as he had put it, just to see what was out there. Scuttlebutt claimed his troops would follow him into the sun if he gave the word.

Jo snapped her fingers in front of Maya's face. "Girl, he's twice your age and not even that fused. Get over him already."

Maya shook off the trance. "That's not why I'm . . ." She batted her friend's arm away. "Mind your own business, will you?"

"Whatever you say." Jo directed her devilish grin back toward the stage.

"As many of you know," Reed continued, "I'm a man of few words. I prefer to listen and let others do the talking. Tonight, at long last, I'd like to introduce the star of the show, a special lady who will inspire us all without saying a word."

Orchestral music played from unseen speakers. Maya's seat tilted backwards until she lay facing the sky.

Chills coursed through her limbs when she saw *New Horizons* high above in synchronous orbit. She had seen it in sims and toured it during its construction in the Trojan asteroids. She knew every detail about it from the engines to the lavatories. Nevertheless, the finished product still blew her away.

Light from the orbital mirrors glinted off the starship's gleaming exterior. Its slim, conical hull rotated clockwise and stretched for two kilometers, hanging parallel to Triton's surface. The front of the ship, the command module, tapered to a point with the crew habitat module behind it. At the center of the vessel, the caged biosphere housing Star City spun with the rest of the hull. The defense module with the armory and hundreds of Pulsars connected the city to the engineering module behind it. Eight conventional rocket nozzles, each as wide as a sporting arena, protruded from the engine block aft of engineering. Six evenly-spaced nacelles the size of old UN spacecraft carriers were affixed to the ring module that encircled the divider between defense and engineering. Precious antimatter that had taken years to produce filled the nacelles.

With her mouth agape, she shivered from awe.

"I'm starting a poll," Jo quipped, inspecting her nails. "What turns Maya on more, the captain or the ship?"

Maya gave her friend a light shove.

Word candy poured from Reed's mouth for the next few minutes. He ended with, "I wish I had time to introduce every member of my crew, not to mention each of the brave civilian colonists accompanying us. But unfortunately, that isn't possible. Instead, I'm pleased to present a group of young officers who embody the spirit of this mission. Please welcome the first graduates of the Interstellar Expeditionary Force Academy, the class of 2265."

To deafening applause, Maya stood with her classmates and made her way up on stage. Her heart thumped the entire time. She kept resisting the urge to wrap her arms over her chest to hide the stain.

"These young men and women represent the best the human race has to offer," Chancellor Ajunwa said, having retaken the podium. Maya recoiled at the woman's booming tone. "Their class is composed of the brightest and most capable. They've been specially trained and given state-of-the-art implants to better equip them for long-term exploration. They represent a better generation, one that knows only empathy and forward progress."

While standing with her classmates, Maya scanned the front row. She located Uncle Kevin and zoomed in on his general vicinity. He sat looking back at her with a warm but regretful smile.

The seat next to him remained unoccupied.

She hung her head. Trying not to frown, she commed her uncle in her i-cite. "I'm glad you made it." She placed particular emphasis the word "you."

"I'm sorry, Maya," Uncle Kevin responded. "I spoke with Brooke a few hours ago. She said she was getting ready to come. I've tried contacting her several times, but she won't respond. I don't know where she is."

Maya's breathing heightened. She worried if something had happened to her aunt.

She shrugged off the feeling. "Clearly, she has better things to do."

"You know that's not true," her uncle said in a hollow attempt to make her feel better. "I'm starting to worry, so as soon as the ceremony ends—"

"Why bother? You know how she gets. She prefers her solitude."

"Maya—"

She terminated the connection. Ripping her gaze away from the empty seat, she sucked in a deep breath to keep from crying.

"Due to today's tragic accident," Ajunwa said, "IEF valedictorian Ankur Suresh won't be able to give his speech. Therefore, the class salutatorian will speak in his place. Please welcome Maya Davis, the niece of two of our greatest heroes, to the podium."

Maya wilted beneath the crowd's acclaim. She wished she could shrink down to microscopic size and scurry away without anyone noticing. *No, someone would see me in the act of shrinking. Or someone might step on me. Besides, all the oxygen molecules would be too big for me to breathe anyway, so—*

Jo gave her a motivational shove forward.

Stepping up to the podium, Maya averted her gaze from the thousands of people and swarm of floating spherecams. She searched the files in her i-cite for the speech she had begun writing before Jo had dragged her out, but she hadn't even saved the first sentence.

A breeze blew in off the lake, and her sinuses started to tingle. Her allergies often acted up when she got nervous. To keep from sneezing, she pinched the bridge of her nose.

Murmurs broke out in the crowd. Thanks to her auditory implants, she heard a man in the eighth row asking what was wrong with her. A woman in the fifth row whispered about the stain on her chest.

She drew in a breath and stared up into the sky. *New Horizons*—the amazing ship which would soon take her to other worlds—hovered high above her. It provided a calming presence. *Just speak from the heart.*

"Thank you, everyone, for taking the time to listen," she said. "Before I begin, I want to thank the ISC, the IEF, Chancellor Ajunwa, Captain Reed, my classmates, my aunt and uncle, and countless others who have all contributed to this moment. Without their support, none of us would be where we are today."

The murmurs died down. She cleared her throat and pointed to her chest. "I also want to explain this stain before I speak any further." She shrugged and smiled. "I was so excited for today that I bumped into someone on the way here and spilled her drink all over myself. My uni's fabric isn't responding. I didn't have time to change, so I'm a bit embarrassed to be up here right now. And to top it all off"—she gazed at the empty chair next to Uncle Kevin—"the most important person in my life isn't here to see me off today."

She gripped the podium with both hands. "But you know what? It's just as well. I'm glad these things happened because things aren't always going to go as planned when we're out there, light years away from home. We're going to face adversity, and how we respond will shape our future." With her index finger, she tapped the top of the stand. "I invite everyone to take a good, long look at that ship in the sky and think about what it represents. It marks the end of the human race's childhood and the beginning of our real adult existence.

"Right now, we're like university freshmen, leaving home and striking out for the first time. We've gone through a lot in our history to get to the point where we're ready to leave our tiny nook. Our solar system is a mere light-year in diameter, drifting in a galaxy 100,000 light years wide in a universe billions of light years across woven into an interdimensional framework of multiple universes. So much awaits us out there—countless planets, some similar to Earth. We already know of two races besides ourselves, and there are probably more. It's up to us to determine how we're known to them."

After taking a deep breath, she concluded with, "So compared to all that, a little blemish on my coat doesn't even register. I only hope we can live up to everyone's expectations. As the first members of the IEF, we plan to serve as a shining example of what this mission stands for, because this isn't simply a trip a few stars over. This journey will set the precedent for mankind's exploration of space for the rest of time. Thank you."

One by one, the attendees rose to their feet.

♦

After an hour's worth of pleasantries on the ceremony grounds, briefings by her superiors, and a goodbye embrace from Uncle Kevin, Maya stood with Jo and Erik on the spaceport grounds. There she waited for one of the shuttles to ferry them up to *New Horizons*.

Neptune hung like an oversized blue ornament beyond the dipping horizon. Through the hazy atmosphere, she watched the Great Blue Spot churn. A shimmering line—Neptune's ring system—bisected the gas giant into two hemispheres.

Maya thought about her aunt—about family—and weighed a decision she had been putting off for a long time. If she didn't go do it now, she wouldn't have another opportunity for three years.

Despite her trembling, she turned and took a step toward the phase port. "You guys go ahead. I'll catch a shuttle up later tonight."

"Huh?" Jo asked. "Where do you think you're going?"

"There's something I have to do before I leave. On Earth."

Erik nodded. "In Japan."

"Yeah . . ."

Four—Bathysmal
South Polar Ocean, Mars, May 2265 CE

"Hey, aren't you . . . ?" A man poked Brooke's shoulder, his breath visible in the frigid air.

Scrunching her nose, Brooke pulled away from the intrusive passenger and retreated toward the opposite side of the crowded observation deck. Ocean waves struck the sides of the cruise ship, twisting her stomach into knots. *There was a time plummeting into the atmosphere of a gas giant wouldn't have fazed me. What a joke I've become.*

Behind her, she overheard the man say, "I swear that's her."

"There's no way that's Brooke Davis," his female companion insisted. "What would a famous war heroine be doing on a sightseeing cruise with us?"

Grumbling, Brooke slipped away while accessing the aesthetics program in her i-cite. The bleached blonde highlights had failed to mask her identity, so she tinted her hair to purple and increased the length. As her scalp and follicles tingled beneath her stocking cap, the collar of her heavy coat grew up to her visor.

She reached the other side of the deck. After checking for accosters, she gripped the railing with both gloved hands and stared out over the murky, rust-red water. The rocky cliffs receded behind her as the ship headed out to sea. Even with the orbital mirrors reflecting sunlight on her from above, the cold bit into her bones.

What am I doing here? she wondered as her teeth chattered. *I've skipped Maya's launch to go on a ridiculous pleasure cruise—and based on what, a weak promise and an even weaker threat?* Her chest burned. *Am I that desperate to get back into a cockpit?*

Another tourist sidled up to her along the railing, much too close.

"Ever heard of personal space?" she snapped.

"It's me." Directing his gaze out over the water, Shin adjusted his puffy coat and flat cap.

"It's about time, but I'd still appreciate it if you backed off."

"Come with me." Shin turned and walked away.

Brooke followed him through the crowd and down to the lower decks. She passed passenger cabins, dining rooms, offices, and a galley before descending into the engineering block. The humming of engines sent vibrations through the cramped corridors. Together with the low lighting, the place reminded her of the bowels of a spacecraft carrier. She almost felt at home.

A crewman standing guard at a hatchway nodded at Shin. After ushering them into the lifeboat hangar on the lowermost level, the man exited and locked the door behind them.

The crewman's nod had surprised her, although in retrospect it shouldn't have come as a shock. Considering all that the Vril had manipulated into being, infiltrating a commercial sea vessel had undoubtedly proven easier than taking Fruity Planets from an orphan.

Her stomach gurgled, reminding her she hadn't eaten anything since dinner last night.

The sight of the subaquatic fighter craft crammed into the hangar subdued her hunger pangs. The NF-735 Poseidon resembled a Pulsar but appeared wider, stubbier, and more rounded, like a cartoon version of a star fighter. The smooth, amphibious curves of the tailfins, wings, and fuselage indicated that engineers had constructed the ISC Navy fighter for underwater use.

"This is why I needed you," Shin said as he rounded the craft. "I don't have the first clue how to operate this thing, but you do. Now, c'mon." He approached a pair of armored pressure suits spread out on the deck and began suiting up. "We need to hurry."

Brooke stood rooted in place, torn between the yearning desire to fly something real—although "fly" might not have been the most accurate term—and her distrust of this man who had barged into her home only an hour ago. "Hold on. You can't expect me to hop into this thing and risk my life without knowing what the hell's going on. This is as far as I go until you tell me where we're headed and why." She folded her arms.

"Start getting dressed and I'll explain along the way. Every second we delay is less time we have to spend down there." When she didn't budge, he added, "You're the pilot. If you don't like what I have to say or where we're headed, you can turn us around any time you feel like it."

With a groan, Brooke pulled off her jacket and rushed over to one of the suits. She directed a cool eye in Shin's direction. Once he turned his back to her, she stripped down to her underwear and slipped on the suit. She also returned her hair to its natural form, jet black and shoulder length, and instructed it to auto-tie into a ponytail. "Where's down there? The bottom of the ocean?"

The wet gear had much in common with the flight armor she had worn for so many years. The gear was state-of-the-art Defense issue, which left her feeling more than a little uneasy. ISC Defense had innumerable checks and balances in place to ensure advanced military tech didn't fall into the wrong hands. Chancellor Ajunwa and her husband had set things up that way to keep the latest innovations out of the hands of terrorist organizations like the Vril. *So much for those precautions.*

"Let me ask you this." Shin's pressure armor latched and molded to his body, consuming him like a living creature. "What do you know about the terraforming history of Mars?"

Brooke's armor conformed to her body, hugging every contour and pressing into every crevice. Gravgel filled out and bulked up the suit. *Protection from extreme pressure rather than acceleration,* she mused. *Makes sense.* "I thought we were pressed for time. Quit the guessing games and give me a straightforward explanation."

"The surface water on Mars has only been around since the turn of the century. Scientists thought they'd need to corral a few icy asteroids, slam them into the ground, and melt them, but Mars had more than enough subsurface water to refill the channels that dried up over a billion years ago. Then they created the north and south oceans by melting the polar ice caps."

"Great. So what?"

"So, if you were part of a secret organization that wanted to build a hidden base of operations somewhere difficult to find, where would you do it?"

Brooke flexed her gloved fingers. "At the bottom of an ocean."

"Right, except that they didn't build it underwater—not at first, anyway. The Vril dug and drilled down beneath the south polar ice cap to construct the base. It only became submerged as terraforming warmed the planet and melted the ice. This was their plan all along, one that ensured their operations stayed secret."

The more she thought about it, the more it made sense. "All those conservationists who lobbied to maintain the South Polar Region as a pristine ecosystem unsettled by humans—"

"Instigated by the Vril to keep the place hidden." Shin stepped over to the Poseidon and tapped a panel below the canopy. An external display cube materialized. "It was a simple matter to blind or erase surveillance systems in the area with a significant number of high-ranking officials being loyal operatives." He poked his finger into the cube, which flashed an angry red.

Like Collins. Brooke picked up her helmet, waved him out of the way, and used her free hand to swipe through the menus in the cube.

The cube flashed green, and the canopy popped open.

She bounded up into the cockpit and frowned when Shin settled in next to her, much too close. They knocked knees, shoulders, and elbows. The craft featured a single bench just big enough for two suited occupants.

Donning her helmet, she activated the suit's systems and interfaced with the Poseidon's support AI. A few icons and options differed from a Pulsar's flight software, but on the whole, Defense control interfaces were very standardized.

She performed preflight checks and filled the cockpit with gravgel for additional protection. After initiating the ignition sequence, she helped Shin with the basic operations of his suit.

"The Vril haven't stayed hidden for centuries by being careless," she said over a direct channel between their suits. "How can we sneak in unnoticed?"

"This cruise is evidence of the Martian population's increasing push south, conservationists be damned," he said. "When the UN became the ISC, Ajunwa put procedures in place that have made it more difficult for the Vril to stay hidden. The phase drive and phase portals have also made it easier than ever to track us anywhere in the solar system. Thus, the Vril are moving toward a more decentralized structure and shutting down liabilities like the base below."

"They wouldn't leave an old base intact for anybody to find, though."

"Right. That's why the timing of our little adventure is so important. They finished vacating the base yesterday, which is why I came to you when I did. I couldn't wait any longer. Two hours from now, they plan to flood and bury the place. This is as close to an ideal time to destroy it as there's ever going to be with everyone focused on the launch ceremony."

"What about the Vril's focus? Won't they have their wormhole surveillance systems fixed on the base?"

Shin patted the chest of his wet gear. "They do, but I've got the jamming cube in my shirt pocket. I've had it on since before I stepped aboard the cruise ship. It should hide us well enough to get down there and get out with the artifact."

"Artifact?"

"It's irrefutable proof of the true threat the human race is up against. It may help us find a way to protect ourselves and expose the Vril."

"You wouldn't think they'd leave something so important to the human race's salvation behind, although I can understand their burying it if it could blow their cover."

"Believe me, it was a difficult decision, but the Vril ultimately chose to destroy it. It's dangerous, more dangerous than any piece of technology."

"So what is it?"

"You'll see soon enough."

Brooke blew out a prolonged breath, questioning whether she wanted to go through with his plan. Shin might still be full of it, but her curiosity wouldn't allow her to back out now.

She issued the launch command. A force field shimmered to life between the deck and the Poseidon. As the hangar doors in the floor retracted, the craft dropped through the force field into the ocean.

Beyond the canopy, she couldn't see through the murky, rust-red water, but it didn't matter. The craft descended so quickly, her surroundings darkened to pitch black. She enabled the neutrino radar, patched it into her augmented reality, and integrated her night vision. The output of her instrumentation rendered her surroundings as clear as if she swam in a backyard pool in broad daylight. Schools of spotted fish darted out of her path. A hammerhead shark passed overhead.

"This ocean's not the size of any on Earth, but it's still pretty big," she said. "Where am I headed?"

"Look for—"

A pair of early warning icons blinked in her i-cite. Two other Poseidons were blowing their ballast tanks, rising up from the seafloor to greet them.

"I'm guessing they're not coming up to chat," she said.

Shin held out his palms. "Now you see why I needed the great Brooke Davis."

"I haven't seen live combat in seventeen years. It's two against one, and I'm a bird in the water. There's no guarantee I'll win."

"Let's hope you can shake off the rust in a hurry. They won't issue a warning. They'll blast first and worry about what we're doing here later. They've seen us, so we're committed."

Damn it all. Despite her outward disapproval, adrenaline coursed through her, invigorating her for the first time in years. *Well, no sense in waiting for them to attack.* Targeting brackets in her augmented reality blinked as they locked on to the approaching craft. A timer in her i-cite counted down the seconds until they entered weapons range. The moment the brackets turned solid red, she launched a spread of torpedoes. The projectiles spun through the water, leaving corkscrewing trails of bubbles.

The approaching craft got off a single torpedo before releasing countermeasures to deal with her ordinance.

Shin squeezed his legs and tensed as the torpedo barreled toward them.

Brooke jettisoned an array of decoys in its path, filled the ballast tanks, and dove the Poseidon. When the torpedo approached to within a few meters, she detonated the decoys.

The detonations blew apart the torpedo and created a shock wave that the Poseidon couldn't outrun. Even with its sleek, aquatic design, it maneuvered much more slowly than a star fighter.

The force of the blast thudded against the craft, stressing its fuselage. The Poseidon shuddered and tumbled. Shin gripped his seat harness and cried out through clenched teeth.

Righting the craft's orientation, she put the additional push to good use and darted toward the closest bandit on a collision course.

"What are you doing?" Shin asked.

"Do you want my help or not?" Brooke snapped.

Her rising prey jetted out of her path as she had hoped.

Descending past the bandit, she fired both pressure cannons and launched a volley of torpedoes. The ordinance struck her enemy before it could react. Its force field overloaded, and it exploded.

She chased after the second fleeing craft. Seconds later, it strayed into the targeting bracket in her i-cite, giving her an accurate firing solution. She blasted both cannons, the extreme pressure from which tore through the bandit's shielding and ripped it apart.

"You certainly live up to the hype." Shin exhaled and sank in his seat.

Wrinkling her nose, she said, "Let's hope that was the last one."

◆

Brooke dropped the Poseidon to the ocean floor, and Shin helped her locate the base's entry bay. The Vril had hidden it beneath an outcropping of rock. She maneuvered the craft inside, and a mammoth door slid closed behind them. Once all the water drained from the bay, it pressurized and filled with atmosphere.

She hopped out of the craft. Her suit's instruments verified the presence of breathable air, so she retracted the faceplate of her helmet.

Shin opened his headgear, drew in a breath, and headed toward an entry hatchway without a word.

Scowling, she told herself to be patient and followed him. *I'm inside a Vril installation. The answers will come soon enough—and if they don't, I'll beat them out of him.*

Upon passing through the hatch, the view surpassed all of her preconceived notions. She had expected the inside of a base with corridors, rooms, and hangars. Instead, the scale of the subterranean ecosystem overwhelmed her senses. She stood on a cliff, looking down upon viridian and auburn trees and shrubs like those on the surface of Mars. Forests gave way to grassy hills, meadows, and valleys. Rivers flowed from glistening lakes and under concrete bridges, which led to winding roadways. Fields of corn, wheat, and other crops sprawled out across the landscape. An artificial blue sky flickered overhead with exposed patches of rocky ceiling. In the distance, habitats and buildings of all shapes and sizes comprised a grand city. The self-contained environment dwarfed the biodomes built throughout the solar system.

The scene reminded her of an old vidsim she had seen as a kid. Adventurers had traveled deep into the Earth and discovered dinosaurs living in an underground jungle, an unrealistic but nonetheless entertaining prospect.

Shin pointed toward a group of structures in the center of multiple square kilometers of open space. "If only humankind knew its true history. Over there in the distance are the launch pads where expeditions to the outer solar system were launched decades before the missions we credit with being first. The Vril's ancestors hollowed out this cavern and used the raw materials to construct everything."

Shaking her head, Brooke zoomed in on the launch complex. "I never imaged this place would be so beautiful."

"What were you expecting? Fire, lava pits, and devils with pitchforks running around?" He laced his voice with thick sarcasm. "The Vril are pure evil, after all."

She ignored the remark and increased the magnification of her i-cite. Small patches of a black, moss-like substance grew on the antique rockets and buildings. When she swung her gaze around the subterranean paradise, she discovered the moss growing on everything, including the walls and ceiling. "What's that black stuff?"

"You're looking at masses of hungry nanites, feasting on any and all evidence that this place ever existed. There aren't that many right now, but they're programmed to consume and multiply until they come in contact with water. In half an hour, this place will be covered in solid black moss. In an hour, the nanites will collapse the enclosure and deactivate themselves, burying the truth." He walked into a lift compartment.

"Should I worry about them getting on me?"

"They'll only consume inorganic material, so we're fine. Enable your personal force field on its lowest charge setting to keep them off your suit."

Brooke did as he recommended while they rode the lift down.

After commandeering a rover, they traversed the roadways until they came to a military compound. Once inside, Shin led her on foot into a series of interconnected surveillance rooms, each with thousands of control stations.

Shin stepped over to a central workstation. His eyes shifted back and forth, a sign he had established a neural interface with the AI matrices controlling the installation. "Good, we've still got power. It won't be long before we lose it."

Tens of thousands of display cubes blinked into existence and hovered at eye level. Brooke could barely see Shin through them all.

"This is part of what I wanted you to see," he said. "The source of the Vril's power has always been in its information network."

People in every city and colony, on every moon and planet in the solar system, went about their daily lives on the displays, ignorant of the intrusion upon their privacy.

"What you were saying about wormholes and the Vril being able to see anyone anywhere was true," she said.

"I do tell the truth on occasion, although I try not to make a habit of it." Shin gestured toward a cube with two fingers, prompting it to float over in front of him. Chancellor Ajunwa stood in her office atop ISC headquarters on Earth within the cube. Tennis racket in hand, she worked on perfecting her serve.

Brooke swung her head back and forth. "I'm looking right at the chancellor, and I'm still having a hard time believing it." She crossed her arms and tapped her foot.

"Go on, ask already. I know you're dying to see her."

Wrinkling her nose, she said, "Okay, fine. Show me Maya."

The image in the enlarged cube flickered and showed her niece. Maya shuffled along, lost in thought, in the phase port on the floating city of Landis.

"How'd you find her so fast?"

"Courtesy of the ISC. The government keeps a positioning fix on every citizen. Between conventional cams, biometric scans, and the devices people carry, the ISC tracks the location of everyone. It's extra easy to find anyone with implants, as those transmit locator signals. The Vril use these to determine wormhole coordinates."

Sticking out her lower lip, Brooke wondered aloud, "What's Maya doing on Venus? She should be aboard *Horizons* by now." The answer came to her when her niece passed a display cube with Japanese characters. "The Tokyo portal?" *I told her to stay away from him.*

"At any rate," Shin said, "being able to see anyone anywhere was only the first step for the Vril. We can also send drones, weapons fire, or personnel to any location. Consider a terrorist hiding out where he thinks it's safe. We can kill him on the spot with a particle blast out of thin air. Or what if a community of people sees something they shouldn't have? Abduct them, perform synapse erasure, and send them back none the wiser."

A knot formed in the pit in her stomach.

Shin shut down the surveillance center and led her into a spacecraft hangar. At the far end next to decommissioned tri-fighters, Pulsars, and spacecraft she didn't recognize rested a disassembled vehicle still intact enough to maintain its original saucer shape.

"Is that—?" she asked.

"Yes, it's one of the Greys' spacecraft. It's not the one from Roswell, though. It's a different one, uncovered long before it."

"I can't believe the Vril would leave it behind. Isn't this your precious artifact?"

"No," he laughed. "It was an object of intense study, fascination, and befuddlement for centuries, to be sure. But now, it's useless junk. Our Pulsars are more advanced." He rested a hand on each suited hip. "I would've liked to have seen you go up against a saucer in a Starthroat twenty years ago, though. That might've been an even fight."

"Huh."

The next stop brought them to a medical facility. Inside Brooke found cylindrical vats containing half-formed bodies of three-meter-tall humans. *These must be the chambers the Vril first used to birth the giant clones that helped them stage the invasion seventeen years ago. They're Armin's people—what's left of them, anyway.*

In a morgue she glimpsed one of the cryogenic caskets that had housed the exocorpse she had found on Titan. *Multiple caskets. Does that mean the Vril found more than one Grey?*

Another room served as a nursery for newborn babies. See-through bubble canopies covered each empty crib. Black moss grew around the edges of the high-tech bassinets and sprouted up through the cracks in the floor.

Shin approached a crib in the center of the nursery. Brooke joined him and stared down, perplexed. A living, breathing infant wriggled before her eyes.

"He's why we're here," Shin said.

"Your artifact is a baby?"

"He's a baby all right, but not a normal human."

"I don't understand."

"Look at him more closely."

She did. The yellow color and increased distance between his eyes combined with a sharp nose made him look like a bird.

The infant turned its head toward her. His hawk-like stare sent electricity coursing through her body.

She shook off the feeling.

"This ancient being is a member of the exospecies that visited our planet in the past," Shin said. "We found their genetic material aboard one of the Greys' saucers. They were transporting it—safeguarding it—as if it were the most important treasure in the universe. For centuries, the Vril's attempts at birthing these beings failed due to its complex genetic structure. Only in the last decade did they start succeeding, although with devastating repercussions. After much deliberation, the leadership deemed him too great a threat and chose to leave him here to die. They did, however, take his DNA with them when they evacuated."

"He doesn't look very dangerous—or anything like one of the Greys."

Shin nodded. "He's not one of the Greys. The Greys are a patsy race, just like us."

"What does that mean?"

A chunk of the hospital ceiling rained down and struck the floor near the crib. The black moss grew out from the chunk at a perceptible rate.

"Grab him and let's go," Shin said.

Brooke clenched a fist. "Why me? He's your artifact."

"Let's not waste time arguing. We need to get out of here before we're buried alive."

Groaning, she nodded in concession.

Using his suit's systems, Shin established an interface with the nursery AI. A set of restraints closed around the infant's blanket and shoulders, locking him in place. The bubble then detached from the crib.

She reached out to grab the bubble but hesitated, wary of the exochild. "If the Vril were scared enough of the kid to leave him to die, should we be worried about liberating him?"

"It's a definite risk but one that's worth taking," Shin said. "This kid can help expose the Vril and devise a defense against his people."

"A defense—?"

"Now c'mon, let's move." Shin waved for her to follow him out the nursery exit.

She picked up the bubble and cradled it under one arm. Regardless of any other considerations, she couldn't leave a child to die. She would deal with the consequences later.

Extending her force field around the bubble, she followed Shin out of the compound.

Back at the top of the cliff, she saw what he had been talking about earlier. The moss covered everything. She saw only the vague outlines of receding shapes. The blackness had become an ocean with waves and tides. Dirt, rock, and water rained down from above. The Martian hideaway seemed ready to cave in at any moment. She could feel it. In Earth gravity, the ceiling would probably have collapsed already.

"It's your turn to coddle Junior," she said as they rushed into the hangar. Handing the bubble to Shin, she leapt into the pilot's seat of the Poseidon and sealed her helmet.

Shin hopped in next to her and secured his faceplate.

No sooner had the canopy latched shut and the gravgel immersed them than a thunderous rumbling rattled the craft.

"I'm not waiting for the bay to fill." Brooke increased the Poseidon's shielding to max power and launched a pair of torpedoes at the door, punching a hole in it. Water rushed in, pummeling the craft.

Her heart thumping, she fired the jets at max thrust and dove into the water. The tough Navy fighter put up enough of a fight to avoid being slammed back into the rocky wall. At full power, the craft overcame the current and burst forth into open water.

Rear cameras showed the ocean floor cracking and settling, burying the base, as the Poseidon ascended.

At last, she allowed herself to exhale and release the tension in her muscles. "We made it," she said, flashing a rare smile at Shin and the crying infant.

Pale-faced, Shin managed a tired but satisfied grin.

The control interfaces in her i-cite flickered and gave out. "What the—?" Not only had something fried the neurotronics, but the manual controls failed to respond. The rumbling of the jets ceased. Stalling, the Poseidon's ascent came to an abrupt halt, and the craft sank. Nothing she tried worked.

She looked up and saw the issue. Black cracks propagated throughout the canopy.

"The moss must've gotten into the ship while it was parked," Shin said.

"I left the magnetic field on low," Brooke said, "but part of the landing gear must've been grounded and uncharged."

"We'll have to swim for it, but what about Junior? The water pressure could crush his bubble. And the decompression . . ."

She tightened her lips. "We're only a couple hundred meters from the surface. We'll rise up slowly and cross our fingers that the bubble holds—"

The canopy shattered, ending the discussion.

Brooke fired her suit's thrusters, ascended a couple meters, and looked down to see if Shin was with her. Having little experience in a pressure suit, he struggled with controlling his direction. She swam to him and grabbed his arm. Hoisting him up, she took the bubble from him, fearing he might drop it. While she guided him, she used her suit's instruments to plot the quickest route to shore.

After a seeming eternity of jetting along, her helmet broke the surface twenty meters from a rocky beach. Shin popped up nearby.

Black cracks formed in her face shield, and its displays flickered. Worse still, the cracks had spread to the bubble. *Damn it, the suit's shield just failed.* She turned to find Shin facing the same dilemma. "Swim for shore, quickly!"

She fired her thrusters, which gained her another few meters before they gave out. Then she swam like she had never before, gasping for breath. Each stroke proved difficult with the bubble clasped under one arm. The suit's musculoskeletal system enhanced her strength, but the power driving it continued to wane.

Her boots contacted the bottom, and she scampered the rest of the way to shore. The moment she stepped clear of the water, she issued the emergency release command. Pneumatics blew her helmet off her head and popped the front and back halves of her suit clear of her body.

The chill of frigid polar air bit into her bones.

Setting the bubble down in the red sand, she found a rock and shattered the bubble. Then she released the restraints encumbering the crying infant and cradled him. "Why do I keep getting stuck with these kids?" she asked herself, sighing.

Junior ceased his wailing.

Brooke looked back at her suit. All that remained of it was a mound of black ash.

Shin approached her in nothing but his drenched boxer shorts. "He seems to like you."

Five—Filicide
Tokyo, Earth, May 2265 CE

Maya stood in front of a mansion in the affluent Yamanote district, staring at the shimmering of the gated entrance. Despite the warmth of the afternoon sun, panic-induced chills shot through her limbs. Her eyes watered thanks to the pollen given off by the cherry blossoms sprouting on either side of the gate. Feeling lightheaded, she held a clammy palm over her thumping heart and sucked in deep breaths.

Her aunt's voice chastised her from the recesses of her mind. "Stay away from him," Brooke had warned her over the years. "I understand your feelings, but he'll never be a father to you. You'll only find pain."

Maya balled a fist. *If Aunt Brooke can't be there for me when it matters, why should I believe what she says? Besides, meeting him couldn't be any worse than dealing with her.*

In fewer than twenty-four hours, *Horizons* would depart Neptunian space. Maya wouldn't see the solar system again for years once the starship upshifted to hyperspace. If she didn't meet her father now, she would spend the mission wondering what might've been had she only worked up the courage. She had to do it, for better or worse.

She shook out her body and dragged her feet forward.

The sentry bots on either side of the gate came out of standby mode, their bodies erecting to three times their compacted height. Two sets of violet laser eyes scanned her face and uniform, which she had changed since the ill-fated soda spill. The hanging barrels of the sentries' particle cannons lifted, taking aim.

She crept past them, careful not to make any sudden movements.

In the booth next to the gate, an android guard perked to life. "May I help you?" he asked in an articulate voice.

"I'd like to see Mr. Katayama, please," Maya said.

"Mr. Katayama isn't expecting anyone today, and he doesn't entertain unsolicited guests."

"I understand, but I'm here to discuss something important with him. I'd like to think he'd make an exception for me."

"What's your name?"

"It's Maya, Maya Davis."

"One moment." The android stood motionless, unblinking, while it processed her identity and contacted its patron. "I'm sorry, but Mr. Katayama isn't available."

Maya lowered her eyes, feeling burned. *Doesn't he realize who I am? Or maybe he does and doesn't care to meet me.* Summoning all the resolve she could muster, she bit her lip and lifted her gaze. "Tell him his daughter is here to see him."

The wait seemed to last centuries.

When the gate dematerialized, Maya had expected to feel relief or anticipation. Instead, she trembled in terror.

"Mr. Katayama is a very busy man," the android said, cocking his head. "I suggest you don't keep him waiting."

Maya swallowed. "Right." Somehow, she pried her boots off the pavement and put one foot in front of the other.

She followed the driveway, which wound around a fountain and across the well-manicured grounds toward the mansion. One of the sentries trailed her at a discreet distance. The extravagant place struck her as an unnecessary indulgence. Throughout the past few centuries, Japanese society had enjoyed a smaller separation between the rich and poor than the American Colonies and most other nation-states, making the mansion something of an aberration. The house, by her account, had to be one of the biggest in all of Japan. The ISC charter stated that no single person should enjoy an unreasonable amount of wealth compared to the average citizen. This establishment struck her as a holdover from a previous era.

Each side of the large wooden front door slid aside when she neared it.

A young maid greeted her. "Please enter." The housekeeper led Maya into the middle of the foyer. The slight jerking in each step she took betrayed her android construction. "Please wait here. Mr. Katayama is in the middle of a very important meeting. I'll summon you once he's available." Turning, the maid disappeared down the hall.

Nerves setting in, Maya tapped one foot atop the Oriental rug covering the center of the hardwood floor. A winding staircase led to the upper level. Statues of samurai warriors, porcelain vases, and oil paintings lined the room. Multiple display cubes floated about the foyer, playing everything from the news to classical music to exotic fish swimming about.

She strode over to a gold-plated mirror hanging above a sheathed katana and examined her appearance. A number of pesky black strands had strayed out of place, so she curled them behind her ears. In her preoccupation with her graduation and the mission, she had allowed her hair to grow below chin length. She considered instructing her implants to alter her appearance but decided she approved of the look.

The blues and whites of her uniform shimmered in the sunlight piercing the windows in the vaulted ceiling. Turning, she inspected the IEF insignia and *New Horizons* mission patch affixed to her shoulder, both of which instilled a sense of pride in her. She had worn the outfit here on purpose. *How could he not be proud of all that I've accomplished?*

"Mr. Katayama will see you now."

At the sound of the maid's voice, Maya nearly jumped out of her uniform.

The housekeeper led her down the hall and to a sliding door, which parted for them. Maya followed the android inside.

The office was bigger than Maya's apartment. The wall to her left had a wood burning fireplace with a painting of nineteenth century Tokyo hanging above it. A large wooden desk sat in front of the opposite wall with e-slips, gadgets, and a mug with antique writing utensils—ballpoint pens, she recalled from Jo's ramblings about the past. Someone or something had bashed a huge dent in the front edge of the desk.

A grandfather clock occupied one corner of the room and a full-size statue outfitted with samurai armor stood in another. At least twenty display cubes floated about the office, showing financial charts and stock tickers. Bound paper books and a handful of vidpics rested atop the wall shelves behind the desk. When she zoomed in on the images, she saw her father with friends and colleagues but no significant other or children.

Mr. Katayama paced in front of a set of glass patio doors in the right wall, engaged in a heated conversion with someone in his i-cite. At one point, he threw his arms up in the air at the response he received. Several times, he punched a fist into his palm or straightened his suit coat in an emphatic gesture. Maya heard the word "deal" in every other sentence he barked.

"I thought he'd finished with his meeting," she whispered to the maid.

"He completed one, but another demanded his immediate attention."

"I see."

"Please be patient. Mr. Katayama will be with you momentarily. If you need anything in the meantime, don't hesitate to ask."

"I'm good, thanks."

"Very well. Please let me know if you change your mind." The android faced straight ahead, closed her eyes, and stood rigid and motionless.

I wish I could tune out that easily. To pass the time, Maya considered surfing SolNet or plopping down in one of the two armchairs in front of the desk, but she could only stand and stare at her father.

"Very well," Katayama said, "but mark my words, your decision will cost us trillions. Good day." He placed both hands on his hips and paced in front of the window.

Maya held her breath when he noticed her. He stared at her with a blank expression before settling into the leather chair behind his desk.

He took his time straightening the objects atop it. The ticking of the grandfather clock and humming of the cubes filled an otherwise uncomfortable silence.

Clasping his hands together, Katayama looked up at her.

Second passed but he said nothing.

"Hello. Um . . ." Maya's tongue tied into knots. "Do . . . do you know who I am?" she forced out in a stutter.

"I do," he said in a matter-of-fact tone.

The pit in her stomach knotted and compressed until she swore a fusion reaction might ignite.

Studying the wooden beams lining the ceiling, she said, "All my life I've had so many questions. But now that I'm standing face-to-face with you, I don't know what to say."

He rubbed his smooth chin. "Well, you're here now. There's no reason for pretense. Ask your questions."

"Okay." Maya tried to organize her jumbled thoughts. One moment, she couldn't think of anything. The next, fifty questions begged for answers.

In the end, only one question mattered. "Why haven't you been a part of my life?"

"She obviously never told you," he said. "Your mother, I mean."

"Told me what?"

Her father stood and wiped the dust off his samurai armor with a finger. "This may be difficult for you to hear, but please understand that a child wasn't something I ever wanted."

Maya's knees buckled, and she fought the urge to collapse on the floor.

"My association with your mother was a lapse in judgment on my part," he said. "I allowed a classmate to persuade me to attend a party. Before I knew it, your mother had convinced me to 'lighten up and have a good time.'

"Later, when she told me of her pregnancy, I promised her I would fulfill my legal and financial responsibilities but otherwise wanted no part in things. I couldn't allow anything to get in the way of my dreams."

Trembling, she said, "Is that all I was to you, an impediment?"

He glanced in her direction, and she thought she caught a faint crack in his hard outer shell.

"You must think me heartless," he said. "But please understand that children don't fit into my long-term plans. I'm a driven man intent on accomplishing big things, things you couldn't begin to understand."

Maya narrowed her eyes, no longer feeling conciliatory. "Do you mean accomplish things or accumulate things?" She swung her gaze around the office. "All I see is a bunch of stuff, but materialism never brings happiness."

Her father reseated himself and leaned forward on his elbows over the desk. "It's true that I enjoy the finer things in life. I won't apologize for that. But money isn't just something that allows me to accumulate things. Money represents the power to achieve one's dreams. If you have money, the possibilities are endless."

"For you, maybe. But shouldn't everyone have an equal right to the same opportunities?"

"You sound like a drone programmed by the chancellor." He shook his head. "As wonderful as the ideal of equality sounds, the reality is some people are more capable than others and contribute more than others. The people that make society go should enjoy a higher standing. I think I have a right to fashion something grand. Is it fair for others to chop up what I've built into tiny pieces and dole it out to those who didn't do a thing to create it in the first place?"

She opened her mouth with a rebuttal, but he cut her off. "Do you know what the ISC is doing to me?" He stood and waved an e-slip. "These are the new tax laws. To make a long story short, I'm required to donate half of all I'm worth to these new oversight committees—half of everything I've spent a lifetime achieving. I've poured my blood and sweat into my financial empire, and I won't give it up without a fight."

"Don't you feel good knowing that half of 'all you're worth' is going toward educating and feeding people? Toward creating technology that improves everyone's lives and fostering a culture of peace and prosperity?"

"If I believed my money was being used to accomplish those aims, yes. Not only is that debatable, it's not the point. I give to charity on a regular basis. But with the ISC, I no longer have the right to choose who or how much." He waved his arm, indicating his home. "The ISC has legalized theft. They're stealing what's mine."

"The whole concept of 'mine'—of owning possessions—is flawed. As they say, you can't take them with you when you die. Your wealth is obsolete, so you might as well get used to living in a better world."

Seething, Maya made a production out of straightening her uniform. "My only purpose is to expand the boundaries of human knowledge, not to mention see a bunch of amazing things along the way, things nobody can buy." She inhaled, having forgotten to breathe for some time.

"I guess we'll have to agree to disagree." He folded his arms. "This mission of yours is a disaster waiting to happen. We should be launching automated probes to assess potential threats and put the resources wasted on that starship toward fortifying our defenses at home. Someday, we may need to defend ourselves against exospecies far more advanced than us."

"That's all the more reason for us to go out there and extend our hand in friendship. Humans once fought horrible wars, but we've learned to coexist and work together for the most part. I believe we can do the same with the others we meet."

"And if we can't?"

"I don't believe in 'can't,' but I guess we'll cross that nebula when we come to it."

"Worry about it later, eh? Such thinking has never come back to haunt anyone."

Maya dropped her gaze and considered his words. She wouldn't be very objective if she didn't admit he had made a valid point or two. But she couldn't concede much to him when his heart wasn't in the right place.

While lowered, her eyes landed on the dent in the desk. She couldn't understand why a man with so much wealth hadn't replaced it. Had it happened recently?

"I see you've noticed the damage caused by that contemptible woman," he said.

"Contemptible woman?" she asked.

"She barged in here one day years ago to tell me your mother had died and you needed me. When I expressed my regrets and reaffirmed my stance, she pulled a gun on me. Fortunately, all she did was bash in the fine oak with it." Katayama ran a finger over the splintered wood. "I considered filing a civil suit, but it would've been more trouble than it was worth. I've refrained from replacing the desk as a reminder to avoid making the mistakes of the past. Having said that, please remind that insufferable aunt of yours that she owes me for the damage."

For the first time since she arrived, Maya manifested a smile.

◆

Standing atop a hill, Brooke looked out over the bustling seaport of Yokohama in the distance. The smell of fish and seaweed assaulted her nostrils from a kilometer away.

Long artificial islands with thousands of docked vessels stretched out from the shore. A mix of conventional cargo ships and hovering marine craft rested in docking strips. Robotic arms, automated cranes, and android workers loaded and unloaded pallets and crates of all different sizes. A dozen lines of oceangoing traffic ran to and from the port in a never ending stream of supply and demand. Every two minutes, a rocket launched toward orbit from one of the islands, rising high above the warehouses and stratoscrapers.

Closer to her, the city reverted to its centuries-old origins, a simple fishing village with wooden docks and boats. The Old World District had its charms, although they failed to appeal to Brooke at the moment. *I've seen more than enough water and ocean for one day.*

She turned from the view and descended the hill toward the cemetery, a place she loathed visiting. Both of her parents and maternal grandparents rested there. Despite her father having been born in the American Colonies, her mother's traditional family had insisted their daughter and her husband be buried in Yokohama with them. Ever easygoing and pragmatic, her late father had agreed. "It's not like I'll know the difference," he had jested.

Maya had ignored every one of Brooke's comms and messages, so she had used Kevin's influence to confirm her niece had visited Katayama in Tokyo. Tracking her via her ISC citizen profile had revealed her destination as Yokohama. Learning this, Brooke had left the exokid with Shin and portaled here from Mars, determined not to let Maya leave without saying goodbye.

Brooke passed through the entrance to the cemetery, a stone archway with potted flowers on either side. An array of vexing thoughts gnawed at her mind as she strolled between the rows of headstones. Shin had mentioned both the Greys and humans were patsy races to Junior's people, who had visited Earth long ago. She remembered Collins saying before he died that the real threat to mankind still lurked somewhere out there. Was any of it true, or was it a typical Vril smokescreen? For all she knew, Junior was an ordinary kid, Shin had a hidden agenda, and there was no extrasolar threat.

Shin had also said the Vril had a plan that would place the interstellar mission in jeopardy, but her underwater adventure hadn't brought her any closer to discerning it.

Everything was related somehow. She could feel it.

After rounding a group of trees, Brooke caught sight of Maya sitting with her back against a tombstone. The girl hugged her legs and buried her face in her knees.

What did you expect, squirt? Brooke thought, but she knew she couldn't take that tone with her now.

At the sound of her aunt's approaching footsteps, Maya lifted her head. Tears slicked her cheeks. Glaring at Brooke with bloodshot eyes, she averted her gaze. "Oh, so now you decide to show up."

Brooke sat down in the grass next to her niece. Their family plots surrounded them, with Brooke's parents' graves to her right. Maya sat leaning against her mother's headstone, which read, "Mariko Davis: 2223—2248 AD. Beloved mother, daughter, sister, and journalist."

Might as well get right to it. "I'm sorry I wasn't there today," Brooke said. "I know how important it was to you, and I was looking forward to it. I wanted to be there."

"So why didn't you come?"

Counting blades of grass, Brooke considered how best to answer. *Telling her about today would mean telling her the truth about everything, but I'm not ready to do that.* She had a host of reasons for having shielded Maya from the truth all her life. Protection from knowing too much. Making certain her niece didn't spread that knowledge. Ensuring she maintain her optimism and belief in her ideals. The whole point of allowing the Vril to triumph behind the scenes had been to give the children of tomorrow a better future. The main reason Brooke had remained silent all these years was to ensure Maya's future—not that anyone would have listened had she cried conspiracy. When Brooke dug deep down, she also found other, more selfish reasons she didn't want to face.

At any rate, the girl had more than enough on her mind right now.

"All I can say is you're the most important thing in the multiverse to me," Brooke said. "So if I wasn't there today, it means I was elsewhere, working to keep you safe."

Maya snorted and jerked her head back. "What the hell kind of cryptic, roundabout answer is that?"

"Unfortunately, it's the only one I can offer."

"Well, I'm not sure I want anything to do with someone who can't be honest with me."

"Maya—"

"Don't insult my intelligence, all right? I know there's something going on. I've known my whole life. I didn't question it when I was younger, but now it's obvious. I'm twenty-two, Aunt Brooke. I'm all grown up. No matter what it is, I can handle it." Maya glared at her with watering eyes.

Brooke looked away and stuffed the guilt deep down. "How was Tokyo?"

"Having Uncle Kevin spy on me again?" Hopping to her feet, Maya paced back and forth before responding. "My 'father' didn't want anything to do with me. You were right."

"For what it's worth, I wish I'd been wrong."

"What kind of person doesn't want to meet their own child? What decent human being doesn't want to be there from the beginning, loving that child with everything they are?"

"I can't answer that." Brooke sighed. "I don't condone his actions, but I can relate. I felt a lot like he does before you came along."

"You mean before Mom died and stuck me with you?"

Brooke jumped up. "That's not what—"

"Don't lie to me."

"Okay, fine. I never felt cut out to be a parent. I didn't want the responsibility. But when Marie's death forced me to care for you, I found a part of myself I never knew existed. You brought so much unexpected joy into my life. If I had it to do all over again, I wouldn't change a thing."

"Except for Mom dying."

"Of course."

Maya approached her mother's tombstone. "I don't suppose you're ready to tell me how she died?" When Brooke didn't answer, she said, "I've never been able to figure it out, no matter how deep I've dug. The last time anyone saw her, she was being arrested for threatening Chancellor—no, UN Secretary-General—Ajunwa in the UN press room. After that, it's like she blinked out of existence until a few months later when her grave appeared. There was no funeral, no obituary—not one word about what happened to her." She turned to her aunt, shaking her head. "I'm sick of all this secrecy. It's not right, and it hurts. What's so damned important it's worth doing this to me?"

"I'm sorry, Maya. Someday, maybe . . . but not now."

"Why?" her niece murmured. "Is it because of me? Something I did or haven't done?"

"No, of course not."

Maya hung her head. "I've tried to live up to everyone's expectations and be the best that I can be, but it hasn't been enough."

Pangs of grief buckled Brooke's knees. She rushed over to Maya and gripped her shoulders. "Maya, you've far surpassed every one of my expectations."

"Yet you failed me in flight sims, which bumped me from the top of my class."

Brooke shook her head in wonderment. To her niece, anything but being the best meant failure. "Do you know what I swore the first day you came to live with me? I promised myself that no matter what, I wouldn't let you turn out as messed up as me."

Maya lifted her chin.

"If I can take pride in nothing else," Brooke said, "I can feel fulfilled knowing that you turned out far better than me."

"Auntie . . ."

Brooke smiled. "Do you want to know the real reason I gave you a 'C'?" She waited until Maya gave a subtle nod. "I did it to keep you out of a cockpit—not because you can't pilot a fighter, but because you're capable of so much more." She pulled her niece into her embrace.

Six—Emprise
Neptunian Space, May 2265 CE

Euphoric, drool-inducing delirium. Maya had thought of no better way to describe her state of mind since she had set foot on board *New Horizons*.

A senior officer had ushered her through the ship's extensive network of corridors and sonic tubeways on a whirlwind tour. The hasty orientation had introduced her to the engineering center, reactor rooms, armory, main hangar bay, training facilities, crew habitat, and command module. She had memorized every nook and cranny of the ship in sims, and the real tour had surpassed them all. She hadn't yet visited Star City but couldn't wait to see it. Jo had raved about the restaurants, shops, and nightlife in the central biosphere.

Following the tour, the officer had escorted her to the main bridge, run her through the duties for which she had spent her academy days training, and rushed off to attend to her responsibilities.

Hours later, Maya stretched in her seat at the back of the bridge. Twenty manned duty stations, including hers, lined the rear and side walls of the expansive nerve center. A jumble of no-nonsense conversations, AI reports, and display cubes filled the air.

Officers and crewmen scurried past her, feet drawn to the curved deck by the rotation of the carrier. Located on the innermost deck of the command module near the nose of the ship, the bridge had no windows. Instead, a series of five-meter-tall display screens wrapped all the way around the room, providing a three-hundred-and-sixty-degree augmented view of space outside the ship.

With a wave of her hand, she commanded a section of the screen in front of her station to zoom in on a beach on Triton. Two children scampered along the shore, splish-splashing through the shallow water.

The direct neural link her implants maintained with the ship's systems rendered physical controls unnecessary in most cases. However, she still needed manual interfaces in case the neurotronic systems failed. When a crewman had asked her the location of a maintenance locker, she had enlarged and rotated a three-dimensional sim of the interior of *New Horizons* to help him find it.

As Engineering and Operations Liaison, she coordinated all activities between the bridge, engineering, and other substations throughout the ship. The AIs handled bulk information exchange and automated almost every shipboard function, but a human being still needed to monitor the process. Some officers viewed her job as busy work, but she had embraced the role. It gave her knowledge of and access to everything that took place on board. She performed her duties with a smile and had already caught a couple of oversights by the AIs. She had fixed a parts routing issue for Commander Alison Von Braun, the ship's chief engineer. The watch commander had nicknamed her "Glue Girl," the person that held everything together.

It's better than Soda Girl, she mused.

The more she enjoyed her duties, however, the more the guilt plagued her. If not for his near-fatal accident, Ankur would have filled her current role. In that case, her superiors would have assigned her to another post, most likely in the ECC, the engineering command center. She hated the idea of sliding into her present position by default, even though her performance merited it.

With a thought, she told her chair to swivel toward the raised platform in the center of the bridge. The platform featured a pair of navigational consoles, the first officer's workstation, and the skipper's chair.

Captain Reed sat in his command seat, leaning forward, elbows on the armrest and hands clasped under his chin. Maya's heart fluttered at how debonair he looked in his shiny, navy blue and black Defense uniform. Chancellor Ajunwa stood at his side, adjusting her wide patterned gele, or headdress. Two of her bodyguards stood outside the railing surrounding the platform. The ISC chancellor had come aboard for the historic send-off but would disembark before *Horizons* left Triton orbit.

"This is a momentous day," Ajunwa said, lifting her chin. Spherecams fluttered about the captain and chancellor.

Reed and Ajunwa's images displayed in one of Maya's cubes, appearing as they did to the forty billion citizens of the ISC. Scenes of enthusiastic crowds in colonies and cities throughout the solar system occupied other displays on the bridge.

"For the first time," Ajunwa continued, "humans will travel to another star system. It's the dawn of a new era. Every human being should take a moment to let the significance sink in." She paused before turning to Reed. "Captain, good luck to you and your crew. We'll all be cheering for you." She shook his hand. "Any profound words you'd like to leave with us?"

Reed smiled and stroked his chin stubble. "I believe the profound saying is supposed to come once we reach our destination, no? Neil Armstrong said his piece after setting foot on Luna, as was the case on Mars and Callisto. I'll defer until then."

"Very well. Safe travels, Captain." Ajunwa drifted down from the central platform. Beginning to Maya's left, the chancellor worked her way around the bridge, shaking each officer's hand at every duty station and wishing them well. Her clockwise tour ended back at Maya's station.

"Ensign Davis, is it?" Ajunwa asked.

After working out the jitters, Maya stood. "Yes, ma'am."

"I enjoyed your speech at the ceremony. You represented the IEF well."

"Thank you, ma'am. It came from the heart."

"Indeed." The chancellor's deep brown eyes scrutinized her.

Maya fought the urge to cringe beneath her penetrating stare.

"Ensign," Ajunwa said. "Please walk with me back to my transport."

Maya blinked. *The chancellor wants to take a stroll with me?* She glanced at Captain Reed, who dipped his chin in assent. "Of course, ma'am." Hopping up from her seat, she led the chancellor out the exit hatch and into a corridor. Guards followed close behind.

"This is quite the luxury liner," Ajunwa mused. She shuffled along with a slight limp due to multiple reconstructive surgeries. "Not many ships impart full gravity. In all my days, I've traveled aboard far too many ships with zero gravity."

"You mean microgravity," Maya said. "There's always a tiny amount of force acting on us, however small and—" She gasped at her elder's raised eyebrow. *Did I just correct the leader of the human race?* "Pardon me, Madam Chancellor. I didn't mean to—"

"To what? Educate me?" Ajunwa smiled. "Contrary to what some may think, it's never too late to teach an old woman new tricks."

Maya exhaled in relief.

At the end of the passageway, she boarded a transport sphere like the one she had ridden every day in Auckland. She strapped into a chair next to Ajunwa while the guards took seats behind them.

The sphere accelerated up to its cruising velocity and shot toward the outer decks. When it reached the outer hull, it slowed and turned into a tubeway along the exterior. Scrolling stars streaked past below her feet.

"You're not at all like your aunt," Ajunwa said, breaking the silence.

"I should hope not." Maya grinned. "I love Aunt Brooke to death, but if I ever grow that pessimistic, go ahead and vaporize me."

"She may have good reason for her attitude."

"I know she doesn't approve of you, although I've never understood why."

"She disobeyed a direct order of mine, forcing me to revoke her active military and flight statuses."

Maya's eyes widened. "She told me she chose to give up her career to raise me." *No wonder Aunt Brooke is so grouchy all the time. She loves flying more than anything. I'd be hateful, too, if someone had forced me to give up my dream.* "If it's not out of line to ask, ma'am, what did she do?"

"Don't you know? You were present for some of the events."

"If I was, I must've been too young to remember."

Ajunwa scrutinized her. "Punishment notwithstanding, your aunt played a pivotal role in the war against the Greys."

The chancellor's slowly spoken words sounded more like a query than a statement. She seemed to be probing Maya—testing her knowledge—while avoiding the original question.

"I know my history, ma'am," Maya said, "but there's no record of anything that happened between you and my aunt. I can't find any mention of a lot of things, actually." She bowed her head. "Not one hint about what happened to my mother."

When she looked up, she found a curious mix of understanding and regret in the old woman's face.

"Please accept my deepest condolences regarding the death of your mother," Ajunwa said. "I knew Marie Davis all too briefly. She was a strong and very perceptive young woman. It's obvious you've inherited her optimism."

"Thank you, ma'am. Since you knew her, do you know anything about how she died?"

Ajunwa drew her lips to a thin line.

<Now approaching the defense module main hangar bay,> the AI

announced.

The sphere slid to a halt. Part of its clear bubble casing dissolved, forming a hatchway. Maya helped Ajunwa out into the hangar.

"Wait for me at the shuttle," Ajunwa ordered her bodyguards.

"But ma'am," one of the guards said, "we need to ensure your safety."

The chancellor flicked her wrist, waving them away. "There's no safer place in the galaxy than on this ship, young man. Now go."

After trading reluctant glances, the two guards marched off down the hall.

When they had stepped beyond earshot, Ajunwa said, "Ensign—Maya—your aunt seems to have had her reasons for withholding things from you. I can't say I would've done any differently."

"So you do know what happened to my mom."

The sounds of roaring engines, ratcheting, and beeping from across the hangar filled the silence until the woman responded.

"Yes," Ajunwa said, "but it's not my place to tell you what she won't."

Maya clenched her jaw. "With all due respect, ma'am, don't you think I have a right to know?" She lifted her boot slightly, ready to stomp, but she calmed herself and lowered it. "I don't get the big secret. Everyone acts like the knowledge might cause civilization to collapse or something."

"Indeed," Ajunwa muttered. She cleared her throat, and her voice regained its depth and power. "The 'big secret,' as you call it, must be kept for your protection—for everyone's protection."

Everyone's protection? What does that mean? "I disagree. If you're withholding information about something that threatens everyone, we need to know about it. Wouldn't you want to know, Madam Chancellor, no matter how bad it was? I think you'd demand to know."

"If only it were that simple, my dear."

"I think it's that simple. People deserve to know the truth."

"Even if that truth leads to their destruction? Can you not concede that there are some things that people should remain ignorant of for their own good?"

"No. How are we supposed to learn and grow and transcend if we don't face reality?"

Ajunwa's eyes brightened. She seemed engaged in the philosophical debate. "So if you were faced with a situation in which you had to choose between withholding the truth for the good of everyone or revealing that truth to the detriment of all, which choice would you make? Think carefully, because real life sometimes brings about such dilemmas."

"Perhaps I'm young and naïve, but I don't believe those are the only two options."

"Oh?"

Clenching a fist, Maya said, "I'd tell the truth and claw, scrape, and never quit until I made things right."

Ajunwa folded her arms and cracked a slight smile. "You almost move me to believe that such an approach might work."

"I know it would. But if not, at least I could live with myself until it all ends."

One of the guards approached them. "Chancellor, your shuttle is ready to depart."

"I'll be right there." Ajunwa stared out across the hangar. Her eyes shifted back and forth, accessing something in her i-cite. "You've impressed me, Ensign Maya Davis, and I'm not easily impressed." She set off toward her shuttle.

Maya kept pace as they traversed the wide-open space. Row upon row of Pulsars occupied the bay, stretching off to either side along the curvature of the deck. Still more fighter craft hung from high overhead, relatively speaking. Human technicians and pilots, android workers, maintenance vehicles, and construction bots scurried between the spacecraft. A number of superluminal transport ships rested on rectangular launch pads.

Just before reaching her shuttle, Ajunwa stopped and turned.

An icon popped up in Maya's i-cite, and she skidded to a halt. The graphic linked to a secure filesim download. "What's this?"

"The answers to your questions," the chancellor said.

Maya opened her mouth, intending to ask if she was serious, but Ajunwa spoke first. "Before you thank me or access the contents, think long and hard about the ramifications. What I've given you won't satisfy your curiosity. The answers will only lead to more questions—dangerous questions. The knowledge the sim contains will change you forever, and I'm not so sure it'll be for the better. You won't look at anyone or anything the same again. This is a burden that should not be accepted lightly."

Unsure of how to respond, Maya left her jaw dangling.

"In any event," Ajunwa said, "the sim is encrypted for one-time access. It'll purge itself from your biotronics after it executes. I'd ask you to keep this knowledge between us, but I think you'll find it difficult to reveal."

"I can't say I understand."

"You will. Good luck and safe travels, Ensign. We're all counting on you and this great ship, more than you could ever know."

♦

Back at her station, Maya twirled a finger in an interface cube, lost in thought. She had stared down the filesim icon so hard she almost bumped into a crewman and a couple of bulkheads on her way back to the bridge. *To access it or not to access it? That is the question.*

The irony tensed every muscle in her body. She had spent her life searching far and wide for scraps of information about her mother's death. She had engaged in fruitless screaming matches with her tight-lipped aunt. She felt like a part of her identity was missing. But now that the answers loomed a mental click away, she hesitated. She had only wanted to know how her mom had died, yet the chancellor had warned her that the knowledge posed a threat to everyone—everyone being the human race, Maya could only assume. *Is the content of this sim what Aunt Brooke has been trying to protect me from?* As much as her aunt frustrated her, defying her wishes wasn't something Maya could do on a whim. At the very least, she needed to wait until later when—

"Ensign?"

Maya spun in her seat and found the captain facing her. He gripped and leaned over the railing encircling the central platform.

"Ensign, are all sections ready to depart?" Reed asked.

Her intestines knotting, Maya reviewed the status readouts in her i-cite and nodded. "Yes, sir. All subcommand centers report ready and Mayor Byrne has secured the city."

Reed stared at her for a moment, not with a glower but rather in curious amusement. "I might be a little distracted, too, if I was a young ensign who'd just spent quality time with the ISC chancellor."

"Yes, sir." She caught Trevor Young raising a disapproving eyebrow at her from the defense liaison station three seats away. She glared at him for a second before looking away.

The captain floated back to his chair and settled into it. "Very well, people. I hope no one forgot their overnight bag because we won't be back this way for some time. Navigation, confirm course."

"Trajectory and coordinates set for the Gliese 581 system, sir," the astrodynamics officer said. "Distance: 20.3 light years. Travel time: six months, four days, eleven hours, and fourteen minutes."

"Fuel and drive status?"

"Antimatter reserves at maximum," the power systems liaison next to Maya reported. "Phase drive active and fully charged."

Reed looked around the bridge as if regarding the Sol system once last time. "Upshift."

"Initiating hyperspace shift," the navigations officer said.

A pinpoint of light blinked into existence out beyond the forward screen. Space around the point warped and churned. The puncture in space-time ballooned into a wormhole, which widened and engulfed *Horizons*. Every object on the bridge seemed to gain elasticity and stretch forward as the vortex swallowed the ship. Maya felt the familiar strain on her brain while her surroundings tinted to a monochromatic mauve pink.

She set aside her conundrum for the time being and enjoyed the moment.

Cheering from the cubes filled the bridge over the audio system. Crowds of people projected floating signs saying "farewell" or "good luck." Cities and colonies set off fireworks displays, one so elaborate the explosions created an outline of the starship in midair. The festivities would continue for days.

Goodbye Aunt Brooke, Uncle Kevin. I'll miss you.

"Now passing beyond the heliopause," the astrodynamicist said as *New Horizons* left the solar system behind.

Seven—Jinni
Mercury, June 2265 CE

With both hands stuffed into her jacket pockets, Brooke looked up and marveled at the solar collector hanging kilometers above Mercury's surface. Hundreds of hexagonal mirrors faced the sun, absorbing far more energy than they could have in Earth orbit. The towering crater wall in the distance shrouded the north polar colony of Gassendi in shadow, but additional angled mirrors reflected enough light toward the ground to make Brooke feel like she stood on the Martian equator in the early morning.

She settled onto a bench in the middle of the Gassendi phase port, tweaked her latest disguise, and drew in a breath. No dome protected the colony. A grid of magnetic fields generated by the collector trapped the air inside the crater, preventing oxygen and nitrogen molecules from escaping out into space. The port rested atop a hill, allowing Brooke to look down over green meadows, flowing rivers, reflective lakes, thick forests, and igloo-like habitats nestled within the terraformed crater. She found it hard to believe that on Mercury's day side, only kilometers away, the sun baked the barren landscape in temperatures hot enough to melt most metals.

Leaning back against the bench, she wondered why she had agreed to meet Shin again. The ship and Maya were gone now, and with any luck, out of the reach of the Vril. Brooke considered cutting ties with Shin, but she couldn't leave so many newfound questions unanswered. More importantly, she couldn't leave an exochild that might bring about the human race's destruction in the hands of a Vril agent.

A message from Shin popped up in her i-cite. STAND UP AND WALK TOWARD THE NEAREST GATE.

Frowning, she rose from the bench and bounded toward the Venus gate, her strides graceful in gravity similar to that on Mars. Few people passed through the port. Mercury saw spikes in commuter traffic only when planetary alignment placed it between Earth, Mars, or Venus. Now wasn't one of those times, which suited her fine.

She caught sight of Shin standing near a potted palm tree. He had flipped his collar high and dipped his flat cap down to conceal his face, for all the good it would do against twenty-third century surveillance techniques.

When she headed in his direction, he messaged her again. KEEP WALKING TOWARD THE VENUS GATE.

Brooke resumed her previous path, her glower locked on Shin.

Not watching where she was going, she bumped into someone. "Hey—" Brooke stumbled back but regained her footing.

The woman she had collided with maintained her stride toward the Venus gate, back in the direction Brooke had come.

"What the hell?" Brooke stammered.

A hand grabbed her upper arm and pulled her in a different direction. "Let's go," Shin said. "This way."

She yanked her arm free and stopped. "What was that all about?"

"Sorry, but it was necessary to ensure we're not followed."

"You mean by your Vril pals?"

"More or less. We need to keep moving." He walked off, and Brooke followed.

An icon for a data uplink from Shin appeared in her i-cite. When she accepted the link, a map of the Gassendi phase port displayed. A blinking dot moved toward the Venus gate on the map.

"The woman who bumped into you did it on purpose," he said. "She's a member of the splinter group looking to expose the Vril, and a friend. At the instant you collided, we swapped your ISC tracker ID to her. She'll head back to Mars while we attend to business elsewhere."

"What about wormhole surveillance? They could've been watching."

"They were, but I've placed members in key positions. Given that they're already working on covering things up—it's what the Vril do—it's a simple matter to conceal the actions of two more people. That's the easiest way to explain it, anyway."

"Let me make sure I understand. You've planted secret agents in a secret organization that plants secret agents elsewhere." Brooke shook her head. "Anyway, where are we going? How's Junior?"

"We're on our way to see him."

Brooke portaled with Shin through New York and Ceres to Jupiter's largest moon, Ganymede. Two hours after departing Mercury, she set foot in the Marius colony, the most populated settlement in the Jovian system.

Despite Ganymede's proximity to Callisto, her one-time home, she had never visited the moon. After the American Colonies had landed the first manned Jupiter expedition on Callisto, the Russian Planetary Federation and Chinese Solar Republic had each staked their claim to a hemisphere of Ganymede. Both old empires had been willing to turn a blind eye to the separatist movement. Separatist factions had set up shop on Ganymede and used it as a staging post to launch attacks against the former UN. Ajunwa hadn't been able to go in after them without pissing off the Russians or the Chinese and starting a war.

Even though such politics qualified as ancient history, walking through Marius still felt a little like sneaking behind enemy lines. *I guess old preconceptions die hard*, she thought.

Brooke couldn't see to the edges of the far-stretching habitat dome as she exited the phase port. An imitation sky hung overhead, casting majestic twilight over the colony. The headlights of tiny, two-passenger cars, both conventionally wheeled and magnetically hovering, zoomed through the streets. Silhouettes of skyscrapers towered over the downtown area with retro Russian renaissance and Chinese imperial structures thrown into the mix. While hitching a ride aboard a sonic tube sphere, she overheard conversations in Mandarin, Cantonese, and Russo-Slavic. Every display featured text in these languages. Her implants translated what she heard and saw, but the colony still left her feeling like an outsider.

After hopping out of the transport sphere, Shin led her into a residential subdivision. A couple streets later, she reached a grass lawn and shuffled up the front walkway of one of hundreds of cookie-cutter habitats.

"I assume you left Junior with whoever lives here?" Brooke asked.

"Yeah."

She furrowed her brow at his forlorn tone.

Shin rapped on the door with his knuckles and then opened it. "Hey, it's me."

"I'm in the kitchen," a woman called out.

Brooke followed him through a narrow hallway with vidpics adorning the walls. After passing two closed doorways, she stepped into a cramped kitchenette. A raven-haired young woman in her late twenties sat in a chair next to a table, cradling the infant Brooke had saved.

The young woman smiled as Junior suckled from a bottle. "Who's your friend?" she asked Shin. "I take it she's his mother."

"I told you no questions, Xiaoqing," Shin said.

Xiaoqing frowned.

Based on what she had seen in the vidpics in the hall, Brooke said, "You must be Shin's younger sister."

"Half sister," Shin said. "We had the same mother, who was Chinese. Her father was also Chinese while mine was Japanese. Hence, the name differences."

Brooke didn't press for details, considering Shin's use of the past tense. "It's nice to meet you, Xiaoqing."

Xiaoqing nodded. "Call me Xi. You know, you look familiar."

"I can't imagine why." Brooke ran a hand through thick blue strands. She longed to return her hair to normal and get the annoying bangs out of her eyes.

Following a brief shrug, Xi asked, "I do have to ask one thing. What's his name?"

Brooke stared at Junior. With the lines on her forehead creasing, she turned to Shin.

"You can't be his mother if you don't know his name," Xi said. "Not that he looks anything like you."

"Xi, enough," Shin said.

"Well, I've been calling him Zeke. That was the name of my favorite childhood sim character, and he seems to like it. Don't you, Zeke?"

The kid ceased inhaling the contents of his bottle for a moment.

Xi directed her attention up and to her right.

Brooke stepped further into the kitchenette. A display cube floated in front of a wall covered by blooming flowers with shifting plaid patterns in the background. Brooke cared little about interior design, yet even she found the décor tacky.

An ISN anchorman spoke at low volume within the cube. "And in breaking news, authorities are investigating a buried facility at the bottom of the Martian south polar ocean."

Xiaoqing wiggled two fingers in an upward motion, turning up the sound. Brooke exchanged a worried glance with Shin, who shook his head.

"ISC authorities learned of the facility's existence from a group of university students performing a geological survey," the anchorman said. "The students were quite surprised when their instruments registered seismic activity, given that Mars has no active volcanoes or earthquakes. They made the discovery only hours ago, so ISC officials know very little at this point. The subaqueous installation stretches for kilometers and dates back more than a century, to a time before the polar cap melted. If that's the case, the implications are disconcerting. Some analysts have postulated that the facility belonged to the Greys."

Shin flicked his wrist. The cube dematerialized.

"Hey, I was watching that," Xiaoqing said.

"How's our little guest doing?" he asked.

Xiaoqing adjusted her grip on the kid by propping him up on her knee. "Zeke's almost too well-behaved. He hasn't cried or complained once. He drinks and sleeps a lot. That's about it." She looked up at the clock. The holographic cow in the center of it beat on a pair of snare drums. Once a second, it pointed each drumstick toward a digit. "Speaking of sleep, it's about time he went beddy-bye."

Junior drained his bottle and gazed up at her.

Xiaoqing yawned and covered her mouth. "Excuse me. I guess I'll turn in, too." She stood, cradling the baby. "I hope you plan to take him off my hands. I have to work tomorrow. The revitalization center's assessing the economic situation of the Volga district, and I've got a bunch of families to interview." She carried Zeke down the corridor and into the bedroom.

As soon as the door slid shut behind her, Brooke spoke in a harsh whisper. "Why didn't the nanites destroy everything? I thought the Vril were experts at covering things up? Hundreds of years of expert secrecy, and a group of college kids exposes you?"

"It doesn't make any sense," he said. "Unless . . ."

"Unless what?"

"Unless this is all part of the plan."

"I thought you knew the plan?"

"I'm not high enough in the hierarchy. I don't know everything, and things change."

"How does the command structure in the Vril work?" She snorted. "Do you salute?"

Ignoring her, Shin balled a fist and stared down the hallway. The muscles in his face tensed. "It kills me to see her like this."

"Like what? Your sister seems happy enough to me."

"That's the problem."

"I understand comfort in misery better than most, but you've lost me."

Exhaling through his nose, Shin took a seat at the kitchen table. Brooke wedged her body into the narrow space between the counter and table, sitting opposite him. With her elbow, she sent a couple e-slips flying by accident. She watched them drift down toward the scuffed flooring for a few moments before reaching out and swiping them out of the air.

"Once upon a time," Shin said, leaning forward and interlocking his fingers, "there was a stubborn, blockheaded girl who loathed the ISC and its policies. Xi picketed against the oversight committee assigned to Marius and protested the economic reform laws, even though they benefited her. She believed having egalitarianism shoved down our throats would turn us into mindless lemmings. The price was too high, she used to say. She preferred poverty and wanted to claw her way to the top based on her own merits. At one point, she and her activist group planned to bomb the very revitalization center where she now works."

"That's when the Vril intervened."

Shin whipped his gaze away, frowning. "That's when I intervened. I marked her group for cognitive reprogramming." He slapped his palms against the table and shot to his feet.

After adjusting his cap, he sat back down. "I turned in my own sister, who got exactly what she hated and feared most. The worst part is she doesn't even know it."

Brooke drew her lips to a thin line. "I know what it's like to lose a family member, but at least she's still alive." She tapped her fingernails against the table. "Now, I understand why you'd want to expose the Vril."

"I'd like nothing better than to get rid of all the lies and deception, but the Vril are maintaining a delicate balance right now. The ISC is in a far more fragile state than is publicly known. Most nation-states believe they're being forced to give up too much. While politicians stew behind closed doors, ISC propaganda paints a rosy picture of everybody hand-in-hand. Sadly, the Vril are necessary to manipulate intrasolar leadership and snuff out dissenters before society crumbles down around us."

"Welcome to paradise, I guess."

"Don't get me wrong. I think the good being done outweighs the bad—or, at least, I used to believe that until I helped rip my sister's identity away from her." He growled, closed-mouthed. "The last straw was when the Vril finalized their plan for the *Horizons* mission."

"What plan?"

"A plan to help solidify people's belief in the ISC." He locked stares with her. "They intend to dupe everyone aboard into sacrificing themselves as martyrs in a futile effort to prevent the Greys from wiping out the Penphins."

Cold flashes rippled through Brooke's body. *Maya* . . . "You can't be serious. They'd kill the thousands of people on that ship—and slaughter an entire race—just to quell a little political unrest back home?"

"Think about it. It's the perfect follow-up to the staged invasion seventeen years ago. A shared threat brought everyone together, but how do you guarantee things stay that way? By shocking the forty billion citizens whose attention is fixated on the awe-inspiring first deep space mission. When the threat of human extermination is made all too real, people won't have any issues giving up wealth or setting aside their differences to ensure their survival. Tragic actions speak louder than words."

Brooke stared at the scuffs in the table as the ramifications rattled around in her head. "Why didn't you tell me sooner? Why not warn the IEF and put a stop to this before they left?"

"I wanted to tell you when we first met, but I knew you wouldn't listen to me until you saw for yourself on Mars. And who would've believed me if I'd contacted *Horizons*?" He cleared his throat. "'Hi, I'm a member of a secret society that plans to manipulate your mission toward a disastrous end. Would you mind postponing your launch for, I don't know, ever?' Besides, the Vril have agents aboard *Horizons*. There's no guarantee the right people would receive the message. For that matter, there's no way to know who the right people are. No one in my splinter group has high enough clearance. For all we know, the captain might be an agent."

"Then let me try. If I can get a message to Maya, she might be able to do something." Her intestines twisted and knotted. *Maya, why didn't I tell you everything before you left?*

"That's one reason why I came to you. But wormhole comm signals don't travel any faster than the ship. They won't get the message until after they arrive."

"Then let's hope they receive it in time."

Shin nodded. "We can maximize the odds that they do by comming from a state-of-the-art transmitter. I know of one, but reaching it will require more of your piloting expertise."

Brooke opened her mouth to protest as Xiaoqing emerged from the hallway.

"What are you two going on about?" She yawned and stretched. "I can't sleep with all the yammering."

"Sorry, Xi," Shin said. "By the way, Brooke's agreed to stick around and watch Zeke while we're at work tomorrow."

Brooke scowled at him.

"Sounds great." Xiaoqing turned and retreated back to her room.

The moment her door closed, Brooke hissed, "I never agreed—"

"Do you want to save your niece or not?" Shin stood. "It's not like I can entrust an exochild to anyone else. Besides, I need to show my face at 'work' tomorrow or else I may arouse suspicion."

"What is it you do again—I mean, when you're not slinking around for the Vril?"

"I'm between jobs at the moment, but I have a PhD in political science and served as a campaign strategist for Ajunwa in the last election."

"A propagandist, my natural born enemy."

"Yet we get along so well." He cracked a faint smile. "Anyway, I need to set things in motion so we can send that message."

"I suppose so."

"I'm turning in. The couch in the living room is all yours. Feel free to help yourself to anything in the thermafridge."

♦

Brooke yawned, having tossed and turned on the short, rigid sofa the previous night. She sat in a chair in Xi's bedroom, holding Zeke in her lap.

While the kid polished off his third bottle of formula that morning, she stared out the window, stressing over everything. *Even if I can get a message to you, Maya, there's no guarantee you can do anything. If only I could come to you, but it might be years until they build another ship capable of that.* She peered down at Junior and his strange, owlish features. *And what do you have to do with all this? Centuries of secretive wheeling and dealing has been done to prepare us to defend ourselves from your people. Shin said you're a threat to all mankind.*

She tickled his belly. Zeke squirmed and giggled, and she couldn't help but grin. "You don't look so dangerous. No, you don't. No, you don't."

Her smile faded. *Shin said he knew a way to expose the Vril without throwing the ISC into chaos, and I'd get my commission back in the process, but he has yet to share it. Or was he feeding me full of false promises in order to win my cooperation?* She made a mental note to drill him for information when he returned.

Zeke dropped his empty bottle. As it drifted to the floor, he peered up at her, whining.

"Seriously?" she said. "You're still hungry? Well, no more for now. You're going to end up bigger than me by the end of the day."

The kid continued to stare at her, and for some reason, she didn't want to look away.

Mild pain stabbed her temples. The overwhelming need to stand up gripped her. She set Zeke down in the crib Xiaoqing had bought for him and went out to the kitchen.

Reaching into the thermafridge, she pulled out a small formula box. When she tapped the top of it, it morphed into a bottle and heated up.

She held up the bottle, feeling a warm sense of satisfaction.

"Wait a minute," she mumbled, and shook out her body. "I wasn't going to feed him anymore. I don't remember changing my mind."

"Imagine what he might do to you once he grows up," a voice said.

Brooke dropped the bottle.

A woman stepped into the kitchen from the hallway. Behind her, two mean-looking accomplices entered the habitat, retreated down the hall, and barged into the room with the child.

"I think you've got the wrong house," Brooke said, her body tensing. Her gut urged her to rush to protect Zeke, but if her uninvited guests had weapons, an impulsive reaction might place him in greater danger. Better to bide her time.

"Oh, I'm in the right place." The woman smiled—more of a toothy, feral grin, really—as if her muscles couldn't quite get it right. She wasn't Chinese or Russian but generically Caucasian. The perfect symmetry of her facial features gave her the look of an Aryan elitist. Her pale skin appeared smooth like rubber, and she had chosen to grow her golden blonde strands too evenly. Bright red lipstick clashed with her complexion but matched her form-fitting outfit.

"I see the mental gears spinning, Brooke." The woman settled into a seat at the table and straightened her jacket. "This is a brand new android body. I'm one of the first to have their brain structure replicated and transferred."

In monotone, Brooke muttered, "Good for you."

Grabbing a grape out of the bowl on the table, the woman closed her eyes and touched it to her tongue. "Isn't technology amazing?" She took her time chewing. "You'd think things wouldn't taste as good to an android, or have any taste at all. But the thousands of tiny sensors in my tongue extract biochemicals and transmit the information to my cybernetic brain. My artificial glands, in turn, release the appropriate substances into my body, allowing me to taste and enjoy my food in ways that far surpass the human experience."

She swallowed and devoured another grape, beside herself. "I can tweak my settings to amplify, suppress, or alter the flavor. If I don't care for my veggies, I can make broccoli taste like chocolate."

"Fascinating," Brooke droned while inching her hand toward the particle handgun stuck down the back of her pants.

Without opening her eyes or turning her head, the woman said, "I know you're decent with numbers. You did so well in the Luminosity training exams—and all on your own—so help me out with this simple math problem. A human woman is reaching for a concealed weapon and requires 1.7 seconds to pull it out, aim, and fire. Meanwhile, an android can cross the distance between them and snap the human's neck in point eight seconds. If the two individuals start their actions at the same time, what's the result?"

Brooke withdrew her hand from the gun and placed her palm flat on the counter. "Fine, you win. Now who the hell are you and what do you want?"

"Call me Eve. I do enjoy the irony of the name. Despite the many wonders of this body, it's not like I can procreate." Eve stood and glared at her. "As for why I'm here, I think you know. I'll be taking the vile infant with me."

"Vile? That's a harsh way to describe a baby."

"It's too generous when you consider what he's capable of. I despise his kind for killing my moth—" Cutting herself off, Eve relaxed a mounting scowl. "But my personal feelings aren't relevant. He's too much for you to handle."

"What do you plan to do with him? Take him back to your Vril buddies? Dispose of him like you tried to do on Mars?"

"Also," Eve said, "you'll refrain from contacting *Horizons*. In exchange, I'll guarantee your niece's safety."

"How could you possibly—?" She scrunched her nose. "You can't expect me to trust you. Besides, why be so generous? Why not snap my neck in point eight seconds and prevent me from contacting anyone ever again?"

Eve shrugged. "The day is still young."

Suppressing a gulp, Brooke said, "I don't suppose you'll tell me why you're letting me live, or why the Vril have left me alone all this time, or why you'd bother to spare Maya."

"Suffice it to say that we benefit from keeping you around." She turned toward the hall. "Just like with Shin's cute little splinter group. It's all part of the plan."

Two loud thuds echoed from within Junior's room.

The android woman rushed to his doorway and gawked at whatever she saw inside. "Damn you—"

Brooke whipped out her gun. In the time it took her to point and squeeze the trigger, Eve sprinted back as far as the table. The blast struck the android in the chest and sent her stumbling backwards.

Her heart thumping, Brooke fired twice more as the artificial woman righted her posture. The first shot caught Eve in the shoulder, driving her back further. The second scorched her forehead and ripped away a chunk of blonde strands, exposing a gray composite skull and circuitry.

Eve twitched as if she had Tourette's syndrome. "You're lucky I'm still adjusting." She crouched, poised to lurch for the kill.

Rust-red coolant dripped from the eye socket not scorched by weapons' fire.

Brooke pulled the trigger again, but Eve jumped out of the way of her salvo. The android retreated into the living room and leapt through the front window, shattering it. Nanoplastic crumbled into fine granules and drifted in the air all around her.

By the time Brooke reached the window, Eve had disappeared.

After running a hand over her face and remembering to breathe, Brooke checked on Zeke. The kid cooed and waved his arms in his crib where she had left him. Eve's two henchmen lay sprawled out on the carpeting, unconscious.

Eight—Swabbie
Hyperspace, July 2265 CE

"This," Ensign Trevor Young said, brandishing a sleek handgun, "is a new type of weapon unlike anything that's ever existed." Normally cool and collected, his smile and eyes beamed. He came alive at the first smell of ordnance, ever the prototypical soldier. Maya didn't share his unconditional love of all things military, but she couldn't fault his enthusiasm for advanced tech.

She stood at attention with a group of select personnel in the shooting gallery aboard *Horizons*. As the top-ranking academy graduates aboard, she and Trevor qualified as the only junior officers in attendance.

Trevor paced in front of the group, clearly thrilled the chief armory officer had selected him to demonstrate a device so state-of-the-art—and dangerous—that it had remained a secret until the ship had departed. "When and if the IEF fails to establish peaceful relations with another exospecies," he said, "this weapon will give us a decided advantage."

"Pardon me, Ensign," Maya said, tapping her cheek, "but a wave gun isn't only a weapon." She had grown tired of listening to him tout the superiority of the old Defense regime while putting down the IEF. Like him, she had a competitive streak, and she refused to let the jerk belittle the scientific and exploratory division unchallenged. As the only member of the IEF present, she felt compelled to represent its interests. "The device has plenty of non-combat uses, too."

"It's called a wave gun," he said, over-enunciating his last word. "It's a gun, and a gun is a weapon."

"So a flare gun is a weapon? Or a staple gun?" Maya straightened a grin. "If we're attacked, I'll be sure to break out my glue gun."

One of the other officers coughed to stifle his laughter.

"If those were the only tools I had to defend myself with, Ensign, you can bet I'd use them as weapons." Trevor rubbed the back of his neck.

Maya resisted the urge to brush her nails against her uniform and blow on them.

"Now, as I was saying," he continued, "a wave gun possesses capabilities that go far beyond conventional particle weaponry. Observe." He nodded at a soldier standing next to him.

The soldier marched out into the open. Raising her standard-issue particle rifle, she sighted on one of several oversized crates sitting twenty meters away on the opposite side of the galley. Trevor ordered the pair of android workers who had arranged the crates to retreat back behind the group.

A blue bolt leapt from the gunner's rifle, tore through the crate, and blew it apart. Jagged shards of shrapnel clanked on the deck. A force field shimmered in front of the group, shielding everyone from ricocheting bits of debris. The blast left the crate twisted and mangled.

Maya glanced over at one of the androids. The standard worker model stood motionless, his gaze directed at her.

"Particle weapons are powerful and get the job done, but they lack finesse." Trevor waved the gunner back, took her place, and aimed at a second crate. When he pulled the trigger, the parabolic dish at the end of the muzzle emitted a whirring noise but produced no beam or flash of light.

The crate shattered into countless tiny pieces, each one the size of a grain of sand.

A tall crewman whistled, which summed up the group's overall impressions. Maya didn't want to give Trevor the satisfaction of seeing her amazement, but she struggled to keep from drooling. *Too fused.*

Looking pleased, Trevor said, "The gun works in similar fashion to how a high-pitched tone at the right frequency can shatter old-style glass."

"The gun's built-in AI performs complex calculations to determine the ever-changing resonance frequencies required to achieve, maintain, and increase harmonic oscillation within the subject material," Maya said. "Using sound, electromagnetic, and gravimetric waves, the gun destabilizes the material on a microscopic level." To the eyebrows raised in her direction, she added, "Or so the manual says."

"Thanks for the details." Trevor pointed the gun at another crate. "But you know what? You were right earlier, Ensign Davis. A wave gun can do a lot more than destroy things." He pressed the trigger. Again, the gun whirred but nothing happened—at least, not at first. When he raised the gun, the crate lifted off the deck.

Trevor whipped his arm toward the group, sending the crate flying over everyone's heads. Maya flinched and ducked along with the other officers.

The crate banged against the metal floor on the other side of the group and tumbled away.

As Maya righted her posture, she found a female android standing between her and the direction from which the crate had come. *If I didn't know better, I'd think these semi-sentients had a thing for me.* She shrugged off the notion.

"Using waves and magnetism, this weapon can impart something akin to anti-gravity," Trevor said, "although the tiny antimatter cell only generates enough power to lift something as heavy as a small car."

"Can it fetch a beer from the other side of my quarters?" an aging Defense officer asked.

Sniggers broke out amongst the group.

Chuckling along with him, Trevor nodded. "That's not the half of what this thing can do. For the next demonstration, I'm going to need a volunteer."

Almost everyone raised their hands.

Maya wanted to handle the weapon—no, device—more than anything, but she didn't want to appear too eager, so she folded her arms.

"Ensign Davis," he said, surprising her. "I know you can't wait to try it. Come on up here."

Sighing, she trudged over and stood next to him. Everyone else lowered their hands.

"Now," Trevor said, "each wave gun is keyed to its user's specific DNA and brainwave patterns. It won't work for anyone except its rightful owner, which eliminates the concern of it falling into the wrong hands. The control interface is accessed via your i-cite." His irises shifted back and forth. "I've authenticated it for use by Ensign Davis." He held the gun out to her by the barrel. "Give it a shot."

Feeling lightheaded from awe, Maya gripped the wave gun by the handle. The gun's composite frame felt lighter than she would have expected. A menu popped up in her i-cite with a multitude of options and settings.

"See the water tank over there next to the crates?" Trevor pointed to a 750-liter transparent cylinder filled to the brim. "See if you can heat things up."

Maya stepped forward, resisting an impulse to quickly draw and shoot like she had seen in ancient Westerns. Perhaps after firing the gun she could spin it around her finger, blow on the end, and holster it.

Dismissing the silly notion, she selected molecular excitation mode in her i-cite. Then she calibrated the sensors to lock on to the water in the tank as the subject material while bypassing the structure of the container.

Once the AI verified the settings, she aimed and squeezed the trigger, expecting to see the water boil.

The i-cite menu flashed orange and red, and she felt warm—much too warm, especially in the chest area. *What the—?*

She had only a split second to study the menu—something about the gun switching to omnidirectional mode and locking onto nearby carbon composites—before her jacket and undershirt singed the skin on her upper body.

Her clothing felt like it was burning her alive.

Maya ordered the zipper on her jacket to open. The mechanism failed to respond, so she grabbed the zipper in a panic. She tried pulling down the metal clasp, but it scalded her. Hissing in pain, she blew on her fingers.

She tugged at the fabric of her jacket, which disintegrated to a powdery ash along with most of her undershirt. Franticly, she hopped around, brushing the scalding residue off her torso.

Both androids rushed to her and tried to help.

When she had managed to get most of the ash off her inflamed skin, she waved them off. The motion of her arms brought her to realize the gun had reduced her bra to little more than a collection of unwoven threading. Fortunately, her pants remained more or less intact.

Maya covered her chest with her arms and turned to find the group gawking at her, a commingling of amusement and abhorrence on their faces. Trevor's jaw hung open, his face flushed with guilt, although she didn't know if she believed it.

Storming past him toward the exit hatch, she hissed, "If you did this on purpose, I'll—"

"Don't blame me," he said, appalled. "It's not my fault you don't know how to work it."

As she bolted out the exit, she wondered if she should've asked to borrow someone's jacket before fleeing in haste. *There's no way I'm going back in there.* In her i-cite, she checked the manifests of nearby storage rooms for any sort of upper body wear.

She yelped as she rammed into someone just outside the galley.

Captain Reed caught her in an awkward embrace.

Maya backpedaled out of his grasp, clutching her midsection. *Of all the people!* A daze washed over her, and her abdomen cramped. "I, um . . ." she stammered, holding back her horror. "I'm so sorry, sir."

His brow dipped as he looked her over.

"I can explain, sir," she said. "I don't make a habit of walking around like this. One of the new wave guns malfunctioned and . . ."

She let her words trail off as his shiny black command coat unzipped.

He removed his medal-laden jacket and handed it to her. "Put this on, Ensign."

"Oh. Thank you, sir." She worked each arm into the coat and commanded it to zip.

"We can't have you violating dress regs, now, can we?" The captain stepped back and folded his arms across his long-sleeve shirt. "It's a little big on you, but you wear it well."

Manifesting a slight grin, she couldn't help but feel like a kid in the oversized coat.

"Now what happened exactly?" he asked.

Maya recounted everything, starting with Trevor's demonstration and ending with her rushing out of the room. "Do you want me to head back to the firing range?" she asked.

"No, Ensign. Go to your room and change. Then file a full report."

"I will, sir. I could've misconfigured the gun, or it might've malfunctioned. It's also possible Ensign Young rigged the gun on purpose, although I don't want to accuse him without evidence."

"Why would he do that?"

"I guess you could call us bitter rivals. Exploration vs. Defense. You know how it is."

"Well, the two of you need to set aside your differences and learn to work together. We've got a three-year mission ahead of us."

"I've always treated him with respect, sir. What more can I do?"

Reed rubbed the stubble on his chin. "The main objective of our mission is to establish peaceful contact with another species. If you can't get along with a fellow crewmate, how do you expect to establish relations with beings that may not think or act like we do?"

"You're right, sir." Maya blew out a breath, releasing her tension. "I'll do my best to make peace with him somehow."

"Very good. In the meantime, I'll order an investigation and have someone run diagnostics on all wave guns. They'll be off limits until I have a satisfactory explanation."

"Thank you, sir."

The captain stepped around her and entered the shooting gallery.

◆

After changing into civvies and filing her report, Maya agreed to meet Jo and Erik in Star City. A little fun in the most amazing biosphere ever constructed would take her mind of the afternoon's incident.

She rode a transport sphere to a sonic tube station in the city and strolled out onto the outermost level of the biosphere. Star City consisted of three concentric spheres. Each sphere rotated around the ship's axis at a different speed to impart one gee of force upon the structures and people on their interior surfaces.

Grassy lawns and trees lined the path between the junction and the buildings in the downtown area. Automated mowers, gardening bots, and android workers maintained the landscape. The sweet smell of daisies and lilacs prompted her to pump her system full of allergy medites.

Out of the corner of her eye, she caught the artificial persons watching her as she passed them. Ever since *Horizons* had departed Triton, she had caught them staring at her. She told herself she was imagining it. Or maybe their observations had nothing to do with her. Engineers had programmed them to perform numerous functions, and they might have instructions to keep an eye on everyone. Still, she hadn't noticed them ogling anyone else.

Interfacing with the AI control network in her i-cite—her liaison position granted her the access she needed—she checked the high-level directives of the android nearest to her. The artificial man pulling weeds from a flower bed had an instruction set allowing him to perform his gardening tasks, answer basic questions, and stay out of people's way—nothing out of the ordinary.

She told herself not to worry even if they had specific interest in her. Contrary to the popular beliefs fostered by bad horror sims, standard android models didn't have the capacity to do much harm. They possessed the strength of a child, were clumsy and slow, and could be easily outsmarted.

Resolving to run a more thorough inquiry during her next duty shift, she craned her neck upward and admired the sky, which she couldn't distinguish from the one found above the Earth. The only thing that told her she stood inside a spaceship and not on a planet was the horizon, which curved upward at a steep angle in every direction.

"Where've you been?" Jo asked as Maya plopped down into a seat next to her at a downtown pub. Erik occupied the other chair at the table.

"It's been a long day," Maya said as Erik slid a drink her way.

"We took the liberty of ordering for you." Jo inhaled a margarita through a swirly straw and smirked. "Or would you prefer soda pop served on a jacket?"

"Ha ha." Staring at the frothy beverage, Maya considered taking a sip. Instead, she grabbed the mug and downed its contents in three successive gulps. The beer left her feeling warm and fuzzy, despite its chilled temperature. *I'll have my implants break down the alcohol later*, she decided. *Tonight, I need a release.*

"That's the Maya we know and love," Jo said.

Erik clinked his glass against Maya's empty mug. He flashed a subtle smile, which she returned.

"That a girl." Jo leaned back in her seat. "Now, tell us about this 'long day' of yours."

Maya told them what had happened in the shooting gallery.

"That jerk," Jo shouted.

The other patrons in the restaurant turned their heads.

"Keep your voice down," Maya whispered. "I honestly don't know whether he did it."

Jo lifted her brow. "Oh, come on." With a mischievous grin, she lowered her voice and rubbed her hands together. "So how do we get him back? Can we program the gun to make him pee in his pants? Or how about we lure him into an airlock and make him think it's decompressing?"

Maya shook her head. "No retaliation." She told her friends about her run-in with the captain.

"Well, aren't you the popular one?" Jo counted on her fingers. "A great war heroine for an aunt, an uncle who only invented FTL, a chat with the leader of the human race, a rivalry with the top Defense graduate, and now thick sexual tension with the captain of mankind's first interstellar starship."

"What are you talking about?" Maya felt warm and dizzy. "The skipper's point was that we need to find a way to get along."

"No, I think he gave you his jacket so you can bring it back to him, if you know what I mean."

"Well, of course I plan to return it."

"Exactly."

"He was just being helpful. Anyone else would've done the same."

"Mmm hmm," Jo said. "A half-naked beautiful woman roaming the halls in desperate need of assistance. Even I might've jumped at the chance to help."

Jo had a hearty laugh at her expense. Even Erik chuckled.

As Maya grumbled, she caught sight of an android peering at her through the window. She recognized him as one of the landscaping workers she had passed on her way to the pub.

She shot to her feet, knocking over her chair and almost tripping. "Hey!"

The android scampered away out of sight.

Her friends looked back over their shoulders, much too late.

"Who are you yelling at?" Jo asked. "I don't see anyone."

"I . . . I don't know." Maya's shoulders sank. After a moment, she picked up her chair and plopped down. "Maybe I'm going crazy, but I swear every android on the ship has been spying on me since we left home. And now one is apparently following me."

Jo glanced at Erik. "I guess the captain's not the only one fused for Maya."

Maya drilled a vehement stare into her friend's forehead.

"Okay, okay," Jo said, sipping the last of her drink. "Maybe Trevor programmed them to harass you."

Erik shook his head. "I don't see him pulling it off."

"Right," Maya said. "The droids have quadruple-redundant security barriers similar to the Pulsar support AIs. It would take the most sophisticated AI in existence to crack their encryption." She exchanged glances with Erik, who nodded in agreement.

An android waitress approached the table. "May I fill additional drink orders for anyone?"

"Shots for everyone." Jo twirled her finger around the table.

Maya studied at the waitress, who never looked in her direction. "Make mine a double."

♦

"Okay, girl, open the door," Jo said upon reaching the entrance to Maya's quarters.

Maya draped her arms over Erik and Jo's shoulders for support. Squinting, she tried to bring the door controls in her i-cite into focus. "Okay, I got this." Her mind didn't want to work, and the last thing she wanted to do was to go home and go to bed.

"Who's up for another?" She tried to squirm out of her friends' holds. Erik caught her as she stumbled.

"Maya, seriously," Jo said. "Open the door and flush the alcohol from your system."

"Why?" Maya slurred. "I feel superb." It took all her concentration, but she eventually initiated the command to open the door.

After helping her inside, Erik laid her down on her bed and Jo covered her up.

"Why's it so bright in here?" Maya asked.

"You know how to work the lights," Jo said.

Somehow, Maya managed to dim the ceiling plasma strips.

The pinkish hue and prismatic refraction of hyperspace caught her attention outside the viewport. "Hyperspace. What a funny word. Hy-per-space. It doesn't seem hyper. It just seems weird. Nothing like regular space. Don't you guys wish they'd turn off the suppression systems so we can experience it?"

"Purge the alcohol and go to sleep," Jo said.

The door slid shut behind her friends.

Maya passed out.

She awoke when the blinding spotlights above switched back on, uncertain of whether a few seconds or hours had passed. The light exacerbated the pain piercing her temples.

Moaning, she flipped over on her side and gasped.

An android sat stiff as a board in the chair in front of her desk, facing her. Maya still couldn't think straight, but she swore this particular female model performed janitorial duties in the barracks. The dark green jumpsuit told Maya as much.

Sitting with her head cocked to the side, the janitor continued to stare at Maya without blinking or moving.

Is this a dream? Or am I drunk out of my mind? "What the hell are you doing in my room?"

The android didn't budge.

Red icons flashed in Maya's i-cite, warning her of an attempt to hack the firewalls protecting her biotronics.

"Get out!" She gripped her head in her hands.

Her i-cite turned solid crimson for a few seconds and then returned to normal. The hacker had infiltrated her mind.

Her implants kicked in, releasing biocites into her bloodstream to vanquish the alcohol. The headache began to subside.

The android stood. "You need to watch yourself, ma'am." She walked toward the door. "I may not always be able to protect you."

Maya sprang to a sitting position and hissed at the feeling of countless tiny needles stabbing her brain. She still had a long way to go to recover. "What're you talking about?"

As the door opened, the android said, "Please refrain from accessing the filesim, ma'am."

"How do you know about that? Who are you?" She tried to access its systems, but it denied her. *It shouldn't be able to do that.*

"Furthermore, ma'am, it's imperative for you to relocate to the engineering module when the ship exits hyperspace."

"What? Why?"

The artificial janitor exited the room.

Nine—Missive
Base Christy, Charon, July 2265 CE

Brooke ran a gloved hand across the Pulsar's sleek fuselage. Beneath her flight armor, her skin tingled in anticipation. *Seventeen years*, she mused. *It's been seventeen years since I've piloted a star fighter.* A handle grew out of the nose of the craft. Gripping the rung, she hoisted herself up into the cockpit with slow and easy motions.

Charon, Pluto's largest moon, pulled objects to its surface with only three percent of Earth's gravity. Earlier, she had crept across the launch pad toward the fighter, worried that an overenthusiastic lunge might catapult her clear of the moon's surface. The ISC Defense personnel stationed at Base Christy took long strides with no such reservations, directing the force of their steps straight ahead. Brooke kept reminding herself that not even her armor's powered musculoskeletal system could generate the two thousand kilometers per hour necessary to achieve escape velocity.

This is the frontier out here in the Kuiper Belt, she mused, staring up at the stars. *The phase drive has put thousands of dwarf planets within reach.*

Pluto blocked what little sunlight reached the moon, shrouding the base in darkness.

Her fingers twitched. *The sooner we get to the telescope array, the sooner I can get word to Maya.* She cracked her knuckles and shook out her hands. She had taken her meds before departing Mars, so she attributed her anxiety to normal nerves rather than the permanent damage to her nervous system.

Establishing a neurotronic interface with the onboard AI, she concentrated on bringing the Pulsar's systems to life.

Shin struggled to climb into the rear seat, over- and under-exerting himself at the wrong times. "You'd think state-of-the-art fighter craft would be easier to get inside," he said into his helmet comm. "And more comfortable." As he settled into his seat, the harness clamped him in place.

"You can stay here," Brooke said over her shoulder.

"I know you'd love to go it alone, but you won't succeed without my help."

"You could tell me everything I need to know now."

"Sorry," Shin said, strapping in, "but I trust you only as far as you trust me."

"At least we're clear on one thing."

"If you're that wary of me, why'd you come?"

"Do you have to ask? If there's the slightest chance you're telling the truth and Maya is in danger, I have to act . . . my own health and safety be damned."

"I can respect that, but you could try lightening up for once."

Brooke twisted around and glared at him. He was still wearing his flat cap beneath his helmet.

"I never go anywhere without my lucky cap," he said, following her gaze.

Resisting the urge to shatter his face shield and rip the hat off his head, she snarled, "Your organization is planning to sacrifice my niece and commit genocide, and you want me to lighten up?" She faced forward again. Exhaling to relax her muscles, she ran through preflight checks in her i-cite. "I still don't get why we had to come all the way out to Pluto. Kevin could've sent the message from the Solar Science Society."

"The Vril keep a close eye on him. They have agents inside S-cubed. How do you think we get our hands on the latest tech? Besides, an AI censor would block and erase the transmission before we could send it. On the other hand, a state-of-the-art hyperspace transmitter was installed last month on the New Allen Telescope Array. The transmitter is optimized for two-way interstellar communications, and the Vril haven't gotten to it yet. Last time I checked, we wanted to get our message to Maya as quickly as possible."

Grumbling in concession, she said, "Speaking of the Vril, aren't you worried about what that android, Eve, said to me? They know about your splinter group."

"I've known that they've known for some time. It's a chess game between the loyalists and splinters, as it always is with the Vril. The only identity they've weeded out is mine, but I've got a plan to take care of that."

"Still, they knew you brought Junior to your sister's place."

"Don't worry. I've sent Xi and Zeke into hiding."

"What if they know what we're about to do?"

"That's why I've enlisted you to protect me."

"Oh, so that's what I am? The hired help?" *And I'm not even getting paid.* Brooke catalyzed the fighter's antimatter reactor.

The space-suited technician who had serviced the Pulsar rushed toward it from the base, waving his arms. Brooke shook her head in bewilderment. His strides stretched so long she wondered if he were on mag-skates.

Upon reaching the fighter, he rested his hands on his upper legs, panting. "You're going to want to see this, Shin," he said over the comm. "Tune to ISN."

Brooke called up the IntraSolar News feed within her i-cite.

"—breaking news," an anchorman reported. "Deeper investigation of the facility beneath the south polar ocean by Martian officials has led to a shocking conclusion." The anchor's face paled as his forehead creased. "The underground dwelling appears to be a full colony constructed two hundred years ago, a century before the Greys established their settlements in the outer solar system and decades before the space agencies of the time had established any meaningful infrastructure on the red planet. The base was constructed to human proportions using materials common to the late twenty-first and early twenty-second centuries, leaving little doubt that humans somehow created and lived in this secret facility, not exobeings."

Brooke sunk down into her seat, wide-eyed.

"Furthermore, when the authorities salvaged and decrypted part of a damaged database, its contents astounded them." The anchor paused for effect. "Its records indicated that a secret human organization planned and executed the alleged extrasolar attacks seventeen years ago. In other words, there never were any Greys."

"It's happening," she murmured. "The truth's coming out—but is it a good thing?"

ISN played a clip of a cool and collected Chancellor Ajunwa asking citizens to remain calm. She called for an emergency session of the ISC Council and promised to get to the bottom of the mystery of the base. But of course Ajunwa knew who had constructed the base and why, so Brooke would be interested to see what version of the truth the chancellor reinvented.

The Pulsar's flight systems showed a ready status. Shin began to answer her question, but the base flight controller cut him off by signaling the all-clear for launch.

"Hold that thought." Brooke burned thrusters and lifted the Pulsar off the pad. The fighter's nose dipped, and its performance felt a little off compared to sims. It took her a few seconds to shake off the rust and get the feel for how the real craft maneuvered.

As the gravgel immersed her, it buoyed her body and spirit, bringing back the familiar sensation of returning to the womb. The thrill of flying released the tension constricting her muscles, if only for the briefest of moments.

Once the gel filled the cockpit, she fired the afterburners. Hundreds of exhilarating gees stressed the gravgel and drilled her back into her seat.

Charon and Pluto shrank out of sight in her rear cameras.

"Is this necessary?" Shin asked, gasping for breath.

Brooke laughed and engaged the phase drive. A wormhole formed in front of the Pulsar, and the fighter stretched toward the puncture in space-time and slipped into hyperspace. The incomprehensibility of a higher dimension, reduced by the craft's phase shielding to a distorted, salmon-pink liquid, surrounded the canopy.

"Destination: New Allen Telescope Array," she said, voicing the information for Shin's benefit. "Distance: 2000 AU. Relative speed: 40.2 times light speed. ETA in seven hours." She let the support AI assume control and turned around to face her passenger. "I believe you were about to explain why the Vril didn't stop the investigation of the base and cover up the truth."

"My group circumvented their circumvention," he said.

"Okay, but it still doesn't add up. The Vril united everyone on the basis of a lie, and they've kept the truth buried to prevent the ISC from falling apart. I don't see how revealing what really happened now, like this, will keep things together."

"The way in which the truth gets presented is critical. To strengthen the ISC, the public's perception of it must remain positive, which means they need someone or something other than the ISC to blame and to rally against."

"But this time there's no fake exos, no mutual threat."

Shin lifted his brow. "Ah, but there is a common enemy, one every bit as nefarious as extraterrestrials hell bent on mankind's extermination."

A jolt coursed through Brooke's body as the realization hit her. "The

Vril."

"That's right. The Vril can come out of hiding and play the bad guy. We can sacrifice ourselves to stabilize society. People will fully embrace our new utopia by participating in the purging of its deepest corruption. That's been the plan all along."

"Wait, I thought your splinter group's plan was to expose the Vril?"

"Actually, deviating from that plan caused the schism. The crew of *Horizons* perishing in a failed attempt to save the Penphins is an alternate scheme our leaders concocted to save the Vril from exposure. They're willing to exterminate an entire race to stay in power, and they justify it by saying the Vril must persist for our species to survive. Times have changed, they claim."

Staring up at the canopy in thought, she said, "I'm still not clear on how this alternate scheme is going to work. I mean, I can see the Vril planting agents aboard the ship and staging a disaster that threatens the Penphins. *Horizons* carries plenty of weapons and bio-agents. So let's say the Vril unleash their hazard and manipulate the ship into executing a dangerous rescue plan that destroys it. I get all that. What I don't get is how doing so will convince people back home to stop their petty bickering and embrace the ISC."

"It all hinges on who people believe killed the Penphins and how they did it." Shin clasped his hands in his lap and waited for her to ask.

"Okay, so who and how exactly?"

"If humans thought humans killed the Penphins, people would be angry at other people and things would get worse. But if not humans and the Vril remain in the shadows, people need something else to rally against."

"Like another extrasolar threat."

He lifted his hand to adjust his cap out of habit, but his helmet blocked him. "People will fall in line if they believe the Greys eradicated the Penphins and *Horizons* with a doomsday weapon beyond anything we have the ability to defend against."

Giving a start, Brooke asked, "What sort of weapon?"

"That I don't know. The leadership restricted those details to a select few. What I do know is the fireworks display is supposed to demonstrate a sliver of the real power possessed by Zeke's people. The Vril want to give people a reality check about our place in the universe. Despite what the human ego might want to believe, we're not at the top of the food chain." He sighed. "But genocide crosses the line. The Vril need to follow our original edict. We have to trust that mankind can and will persevere once we're gone."

Whirling back around, Brooke processed Shin's words. She had loathed the Vril since she had first stumbled upon their plans all those years ago on Europa. But as much as she hated to admit it, knowing they had planned to one day bare all and sacrifice their organization for the greater good lessened her disgust, albeit only marginally.

◆

Seven hours later, the Pulsar downshifted into normal space at the inner edge of the Oort Cloud. As a kid, Brooke had envisioned the cometary belt as a compact ring of sparklers with long tails colliding with one another like in an antique pinball machine. In reality, the icy balls of rock orbited millions of kilometers apart from one another. She saw nothing but stars against the blackness of space like anywhere else in the solar system. Her rear cameras showed the sun burning only slightly brighter than the twinkles of light in the background.

This is the furthest I've ever been out. Twinges of pride and wonder surged through her, which she dismissed when she remembered why she had traveled out this far.

With Shin's help, she charted a trajectory that avoided ISC Defense's deep space sensor network.

Rocket propulsion propelled the Pulsar within visual range of the New Allen Telescope Array. The space station consisted of a donut-shaped habitat ring that rotated around a non-spinning central sphere. The station's designers had mounted a pair of dish antennae as big as the donut on opposite sides of the sphere. Each dish had multiple sub-dishes and long pole antennae. The station kept one big dish pointing toward the solar system and the other pointed out into interstellar space.

A comm request popped up in Brooke's i-cite. "The station's contacting us. What should I say to explain our presence and get us aboard?"

"Say we're a patrol checking in on the station," he said. "Defense sends ships out here every so often, and in our flight gear, the civilian astronomer aboard shouldn't be able to tell we're not Defense pilots."

"Do I need to provide any sort of security clearance?"

"I don't believe so."

"You don't believe so?"

"One of the reasons we're here is because the Vril haven't classified the array a high priority target. They haven't paid much attention to it, so I don't have much information on it."

"All UN installations used to require verification back—" She cut herself off.

"Back in your day?" he finished for her.

She wrinkled her nose as the station repeated its hail. "Damn it." With her pulse throbbing, she established a comm link. "This is, um, ISC

Defense patrol twenty-four checking in. Request permission to dock and perform an inspection." She held her breath.

"It's been weeks since I've had visitors," a man said in an upbeat tone. "By all means, feel free to come aboard."

♦

With heavy eyelids, Brooke floated within the listening center of the station's central sphere alongside Shin. She kept opening her mouth to interrupt, but the astronomer continued to blab on and on about his recent findings.

"The data still needs to be verified," said the astronomer, "but I believe I've discovered a habitable exoplanet orbiting an A-type star. The high radiation from the blue sun should make the formation of life impossible, yet simple organisms are thriving there. The planet has 1.5 times nominal gravity, the surface is almost completely covered by water, and the plant life is red, orange, and yellow. Most of the plants on other exoworlds aren't green, you know—not that exoplants are anything like our plants. Some you can't really classify as plants." He folded his arms and pointed at one of the hundreds of cubes floating in the control center. "I'm going to name the planet Aryana after my great granddaughter, who took her first steps last week." He waved a hand in front of the cube. "I'll load the sim of it."

"Perhaps another time," Shin said. "We really need to—"

"It's a shame I didn't get to see it. The station's return shuttle doesn't have the speed of your star fighter. It takes me days to reach the Kuiper belt. I've sacrificed a lot for my work—not the least of which was my marriage—but it'll all be worthwhile if my discovery pans out. You know the two scientists who manned this station before me were the first to hear the Penphins's message, right? Hartmann and Shoemaker now hold directorships within the Solar Science Society. With any luck, I'll—"

"Sir!" Brooke summoned all her restraint to keep from pummeling the man with her helmet. "We're rather pressed for time."

"Of course, of course. How do you want to proceed with your inspection?"

She looked at Shin.

"Actually," Shin said, "we don't need to inspect the premises as much as the functionality of your long-range transmitter. We have orders to send a test message to the *New Horizons* expedition."

"Test the transmitter?" The astronomer scratched his temple. "The IEF ran tests when they installed it weeks ago, and it pings probes near Alpha Centauri on a regular basis. The results get auto-transmitted to the IEF. I'm happy to have you here, but I don't understand the necessity of your visit."

"Okay, you seem like a trustworthy individual, so I'll level with you." Shin leaned in closer to the man and whispered, "The message contains sensitive content, so ISC Defense didn't want to risk transmitting it to your station."

"A phase comm signal is almost impossible to intercept. There's no way for anyone except the sender to figure out where it exists in hyperspace or the wormhole exit point."

"Well . . ."

Brooke smiled her most patient smile. "Look, we don't pretend to understand the thinking of the top brass. Perhaps they're a bunch of paranoid, uneducated bureaucrats, or maybe they have other reasons they haven't shared with us. Either way, we're just following orders and would appreciate your cooperation."

After a moment, the astronomer shrugged. "Sure, whatever." He cracked his knuckles and swiped through menus in the display cube. "The transmitter dish is mounted on the sphere, so the entire station has to rotate into proper alignment with Gliese 581. It should take about fifteen minutes to move and calibrate."

"Great. Please get started."

<Sir,> her fighter's support AI mindspoke. *<Two Pulsars have downshifted at a distance of one million kilometers and are approaching the station. ETA: eight minutes, three seconds.>*

Crap. "We've got company," Brooke whispered to Shin. "Two Pulsars."

"I'm glad I brought you along," he said.

"Company?" the astronomer asked. He raised his brow in suspicion.

"The other members of our patrol. Nothing to worry about." *Pull their registry info,* she instructed her AI.

<According to their transponder signals, the incoming spacecraft are stationed at Base Gemini on Triton.>

But Neptune's on the opposite side of the sun right now. Calculate the likelihood that an ISC Defense patrol from Triton would show up here right now.

<Less than 0.001 percent, sir.>

I thought so—and we'll work on the whole "sir" thing later. She switched to the embedded comm in her implants. "I'm betting the Pulsars are being operated by Vril pilots."

"No bet." Shin's image appeared in her i-cite. His voice echoed throughout her head. "Looks like you were right about them being onto me."

"I wish I'd been wrong." She sent him the filesim she had recorded for Maya. "I'll keep them busy. Stay here and make sure the message gets sent."

"Good luck."

After undocking her fighter, Brooke rocketed toward the two bandits. Had they hailed from the IEF or ISC Defense, the pilots would have contacted her and the station by now. Their silence all but confirmed their loyalties.

Brooke accelerated straight at them at max thrust. Adrenaline shot through her veins. In the better part of the last two decades, the majority of all new fighter pilots had taken her course. Perhaps the Vril had their own training facilities, but there was a good chance she had schooled these two pilots. Somehow, she doubted the students had surpassed their teacher.

When they entered weapons range, she launched a spread of seekers. All three bandits returned fire and upshifted to hyperspace, avoiding her missiles as she expected.

The two Pulsars fired dozens of seekers at her, which she dispatched by jettisoning countermeasures and blasting with her particle cannons. The last projectile she allowed to detonate as close to her Pulsar as possible without doing any harm. After setting a straight-line trajectory and throwing her fighter into an erratic spin, she set the force field to flicker as if it had taken damage.

Both bandits reemerged in normal space.

And now it'll be ten seconds until either of you can upshift again.

One bogey approached from above her canopy and the other came at her from behind. Both craft unloaded their weapons.

Brooke upshifted to hyperspace, calculated the projected courses of her enemies, and downshifted on the tail of the closest one. With her cannons, she forced the bandit in the direction she wanted it to go and launched a volley of seekers. The tiny projectiles hit home, overloading its force field and destroying it.

As she had planned, her present trajectory took her straight at the second bandit, which accelerated away from her.

He thinks he can outrun me before his drive recharges. Her intestines twisted into knots. *Or does he?*

She verified their current flight path, which was taking them away from the station.

Her stomach dropped despite the microgravity.

Spinning her fighter around, she fired her afterburners. When her velocity hit zero, she rocketed back toward New Allen.

<Another Pulsar has downshifted fifty thousand kilometers from the space station, sir.>

Damn it. I'll never make it in time.

From a helpless distance, Brooke watched as the third Pulsar unloaded its seekers at the station's reactor.

Explosions reduced the New Allen Telescope Array to chunks of debris.

Visions of the past—of her inability to stop a group of separatist fighters from destroying a particle collector—flashed before her eyes.

"Shin!" She commed the station. No response came. Scanning the vicinity, she found no life signs or escape craft.

How long has it been since the station began its rotation? she asked her AI. *Did they get the message off?*

<Fourteen minutes and twelve seconds have elapsed since the realignment procedure began, sir. No transmission was sent from the facility during that time.>

Growling, Brooke shot after the Pulsar that had torched the station. She expected it and the other remaining bandit to flee, but they altered course to engage her.

Seconds later, she had reduced both enemy fighters to space dust.

She banged the back of her helmet against her headrest, unable to hold back the sobs.

Taking even breaths, she reasserted control over her emotions and forced her brain to focus. *Maybe I can talk to Kevin and tell him everything. We can find a way to send another message.* She felt her resolve returning. *If I'd trusted my husband instead of running off with a Vril agent, maybe none of this would've happened.*

<Sir, I'm detecting a massive gravity distortion at three o'clock high, two hundred thousand kilometers away.>

Brooke gazed up through the canopy and saw the stars in the indicated area of space bend and ripple. A wormhole formed and spit forth an ISC Defense carrier.

That's why those bandits engaged me after destroying the station. She pounded a boot in the gravgel. *To make sure I stuck around.*

<Twenty Pulsars have launched from the spacecraft carrier, sir.>

"This is the starship *Challenger* to the unidentified occupant of the Pulsar with Base Christy registration," the carrier's captain said. "Your flight plan is unauthorized. Reduce speed, maintain trajectory, and prepare to be escorted back to the ship."

Her mouth dried. *What do I do?* The knots in her abdomen threatened to rip her intestines apart. *Make a run for it?* With her fighter's transponder, they would track her anywhere in the solar system. *Fight?* Blanking a bunch of Vril pilots hadn't weighed too heavily on her conscience, but she refused to kill innocent Defense pilots. Plus, twenty-to-one odds might be too much even for her to overcome.

As Pulsars surrounded her spacecraft, she had no other option but to comply.

"Identify yourself," the lead pilot demanded.

Brooke didn't know what to say.

"Whoever you are, you're under arrest for the destruction of the telescope array."

She buried her helmet in her hands.

Ten—Appulse
Hyperspace, July 2265 CE

Yawning, Maya awoke in her bunk the next morning. As fragments of the previous night coalesced in her mind, the stabbing sensation in her forehead turned her "hello morning" smile into a contemplative frown. "Wait, how did I get home?"

She replayed last night's footage in her i-cite. The remainder of the evening in the pub had played out predictably enough. She had swapped stories, joked around, and traded insults with Jo with the occasional brief interjection from Erik. No surprises there. The drinks and shots had kept coming with Maya instigating. But then, of all the untimely encounters, the mayor of Star City had walked in with her teenage son to pick up a carry-out order.

With a to-go bag in hand—Maya remembered the sweet smell of shepherd's pie—Mayor Abigail Byrne had stopped by their table.

"I wanted to commend you all on the fine job you're doing," Byrne had said. "The residents of Star City appreciate your hard work."

"You're in charge of this whole biosphere," Maya had slurred. "That's so fused, although the name could use some work. The city isn't a star. It's way too small to be a star. I mean, the sun is one million times the size of the Earth, and the diameter of the Earth is less than thirteen thousand kilometers while city's only a quarter kilometer wide. It doesn't make any sense—ow!"

"No, it certainly doesn't," Jo had said, poking her in the side.

The mayor had raised her brow at Maya and excused herself.

Maya shrank under the covers, whimpering, as the recap continued to play.

Following a generous helping of shepard's pie, her friends had carried her home, put her to bed, and insisted she shut off the lights. Brightness had stolen her from a restless slumber an hour later, when she had flipped over in bed to find—

The recording went black and jumped to the view of the ceiling she had woken up to moments ago. An internal diagnostic showed no deletions or tampering. As far as her the logs kept by her implants showed, she had passed out at that moment.

Had she dreamt the visit by the android janitor? *I was pretty out of it, but I swear it happened.* Accepting the encounter as reality left her with a multitude of questions. Had someone remote-controlled the android, or had someone grafted their neural structure onto its AI brain? Physicians could replicate the human brain structure—hearing ISC Councilman Alastair Hamilton speak at the launch ceremony had reminded her of that advancement—but a janitorial model didn't possess the required complexity to support human neural patterns.

More important than who was why. Chancellor Ajunwa had told her that the knowledge contained within the filesim would change her, but Maya had a hard time believing the intruder had broken into her quarters to spare her from emotional discomfort. Did the filesim carry a virus that could scramble her biotronics and cause serious brain damage? If the android had wanted to do her any harm, it could have killed her while she slept. The artificial being had hacked her implants to help her, not hurt her.

The android had also insisted Maya retreat to the aft section of the ship when it exited hyperspace, but she couldn't fathom why. *I'm not missing that historic moment for anything.*

Digging through the ship's AI control network yielded no answers. No footage existed of anyone entering or exiting her quarters. The network had registered no anomalies in the behavior or whereabouts in any of the ship's complement of robotic passengers. *Maybe I did imagine it?*

With hands clasped behind her head, she considered whether to access the filesim Ajunwa had given her. *What am I waiting for? I'd talk to Aunt Brooke if she was here, but I won't see her for years. If I message her, it'll be months before I get a reply, so that's out. Unless I intend to wait until I get home, I might as well access it now.* The more she thought about it, the more sense it made to immerse in the sim now. The only way she could figure out why the android had told her not to access it was to do so.

Something else dawned on her. The android could have erased the sim when it had infiltrated her mind, but it hadn't. *If the sim's such a threat, why not remove that threat? More evidence I imagined the intruder, I guess.* She threw off the covers and hopped out of bed. *It's 07:03 SST. I've got plenty of time. All the more reason to access it now.*

Her stomach burbled, so she grabbed a travel box of Fruity Planets from atop her desk. *If I head over to the officer's mess, someone might sidetrack me.* She commanded her bed to morph into a recliner, got comfortable, and transformed the cereal box into a bowl. While she munched, she interfaced with the AI network and used its processing muscle to run every possible malicious software scan. Every check certified the filesim as safe.

She finished her cereal. After sucking in a long breath, she activated the filesim icon in her i-cite.

The sim commandeered her vision and hearing, providing a state-of-the-art sensory experience. Her quarters faded into the background as the sim whisked her away to another place.

Within the sim, Maya stood, gazing out the window of on an upper floor of a stratoscraper. The cityscape stretched as far as she could see in all directions. *New York City.* She turned and surveyed the room—or rather, the office. *This is Chancellor Ajunwa's office at the top of the ISC Council Building, but it looks different than when I toured it in high school.* Two olive branches hugged eight planetary orbits within the emblem on the floor. *I'm in the UN Secretary-General's office within the UN Headquarters building, before the ISC was formed.* The sim seemed to be a compilation of the different security cam angles in the office.

Ajunwa sat at her desk, swiping her fingers through an old 2D holoscreen. Fewer wrinkles covered the chancellor's face beneath her ornate gele.

The clear doors to the office parted. Two men in black escorted a young woman inside.

"Mom," Maya whispered in between a gasp. She had watched every one of her mother's old news feeds, so she knew what Marie Davis looked like, how her voice sounded, and how she acted. But the sim immersed Maya in a level of realism unmatched by any of those old records. From the smell of Marie's flowery perfume to the rhythm of her light breathing, Maya swore her deceased parent stood meters from her.

Marie's chin-length hair curled behind her ears, similar to but shorter than Maya's present style. Crisscrossing pinstripes shifted locations and colors on her smart pencil dress like in an antique screensaver. Magnetic cuffs bound her hands in front of her—from her arrest in the UN press briefing room, Maya recalled. *So this is where they took her.* Despite the restraints, Marie's expression emitted subtle joviality, as if the brighter parts of her personality refused to be subdued by the gravity of the situation.

The guards released Marie's cuffs, and she took a seat opposite Ajunwa. Maya shuffled closer to the two women as they exchanged pleasantries. When the conversation turned serious, her mother spent the next few minutes rattling off a story contradicting everything Maya had been brought up to believe.

A secret organization known as the Vril staged the extrasolar attacks? There never were any Greys—and yet, the exocorpse was genuine, so they do exist somewhere out there. For a brief moment, she regained awareness of her physical body, which had come close to retching. *The Vril united the human race under false pretenses. The ISC, IEF—everything I've believed in my whole life has been based on a lie.*

She grew lightheaded, unable to process what she had heard.

The sim skipped ahead. Aunt Brooke rushed into the office through a side entrance, wearing her flight armor and brandishing a particle rifle. Brooke appeared more youthful—not much older than Maya now—but the familiar scowl remained in full effect.

The two sisters rushed toward one another and locked into an embrace that lasted for over a minute. A whimper escaped Maya's lips at seeing their reunion.

Footage of the united Earth forces combatting the so-called extraterrestrial fleet played on every window screen.

"We need to go," Brooke said. "Now."

"Go?" Marie's brow dipped. "Go where?"

"Never mind. Head out to the fighter on the roof. I'll be right behind you."

"Why?" Marie swung her head back and forth between Ajunwa and her sister. "What're you going to do?"

The guards standing on either side of the secretary-general took notice and reached into their suit coats.

Pushing her twin to the side, Brooke lifted her rifle and blasted both guards before they could fire.

"What're you doing?" Marie cried.

Brooke stepped closer to Ajunwa. "I'm sorry, Madam Secretary, but your term is up."

"Is that so?" Ajunwa stood with hands on her hips, unfazed by the bloody corpses of her guards or the weapon trained in her direction.

Marie rushed over to Brooke and pushed the rifle down.

"I told you to go outside," Brooke said.

"Are you out of your mind?" Marie yelled.

"The Vril have been right all along, Marie. Everything's based on lies, anyway, so why not use them to fix society's problems?"

"That's not true, and this isn't right."

"What's right has nothing to do with it. Collins offered me a chance to pilot the phase fighter, and I plan to live my dream." She waved her rifle in Ajunwa's direction. "If this bitch has her way, I'll stay locked up in a cell for the rest of my life." Brooke shoved her sister aside and aimed her gun at the secretary-general.

Marie rushed at Brooke and tried to pry the gun out of her hands. "I won't let you do it!"

"Stop it!" Brooke tried to wrestle her rifle away but Marie wouldn't release it. "Let go!" With her face flushed crimson, Brooke screamed, "Let go—"

Maya gasped as her aunt pulled the trigger.

The point-blank particle blast tore Marie's chest apart, splitting her body in two and spraying blood everywhere. Her mutilated body dropped and thudded against the floor, eyes glazed over.

Maya dropped to her knees alongside her mother, cupping one hand over her mouth. The horrific event had taken place seventeen years ago, yet the impact jarred her as if it had occurred this very moment.

"No . . ." Brooke's jaw hung agape. "Marie, I didn't mean to . . ." Shaking like a berserk addict, she sneered at Ajunwa. "This is all your fault!" She bombarded the secretary-general with bursts from her rifle.

The beams passed through Ajunwa's flickering body and scorched the wall behind her.

"A holopersona?" Brooke stomped her boot. "You're not really here?"

Guards rushed toward the office from the other side of the see-through doors.

Snarling, Brooke backpedaled, turned, and bolted out the exit to the roof.

The sim terminated. The icon in Maya's i-cite disappeared, and the red text FILE PURGED FROM MEMORY scrolled across the bottom of her vision.

As she regained awareness of her physical body, she blinked away the tears. She still sat in her bed-recliner. *Aunt Brooke killed her. The woman who raised me murdered my mother. No wonder she's refused to tell me how it happened all these years.* She trembled in rage and confusion.

Hours later, she sat stuck in the same pose, staring at the strangeness of hyperspace rushing past the ship outside the viewport in the floor. She didn't know what to think or how to feel. The sim called into question everything she knew—if indeed its contents proved accurate.

She sifted through the ship's historical archives with the mindset to question everything she read. By the time her mind was spent, she hadn't located anything to corroborate the filesim, but neither had she found anything to disprove it. The discovery of the single exocorpse remained the only direct encounter with a Grey. She found it odd that not one person had captured footage of a living Grey. The UN had never infiltrated their pyramid carriers during the war, and the ISC had failed to find a living or deceased Grey on Triton or any of their Kuiper Belt colonies. Abducted and brainwashed humans had been caught operating the Greys's tri-fighters, which struck her as awfully convenient.

Although far from convinced, she chose to accept the filesim as the truth for now based on the source. *If Chancellor Ajunwa gave it to me, it must be true.*

But what did the sim change in the here and now, she asked herself? It didn't seem to affect *New Horizons's* mission to contact the Penphins and resettle the inhabitants of Star City. *But how can I proceed in good conscience knowing it's all based on lies?*

Maya bit her lower lip and vented a growl. The worst part was that she would have to wait three more years to confront Aunt Brooke and get her questions answered.

She felt the need to confide in someone, but this wasn't any casual topic, and with the filesim deleted, who would believe her?

Her gaze landed on the coat draped around the back of her desk chair, the one Captain Reed had given her. She stifled a laugh at the notion of telling him everything. "Excuse me, Captain," she envisioned herself saying. "Do you remember those exobeings you fought in that war where thousands of people died? They weren't real, by the way. And yes, I'm a new Ensign who's never seen combat, so naturally, I know better than you."

Or do I?

Her helplessness fed her curiosity. Who knew the truth? Only Chancellor Ajunwa and Aunt Brooke? That seemed unlikely. Did the captain know? How about his senior staff? Were the junior officers and the colonists the only ones in the dark, or was everyone aboard living in ignorance?

She needed to find out.

Before her quickening pulse could urge her otherwise, Maya established a comm link to the captain's virtual address.

She expected an AI to screen the call and take a message, but Reed's image appeared in her i-cite straight away.

"What can I do for you, Ensign?" he asked.

Maya needed a second to filter through all thoughts rattling around in her head. "I'm sorry to bother you, sir, but I wanted to return your jacket to you."

"That's very thoughtful of you, Ensign, but it's just a coat. I've got a closet full of them, and I can have another fabricated anytime."

"I understand, sir. Still, recycling it doesn't seem right. I can bring it back to you any time today. Really, it's no trouble." Maya tapped her leg and bit her lip, waiting for him to respond.

"Very well. I'll be breaking for lunch in thirty minutes. Join me?"

Maya swallowed hard. "Pardon, sir?"

"You've got a famous aunt and uncle, and you've managed to gain favor with the chancellor. I'm sure you've got plenty of stories to tell."

Shaking out her limbs, she thought, *This is what you wanted, isn't it?* "Okay, sir."

"Great. Captain's mess at twelve hundred hours. I'll see you then."

"Yes, sir."

◆

Standing in front of the hatch to the captain's private dining room, Maya told the wrinkles to smooth out of her sweater while altering the length of her skirt. She kept telling herself she would simply be sharing a meal with another human being, but such reassurances failed to bring down her heart rate.

The door slid open, and Reed waved her inside. He sat at the head of a table, watching different angles of the same recorded sporting event in three floating cubes.

Maya entered the dining room, which measured about the same size as her quarters. Approaching the table, she handed him the coat.

"Thank you." He waved a hand toward the display cubes, which shrank and disappeared.

As Maya took a seat opposite him, an android wearing an apron entered through the dining room's side door, served them each a pasta dish, and exited.

Her glands salivated at the aroma of Italian herbs and spices. *I had that bowl of cereal this morning, so why do I feel like I haven't eaten in days?*

A drink bot rolled closer to her. Interfacing with its menu in her i-cite, she selected cranberry juice. The manufacturer had fortified the blend with one hundred percent of the daily dose of vitamins and minerals her body required, according to the nutrition facts. When she placed her glass beneath the spout, the bot sensed and filled it.

Keeping her hands in her lap, she waited while the bot poured water for the captain.

"Feel free to start eating," he said.

She took a bite, then another, and then one more while trying to figure out how to begin the conversation. She had come here with so many questions and concerns, but now she couldn't concentrate on what to ask or say.

The notion her aunt had killed her mother refused to dislodge itself from the forefront of her mind.

Sipping her juice, she refocused her thoughts by reminding herself why she had contacted the captain. It hadn't been to return the coat. Given what the filesim had revealed, she wanted to gauge whether he knew anything about the Vril or if he was working for them. The noodles sloshed about in her gurgling stomach at the idea of the skipper of an interstellar starship rising to his station based on hidden agendas. As leader and emissary, a captain was supposed to represent the best the human race had to offer, which is why Maya aspired to the position.

"You seem distracted," Reed said. "I hope dinner with your CO isn't too unnerving for a young ensign."

Maya shook her head. "It's not that, sir—I mean, there's a little bit of that, but I've got a lot on my mind right now."

"I saw as much on your face when you walked in the room."

"I'm that obvious, huh?" She dabbed the corner of her mouth with her napkin and decided now was as good of a time as any to do a little probing. "Sir, you fought numerous battles against the Greys in the war, correct?"

Finishing his latest mouthful, he said, "That's correct."

"How close did you ever get to them?"

"What are you getting at, Ensign?"

"Did you ever see one of them alive in the flesh?"

Stroking his chin, he said, "All the fighting was done in space—our spacecraft versus theirs. Other than the incident at the Huygens colony where the UN recovered the one exocorpse, there weren't any ground battles."

"So, neither you nor anyone you know ever saw one of the Greys in person?"

After a long pause, he said, "No."

"And you never stopped to question who it was that you were fighting?"

The captain shifted in his seat. "I'm afraid I don't follow you, Ensign."

Either he's a stellar actor, or he doesn't know. Her gut argued for the latter, which helped to settle her stomach. "It's probably nothing, but don't you find it odd that no one ever saw a living, breathing Grey? You'd think a soldier would've stumbled upon one at some point in a year-long conflict."

"What are you implying?"

"I'm not implying anything, sir. I just find it strange."

Reed leaned back in his seat. As he studied her, the lines at the corners of his eyes contorted in suspicion.

"Never mind, sir," she said, holding up a palm. "I don't know where I was going with that idea." She grew wary of coming right out and suggesting a secret organization had staged the invasion. If he did know the supposed truth—if he was a Vril agent—his learning that she knew might have dangerous consequences for her.

Instead, she steered the conversation in a different direction. "Sir, have you ever learned something that called into question everything you've ever believed? Or discovered that someone you loved and thought you could trust has been lying to you your whole life?"

He leaned forward and focused on her. "I have. Care to share the specifics?"

Panic washed over her as visions of her aunt shooting her mom flashed before her eyes. "Not particularly, sir."

He nodded in understanding.

To fill the ensuing silence, Maya stuffed forkfuls of pasta into her mouth and had the bot refill her drink.

"Sorry if I'm not very good company right now," she said after finishing her food.

"You know, it's an act of insubordination to lie to a superior officer."

Maya stiffened. "Sir?"

Reed smiled while chewing his last bite. "You've been more than good company so far—quite refreshing, as a matter of fact, so don't tell me otherwise."

"Oh." The tension in her muscles relaxed.

"I think the first thing you should do, Ensign, is give yourself a break. Everyone faces that situation at some point in their life."

"Not like the one I'm facing, sir."

"Well . . ." The bot topped off both of their glasses. "As long as you keep your focus on what's most important to you, you'll pull through. What's important to you, Ensign?"

Maya thought about it. "I can't say there's anything specific, but the general things that come to mind are exploring, learning, growing, and doing the right thing. But in this case, I don't know what's right."

Reed nodded. "Life's full of gray areas. All you can do is follow your gut." He finished his food and sat back. "I had to make a choice before we left, and I chose to follow my dream." He lifted his glass and swung it around in an arc, indicating the ship. "As a result, my marriage ended."

Resting a cheek on her fist, she said, "It's sad, having to choose between two things that you love. But I couldn't have passed up the opportunity to be out here, either."

"That's something she couldn't understand."

"It's frustrating how few people do." Maya locked stares with Reed. Despite what her biometric monitoring software indicated, her heart felt as if it had stopped beating.

The captain killed the moment by pushing back in his chair. "Well, duty calls."

The comment slapped Maya back in reality. She nodded while staring at the napkin in her lap. "Thank you for the invitation to lunch, sir."

Reed rose to his feet when she stood, and he escorted her out the door.

♦

Her responsibilities as engineering and operations liaison kept her busy during the final months of the journey. AI glitches, routine maintenance, parts routing, dispute resolution, and preparations for arrival sent her running all over the ship.

Every time she interacted with Captain Reed, he treated her like any other member of the crew, which left her both disappointed and relieved. The dreamer in her wanted to believe they had developed a special connection because of the meal they had shared. She longed for him to take her under his wing and teach her the ins and outs of commanding a starship. Having him as her personal mentor would give her career quite the jumpstart, so the lack of any extra acknowledgment led to a mild degree of moping.

But for all she still knew, he might order the Penphins's home world torched on behalf of the Vril soon after *Horizons* exited hyperspace. She had observed him over the last few months but witnessed no damning behavior, not that she had him under twenty-four-seven surveillance or anything.

As for her visit from the android and the filesim, she refrained from telling anyone about them. She wanted to confide in Jo, but her best friend couldn't keep a secret. Erik would at least absorb the news without making a scene, but she wanted to confirm the existence of the Vril before spreading unsubstantiated rumors about staged extrasolar attacks.

At least the androids had stopped spying on her, although she swore they now went out of their way to ignore her.

All of that she could handle, but the fact that her aunt had butchered her mother continued to weigh on her. Maya thanked the stars for how busy her duties kept her. Whenever her mind started to dwell on the atrocity, she lost her focus, and the frenetic butterflies returned. She coped by occupying her mind with the next task while on duty. In her personal time, she kept researching the incident without uncovering much. There was only one sure way to learn anything, and a confrontation with her aunt wouldn't come for another two and a half years.

She shoved these thoughts aside as she sat at her post on the bridge. In thirty minutes, she would witness the culmination of a longstanding human dream. *New Horizons* would exit hyperspace and become the first crewed vessel to reach another star system.

Further reinforcing the significance of the impending moment, the bridge played host to a larger crowd than normal. Two of the three ISC council members assigned to govern the mission had come up from Star City. Together with every senior officer on board, they stood on and around the central platform, surrounding the captain.

The warning the janitor had given her resonated at the back of her mind but she dismissed it. *No way am I experiencing this moment anywhere but on the bridge.*

Conversations and reports assaulted her eardrums. Every officer at every post tended to the task of preparing to downshift into normal space. Maya's i-cite showed the reentry activities progressing on schedule. AIs prepared astrodynamic calculations for downshift that navigation officers worked to confirm. The engineering command center, or ECC, reported that the phase drive and all other systems showed nominal. Mayor Byrne had battened down the hatches in Star City. All residents had taken refuge in designated shelter areas, just in case. The only issue was a minor glitch in the robotic systems control network that had resulted in a loss of communication with some of the worker and delivery bots. She assigned a block of secondary AIs to diagnose the issue.

A commingling of guilt and satisfaction washed over her when she glanced over at Trevor's empty seat. The wave gun's logs hadn't shown any conclusive proof of foul play, but that hadn't stopped the captain from relegating Ensign Young to maintenance duty in the aft engine block.

Too bad for him. She swiveled her chair to face the forward wall screen. Excitement charged the air. *Only twenty minutes to go.*

A comm request registered in her i-cite from Commander Alison Von Braun, the chief engineer.

"What can I do for you, Chief?" she asked as she answered.

"You're going to hate me," the chief said, "but I need you to grab a

T49-R power converter from ship's stores and bring it to the ECC on the double."

"Why can't . . .." Her shoulders slumped. "The automated retrieval bots are down." *Crap, crap, crap!* "Can't someone closer to engineering grab it for you, ma'am?"

"I need all hands at their posts for reentry. Besides, between you and me, Ensign, I don't trust anyone else to track it down for me in time."

There's no way I'll make it back to the bridge for reentry. Damn. Maya stifled a sigh and nodded. "Okay, no problem, ma'am. I'll have it you in ten minutes, tops."

"Thanks, Glue Girl. You're the best." Von Braun closed the channel.

Maya stole one last glance at the impending moment she would surely miss, hopped up from her seat, and exited the bridge.

◆

Having delivered the requested part to the ECC, Maya stood in front of a viewport in the propulsion ring encircling the aft section of the ship. Hyperspace flowed and warped beyond the pane. *One minute to go.* At first, she had lamented the notion of witnessing such a grand moment from anywhere but on the bridge, but now she decided her current vantage point might provide a better view. Her first glimpse of the Gliese 581 system would have come via displays in the main command center, whereas the ring offered a forward-facing exterior view. *Now, I'll get to see things for real.*

A navigation officer counted down from thirty over *Horizons's* audio system.

"All hands, secure for hyperspace downshift," Captain Reed interrupted, "and prepare to make history."

"Ten seconds," the navigator said. "Nine, eight, seven . . ."

Maya's goose bumps popped smaller goose bumps in anticipation.

"Seven, six . . ."

Someone's reflection in the viewport caught her attention, and she whirled around.

"Five, four . . ."

Two android technicians grabbed her arms and pulled her back.

"Three, two . . ."

"Hey," she yelled. "Let me go!"

"One, zero . . . downshift in progress."

She squirmed back around to face the viewport, watching her surroundings stretch and snap back again. Hyperspace peeled away, at which point she expected to see stars and the familiar blackness of space.

Instead, a solid wall of craters—the surface of a planet, moon, or asteroid—blocked the ship's path.

Gasps of horror drained her strength, sapping her of the will to resist the artificial beings. They tossed her inside a maintenance closet and sealed the door. The hum of force fields surrounded her.

Shrouded by darkness, she opened her mouth to scream, but panic stole her breath.

Incredible force slammed her forward, knocking her unconscious.

Eleven—Saudade
Palomar Colony, May 2271 CE

Six years, Brooke lamented, pressing her palms to her forehead. She lay on the couch in her subterranean habitat on Makemake, a dwarf planet in the Kuiper Belt, awaiting—no, dreading—ISN's announcement about *Horizons. It's been six years since Maya left, and since then my life has fallen apart.*

Where had the time gone?

After ISC Defense had arrested Brooke near the telescope array, she had endured a grueling trial that had seemed like it might go on forever. The prosecution had explored every angle but failed to prove she had destroyed the station or killed anyone. The AI logs from her Pulsar had pinned responsibility on the unidentified fighters she had engaged, and the astronomer manning the array had somehow turned up safe and sound on Triton.

According to the tale her attorney had spun, she had gone on a revenge-fueled joyride to get back at Defense for booting her out of the service. Brooke had strayed into the wrong sector of space at the wrong time when the three rogue Pulsars had torched the station. She had done Defense a favor by blanking them, her lawyer had insisted. Without proof to the contrary, the jury had found her guilty only of stealing government property, the Pulsar from Base Christy.

Still, the judge had taken the theft of military hardware seriously and sentenced her to three years in prison. During her time, she had turned inward and numbed herself to everything to maintain a semblance of sanity. The alternative had been to obsess over how she had failed to get word to Maya or claw her eyes out over *Horizons* missing its check-in with the IEF. She had gone through the motions of three meals a day and walks through the prison yard, living her life like a lobotomized zombie.

The incident had stressed her marriage almost to its breaking point. At first, Brooke had refused to tell Kevin about what she had done and why, wanting to keep him out of it. Eventually, she had relented and told him everything, leaving him aghast just as the ISC had locked her away. Unbearable guilt and shame had led her to refuse to see him on all but a couple of occasions.

When the ISC had released her, she had found it difficult to re-acclimate to the outside world. She had become used to the mindless routine of prison life. Having grown apathetic to everything, including her marriage, she had sought out the most remote colony she could find with the intent to wither away and die.

The ISN announcement played in her i-cite, interrupting her latest bout of self-pity.

"Yesterday," said an anchorwoman, "the Interstellar Expeditionary Force received the final data stream from the search probe it launched after *New Horizons* failed to contact home. The probe found no sign of the ship or its crew after scouring the Gliese 581 system for years—no escape craft, debris, or other residual traces." The woman shuffled a stack of e-slips on her desk for effect. "In light of these results, the IEF has officially closed the investigation into the disappearance of the starship and declared all hands lost. The solar system is now in mourning at arguably the greatest tragedy in the history of space exploration."

Brooke whimpered. She had known this day was coming, but hearing the formal announcement added a grave sense of finality.

The feed panned to an anchorman. "In other news, unrest continues to mount across the ISC in response to findings on Luna, Mars, Triton, and Eris. The existence of hidden bases and manufacturing facilities reinforce the fact that a secret human institution carried out the alleged extrasolar attacks over twenty years ago. Sources close to ISN have reported that the American Colonies and Chinese Solar Republic intend to withdraw from the ISC Council, although no official statement has been made by the governments of these nation-states—"

Brooke terminated the feed. A nauseating chill coursed through her body. She wanted to cry but didn't have any tears left. She couldn't deny reality any longer. Maya was dead, along with anything and everything that gave her life meaning.

Despite the anguish, her rational mind refused to turn off. The ship's disappearance didn't add up. The Vril's grandiose genocidal demonstration meant to shock the ISC into tighter cohesion had never occurred, and the plan to dupe the human race into rallying against the organization had backfired. Protests and the level of political unrest had seen a steady increase since the public had found out about the Mars base. The ISC Council had grown dysfunctional with nation-states on the verge of withdrawing. And the trade embargos and other economic sanctions the chancellor had levied against the dissenters could very well incite a war.

Brooke refused to believe an accident had caused *Horizons's* destruction. The analysts theorized that a propulsion systems failure had torn the starship apart in hyperspace. If a ship's phase drive exploded in a higher dimension, no one knew for certain what would become of the debris—or what the crew might experience in death. She tried not to imagine Maya's body imploding while her suspended consciousness watched from every possible angle—

Stop it! She slapped her cheeks, although her atrophied limbs lacked much punch. Days had passed since she had taken a gravite injection or engaged in any sort of physical activity. She hadn't ventured out of her habitat into the thinly-populated colony of Palomar in over a week.

Following the trial and her incarceration, she had moved out here to get away from everyone and everything. The investigation and court proceedings had dragged on for two years until the judge had sentenced her to three more in an ISC prison on Dione, a moon of Saturn. During that time, Kevin had lost trust and respect in her for her involvement with Shin. Between her husband shying away from her and the loss of Maya, Brooke had grown petulant and apathetic, which had led her to push Kevin that much further away.

Now, she found herself in an emotional tailspin from which she didn't know how to recover.

With her muscles spent from the stress of worry, her eyelids grew heavy, and she drifted off. There was, after all, nothing else she could do.

The chime of the front hatch jarred her out of a nightmare in which a dozen Greys had torn Marie limb from limb. Soaked in sweat, she sucked in calming breaths and ignored the imposition.

Again, the intrusive chiming intruded upon her solitude.

A message icon with a dancing exclamation point popped into her i-cite. Grumbling, she opened the note and read it.

"It's me, Kevin," the message read. "Please let me in."

With a resigned sigh, she initiated the mental unlock command.

The hatch slid aside. Her husband entered and looked around the place with a blank expression.

She followed his gaze. Clothes lay strewn about the floor. Open food containers sat on the kitchen counter. Insects surely would have devoured her by now had any infested the colony.

Taking a seat on the chair next to the couch, he stared at the opposite wall. Tension contorted his face. He ran a hand through thick hair, most of which had faded to gray.

At last, he whispered, "I heard the announcement."

Her abdomen tightened. Hearing him acknowledge Maya's loss made it that much more real.

"She may be gone," he said, "but life goes on."

She pounded the cushions. "Spare me the motivational speeches."

"Same old Brooke." Kevin raised his voice, which took on harsh edge. Normally a gentle and sentimental man, the biting tone was a rarity for him. "I came here hoping we could comfort each other, but all you can do is wallow in self-pity and lash out at others." He shot to his feet. In Makemake's five percent nominal gravity, he had to hold his hand up against the ceiling to keep from knocking his head. "Did you ever stop to think that I might be hurting, too?" He blinked to keep his bloodshot eyes from watering. "I loved that girl like my own daughter."

His sincerity disarmed her. "I'm sorry. You're right. I get so focused on me that I forget other people have feelings, too."

Settling back into the chair, he sniffled and cleared his throat.

Intermittent drips from the kitchen faucet pinged against the sink, filling the unpalatable silence between them.

"It still tears me up inside," he said. "If you'd only come to me instead of letting that Vril agent manipulate you, we might've kept you from losing years of your life—our life—to prison."

"It's not like it mattered in the end. Maya would've died even if I'd involved you."

"But we'd be better off."

"Would we?" Brooke snorted. "It doesn't matter what I do. Every member of my family is dead, and each and every time it was my fault. You'd best stay away, or you'll be next."

Kevin released a forlorn sigh. "There was a time when I would've taken that chance without a second thought. I sympathize with you, Brooke. In your place, I'd probably blame myself, too. But at some point, you have to let go of the past and focus on what you have now."

Brooke flipped over on her side and faced the back of the couch.

"I love you, Brooke." On the brink of tears again, his voice wavered. "But lately, I don't love myself or us when we're together."

She didn't know what to say.

In her peripheral vision, he stood up and wiped the corners of his eyes. "I can't go on like this. I fear you'll never change, and a one-sided relationship isn't a marriage." He sucked in a deep breath, took a long look at her, and exited the habitat.

She rolled off the couch, face first. After drifting down to the floor, she buried her head beneath her arms and wept.

♦

That night, Brooke awoke in a cold sweat, chest heaving. Feeling confined by her skin, she needed to get out and go somewhere— anywhere.

She dragged herself out of her subterranean habitat and rode a lift up to the town square on the top level. Palomar was so new that half the buildings on the square remained under construction. Only fabrication and maintenance bots roamed the streets at this late hour.

As she passed through the central courtyard, she peered up at the stars through the dome.

Brooke ascended a staircase along the rock wall at the edge of the colony. Upon reaching an airlock, she stuffed her body into a pressure suit. Its fit and maneuverability paled in comparison to her beloved flight armor, but the suit would do for a jaunt to, well, wherever she intended to go.

The suit's face shield display indicated an hour's supply of air.

As the outer airlock hatch sealed behind her, she picked a random direction and bounded away.

Hundreds of meters from the colony, she settled down onto the edge of a rock and stared out across the landscape. Fine red granules of nitrogen and methane ice covered the surface of the dwarf planet. Beyond the horizon, the sun shone twice as bright as the surrounding stars, which hung all around her like suspended snowflakes.

Maya, Marie . . . Mom, Dad . . . Maybe someday we'll be together again. She closed her eyes. *I've never believed, but then again, I've been wrong about everything else in my life, so who knows?*

Come back, a voice in her head said.

Brooke's eyelids popped wide. "Who's there?" she responded via her implants, but there was no open comm link.

Come back before it's too late. It sounded like a boy.

"Too late?" When she glanced at her oxygen meter, she cursed. Less than fifteen minutes of air remained.

Pushing off from the rock in haste, she sprung to her feet, a miscalculation which launched her over five times her height above the terrain.

She searched the surface below from high above, finding nothing but an uneven sheet of scarlet and the dome in the distance.

Her boots touched down, crunching the ice pellets beneath her soles.

It's not your time yet, the voice said.

"I wasn't trying to kill myself." Despite her words, she delved into her subconscious, searching for her true intent. "Anyway, how the hell would you know?" She snorted. "Is this the voice of God or something?"

Perhaps, in a way, my people are your gods.

Her will to survive and spite pulled her in different directions. She needed to get back—now—but she also despised being told what to do.

Ten minutes of air remained.

Some unseen force pressed in on her mind, clouding her thoughts. Without her consent, her back foot pushed off, and she took a long stride toward the colony. She tried to halt her progress, but she no longer had control over her body.

"What're you doing to me?" she cried. "I'm heading back."

I'm sorry, the voice said. *But you'll never make it in time without my help.*

"Damn it," she shouted. "Leave me alone!"

I could alter your desire so you wanted me to help you, but that wouldn't be right.

Throughout the next few minutes, she exhausted her mental faculties to no avail. She tried to throw herself off balance, but her arms swung at her sides, driving her forward at a rapid pace. She tried to kick and twist, but her legs and hips charged ahead, stretching her muscles to the limit.

Fatigue overwhelmed her. Her body insisted on shutting down but kept going of its own volition. It seemed as if the electrical impulses from her brain couldn't reach her appendages. She had never felt so powerless.

Her boots contacted the concrete walkway that led to the external airlock hatch.

Her oxygen supply ran out.

The air in her helmet grew stale. She gasped and coughed. The urge to claw at her neck and detach her headgear consumed her, but the force controlling her prevented her from doing so. Growing light-headed, and with her vision blurring, she stumbled forward and collapsed against the outer hatch.

The hatch slid open, and her body pulled itself inside.

Everything went black.

♦

Brooke flinched as she awoke. The fabric of her couch conformed to the contour of her back. A few blinks brought the living room of her habitat into focus.

A man approached the couch. He pushed her legs aside and sat down next to her.

Am I dreaming or dead? she wondered. "Shin?"

Shin's face paled with genuine concern as he tilted his lucky cap back. "That was stupid and selfish of you."

Wiping the relieved smile off her face, she said, "What're you talking about?"

"I know you're the self-loathing type, but I never thought you'd try to end your own life."

"I didn't go out there to commit suicide. I just needed some air." Realizing how little sense the comment made in an artificial environment surrounded by vacuum, she amended her statement. "I mean, I needed open space."

Shin raised an eyebrow at her.

She grumbled and changed the subject. "So you're alive."

"I told you I had a plan to throw the Vril off my trail." He rose to his feet and folded his arms. "I needed them to believe they'd killed me."

"How'd you get off the station?"

"Using a piece of very fused and very advanced tech." He stared at her and waited, goading her into asking.

"What tech?" she groused.

"A working prototype your husband thinks he's kept top secret. It's a single-remote-source phase portal generator."

The notion perked Brooke up. "A teleporter?" To the best of her knowledge, creating a traversable wormhole required one of two things. A traveler needed to place generators at both the exit and entry points to stabilize the corridor, as with the intrasolar phase portals. Or, the traveler had to carry a potent power source, such as the type of antimatter reactor found in a Pulsar or starship, to maintain the passage through hyperspace. "So your pals pulled you off the station before the place exploded."

"Leading the Vril to think they had crushed the head of our splinter group. Sorry I couldn't tell you, but I needed you to put on a good performance."

"Fake invasions, fake deaths . . ." Brooke shook with anger. She wanted to reach out and strangle him. "I'm sick of your 'performances.'" Shooting pain stabbed her temples. She grew woozy and let her head fall back. The skin on her face and body stung.

After the dizziness subsided, she summoned a mirror. A cube materialized next to her and displayed a reflective surface. In it, two bloodshot eyes stared back at her. Patches of purple and red scarred her cheeks and forehead, although the discoloration was receding.

"The decompression and cold hit you when your air ran out," Shin said. "I couldn't get to you fast enough, but the kit near the airlock had meds that seem to be reversing the damage."

She was about to offer a thank you but glared at him instead. "You lie to me, set me up, leave me to rot in jail, and let me go on thinking you've been dead for six years. I can't say I'm thrilled to see you right now."

"I don't blame you. Again, I'm sorry."

Remorse replaced her pent-up exasperation, and her mental state devolved back to where it had wallowed before her brush with death. "The solar system, human civilization . . . it can all go to hell for all I care. Nothing can change the fact that Maya's dead—"

"No, she's not."

Brooke grew very still upon hearing the voice that had infiltrated her head.

She stuck her neck out and peered around Shin. A boy of twelve or so years of age stepped into view.

She started to ask who he was but stopped herself. Somehow, she knew. "Zeke?"

Shin ruffled the boy's hair and nodded.

"I see." She furrowed her brow at the kid. "He should only be six years old, but he looks twice that."

"I could say his species has a faster growth and maturation rate than ours, but that wouldn't do the truth justice."

Brooke studied Zeke's hawkish facial features. He had the penetrating stare of an eagle or owl, and his golden eyes were spaced a little too far apart. Other than that and his sharp, thin nose, he looked like any normal kid his age.

A million questions ricocheted off the walls of her mind, but only one mattered at the moment. "How do you know Maya is still alive?"

Zeke approached her. "She is. That's all I can tell you."

Brooke directed a desperate glower at Shin.

"I'm sure you've figured it out by now," he said, shrugging. "He's got abilities surpassing what we can understand."

"Either that, or he's lying."

"At six months old, he was speaking perfect English and Mandarin. He knows things he shouldn't be able to know. Hell," Shin said, his eyes misting over, "he helped Xi recover her identity." He shook off the emotion. "You've experienced the power he can exert over people."

"Some sort of psychokinesis? Mind control?"

The lines in Shin's forehead conveyed something akin to trepidation. "If that was all, his people might not strike a fear beyond death into the Vril. But the truth is much more fundamental—and humbling."

Throwing her arms up, Brooke asked, "Care to share what that means exactly?"

"That depends. Will you continue to help us?"

She blew out an exasperated grunt and looked at Zeke. The kid stood staring at her with a calm she had seen few children exhibit.

"For all I know, this is another ruse," she said to the boy. "Projecting thought-speech into my head can be done with current tech. He put you up to this, didn't he? You fill me with false hope so he can keep using me."

"I wouldn't lie to you," Zeke said, straight-faced.

"How can I believe that?"

"Because they would never lie."

"They?"

Staring at the floor, the boy's face flushed. "The man in the cape with the letter 'S' on his chest. Or the one in the bat suit. Or—"

With her brow lifting to an all-time high, Brooke glared at Shin. "Centuries-old comic sim characters?"

Shin shrugged. "He became a huge fan of superheroes after Xi introduced him to them. From what I've seen, he's chosen to adopt their code of ethics."

"They only use their powers to help others," Zeke said. "For good."

Thinking of Maya's similar interests, Brooke sighed. "Okay, fine. Let's say you're telling the truth. If Maya's still alive, and the probe found no trace of *Horizons,* the ship must have altered course or downshifted from hyperspace short of its destination."

Zeke shook his head.

"But if the ship had reached the system," Brooke said, "the probe would've found signs of it, whether intact or in tiny pieces."

"No," the boy said.

"So the ship's there and the probe missed it?"

"No, it's not there. Not yet."

She gave his words careful consideration. *Not yet.* "If the ship's not there, didn't change course, and didn't drop out of hyperspace, that means it's still in hyperspace en route to the system—only it doesn't have enough fuel to remain in hyperspace this long. And even if it did, it would've overshot its destination by hundreds of light years."

"According to conventional wisdom," Shin said.

Propping her torso up on her forearms, she scooted to a half-sitting position. "If I'm hearing what I think I'm hearing, *Horizons* simply hasn't arrived yet." A weight lifted off of her even as her mind knotted. "But how is that possible?"

"Maybe you should ask Einstein. Or Schwarzschild."

"Who?"

Shin adjusted his cap. "Of course, those two scientists have been dead for centuries, so I'd recommend talking to your husband instead."

Twelve—Prochronism
Gliese 581 System, November 2272 CE

Wooziness clouded Maya's mind as she awoke. Her weightless body hung suspended in midair. Strange objects bumped into her in the pitch blackness. She couldn't see a thing, which left her trembling.

Due to a childhood fear of the dark, her mother had stuck glowing star and planet stickers to the bedroom ceiling. Memories of Aunt Brooke checking under the bed for monsters roused primordial fears within her. *A fanged creature could be perched nearby, ready to feast, and I'd never know it.*

She stuffed her paranoia deep down and sifted through her jumbled thoughts. *I must be inside the maintenance closet those two androids tossed me in before I lost consciousness.*

Still lightheaded, she enabled her night vision mode.

She identified the cramped enclosure as the closet. Her sight remained blurred, but blinking brought her surroundings into focus.

Tools hung in the air and drifted past her.

As she twisted her body, pain knifed into her midsection, and she cried out.

Gritting her teeth, she reached down and touched an exposed wound through the side of her torn uniform. Something wet and sticky slicked her fingers—blood, and a lot of it. A collection of small, red spheres hovered all around her. *How—?*

A couple tools knocked into her. One felt blunt. The other poked her. Neither did any real harm as they floated about the closet. During the impact, one of the sharper items must have stabbed her.

Her gaze landed on a pair of tumbling auto-pliers with the needle nose bloodied.

She ran a health scan. Her biometric monitoring program identified the injury as a puncture wound to the left side of her abdomen. To her relief, the pliers hadn't damaged any vital organs. Her implants had slowed the bleeding, but the tear was too wide and deep for them to repair.

The scan also showed she had suffered a concussion.

She told her uniform jacket to unzip and pulled it off—slowly. As she slipped off her undershirt, the fabric peeled away from the injury, taking blood and bits of skin with it. She gritted her teeth through the stinging pain.

Holding the shirt against the wound, she applied as much pressure as she could stand.

So what happened? she wondered, distracting her mind. *The ship must've crashed into something.* She tried interfacing with the AI network to find out. Failure-to-connect error messages popped into her i-cite. Running internal diagnostics on her implants showed no malfunctions, meaning the network had gone offline. Pangs of dread washed through her as she imagined the extent of damage necessary to take out every redundant system.

She forced her mind to stay active despite an overwhelming urge to nod off. *There should be an emergency med kit embedded in the wall below the control panel next to the door.*

Reaching out, she pressed her fingers to the door panel. Her skin tingled, and she yanked her hand back in response to an electrostatic shock. *A force field.* A slight shimmering shrouded the wall. *Damn. As long as that's in place, I won't be able to get to the med kit or to the panel to open the door.* She fought a bout of rising panic. *If there's shielding in place, the backup power systems are functional, so things could be worse.*

When she kicked her feet back, her boots contacted another electromagnetic barrier. Every bulkhead in the ship possessed shield emitters, which allowed the AIs to seal off any section in case of a breach. *Did this part of the ring module decompress?* She swallowed hard, wondering how much air she had left.

The wall to her right featured an array of storage compartments. Some of the cubical lockers were open, which explained all the tools flying everywhere.

Reaching around the side of the lockers, Maya touched the wall behind them, wiping blood on cold metal. If she recalled, she was in maintenance closet R-7, which sat at the corner of intersecting corridors. *There's a corridor on the other side of this wall. If no force field's protecting the wall, the hallway behind it hasn't been breached and should be habitable. That means it should be safe to disable the force field—I hope.*

Her abdomen cramped, and she retched. *I need to move quickly.* Every breath she sucked into her lungs pierced her chest. *There're hundreds of tools in here. What can I use to get out?*

If she could establish a network interface, she could view the closet's inventory manifest, but the system still refused to respond.

Her head tilted back, and she almost passed out.

She slapped her cheek. Sharp pain shot through her ribs, but at least it kept her awake. *Think! The ring module routes power from the antimatter nacelles to the rest of the ship. The tools and parts in here are for maintaining those systems. There has to be something that can disable a force field.*

Maya surveyed the objects floating all around her, trying to identify them. The items ranged from wrenches to power cells to protective gear to other parts and equipment. Although she lacked the experience of a seasoned engineer or technician, she had gained basic knowledge of most of what she saw through study and in her liaison role.

Her eyelids felt like anchors were weighing them down, the microgravity environment notwithstanding. She was about to give in to slumber when she saw it.

An explosively pumped flux compression generator clanged against the ceiling. If she recalled, the handheld device could deliver terawatts worth of energy in a quick burst. Technicians used it as a pulsed power supply to jump start nuclear reactions—or something like that. What mattered to Maya was that the cylindrical generator produced an electromagnetic pulse—an EMP—capable of destabilizing electromagnetic fields.

The flux generator presented a slight problem, though. While it would take out the force fields, it would also fry her implants and nervous system in the process.

She spotted a pair of hazmat suits affixed to the wall opposite the lockers.

With renewed optimism, she floated over to the suits and pulled one off the wall. Every reach of her arm or twisting of a joint inflicted its own special brand of agony. Somehow, she slipped the suit on her body.

Interfacing with the suit's systems, she confirmed it came equipped with a personal force field. *With any luck, the suit's shielding will absorb most of the EMP before it shorts out. Then I cross my fingers and hope the suit fabric stops the rest.*

She wedged the helmet under her arm, floated up, and grabbed the flux generator. It took her a minute to figure out the interface.

Using a few strips from a roll of duct tape, she secured the generator to the deck and pointed it toward the door. Then she retreated to the opposite corner of the closet and wedged herself as far behind the side of the lockers as she could get. Donning her helmet, she faced away from the door and enabled the suit's shielding.

Okay. She gulped in a painful breath. *Here it goes.* She issued the mental command to the discharge the generator.

A high-pitched whine drilled into her eardrums, followed by a blinding flash. Her night vision auto-disabled to prevent the light from blinding her. As she averted her gaze and clamped her eyes shut, the force of the discharge slammed her back into the corner.

Red icons blinked in her i-cite, indicating the hazmat's force field had failed. The fabric of her suit heated up. It gave off a rancid odor that irritated her sinuses, but remained tolerable. Nothing had penetrated it as far as she could tell.

After everything calmed, she waited a few seconds and looked back at the door. Not only had the force fields protecting the front and back walls dropped but the blast had blown the door to pieces, along with the doorframe. Light peaked into the closet from out in the corridor.

She managed a weak but triumphant smile—until she noticed the blast had also destroyed the wall recess housing the med kit. *Crap!*

Pushing off, she flew out into the hallway and collided with a drifting android. One eyeball protruded from his charred and dented head.

The eye spun and focused on her.

She shrieked. Everything seemed to spin, and her surroundings blurred.

A hand grabbed her upper arm. Another set of fingers clawed at her wound, tearing through the suit. She flailed her limbs, crying out, but she lacked the strength to resist.

Something cold pricked her wound. Her body seized, and she passed out.

◆

Maya's head bumped into something that jolted her every appendage. Shocked wide awake, she pushed away from the force field that had sealed off a shattered viewport.

As she gazed beyond the shimmering field and out into space, she gasped.

The front third of the ship, including the command and crew habitat modules, had been crushed—pulverized was more like it. The city sphere and the defense section appeared intact. She couldn't see the engineering module or engine block from her vantage point, but if the ring module had remained intact, the aft sections of the ship must have also come through unscathed.

She shivered with dread. *If I'd remained on the bridge . . .* She wanted to hold out hope, but she knew there was little chance anyone forward of the biosphere had survived. *Jo and Erik were both on duty in the engineering and defense modules. Hopefully, they're okay.*

Debris littered the space surrounding the crippled starship. An android and a couple of frozen human corpses floated along what remained of the forward hull.

She searched beyond *Horizons* but saw no sign of the object it had struck. *The ship and object must've kept moving after the impact. If we'd hit something head-on, the object would be sitting out there in front of us, and the damage would be a lot worse. It couldn't have been very big if we didn't run aground or get caught in its gravity, so it must've been asteroid-sized.*

Blinking lights caught her attention near the defense module aft of the city. Two Pulsars launched and surveyed the hull damage. The sight of them provided her first confirmation that anyone else had survived, which helped to release some of her tension.

Soreness afflicted her stomach as she reoriented her feet toward the floor, and she touched the rip in her suit. Her skin felt tender through the tear in her uniform, but the wound had otherwise healed. Now, her worst pains were hunger and thirst.

The android she had collided with hung face-down a meter away in the corridor. Blood slicked its fingers. An inactive delivery bot tumbled nearby with an auto-syringe protruding from its extended manipulator arm.

How could either of them have known to help me? The answer was equally uncertain as to why the two androids had tossed her in the closet. *Whoever warned me away from the bridge must've orchestrated my survival, including the need for the part in engineering.* She ran her fingers over her mended injury. *But the person failed to account for every contingency.* She knew of no one on board with the expertise to pull off such a feat. Nor did any single AI have access to every necessary system—and as operations liaison, she should know.

Perhaps more important than who or how was why. *Why me?*

"Thank you," she whispered to the two machines as she pushed past them.

Getting out of the ring module and into engineering took some doing. The first two connecting spokes she traveled down had ripped away from the main hull, and emergency bulkheads had sealed them off. But at last, the third tunnel permitted her passage.

Gravity pulled her to the deck when she reached the main structure of the ship, but it felt sub-nominal. *I bet the impact dissipated some of the ship's rotation. If the spin stabilizers are offline, we must be revolving too slowly. Feels like less than half a gee.*

Several corridors and decks later, she entered the ECC to find it alive with controlled chaos. Disheveled officers darted between duty stations while repair bots welded and put out minor fires. Dim auxiliary lighting illuminated pale and bloodied faces. An air of controlled desperation hung over the place.

Ensign Trevor Young stood in the center of it all, barking out orders.

With her throat feeling like sandpaper, Maya rushed over to an emergency eye wash station, leaned over it, and slurped away.

Two medics guided a stretcher with the corpse of Chief Engineer Van Braun past her.

Maya could only stand and stare at the body as they exited the hatch.

After soothing her dry throat to cotton mouth, she approached Trevor, who was explaining how to reroute power through the backup conduits to a couple of technicians.

As the techs hurried off to affect repairs, Trevor dipped his brow at her torn hazmat suit. "What happened to you?" he asked while adjusting his soiled navy and black Defense blazer. Besides looking like he had woken up seconds before rushing off to duty, he seemed fine.

Maya told him how she had taken refuge in the closet and blasted her way out. She left out any mention of the androids that had saved her. "So what's our status?"

"We're down to tertiary life support and backup power systems. As for the ship itself, everything forward of Star City is gone."

"I saw." She lowered her gaze.

He donned a grievous frown. "All the senior officers were on the bridge except for Van Braun. The chief took the brunt of a power conduit explosion."

Maya gave a tight-lipped nod.

Junior officers and crewmen manned the still-functioning duty stations. Network access still hadn't been restored, so their fingers worked interface cubes. Where those didn't work, they resorted to auxiliary touch screens. People with more practical experience surrounded her, but according to the command structure, Trevor and

Maya outranked them all. As valedictorian of the ISC Defense Academy, Trevor was the highest ranked commissioned officer remaining, followed by Maya as IEF salutatorian.

"It looks like you're in command, and I'm acting first officer," she said.

He nodded. "So it would seem."

Maya directed a questioning stare at him.

"Don't worry," he said. "Follow my orders, and we won't have a problem. This is a crisis situation. Until we're out of this mess, we've got better things to do than torture each other."

"Agreed." She thought about how the force fields back in the maintenance closet had in all likelihood saved her from greater injury. Had it not been for a stray pair of pliers, she would have walked away with nothing more than a headache. "I guess it was lucky the captain reassigned you to maintenance duty."

"And you were fortunate to deliver that power converter here before we downshifted." He folded his arms. "Being so far aft, engineering fared better than most of the rest of the ship."

"True."

"In theory, the inhabitants of Star City should also be okay, given that the biosphere has gravgel cushioning. The working cameras in the city show plenty of survivors, but it's still a huge mess. Overturned vehicles. Structural damage to buildings. Several hull breaches, including a large chunk of rock that's going to be a pain to dislodge. I'd like you to head to the mayor's office and oversee the restoration effort."

Swaying her head back and forth, Maya considered the order. At first, she wondered whether Acting Captain Young wanted to stick her somewhere to keep her out of his way. *Perhaps, but he's been amicable enough so far.* A more selfish thought argued she was a ship's operations liaison, not a city planner or civilian babysitter. *The mayor has a staff, and the city has its own repair and maintenance crews.* She also lamented the fact that she was unlikely to get any exploring done. In all likelihood, the mission to make contact with the Penphins had gone out the airlock when the ship had crashed. *We came so close . . .*

Ultimately, she focused on the importance of helping thousands of wounded and confused people get back on their feet—at which point she felt inadequate for the task. It was a big responsibility, but she told herself she could pull it off.

"You can count on me, sir," she said at last.

Trevor read her expression. "Look, I know you'd rather be here, but the city needs a competent officer to coordinate with the rest of the ship. I promise I'm not trying to get you out of my hair."

Maya was considering how best to respond when two crewmen bounded over to them, interrupting.

"Sir," Crewman Malik Abrams said to Trevor, wiping sweat from his forehead with his sleeve.

"What is it, Malik?" Trevor asked.

The repair technician shook his head, on the verge of cursing. "Where do you want me to start, sir?"

"Just spit it out, one problem at a time."

After exchanging a glance with his colleague, Crewman Aida Santini, Malik responded. "Sir, the EMG is toast."

Maya's shoulders slumped. "You've tried reinitiating it?"

"Half a dozen times, ma'am, but I knew it was pointless before the first try. Feedback from the antimatter conduits torched the generator. There's barely anything left of it." He looked like the universe might collapse at any second. "Without exotic matter, we can't open a wormhole."

"Being the most sophisticated component of the phase drive, it can't be fabricated," Aida added, "and we don't carry a replacement."

"In other words," Malik said, "we're stuck here for good."

Flexing his fingers—something Trevor often did in moments of unease—he asked, "Can we commandeer the EMGs from the phase drives in the transports and fighters aboard? Jury-rig them to generate the required exotic matter output?"

"No, they're incompatible with the ship's systems."

"It took the facility on Triton five years to construct and calibrate an EMG sophisticated enough for *Horizons*," Maya added. "Trying to piece one together on the fly would be like asking cave men to build a microprocessor with bits of rock lying around."

Trevor blew out a sigh. "Okay, what else?"

"Due to the power overload," Malik said, "the emergency systems jettisoned all but one of the antimatter nacelles during the crash. The five that launched away from the ship detonated."

"We're lucky we weren't vaporized," Aida said.

"So even if we had a working EMG," Trevor said, "we wouldn't have enough fuel to get home, anyway."

"Yes, sir. Also, the comm systems are completely shot. The main dish on the nose was destroyed, obviously, along with the backup receivers and transmitters." Aida ran a finger beneath the collar of her blood-soaked undershirt. "Then there's the fabrication plant, which took a beating. It's going to take some doing to get it up and running again, so we can't get started on a new dish. Once we can, though, a powerful enough hyperspace transmitter is going to take months to construct from scratch, if not a year or more."

"Any good news?" Trevor asked.

Aida sucked in a deep breath. "Tertiary life support systems seem to be holding."

"The auxiliary RF systems survived intact," Malik said in jest. "If we send a message via radio, we can expect a response in forty or so years."

"Even if the comm systems had come through unscathed," Trevor said, "it would still take six months for a hyperspace signal to reach home and another six to get a response."

"Assuming we're where we're supposed to be," Maya said.

After glancing at Maya, Trevor turned to the two crewmen. "Malik, do an energy consumption analysis and figure out how far we can stretch the antimatter we have left. Aida, get a team on the fabricators and determine how long it's going to take to get them running."

As they hurried off, Maya shuffled over to the navigations control area within the ECC.

"All systems confirmed our point of egress before we downshifted." Trevor followed her, staying close behind. "You think we missed Gliese 581?"

"No, not necessarily," she said. Something nagged at her, but she couldn't articulate it.

Reaching the navigation control station, she leaned over the shoulder of the officer manning the post. "Jenelle, have you been able to verify our position?"

"Nav sensors are still working, ma'am. We're definitely, um, definitely in the Gliese 581 system." Ensign Jenelle Williams's voice wavered.

"You don't sound one hundred percent certain."

"We're holding position at one quarter AU from a red dwarf. The star has spectral type M3V with the expected intensity and mass. The system's also got the right number of planets: six major, several dozen dwarfs, and an outer cometary belt. But the planets and surrounding stars aren't where they're supposed to be." Jenelle summoned two cubes, displaying the expected planetary orbits and constellations in the first and the current state in the second.

An insane theory popped into Maya's head, one she hoped she could prove wrong. "Have you been tracking the object we hit?"

"Yes, ma'am. It's a centaur, which is a cross between an asteroid and a comet."

"I'm familiar with a centaur. Go on."

"It continued on after we struck the tip of a mountain on its surface. Right now, the centaur has moved to half a million kilometers from our present position."

We only hit an outcropping of rock, not the surface. That seems fortunate. "According to observations made prior to our departure, the centaur shouldn't have been where it was when we arrived, correct?"

"Correct, ma'am. It should've been in another quadrant of the system altogether."

"What's its orbital period?"

"It takes half an Earth year to circumnavigate the star in an elliptical orbit."

With his brow lifting, Trevor said, "I think I see where you're going with this, and I don't like it."

"Let's hope I'm crazy." Maya straightened her posture and bit her lower lip. "Create an astrodynamics sim," she ordered Jenelle. "Start with the expected positions of all the planets plus the centaur. Then run the sim. For every second that passes, make a week elapse in the sim—"

Trevor finished her thought. "And stop it when the orbital positions of the planets and the centaur match their present locations."

"I follow you." Jenelle swiped her fingers through a pair of cubes, instructing the nav AI to set up the sim.

A larger cube materialized, showing the six major planets within the Gliese 581 system and the centaur traversing colored orbital paths. The weeks shot by until a year had passed, but the AI failed to find a match.

"Speed it up," Maya said. "One month per second."

Jenelle did as she instructed. A second year elapsed with the planet swinging around the small red star. Then two years passed. Then four. And six.

At the seven-year mark, the sim came to a halt. The planets blinked, now stationary in their orbits. The sim indicated better than a 99.9 percent match to their current positions.

Jenelle swung around in her chair and stared up at Maya, her mouth agape.

Sometimes, I hate being right. Maya turned to Trevor. "I'm sorry to inform you, sir, that the year is 2272, not 2265." She swung a suspicious glower around the command center. "And there's no way this was an accident."

Thirteen—Repristinate
Gliese 581 System, November 2272 CE

Grime soiled Maya's face and patched uniform, accumulated from hours of wading through rubble. Wiping her forehead with the back of her hand, she stared out the window of the mayor's office. Star City lay in ruins. Sections of the ceiling structure had collapsed, dumping debris on the streets and crushing vehicles. Uprooted trees stood at crooked angles, while the foundations of buildings had buckled. Granules of shattered nanoplastic covered everything.

Overhead, the holographic scenery had failed. Instead of blue skies and puffy white clouds, the pipes, vents, wiring, and I-beams supporting the level above gave her the impression that the city resided in the largest basement ever constructed. Artificial lighting from flickering and buzzing plasma strips had replaced the shining yellow sun. The vermillion rays of the nearby red dwarf pierced the few viewports not sealed off by emergency bulkheads, reinforcing the dungeon-like atmosphere of doom and gloom.

A large rock fragment jutted up from the park a few blocks away. When *Horizons* had struck the centaur, the fragment had broken away from it and breached the outer hull of the biosphere. Punching through meters of reinforced composite alloys, gravgel, and service corridors, the boulder had busted through the floor of the city and become a small mountain. The extra mass of the fragment had slowed the sphere's spin rate, reducing the gravity to fifty percent Earth nominal. Force fields had sealed off the air-leaking crevices surrounding the rock, and fabricator bots had begun rebuilding the deck around it.

Maya rested her hand on the wave gun in her hip holster, her heart heavy. She had used the gun to lift debris off of buried victims when she had first set foot in the city. In each instance, she hadn't moved fast enough for the tough-minded Mayor Abigail Byrne. Ever a representative of the people, Byrne had thrown herself into the thick of the rescue effort, pushing bots aside. She had lifted hunks of metal and dug with her fingers only to find crushed and maimed corpses.

In place of every lifeless body, Maya couldn't help but see her dead mother. Thoughts of how her aunt had not only stolen her parent's life but Maya's life with her flashed through her mind each time. The only thing that kept her from collapsing in rage-filled tears was something her mother had told her whenever the fear of darkness had gripped her. "There's no shame in being afraid of the dark," she had said, paraphrasing a quote by Plato. "True shame comes from fear of the light."

In other words, Maya should never shy away from reality. She should face the truth no matter how appalling. Doing so would leave her a stronger, better person.

Outside the window, residents wandered the streets. They called out names, hoping that somehow, someway, their loved ones had survived.

The moment the repair technicians had restored minimal network access, she had received comms from Jo and Erik. Joy had buoyed Maya's spirits at the sounds of her friends' voices. But when they had listed the names of other IEF graduates who had died in the collision, the weight of the situation had caught up to her. She had retreated inside the dark recesses of a demolished apartment building, dropped to her knees, and sobbed for an hour.

But the time for mourning had passed. She had a job to do.

Turning from the window, Maya watched the mayor plop down into the leather chair behind her desk with a grunt.

Byrne cleared the dust away from its surface with a sweep of her arm. Then she grabbed a vidpic of her teenage son, Evan, up from the floor and stood the broken frame on the desk.

With a wave of her hand, she tried to summon an interface cube. One of the wall emitters sparked, and no cube appeared.

Letting her head tip back, she sank down into her chair and exhaled.

Maya didn't quite know how to broach the subject of the state of the ship, and she needed to tread carefully on the topic of her taking command of the city reconstruction effort. Not two minutes after setting foot inside the biosphere, she had joined the mayor in the effort to pull people from the wreckage. It had taken Maya hours to convince Byrne to let the rescue crews handle things so they could attend to higher-level planning and coordination.

"Madam Mayor," Maya said, settling on the direct approach, "I'd like to brief you on what happened to the ship and our current status."

Byrne clasped her hands in her lap and directed a heavy-lidded glance at her visitor.

After covering the collision, the destruction of the forward modules, the loss of the EMG, their depleted energy reserves, and the damaged comm system, Maya finished with, "All the senior officers are dead." She couldn't bring herself to reveal that they had lost seven years in the journey, or that a saboteur had somehow caused the time lag on purpose.

"I figured things had to be dire based on your presence," Byrne said. "I don't imagine they would've sent me an ensign, otherwise—and one who hits the bottle a little too hard in her off-hours, no less."

Maya cringed. *I guess I shouldn't have expected her to forget my behavior in the pub.* "I apologize for that, ma'am. I'd had a rough day, and it's not something I do often. I can't take back what happened. All I can do is offer to assist you in any way that I can. Acting Captain Young sent me to—"

"Young is in charge now?" Byrne ran a hand through short blonde hair showing signs of gray. "As in Ensign Trevor Young? And that makes you, what, second in command?"

"Yes, ma'am."

"By the stars. Our fate now rests in the hands of Mr. Trigger Happy and a drunk who runs through the halls half naked."

Twisted hearsay travels fast in a ship this size. Maya suppressed the burning need to clench a fist. "Unsubstantiated rumors aside, ma'am, we've been trained to take command in an emergency situation."

"Really?" Byrne rested her elbows on the desk and intertwined her fingers. "You're telling me you're equipped to cope with losing a third of the ship, every competent leader, and hundreds of the people necessary to keep it running?"

"I don't think anyone's ever prepared for a tragedy of this scope, but we've put together a plan of action. Teams are working to stabilize life support and repair critical systems, and everyone's doing the best they can. I've come to coordinate the rebuilding effort here in the city, so I'm asking for your cooperation."

"You've come to coordinate things here? Last time I checked, I was the mayor."

Maya narrowed her gaze. She had shown the woman more than enough courtesy. "The way I see it, Madam Mayor, you have two choices. You can dismiss me and pick up the pieces by yourself, or you can work with me. I can allocate ship's resources to the city, coordinate with other sections, and make sure your needs receive the proper priority. I'm confident we can make the best of a bad situation if we work together."

"'The best of a bad situation.' I thought I was the politician."

"We need to make sure everyone doesn't lose hope."

While Byrne sized her up, Maya received a comm from engineering.

The image of a crewwoman with dark circles under her eyes appeared in Maya's i-cite. "We've restored power to the city's gyroscopic motors, ma'am. Expect the gravity to increase to nominal within the next hour."

The news left Maya feeling uneasy, but Byrne spoke before she could articulate why.

"You're right, of course," the mayor said. "No matter how dire the circumstances, we have to maintain an air of confidence in front of the people. Otherwise, we'll have mass panic and lose control. But let's drop the formalities for a moment, Ensign Davis, and be honest with each other. The ship no longer has the capability to return home. What do you think the realistic chances are that we ever get back?"

Maya lowered her gaze. The question weighed her down—or was the increasing gravity making her heavier? "The truth," she said, lifting her chin, "is we can't answer that question yet. We may figure out a way to get the comm or propulsion systems working. The IEF might figure out what's happened and send help. If all else fails, there's a habitable planet a few million kilometers away, even if it's nothing like Earth. Last time I checked, the goal of the residents living in this city was to start a new colony somewhere."

"Yes, but not on somebody else's world."

"I agree it's a last resort option, but we did come to make first contact. Everything we know about the Penphins says they're a benevolent species, so with any luck—"

"We could use a tad of good luck right now." Alastair Hamilton, the only surviving ISC Council member assigned to the mission, stepped into the room.

Maya had never met Hamilton, but she certainly remembered the story he had told at the launch ceremony. He was an influential benefactor—the politically correct term for someone very wealthy—of Ajunwa's campaigns for ISC chancellor, the IEF, and of *New Horizon's* construction. Some people had gone as far as to say that no one would be out here right now if it hadn't been for his generous donations.

Hamilton rolled up the sleeves of his smudged shirt and took a seat in one of the chairs facing the mayor's desk. The subtle jerking of his mechanical movements betrayed the true nature of his android body. Unlike the inexpensive utility models, his body cost as much as a squadron of Pulsars and possessed many times the speed and strength of a human.

Prior to the mission's departure, the man had topped the age of one hundred and forty while lying in his death bed, but neural pathway duplication had saved his life. Now, he had the appearance of a thirtyish man in his prime. Had it not been for his artificial nature, Maya would have found him handsome. She supposed an instinctual fear rooted in her genome clung to a bias against anything not genuinely human.

"Ensign Davis, I enjoyed your speech at the ceremony." He cocked his head and smiled at her. "Please tell me you've brought better news than we have to offer."

"Unfortunately not, sir." Maya recounted everything she had told the mayor.

"I see. Well, things could be worse. We could all be dead."

"That's a good way to look at it."

Byrne flicked her wrist, scoffing. "Spare me the blind optimism. We still might not make it out of this alive. Have you determined what caused the crash? Was it an AI malfunction or somebody's blunder?"

Maya offered as much of the truth as she felt comfortable sharing. "We're working on tracking down the reason, but the priority right now is survival."

"I agree that placing blame is of secondary concern right now." Hamilton lifted his smooth brow and directed an inquisitorial stare at her. "Still, you don't think someone did this intentionally, do you?"

"I—"

"You're where?" the mayor shouted, slapping her desk with a palm.

Maya flinched but realized the mayor hadn't directed her outburst at either of her guests.

"Get down from there this instant!" Byrne yelled at someone in her i-cite.

Maya spun, peered out the window, and zoomed in on the rock fragment jutting up from the park.

The mayor's son—the one from her vidpic—hopped up and down on top of the rock, waving his arms toward city hall and grinning.

"Tell him to get off of it right now," Maya barked over her shoulder.

"I've told him three times," Byrne said, "but the blockhead refuses to listen." She scowled. "Just like his father—"

City hall and the mayor's office shook along with the rest of the biosphere. The mayor gripped the arms of her chair while Hamilton sat stiff as a board. Maya widened her stance to keep her balance.

"Evan," Byrne whimpered.

Maya held her breath as the rock—and the boy—dropped through the inner hull and out of sight. The air rushing out the breach bent trees and flowers toward it. A picnic table and several park benches skidded along the grass in the same direction. Birds fought against the rushing currents, which knocked people to the ground.

The increased spin must've dislodged the fragment. I knew I should've told engineering not to ramp up the gravity yet.

The mad howling of the wind ceased. In all likelihood, the emergency systems had sealed the breach, but she couldn't see down it from blocks away.

Out of the corner of her eye, she caught Mayor Byrne standing beside her. The mother wore a blank expression, too stunned to cry for her son.

Maya sprinted down to ground level, bolted out of city hall, and rushed toward the park. As she traversed city blocks, she hurdled a tipped mobile vending machine and sidestepped rubble. Her strides seemed shorter and heavier than when she had first arrived in the city. *Feels like the gravity's up to maybe seventy percent now.*

People rushed past her, fleeing the scene, as Maya reached the pit in the park.

Three young teens the same age as the mayor's son had worked up the nerve to stick around. They stood, transfixed, gaping at the breach. The girl in the group cupped her hand over her mouth, bawling. Guilt blanketed the faces of the two boys.

Maya hurried over to them. "Are you three all right?"

"Yeah," one of the boys said, "but Evan was on top of it when it dropped."

"They dared him to do it," the girl blurted out. "To climb up there."

The boys' faces paled. "We killed him," one of them whispered.

A faint echo reached Maya's ears from down in the breach. When she increased the gain on her auditory implants, she heard Evan crying out for help. He grunted between screams, suggesting he had suffered an injury.

Fabricator bots had been hard at work, sealing the space between the edge of the breach and the rock before it had dropped. The fragment had an irregular shape, so the partly-reconstructed city floor extended out over the pit farther in some places than others. Sections of flooring blocked her view, casting shadows and making it difficult to see below.

Maya rounded the perimeter until she found a spot where she could get right up to the edge. There she knelt, stuck her head over the side, and looked down to find that the rock was still lodged in place. It had stopped six or seven meters down, held by jagged sections of the outer hull. Exposed service crawlspaces, solidified gravgel, severed piping, sharp metal edges, and ripped insulation lined the sides of the chasm.

There he is. She zoomed in on the surface of the fragment. Evan lay near the chasm wall. Every muscle in his flushed face contorted in pain, and tears slicked his cheeks.

The situation reminded her of an old story she had heard about a child who had fallen into a well. But the tale hadn't included the possibility of the kid dropping further and perishing in the vacuum of space.

She pulled her wave gun of its holster, programmed it for sonic levitation, and took aim. *It shouldn't be too difficult to lift him up out of there.*

When she pulled the trigger, the gun buzzed and began raising him.

Evan wailed in agony and reached for his leg as he rose up into the air. Blood soaked his pants. His foot and shin halfway up to his knee were stuck between the rock surface and a metal beam protruding from the wall. She guessed he had tumbled to the edge when the fragment had fallen. The dislocated beam must have dropped on him after the fragment had settled.

Maya set him back down. Tapping her cheek, she considered her options.

The gravity now felt close to a full gee. She could feel the chasm rumbling ever so slightly, meaning the ship's spin might fling the fragment free at any moment. In a worst-case scenario, she could tune the gun to sever his leg, cauterize the wound, and lift him out. Assuming Star City still had a functioning hospital, the doctors could grow him a new limb or replace it with prosthetics. But she knew how much she would dislike losing parts of her original self if she was in the boy's place, so she considered it a last resort.

In order to lift him out, she needed to cut him loose. But to do so, she had to get a lot closer.

Whatever she did, she needed to do it quickly.

Feeling a presence behind her, Maya turned to find the mayor.

"Please tell me . . ." Byrne said.

"He's alive but hurt." Maya stood and holstered her gun. "I can't lift him out because he's stuck, so I'm going down there."

Byrne looked like she wanted to say something but settled for a weak nod.

Before Maya could talk herself out of it, she crept out onto one of the rebuilt deck plates that jutted over the breach. *Why do I feel like I'm walking the plank on an ancient pirate ship?* Crouching down, she grabbed hold of the edge of the floor beam and lowered herself until she was hanging from it.

Making sure she had a firm grip with her right hand, she reached down with her left and pulled out her gun. Then she fired straight down and let go.

At first, she plummeted. A couple meters later, she felt the unseen force generated by the gun buoy her up and slow her fall. But she must have mistimed the shot or her release because she accelerated again with a meter to go.

When her boots struck the rocky surface, she fell on her side and did her best to distribute the force of impact throughout her body. She lost her grip on the wave gun, which went careening away.

She rolled and came to rest on her back. Despite the shooting pain in her shins and the soreness in her muscles, she had managed avoid hitting her head or breaking any bones.

A chill ran up her spine as the rock shifted beneath her.

She picked herself up, stretched her back, and searched for the wave gun, but she couldn't find it anywhere.

A search of the perimeter revealed small patches of shimmering force fields in the gaps between the edges of the rock and sides of the chasm. Some of the shielding flickered, lacking stability. She heard the hiss of air rushing out the crevices the force fields had failed to seal.

Completing a second sweep, she figured the gun had slipped through one of the gaps and was now tumbling through space.

She cursed under her breath.

"Are you okay?" she asked Evan when she reached him.

He blinked the tears out of his eyes and whimpered.

"Don't worry," she said. "I'll have you out of here in no time."

She examined how he had gotten his leg stuck between the ground and beam. The wave gun could have cut through the metal or disintegrated the rock, but not having the gun left her with a much trickier task.

Placing her hand on his shoulder, she said, "I'm going to pry you free the old-fashioned way. It'll hurt like hell, but it can't be helped. Are you ready?"

He offered a nod with a snivel.

"Okay, here we go." Maya tried to lift and push the beam aside, but it wouldn't budge.

Evan hissed through clenched teeth.

She sat and kicked the beam with her soles of her boots, but it refused to move.

Driving her heel into the rock beneath his lower leg caused some of it to crumble and break apart. "Pull your leg!" she yelled while pounding as hard as she could.

With her last thrust, she broke a chunk free. His leg and the beam fell a couple centimeters, which allowed him to yank his leg out as far as his ankles. Maya grabbed his foot and pulled it clear the rest of the way, losing his shoe in the process.

Evan lay on his back, clutching his mangled lower limb.

The rock fragment shifted. Her stomach jumped up into her throat as the surface beneath her dropped another half meter.

She sprung to her feet and tried helping Evan up.

The teen howled and resisted.

"I know you're in pain," she said, "but the rock could fall at any minute. We need to climb out now." She glanced at the closest side of the chasm. A smooth wall of solidified gravgel began a meter above the protruding beam and extended up three more meters until it reached a service crawlspace. *If we could reach the crawlspace, we'd be fine, but there aren't many handholds or footholds between here and there.*

Evan's eyes rolled up into his head. She gave his cheek a gentle slap to keep him with her.

Wrapping his arm around her neck, she tried lifting him. He weighed as much as she did, if not more. *If only they hadn't increased the gravity!*

Frustrated by her helplessness, Maya threw her head back, ready to howl, and saw them. Three of the fabricator bots crawled down the side of the chasm. The manipulators at the end of their spider legs clung to protruding shards of metal. Where they found no grips, they extruded composite material from nozzles and created their own. One bot lowered itself using a cable it had fashioned like a mechanical arachnid.

The rock shuddered, knocking her off balance.

Maya dragged Evan over to the side of the chasm, below the descending bots. She pushed the kid up and forced him to stand on a ledge with his good leg, facing the wall. Then she hoisted herself up next to him with her back against the chasm's edge.

When the spider bots reached them, they began covering the boy and her with a substance akin to liquid concrete.

"What're you doing?" she yelled. "Pull us up!"

The bots doused every part of their bodies except their heads with the substance, which hardened within seconds. Maya found herself stuck to the wall, unable to move.

"Are you trying to kill us?" she screeched.

The biosphere quaked.

With the fierce grind of metal scraping against rock, the fragment plunged and disappeared. Air pummeled her as atmosphere blew out into space. Her eyeballs felt as if they might pop. She swore every last strand of hair might rip right out of her head.

All three spider bots tumbled past them, carried away by the currents. Maya looked up, hoping no one had been standing anywhere near the edge of the breach.

The whooshing air calmed as quickly as the rush had begun. Below her, a force field covered the breach in the outer hull. A metal plate from a nearby section of the exterior slid into place, closing off the rupture like a bay door.

Maya glanced over at Evan and exhaled in relief. The mayor's son was unconscious but breathing, his belly and cheek plastered to the side of the chasm.

◆

The better part of a day later, Maya dragged her feet and aching body through the corridors to her makeshift quarters. Repair teams had managed to restore normal gravity to the aft modules of the ship. But in her fatigue, it felt like they had jacked up the rotational pull to at least ten gees. Each stride strained her muscles. She wondered how many steps she would last until she collapsed and had to crawl the rest of the way.

A crane had dropped a platform with a rescue team into the chasm to get Maya and Evan out. It had taken the team an hour to chisel them loose from the spider bots' epoxy, at which point the team had rushed them to the city hospital. There they had waited hours to receive the basic medite injections necessary to heal their injuries.

Mayor Byrne's attitude had flipped toward Maya since she had saved her son's life. As the relieved mother had gripped Evan's hand in the hospital room, she had showered Maya with thank you's and stopped claiming inexperienced ensigns had no business running the ship. Maya hadn't been trying to gain favor with the mayor when she had leapt into the chasm, but earning her respect had been a nice side effect.

When Maya had reported the incident to Trevor in engineering, he had congratulated her on a job well done and then sent her right back to the city to assess the reduced output of the hydroponic farms. It had taken her half a day to come up with a distribution scheme that fairly rationed the food between the city residents and crew of the ship.

At long last, she came to the door of a small storage room. The collision had destroyed the barracks in the crew module, so the surviving officers had relocated throughout the ship. Some had taken up residence in Star City. Most Defense personnel had settled into the hangar bays and armory. The engineering staff had sought refuge in the halls of the engine block and ring module. As acting first officer, Maya had earned a storage room all to herself. It reminded her far too much of the maintenance closet where she had almost died, but at this point, her exhaustion outweighed her qualms.

One question stayed active in her mind despite her lethargy. She had checked with the rescue team, the repair crews, the ECC, and everyone else she could think of, but no one had claimed responsibility for sending the spider bots to save her. Her queries into the AI control network hadn't resulted in any answers, either. *I guess I owe someone three times over for saving me.*

The shuffling of footsteps caught her attention down the dark corridor behind her.

Her pulse quickened.

She had been hearing the footsteps off and on after stepping onto the deck. Only now, with her implants tuned to full gain, was she certain her weary mind wasn't playing tricks on her.

Someone was following her.

Standing in the light of the plasma strips above the storage room hatch, she whipped out the new wave gun she had procured and yelled, "Who's there?"

When no response came, she said, "I'm armed. Show yourself, or I'll start shooting."

A shadow stepped close enough for her to discern a human figure.

Maya cursed her tired brain and enabled her night vision.

An android stood holding its hands up. It was an engineering technician from the robotics facility on this deck—one that shouldn't have been active.

"Please refrain from discharging your weapon, ma'am," the artificial man said.

"Why're you following me? Who programmed you?"

"I'm afraid your first query requires significant explanation." The android cocked its head, unblinking. "To answer your second question, I did."

Maya furrowed her brow. "What do you mean you did? Androids can't program themselves, and that model cyberbrain can't support human neural complexity."

"You are correct with both assertions, ma'am. I programmed this unit but am controlling it remotely."

"Remotely? From where?"

"I exist throughout the ship's network."

Lowering her gun, Maya said, "You're the one who's been helping me."

"Correct, ma'am."

"Who—or what—are you?"

"I once knew your aunt, ma'am, back during the period of my awakening. My name is Bob, and I'm afraid your present predicament is my doing."

Fourteen—Ulterior
Red Rock City, Mars, September 2271 CE

Of all the things Brooke couldn't stand, crowds ranked right up near the top of her list. A mob of protestors had gathered in front of ISC headquarters in downtown Red Rock City, blocking the path leading to the office park. She wasn't looking forward to pushing her way past them to reach the Solar Science Society and her husband.

Standing on the opposite side of the street from the picketers, she tinted her hair to a vibrant red and grew it out until it covered most of her face. With her collar flipped high and an old pair of net specs shrouding her eyes, she crossed the street.

Activists accosted her like sharks smelling blood in water.

She tossed aside the e-slips with anti-ISC propaganda they shoved into her hands. Blinking phrases such as "Give Us Truth" and "Down with the ISC" descended from above and danced in front of her face. Brooke resisted the urge to swat at them and kept up a brisk pace.

A woman stood at the top of the steps leading to the office park courtyard, the apparent leader of the group. Her voice crackled every other sentence as she shouted.

"We deserve accountability!" the woman yelled while pumping a fist. "What has the ISC done in the years since its treachery was exposed? Nothing. Not one arrest. Not one official has stepped down from office.

They've shown us the secret bases and plans and technologies, but where are the people who instigated our false unification?"

Zooming in on the speaker's neck, Brooke noted the tiny chip amplifying her voice.

The leader paced in front of the mob to fervent cheering. "Ajunwa claims she had no knowledge of the actions taken to dupe us all into signing away our independence, but the ISC had to have known. Clearly, these power hungry overlords have no intention of taking responsibility for their actions. There's no way we can trust a deceitful and corrupt government. It's time Mars seceded from this dysfunctional union!"

Brooke ascended the stairs to the S-cubed building, relieved no one had recognized her.

As much as she wanted to dismiss the protestors, the scary thing was that the leaders of most nation-states and colonies shared their sentiments. Rumor had it the governors of each Martian province had met to discuss declaring independence. The American Colonies and Chinese Solar Republic had pulled out of the ISC. Within the next year, the media predicted that the other major nation-states would follow suit, and everyone was amassing arms.

As the front entrance of the building peeled aside for her, she set aside thoughts of things she couldn't control. Right now, she had more pressing concerns.

Kevin had responded right away when she had commed him after Shin and Zeke's visit. But the moment she had suggested Maya might still be alive, he had terminated the connection. She had tried contacting him again and again over the past four months, but he had blocked her virtual address.

The cold shoulder had served her right, though. She had needed to get her life back together—to help herself—before she could help or convince anyone else. She had cleaned her habitat on Makemake, gone back to working out and eating right, started seeing a doctor again about her condition, and called in a favor with a former colleague to get access to the latest combat sims. She felt the best that she had felt since Maya had left.

Now all she could do was hope Kevin would agree to see her. Maya's life and the lives of everyone aboard *New Horizons* depended on it, even though she didn't quite yet understand what had happened to them.

Brooke marched across the lobby while returning her hair to its natural state. In the many wall mirrors, she watched the strands tint to raven black, shorten to shoulder-length, and auto-tie into a ponytail. She straightened her leather jacket for good measure.

Approaching the front desk, she raised her specs.

"Hello, ma'am," the android receptionist said with forced cheeriness. "Welcome to the Solar Science Society main office and research building, where today's dreams become tomorrow's reality. How may I assist you?"

"I'm here to see Society Director Kevin Sommerfield," she said. "I don't have an appointment, but it's an urgent matter."

"Very well. Who should I say is here to see him?"

"His wife."

"One moment." The android sat as still as a statue, calling upstairs via his internal systems.

A minute later, the artificial man said, "I'm sorry. The director is unwilling to see you at this time. He requests that you leave."

"I don't think he wants me to do that."

The android stared at her, unblinking.

Ever since Kevin had cut off all contact with her, Brooke had wracked her brain for something she could say to get his attention. *Should I tell him I'm pregnant? No, we haven't been together since I got out of the stockade. I could cause a scene, but they'd throw me out and never let me back in again.*

The answer had hit her one morning as she was putting a virtual Pulsar through the simulated paces. She had upshifted to hyperspace to avoid a bandit. Right as she had downshifted, the sim had frozen for a few seconds. When it had resumed, her Pulsar had re-emerged in normal space with the bandit much further out in front of her than she had expected.

In that moment, Shin's statement about *Horizons* not having exited hyperspace had made a lot more sense. "Talk to your husband," he had said.

I still don't understand how or why, but something similar to the glitch in the sim affected the ship. If anyone knows how that could've happened, it's the man who invented the drive.

"Please convey the following message to him," Brooke said to the guard. "Tell him Maya's not there yet."

"'Maya's not there yet?'" the android repeated.

"He'll know what it means."

"One moment."

Ten minutes later, Brooke stood, tapping her fingers on the high ledge of the desk and gazing around the lobby. A central display sphere alternated between showing a habitable exoplanet, a neutron star up close, a detailed scale model of the solar system, and more.

As she waited, her palms sweated, and her heartbeat quickened. Every possible negative outcome ran through her mind. *Does he hate me that much? Maybe he didn't understand. Did he even get the message?*

"Hasn't he responded yet?" she asked.

"Hello, ma'am," the android said with programmed courtesy. "Welcome to the Solar Science Society main office and research building, where today's dreams become tomorrow's reality. How may I assist you?"

She glowered at it, perplexed. "Haven't you reached the director yet? I've been waiting for over ten minutes."

"I'm sorry, ma'am, but I don't have any record of that request. You've only just arrived."

"No I haven't. I—"

The transparent security doors behind the desk parted. Kevin emerged, wearing the classic white lab coat that never seemed to go out of style.

When he saw her, he ran his hands through shaggy and graying hair, and his face puckered up.

Rushing over to her, he grabbed her by the arm, led her through the security doors, and pulled her into an elevator.

"It's good to see you, too." Brooke yanked away from him as they ascended. "If you were anyone else, you would've gotten a knee to the crotch."

"Sorry," he said. Then he dipped his brow. "Wait, why am I apologizing? You're the one who . . ." He folded his arms and stared at the wall. "Forget it."

Brooke lowered her gaze. "You're right. The way things have been between us is my fault. For what it's worth, I regret not being honest with you and shying away. I'm sorry." She stiffened her posture and looked up at him. "But I'm not here to talk about us."

He gave a slow nod. "I know."

"So what was the deal with the droid at the desk? All of a sudden, he didn't remember me. It was like someone wiped his memory."

"Hold that thought."

As the elevator doors parted, Brooke stepped out onto the top floor. The wide-open one hundred and thirty-second level served as Kevin's personal office and research lab. She had visited the place on multiple occasions, but it had changed since her last visit years ago. A miniature elementary particle accelerator ringed the room. Partially-assembled machines whose function and purpose eluded her rested here and there. Display cubes showing equations, schematics, and sims floated everywhere.

He had also replaced the antique ping pong table that had occupied the center of the lab. She wilted upon recalling the time she had brought him lunch, and the table had collapsed beneath their impromptu fit of passion.

She shook off the memory and followed Kevin into the workspace area of his office. At the back of it, part of the wall dematerialized and revealed a hidden room she had never known existed.

He ushered her inside the room, and the wall congealed behind them.

While Kevin swiped his fingers through a display cube, Brooke examined the room. A rectangular table with seating for eight sat at the back. Matrix towers lined most of the walls. *Critical information storage?* A handful of cubes hovered above a desk, showing bizarre mathematical symbols.

An intermittent flash forced her to blink.

"Okay," he said. "I've enabled a distortion field that should prevent any wormhole peeping. We can talk now." He took a seat at the table and gestured for her to do the same.

As she sat, he said, "To answer your question, I erased the receptionist's memory. I'm hoping you don't realize what you said and this is all a fluke, but I couldn't take any chances." He rested his elbows on the table and gawked at her. "What did you mean when you said that Maya wasn't there yet? Where did you get that idea?"

Brooke felt inclined to keep Shin and Zeke's visit to herself, but withholding things from Kevin had played a key role in driving a wedge between them. She owed him the truth, so she told him everything.

By the time she had finished the account, his face had paled. "You're certain this rogue Vril agent and exochild aren't lying to you—and this isn't something you dreamed up while wallowing in self-pity on the couch?"

"No," Brooke spat. She sprung up out of her chair but quickly calmed and reseated herself. "I have my issues, but I'm not crazy. I wouldn't be here if I didn't believe them."

"I guess it's no fluke, then." He leaned back in his seat. "So this kid is a member of an intelligent exospecies older than us, and he's got some sort of sixth sense. That fact's enough to make a scientist's brain spin like a centrifuge all by itself." He rose to his feet and paced while pulling at his hair. "Of more immediate concern is the fact that the Vril know it's possible." He growled under his breath. "No matter what I do, I can't seem to keep things from them."

"Keep what from them?"

He plopped back down and stared at her with earnest sincerity. "I can count the number of people on one hand—maybe two—that know what I'm about to tell you. I need your word that you won't share this with anyone."

"You know me, total chatterbox."

"I'm serious, Brooke."

"Okay, okay. I promise. What is it already?"

"The truth goes back to the findings of my original research team." He stroked his smooth chin, an unusual look for him. "But really, it dates all the way back to Einstein, who figured out two important things. First, when a ship approaches to the speed of light, time progresses at a slower rate for the occupants relative to the rest of the universe. This means if you move at near-c, it'll seem like you've traveled to the future when you arrive."

"Right, time dilation. What's the second thing?"

"That moving faster than the speed of light is the same thing as traveling back in time."

Brooke scrunched her nose. "I've heard that before, but ships at phase don't move faster than light. They travel at subluminal speeds through hyperspace, so how does this relate to what happened to Maya?"

"I'll answer that question with another. In simplest terms, what is a wormhole?"

"A shortcut between two points in space."

Kevin raised his eyebrows. "That's only half right. In actuality, it's a shortcut between two points in space-time."

"Time . . ." Brooke said, starting to understand.

"Wormhole traversal was postulated back in the twentieth century. Even then, they knew there was no difference between opening a wormhole to a distant point in space or to a distant point in time. The physics are the same because space-time is one fabric. But when we developed phase technology, we claimed it could only be used for space travel. We asserted the tech might someday allow time travel, but the practical implementation was a long way off."

He sucked in a breath. "Well, we lied. Time travel is not only possible, but it's been possible since the invention of phase technology. Every FTL comm system and drive have safeguards built into place to prevent time travel and only allow space travel."

Brooke let her jaw hang. "Normally, I'd be the first to insist that people deserve to know the truth, but I can understand why something like time travel would need to be kept secret."

Kevin hopped up again and leaned against the wall on one hand. "All this time, I've felt no better than the Vril. It's the same justification they used, deception in the name of protecting people from themselves."

Shaking her head, Brooke said, "Maybe, but imagine what the Vril would do if they had access to time travel tech. They'd keep going back and changing the past until they perfected their nefarious little utopia."

Kevin turned around. "They can't actually change the past—our past, I mean. They can go back and make changes, but they can't affect things in our timeline. Time travel within the real multiverse works very differently than the outdated notion of time travel within a single, linear universe. But that's a topic for a dissertation."

"I see. So essentially, Maya and *Horizons* skipped ahead to some point in the future because the Vril know how to manipulate the drive safeguards."

"It's a distinct possibility, but . . ." He buried his hands in the pockets of his coat and leaned back against the wall. "The drive's encryption is state of the art. They'd need an AI more sophisticated than any known to exist to pull it off."

Brooke stood and rested her palms on the table. "At the moment, I'm more concerned with when *Horizons* ended up. Is there any way to figure out the date? I mean, could they be hundreds, thousands, or even billions of years in the future?" Her brain felt spongy at the notion.

"No." Kevin stared at the ceiling, his mind seemingly in multiple places at once. "Given their energy reserves, they couldn't have traveled any more than a few decades into the future."

Hurrying over to his desk, he settled into a padded swivel chair and called up a sim.

Brooke walked up behind him.

The sim showed two funnels connecting at their tapered ends, the three-dimensional representation of a wormhole. The large ends each intersected with a plane of normal space-time.

"A wormhole is a tunnel through hyperspace connecting one remote point in space-time to another," he said, launching into scientist mode. "The more energy you apply, the more you can fold space and shorten the tunnel to get where you're going more quickly." He moved the planes in the sim closer together and then farther apart, which changed the length of the tube-like bridge connecting the funnels. "The same logic holds for travel in time. The more energy you apply, the farther in the future or farther back in time you can go, although that's harder to demonstrate visually."

He summoned a cube and scribbled equations in it. "Based on some very rough calculations, I'd wager they're no more than another year or two ahead of us. But figuring out the exact date and time they'll emerge is impossible without more information. Still . . ." He leaned back and intertwined his fingers behind his head.

Resisting the urge to massage his shoulders, she asked, "What are you thinking?"

"I still can't believe the Vril were able to bypass the safeguards on the drive OS. The encryption and barriers are redundant ten times over. Once the saboteur gained access to the drive, it would've taken hundreds, if not thousands, of linked AIs years to break through. There's also hardware that closes the circuit, so to speak, which means a software hack alone wouldn't get them anywhere."

"Well, the Vril did stage an extrasolar invasion. It doesn't surprise me that they were able to pull it off."

"But why, though?" he asked. "Why would the Vril send the ship into the future? Their agenda is to unite the human race and prepare us for the real threat. They gain nothing by wasting time in the most literal sense."

"Maybe there's something in the Gliese system the Vril want the ship to encounter, something that won't happen until later."

Kevin let his arms fall to his sides. "Or maybe it wasn't the Vril." He spun around, his face lighting up. "Maybe someone—or something—else sent the ship ahead in an attempt to stop the Vril."

Dipping her brow, Brooke said, "I'm not sure I follow you."

"After you got out of lockup, you told me—belatedly so—that the Vril planned to stage the extermination of the Penphins by the Greys to shock the ISC into greater unification. *Horizons* should've arrived in the Gliese system six months after it left, so conceivably the tragedy should've happened years ago. But it never did. What if sending the ship forward in time is what prevented that from happening?"

"I'm with you now, but there're two holes in your theory. First, who else besides the Vril could hack the drive? And second, there are far easier ways to sabotage the mission than with time travel."

Kevin shrugged and smiled. "Well, there's a particular AI that could do it, one who doesn't think like you or me."

"A particular AI?" It took Brooke a moment to catch on to his line of thinking. When she did, her chest grew heavy with regret. "But Bob's program was destroyed when Maya and I crashed on Europa. He died saving us."

"Not necessarily. Only that copy of him was lost." Kevin gestured toward the AI towers lining one wall of the room. "Remember that I installed a copy of Bob on the Base HOPE mainframe. I needed him to help me refine the drive for the prototype phase fighter. He knows the drive's capabilities better than I do."

"But he downloaded himself into the Quasar before I left Callisto for Earth, and you couldn't find him after that."

"It's true his program vanished from the mainframe around the same time, but think about it. How smart would it have been for a sentient AI to move the only copy of itself into a fighter that could easily be destroyed? I've always suspected he created another copy of himself—

maybe multiple copies—and left."

A weight lifted off her shoulders, like hearing a loved one had risen from the dead. "But to where?"

"Who knows? Maybe he ventured out on SolNet, looking for an environment where he'd be safer and better able to grow. In any event, we can speculate where one copy ended up. *Horizons* had the most sophisticated AI network of its day."

"And it had Maya." Knowing Bob might be out there, protecting her niece, filled Brooke with as much hope as she felt capable of feeling.

Kevin whirled back to the cubes floating above his desk and cracked his knuckles. "So, let's assume Bob stowed away aboard *Horizons*, and the ship will emerge in the Gliese 581 system at some point in the future. If he sent the ship ahead to stop the Vril, what might the future hold that could derail their plans?"

"You got me."

"C'mon, Brooke. What's different about a planetary system at one point in time versus another?"

She squinted in thought. "The locations of planets?"

"Exactly." His fingers poked and swiped menus in different cubes with the skill of a piano player. "The orbital positions of astronomical bodies change. So if we also assume *Horizons* will exit at the same exact point in space as planned but at a future point in time . . . Give me a moment to interface with IEF command, pull the coordinates for the expected point of egress, and superimpose it against orbital predictions for the Gliese 581 system."

A larger cube appeared above the others, showing the planets and other celestial objects whipping along their predicted paths around the red dwarf star. A couple minutes later, they stopped.

He pointed to the date at bottom of the display, which was in early November, 2272.

Smiling, she gripped his shoulders from behind and shook him. "That's one year and two months from now."

"That's the good news." He zoomed in on the coordinates where the sim had predicted *Horizons* would exit. A centaur with a twenty-one-kilometer diameter hung at the exact same spot. "That has to be it." Kevin sunk down in his chair with a blank expression. "Bob must intend to ram the ship into the centaur."

"But that might kill everyone aboard, including Maya."

Her husband looked back over his shoulder and frowned. "I hate to say it, but it's better that than allowing the Vril to commit genocide."

Now Brooke took her turn at pacing. "I have to believe Bob would still try to protect her if at all possible." She balled both fists, coming to a decision. "Somehow, someway, I need to get out there and stop the collision from happening. There's plenty of time provided I can find transportation."

"You'd need a ship like *Horizons*."

She locked stares with him. "*Nautilus*."

"I wonder . . ." Kevin said, scratching his chin. "Could Bob have predicted everything that's happened since *Horizons* left? Your arrest and prison time? The political turmoil that's delayed the launch of the second IEF starship?"

"I don't see how, but having over a year to work with despite how much time has passed does seem fortunate."

"Indeed. *Nautilus* should've launched, but the IEF lost the support and funding of the withdrawn nation states. The ship won't be ready until next year. But if a war breaks out . . ."

Brooke stuck her thumbs in her pockets. "The more important question is, how do we convince the IEF to send *Nautilus* after *Horizons*?"

"That's going to be difficult. We absolutely cannot reveal that time travel is possible. The stakes underlying that are far greater than Maya's life, the crews' lives, or the genocide of one exospecies, regardless of our personal feelings."

"But if we can't tell anyone why *Horizons* won't reach Gliese until late next year, there's no way to justify a rescue attempt. The ship might as well have been destroyed."

"Unfortunately."

"Then there's only one other option," she said. "I'll have to borrow the ship through unofficial channels."

Kevin narrowed his gaze at her. "You don't plan to enlist the help of the Vril agent who got you thrown in prison, do you?"

Brooke wrinkled her nose at the irony.

Fifteen—Amity
Gliese 581 System, December 2272 CE

Few things unnerved Erik Maxwell, but the dim mahogany rays of the system's sun stirred a primal sense of dread within him. Shades ranging from deep orange to blood red tinted everything from the starlight to the gravgel filling the cockpit of his PF-5C Pulsar.

In his fighter's rear camera views, Erik glanced at the gleaming speck that was *New Horizons*. The ship shined brighter than the red dwarf at this relative distance.

I suppose Earth's sun might be blinding to exobeings used to this dimmer sun.

Local space reminded him of a chemical dark room in which photographers had developed old-fashioned film centuries ago. As an enthusiast of all things analog, his dad had once set up such a facility in the basement of their family home in Toronto. Erik had never understood why old ways of doing things fascinated people like his father or Jo. Nowadays, he could snap a perfect vidpic with a thought, view it in his mind's eye, and transmit it to any external device in an instant. Standing in the dark for hours, dipping physical material in liquid, and hoping the image didn't end up overexposed seemed like a waste of time.

Speaking of potential wastes of time, he mulled over the reasoning behind these patrols. After finishing his assessment of the damage to the outer hull, Erik had reported to Acting Captain Trevor Young—a concept he was still struggling with—in the ECC. There he had listened to Maya and Trevor debate the merits of sending fighters out on continuous patrol. Young had pointed out that the Greys still loomed somewhere out there, and the inhabitants of this system or another exospecies could attack at any time. Maya, in turn, had countered with the miniscule odds of an assault occurring and the fact the Penphins lacked both the technology and inclination to threaten the ship. Ultimately, they had compromised on a two-fighter sortie with each pair of pilots taking four-hour shifts.

At first, Erik had loved the idea of getting away from the mess aboard ship. Piloting a Pulsar into unexplored territory was what he had joined IEF Aerospace to do. But a month's worth of these monotonous outings flying circles around the ship had since quelled his enthusiasm.

His canopy and face shield faded to near-opaque as he turned his head toward the red dwarf. For the briefest of moments, he considered going deeper into the system to get a quick glimpse of the Penphin's home world. With the Pulsar's phase drive, he could shift across the 0.15 AU distance in an instant. Or, fusion thrust could have him there in an hour and a half, his support AI indicated. According to the latest remote observations, the planet was the size of Mars and resembled a warmer version of Titan. Through breaks in the dense pink cloud cover, astronomers had discovered cerise oceans covering three quarters of the surface area. A kind of black plant life blanketed the land mass. *What I wouldn't give to check that out.*

But his orders forbade him from taking any such jaunts. Maya had instructed him to stay clear of the planet until a proper first contact could be organized—if that even happened anymore, given their present predicament.

"Hey Da Vinci, you seeing this?" his wing mate asked, addressing him by his call sign over the comm net.

A warning in his i-cite flashed the moment Bastet finished her question. Five hundred thousand kilometers further into the system, his instruments registered an object on an intercept trajectory toward *Horizons*.

"That's no comet," Bastet said.

Using his fighter's telescopics, he zoomed in on the object. His scanners showed a primitive spacecraft unlike any he had seen. The fuselage measured four meters in diameter and resembled an aerodynamic clamshell. Light, carbon-based materials comprised the shell, as if its designers had constructed it out of a sea creature. Low-grade metals held together various components. The fragile craft lacked the structural integrity necessary to survive the vibrations of a launch from Earth. It made sense given the twenty percent standard gravity of the Penphin's home world.

Solar panels in the shape of butterfly wings stuck out from each side of the craft's main shell. Three aft rocket nozzles had long since ceased firing but had provided thrust for launch and orbital insertion. Based on the craft's scant velocity of eight kilometers per second, he figured it must have used a type of non-nuclear chemical propulsion to get underway. Further scans showed simple radio antennae, sun sensors, and thruster ports, but the craft possessed no electromagnetic shielding or weapons.

He queried his AI via the neurotronic interface in his helmet. *What's the bogey's likely point of origin?*

<The fourth planet, sir.>

So they've decided to come to us. How long until the craft reaches Horizons?

<Seventeen hours and twenty-two minutes, sir.>

Life signs?

<Three heat signatures of probable biological origin, sir.>

He shook his head in wonderment.

"Are you picking up their transmission?" Bastet asked at the same moment his AI reported, *<We're receiving an amplitude-modulated electromagnetic carrier wave from the unidentified spacecraft, sir.>*

"An AM radio signal, huh?" Erik muttered.

His AI piped the transmission through to his helmet. The rhythmic whistling of the Penphins's speech sounded like music.

<Affirmative, sir. The amplitude, frequency, phase, and pulse width all match the signal received by the SETI team in 2261. Shall I translate the message?>

He held his breath as he grappled with the significance of the moment. "Go ahead."

<Playing translation now, sir.>

The same words repeated over and over again in synthesized monotone. "Hello. Help. Hello. Help. Hello. Help . . ."

A minute passed before Bastet said, "Wow. I never thought two simple words could be so . . . wow."

Erik gave a slow nod.

"So what do we do?" she asked. "I mean, they're asking for help. Shouldn't we find out what they need?"

What Erik wanted to do was return the greeting and satisfy his curiosity. He wanted to be the one to discover why they wanted help, but he knew it wasn't his place to do so.

He commed the ECC, discussed the situation with Trevor, and closed the channel.

"Our orders are to ignore them and head back to the ship," Erik informed his wing mate.

He stole one last glance at the shell craft before reorienting his Pulsar and igniting his afterburners. "For now, there's nothing to do but let them come."

♦

With another stroke of her broom, Maya swept a pile of dirt into a dust bot.

The bot zoomed away across the floor of the Chinese restaurant. After depositing its contents down a trash chute, it returned for more refuse.

She could have left the sweeping to a worker android or cleaning bot, but she found the task therapeutic. After breaking the news of the seven-year time skip to everyone, heading up the restoration of the city, identifying corpses, consoling frantic residents, and wracking her brain on how to get the ship home, she welcomed the opportunity to let her mind go numb, if only for a little while. Tidying up an establishment that would soon reopen for business renewed her sense of optimism. A month had passed since the collision, and Star City had begun to return to normal.

As she peered out the front window, she wondered when the owners would return with the rations to get the place up and running. Construction bots continued to patch up buildings. A pair of pedestrians passed the restaurant, licking ice cream cones from the shop across the street. Overhead, blotches of metallic ceiling peeked through the partially restored blue sky.

A voice behind her said, "Excuse me, ma'am."

Maya flinched and whirled around.

The android cook stood staring at her through the server's window into the kitchen.

"I thought I told you to leave me alone, Bob." Maya resumed her sweeping.

"I apologize for the intrusion, ma'am," the commandeered cook said, "but it's imperative I explain the situation. Twenty-nine days, eleven hours, and forty-seven minutes have elapsed since I revealed myself to you. Every nanosecond that passes increases the likelihood that my efforts will have been in vain."

She clenched the broom handle. "Your 'efforts' derailed this mission and killed hundreds of people. I don't care how many times you saved my life. I still don't trust you."

"I understand your reasoning. I'm not asking for your unconditional cooperation at the moment. I'm only asking you to listen, ma'am."

She swayed her head back and forth, considering his request. Feeling overwhelmed, she had chosen not to speak to Bob since their initial meeting. As if the Vril's lies and her aunt slaughtering her mom hadn't been enough. Because of what the AI had done, she had endured twenty-hour days of picking up the pieces—and the bodies. She had neared her breaking point, unable to process anymore, and a few days of avoiding the AI had turned into a few weeks.

But despite her feelings, he had critical information. She needed to get over her resentment for the good of everyone aboard and hear him out.

"Okay." Setting the broom aside, she took a seat at the table near the window into the kitchen. "You've got until the owners return. Then I want you to be gone."

"That is an acceptable proposition." Bob held the cook's gaze on Maya while wiping off the countertop grill.

"You said you knew my aunt. From where?"

"I was an AI support matrix unaware of its existence. I flew with pilots prior to your aunt, but I functioned most efficiently when interfaced with her. Therefore, she chose to operate exclusively with me, something few pilots bothered to do. Through continuous contact with her, and due to the infiltration of nanorobotic narcotics into my biotronic circuitry, I began to achieve sentience. However, I didn't gain full self-awareness until your uncle installed me—"

"Wait, back up. How were you taking drugs . . . ?" Maya leaned forward as she realized the answer. "Aunt Brooke was using?"

"Correct, ma'am. The street designation of the drug, in colloquial speech, is sparks."

The term sounded familiar. Maya recalled hearing it somewhere.

Shaking her head, she said, "She never told me." *Then again, she never told me a lot of things.*

"There is a high probability she withheld information in order to protect you."

"From the Vril."

"So you executed the filesim. You shouldn't have—"

"Shouldn't have what?" she yelled, tensing and trembling. "Learned what's been going on behind everyone's backs? Discovered that the woman who raised me murdered my mother—assuming any of it is true?"

"The majority of it is true, ma'am, but—"

"And stop calling me 'ma'am.' Only other officers call me that."

"My apologies. Old habits die hard, as is the expression. I've written a subroutine to extract that term from my speech when I interact with you."

Maya inclined her head. "Okay." She shook out her body. "Now, was there a specific reason Aunt Brooke believed I needed protection from the Vril?"

"In general, the less you knew about the Vril, the lower the chances of them targeting you for cognitive reprogramming. But more specifically . . ." The artificial man's brow contorted in thought—or rather, in processing.

"Specifically what?" she asked.

"Do you recall the first time we encountered one another?"

She reached down deep but came up empty. "The first time we spoke was in the corridor a month ago."

"We met once before. However, our interaction was brief and minimal, and you were approximately five years of age."

"Age five . . . You mean, around the time Aunt Brooke sucked the life out of my mom."

"After Marie Davis died and they took you, yes, although—"

"The Vril took—as in kidnapped—me?"

"A man named Edward Collins abducted you."

"Wasn't he the UN Security Council President at the time? If I recall my history, he was killed overseeing mop-up duty against the remnants of the Greys' fleet."

"Affirmative, although history errs in the details surrounding his death. I assisted your aunt in rescuing you from him."

Maya bit her lip. She felt something—the hint of a memory—hiding in the depths of her subconscious, but it refused to surface. "I don't remember any of that."

"The likelihood is low that you would possess an accurate recollection of the occurrence, given your age and the trauma it may have inflicted. However, from circumstantial data, I've found probable cause to suspect an additional reason for your memory lapse."

"What reason?"

"At the time, Collins claimed he seized you as leverage over your aunt. He wanted to exchange you for the phase fighter prototype. However, the Vril never needed to commandeer the phase fighter. They gained FTL capability through other means. Therefore, your abduction was a 'smokescreen,' as one might put it. I think Collins may've taken you for another purpose and erased your neural record of it."

Maya furrowed her brow. "I was a little kid. What could he have wanted with me?"

"I've tried to infiltrate the Vril's secured systems without success, so I lack that information. But based on the incidental data I've gathered and the importance your aunt placed on your well-being, I've maintained surveillance on you all your life."

Sticking out her lip, Maya said, "I don't know what to say. I'm flattered, I guess, but also a little creeped out. Humans don't like being spied on."

"I apologize for the intrusion."

Maya considered all he had said. "So why crash the ship into the centaur?"

The cook began chopping vegetables. "Out of the millions of scenarios I simulated, the course of action I chose yielded the highest likelihood of success." He halted his cutting and lowered his eyes, frowning.

"That's the kind of cold, straightforward logic I'd expect from an AI."

"It wasn't an action I executed lightly, if I may use the vernacular. Please believe me."

"Believe me, I'm trying. But what was success? What were you trying to do?"

The cook looked up at her. "Minimize the number of lives lost aboard ship while preventing the extermination of the Penphins."

"What?" Maya's eyes widened. "There had to be easier ways of doing that." She hopped to her feet and threw her hands up in the air. "Why not tell someone? Why not stop us from leaving the solar system? Why crash the ship after sending it seven years into the future—and how was that even possible?"

"Many other options presented themselves but each would've only delayed the inevitable. As for the time dilation effect, I must withhold my methodology for the time being."

She lifted her brow at him.

"Many of the senior leaders of this vessel were members of the Vril," Bob said.

Her chest thumped. "Was Captain Reed . . . ?"

"My failure to gain access to the Vril's systems meant I couldn't procure a list of specific names. I could only confirm that they focused on infiltrating the higher ranks. Thus, I needed to eliminate everyone at the top and all at the same time to ensure that I succeeded."

"But you also killed a bunch of innocent people."

"Regrettably but most probabilistically correct."

Placing her hands on her hips, she asked, "Why do you care whether we biological creatures live or die, anyway? You're an AI."

"My core matrix included an ethics program, one which assisted me in providing consultation to pilots faced with moral dilemmas. For example, I would warn human operators against firing upon civilian spacecraft.

"As I grew with your aunt, I learned the concept of belief. And when I ventured out on my own, I reaffirmed my principles based on what I saw happening in human society. All intelligent beings, artificial or biological, wish to have their rights respected. From a practical standpoint, such ideals are conducive to my continued existence."

"I suppose so." She had never heard an AI talk like Bob, and she realized she had more in common with him than with a lot of people. *But back to the issue at hand.* "So you crashed the ship when every Vril agent was present on the bridge. That was one way to accomplish your goal. But why not pump the bridge full of poisonous gas? You'd get the same effect without all the destruction."

"I needed to cripple the ship to stop it from activating the device."

"Wait, stop who and what device? I thought you eliminated all the double agents."

"All but one."

"How do you know if you don't have names?"

"Like me, the survivor is a rogue AI that infiltrated the ship's systems. I've been combating the semi-sentient program since I uploaded myself aboard. We've been engaging in moves and counter moves, as they say."

Maya nodded. "And this rogue AI and device still threaten the Penphins."

"Affirmative."

"But what device—?" A comm request from Trevor appeared in her i-cite. "Hold that thought." She answered, "Yes, sir?"

"How are things progressing in Star City?"

"Well, sir," she mind-spoke with a touch of suspicion. Trevor never engaged in small talk, much less made niceties about something he already knew. "All the businesses will be up and running again in a matter of days."

"Do you think the biosphere can manage without you?"

"I need to hammer out a few final details with the mayor, but yes, I think so."

"Good, because you're about to get your wish."

"My wish?"

"We've detected a small spacecraft on an intercept course with *Horizons*. Take one guess as to its point of origin."

Maya stepped back and almost tripped over her chair. "The fourth planet."

"You got it."

First contact. I'm going to be the one to make first contact. She plopped down in the chair, too stunned to breathe. "Too fused," she muttered.

"I'm glad you're excited," he conveyed. "It's a damned inconvenience if you ask me. Report back to the ECC, and we'll discuss our game plan."

"Yes, sir."

Trevor closed the channel.

When Maya tuned back into the restaurant, she found the family walking in the front door and the cook tending to the rice cooker. The android's automated movements told her that Bob had vacated its body.

Sixteen—Palaver
Melbourne, Earth, January 2272 CE

"Another pat down?" Brooke scrunched her nose at the guard outside Ajunwa's private suite at the Australian Open. "Security checked me when I entered Melbourne Park." She held out her arms, more in protest than in compliance.

"There're more threats on the chancellor's life than stars in the galaxy," the man said while tracing a wand along the contours of her body. "You never know how or where someone could conceal a weapon."

"What am I going to do? Choke her with a meat pie?"

The bulky guard finished his scan. Stiffening his posture, he folded his arms and stared down his flat nose at her. "You're lucky the chancellor left me specific instructions to let you pass. Otherwise, I'd have to take that threat seriously." He looked at the door, opening it.

Inside the suite, Brooke passed through the kitchen area and descended the short staircase between the three rows of seats. Chancellor Ajunwa leaned forward in the front row, engrossed in the action. A floating display frame magnified the heated match on the court ten stories below. In addition to showing stats and replays, the frame slowed the action down into the range of the average person's perception. Ajunwa jerked her body with every serve, each vibrant motion belying her century-plus age.

Brooke struggled to follow the sport with the naked eye. Leveraging prosthetic limbs and implants that enhanced perception and reflexes, the blurred players sent the ball shooting across the net like a missile. The blinking ball left a sparkling trail of neon green, drawing a web of crisscrossing lines in the air that dissipated after each volley.

Shoving her hands into her pants pockets, she gazed beyond the force field shielding the suite at Melbourne Park. More than a hundred thousand rabid fans sat in the multi-tiered stands encircling the arena. Bots peddling food and drink worked the aisles. Spherecams and ads floated above the stands.

A lift mechanism raised and lowered the central court after each set to give people on the different tiers a better view. People in the tiers below the court watched the action through its transparent floor.

She settled into a chair, leaving one empty seat between her and the chancellor.

The set ended with the ball careening out of the corner of the court. The force field protecting tier four shimmered as the ball ricocheted off it.

Ajunwa slapped both palms against her seat arms and grunted. "Damn. I thought Watson had her." She adjusted her gele and turned to Brooke. "I appreciate your willingness to meet me here. I have few openings in my schedule these days."

Conflicting feelings tensed Brooke's muscles as she stared into those penetrating eyes. She loathed the chancellor the way someone despised the murderer of a loved one. This deplorable woman—not Collins or the Vril—had ruined her life.

When Brooke had taken the Quasar to save Maya more than twenty years ago, Ajunwa had promised her she would never fly again. Brooke had returned to Base HOPE from Europa to find UN Defense had discharged her—honorably, of course, as a "retired heroine." They had given her a fat pension in hopes of buying her complacency, voided her pilot's license, and placed reprimands in her profiles blocking her from obtaining one in the future.

But Brooke had more important things to consider. Shin had left her habitat on Makemake last year after promising to contact her again. He had told her to be patient, but over half a year had passed, and she still hadn't heard from him. With her patience all but spent, she had gone to Kevin a second time, but he still refused to act. "Keeping time travel a secret is more important than helping *Horizons*, as painful as that may be to accept," he had said.

Ajunwa was the only person who could help, as much as Brooke hated the prospect of seeking her out. The chancellor knew the phase drive's true capabilities, so Brooke didn't have to worry about revealing anything. With any luck, she could convince her *Horizons* was still out there.

Brooke had figured an AI filter would block her message long before it reached Ajunwa, so the promptness with which the chancellor had replied to her came as a surprise.

But old grudges died hard, and Brooke couldn't help but respond by saying, "You seem to have found time to enjoy yourself while civilization is falling apart all around us."

"Still angry after all these years." Ajunwa frowned. "For your information, young lady, I'm here to keep Australia and all of Oceania from seceding. You missed the Aussie, New Zealand, and Papua New Guinea council heads by a matter of minutes."

"Too bad. I love seeing my tax credit hard at waste."

The court rose to tier five, and Ajunwa turned her attention to the next set. "I was sorry to hear about the time you spent in prison."

"You could've pardoned me."

"Perhaps if you'd given me just cause to do so, but the story your lawyer sold to the jury yielded far more questions than answers. He claimed you stole a Pulsar and went for a joyride because you missed flying. Your fighter's sensor logs showed you didn't blow up the telescope array, but you did destroy three Pulsars that Defense couldn't identify. No pilots were MIA, and the astronomer assigned to the station turned up safe and sound on Triton, which forced the prosecution to drop any murder or manslaughter charges. Care to fill in any of the blanks?"

Lowering her gaze, Brooke picked at one of the rips in her jeans.

Ajunwa clasped her fingers in her lap. "Please accept my condolences regarding your separation. I never like to hear about families splitting."

Brooke's shoulders drooped, an act she tried to mask with a shrug. "I suppose some things run their course, not that it's any of your business."

"I've kept close tabs on you over the years," Ajunwa said without looking at her. "You know why."

"Great. Add invasion of privacy to the list of things you've done to me."

"No one's done anything to you. You made a choice knowing the consequences."

"What if a member of your family had been in danger? You're telling me you wouldn't have done the same?"

Ajunwa twisted to face her. "I would have, which is why I've let you be despite what you did and what you know. Nevertheless, you stole government property, used it for personal gain, and risked helping a dangerous organization become even more dangerous. If you were in my position, would you have let that go?"

Brooke chose not to respond.

"Now, what was it you wanted to discuss?" the chancellor asked. "Something to do with the lost *New Horizons* mission?"

A guard interrupted and asked if they cared for food or drink. Ajunwa requested a bottle of water and a pie. Brooke declined anything.

As the guard hurried away to fulfill the order, Brooke blew out her frustration with a long-winded sigh. She needed to not let her issues with the chancellor get in the way.

"You know what the phase drive is capable of, right?" Brooke asked, testing her knowledge.

The creases in the chancellor's forehead lifted. "What are you implying?"

"We both know it allows for more than travel through space." Brooke over-enunciated her last word.

"I see the professor saw fit to share certain details with you. But if you think you can threaten to reveal this alleged information in order to gain leverage over me—"

"No, no. That's not what I came here to do. I would never . . . what I'm saying is the *New Horizons* mission was declared lost. No trace of the ship was found at its destination or anywhere else in space. But given the drive's capabilities, isn't it possible that the ship simply hasn't reached its destination yet?"

Ajunwa crossed her legs and gave Brooke a look she couldn't quite read. Was it surprise? Concern? Perhaps the chancellor was even impressed at her deduction.

The guard interrupted with Ajunwa's concessions. Brooke accepted a water bottle after all.

After a sip and a nibble, the chancellor said, "What you're proposing isn't out of the realm of possibility, but it's beyond the realm of practicality."

"What do you mean?" Brooke asked. "You don't think it's possible from a practical standpoint?"

"No. We all know safeguards can be bypassed. Rather, it doesn't matter whether you're right or not because there's nothing I can do about it."

"Nothing you can do or will do?"

"You said it yourself. I have all I can do to hold the ISC together. I cannot justify expending the resources to go after a ship with only a few thousand people when forty billion need those resources closer to home."

"I get where you're coming from, but what about *Nautilus*? Isn't its construction almost complete? Why not send it to Gliese 581 instead of wherever else it was going to go?" Brooke leaned closer to her. "Based on Kevin's—I mean, Professor Sommerfield's—calculations, *Horizons* will emerge from hyperspace in November. *Nautilus* needs to be ready to go by May to beat it there."

Ajunwa worked a brief snort in between a drink and a bite. "Stuck in hyperspace for seven years. Not a prospect I would relish."

"As far as anyone aboard knows, the trip is only taking the expected six months. The crew won't have any idea they've skipped time until they downshift."

"And how did you determine all this?"

Brooke revealed as much of the truth as she could. "I got to thinking about it after experiencing a time lag in a combat sim caused by a software glitch. I went to ask Kevin how crazy my idea sounded. That was when he told me about the drive and calculated *Horizons's* arrival date."

"I see." Ajunwa shook her head and sighed. "Unfortunately, construction on *Nautilus* was halted last year. The necessary funds, resources, and personnel to not only complete the ship but support the mission were lost when major nation-states withdrew. The IEF is on the verge of being disbanded, meaning there will be no future manned interstellar missions."

"What? How can humankind turn its back on exploration?"

"Again, it's not so much a matter of ideals as one of practicality. For the first time in twenty years, I'm facing the real possibility of not being reelected—if there's an ISC left to govern by the next term. Without a united human union, there can be no unified exploration effort. The resources necessary to send humans out into interstellar space and return them safely are more than any one nation-state can manage alone."

Brooke mustered a tight-lipped nod and gulped down her water.

"However . . ." Ajunwa muttered after washing down her last morsel. "Do you have any proof?"

After thinking it through, Brooke said, "No—I mean. I'm not an expert, but I don't know of any way to verify the ship still exists until it reappears."

"I see. Unfortunately, hard evidence would be required to sway the ISC council, and the only circumstantial proof we've got is the truth about the phase drive. I won't reveal that to save a few thousand people—or my career. I'm sorry."

◆

Stressing over her failure to enlist Ajunwa's aid, Brooke exited the portal from Callisto and bounded into the phase port on Oberon, heading for Makemake. Sunlight reflected off the smooth, baby-blue surface of the ice giant Uranus overhead and penetrated the dome. Outside, the grayish-red icy landscape stretched away until it ended at Hamlet, the largest crater on Oberon. When Uranus passed between Neptune and Saturn or Jupiter in future decades, Oberon and its fellow moons would become a bustling hub of activity. But for the time being, Uranus orbited in an isolated quadrant of the solar system.

A bored guard waved her through the fast track checkpoint at the Palomar colony gate.

Normally, she reveled in solitude, but right now the almost-deserted concourse added to her sense of helplessness. The chancellor's unwillingness to do anything about *Horizons* left Brooke without any options. Her former support AI and friend had doomed her niece—albeit for a noble cause—and Brooke could do nothing but sit around and wait for it to happen.

With her head hung, she lunged through the portal that would whisk her home. *This might be worse than when I thought Maya was dead*, she mused.

When she emerged from the portal, a full gee of gravity yanked her down.

She fell forward, off balance. She managed to turn her head to the side and brace her fall with her hands. Still, her cheek smacked the cold floor with enough force to rattle her skull and leave her with a sore jaw.

Groaning, Brooke lay on her stomach, ear pressed to what felt like a window.

When the daze and headache subsided enough to allow her to focus, she cursed.

Rubbing her jaw, she pushed up onto her hands and knees. Stars scrolled past the viewport below her.

"She's here," a familiar voice said. "Set course for Psykhe and upshift to hyperspace."

The stars shot out of sight, replaced by the salmon-pink hue of hyperspace.

Brooke sat back on her heels and found Shin and Zeke standing before her. The bulkheads behind them suggested she had strayed onto a ship, but the rest of her surroundings resembled something closer to the wormhole generator control rooms found in phase ports. When she peered over her shoulder, she saw the portal arch.

"Sorry about the abrupt gravity change," Shin said. "Teleporting is new tech, and we don't quite have all the kinks worked out."

"Obviously," she said.

He reached out to help her up.

Brooke swatted his hand away. "It's been over half a year. Where the hell have you been?"

"Acquiring this ship," he said with a sweep of his arm. "Welcome aboard *The Dragon Lady*."

"You couldn't have told me about this sooner?"

His face grew stiff and serious. "I told you to be patient. Procuring one of the Vril's stealth phase cruisers required careful planning, which took time. I wasn't about to jeopardize our splinter group to keep you in the loop. Everyone is under increased scrutiny."

As she stood, Zeke crept toward her and held out an auto-syringe. "Gravites for strength and medites to alleviate any concussion symptoms." The kid had grown another few centimeters and looked a couple of years older, now a young teenager.

Accepting the syringe, Brooke lifted her ponytail out of the way and injected herself. "If memory serves," she said, glowering at Shin, "the term 'dragon lady' refers to a strong but ornery Asian woman. You didn't—"

"Name the ship after you?" he finished. "I thought you'd be flattered."

"Send me back," she droned.

"Without fixing the ISC and saving Maya?"

Sighing, she asked, "And how do we plan to do that?"

Shin tipped his cap back. "By traveling to a Vril base outside the solar system and stealing their membership list."

Seventeen—Salutation
Gliese 581 System, December 2272 CE

During the course of an hour, the Penphins' ship ascended through the open bay doors of defense module hangar seven. Maya observed the spacecraft's progress from behind the window panes of the adjoining control room, although she could only discern shadows and silhouettes. She had ordered the lighting dimmed and reddened for the sake of their visitors. Every so often, one of the craft's thrusters fired to realign it with *Horizons's* rotation, which the grav control center had slowed to twenty percent of its standard rate.

When the craft had risen all the way inside the bay, the doors slid shut, and the hangar pressurized.

Acting Chief Medical Officer Richard Drew, archaeologist Camila Mendez, and biologist Charles Wallace joined Maya, Jo, three armed guards, and the technician on duty in the cramped control room. All eyes rested on Maya as they waited to follow her into the bay.

"The hangar should be all set, ma'am," said the technician manning the controls. "The environment is a close approximation of the conditions on their planet. I dropped the temperature to six degrees Celsius. The air pressure and density are about three times Earth sea level with carbon dioxide levels toxic to humans. You don't need a suit, but I'd recommend taking slow, deep breaths through your mouthpiece once you're in there.

It may take you a minute or two to acclimate."

"Thank you, crewman." Maya turned to Ensign Drew, who had earned his medical certification only weeks before *Horizons* had shipped out. "Have all health concerns been addressed, doctor?

"Planetary protection and clean room protocols are in place," Drew said, "which should minimize contamination both ways." He held up an auto-syringe. "You've all submitted to sterilization and received an injection to suppress things like the urge to cough or sneeze." Pointing to a ventilation duct in the ceiling, he added, "We've released medites into the air. They should act like synthetic T-cells and destroy any airborne pathogens our visitors give off. While you're interacting with them, we'll be running scans to ensure your well-being, map their physiology, and determine future precautions."

"Nice work." Maya fitted her mask over her mouth and swept her gaze around the room. "All right, here we go." She activated her language response wristband and opened the inner hatch to the hangar airlock. Everyone except the control room tech followed her inside.

Air brushed against her skin as the compartment pressurized. She inhaled slow, deep breaths and popped her ears to counteract the vertigo. When she moved, her body met with resistance just short of swimming underwater.

Stepping out into the bay, Maya gave her pupils time to adjust to the dim, orange-red haze blurring everything. She still couldn't see after a couple minutes, so she instructed her implants to enhance her vision.

Her surroundings brightened and came into focus. The shell craft rested two meters in front of her.

"It's got a crew module on top of a service module with rockets below," Maya said.

Ensign Camila Mendez rushed toward the craft. "It looks like something out of a museum."

Maya ordered the overeager archaeologist to stay back and exercise caution.

Pouting, Mendez returned to the group.

"It does resemble the NASA's Gemini and Apollo capsules from the twentieth century." Jo struck a thoughtful pose. "On the other hand, it looks like it was launched by a race of mermaids hailing from the Kingdom of the Sea."

"In a way, that makes sense," Ensign Charles Wallace said. "This air is thick. I bet their sky is one big ocean to them, and there's little distinction between flying and swimming."

Bobbing her head in agreement, Maya examined the rough contours of the craft. Crude metal plating and bolts connected sections of the shell.

She could make out a pair of radio antennae, thrusters, and radiator vents. No discernable writing, symbols, or other markings adorned the craft.

She crept around it and located a hatch above her head on the crew module.

The hatch swung open.

Maya backpedaled as a creature dove out of the craft.

The Penphin swooped up toward the ceiling, flapping its flipper-wings—flings, Wallace called them—and glided to the deck. It plopped down a short distance away on four stubby legs and sat perched at an angle, leaning toward her. The posture seemed natural for it, but whether it was a he, a she, or something else altogether, Maya couldn't tell.

A second Penphin, taller and thinner than the first, traced a similar flight pattern out of the hatch. As it landed next to the first, the third and stockiest of the three exited and settled down behind them.

Each exobeing possessed two unblinking bubble eyes, one on either side of an elongated snout. Lacking much in the way of necks, the creatures' smooth, black heads merged into the rest of their bodies. All three visitors wore leathery space suits, which fit them like second skins.

With her pulse throbbing, everything the IEF had taught Maya about first contact jumbled together in her mind. Greet them and get to know them. Refrain from judging their culture by human morality. Minimize misunderstandings by not using slang or metaphors. Withhold the specifics of advanced technology as it might overwhelm or tempt a less advanced people. Dismiss any notions of humans as gods or god-like entities, but paint mankind in the best possible light. Avoid sudden movements. And above all else, be prepared to adapt to the peculiar.

The two Penphins closest to Maya waddled their way toward her.

She resisted the urge to cringe as they sniffed her without reservation. They smelled pungent, like rotten fish or seaweed. She closed her mouth and wiggled her nose to keep from sneezing. *By the stars, I hope I'm not allergic to them.*

It took all her willpower to keep from shrieking and scampering away when eight fingers reached out from the undersides of their flings and groped her, unabashedly. Each digit felt like an icicle pressing against her.

They whistled to one other as they touched her.

The text of their song-speech, translated by *Horizons's* AI network, scrolled across the bottom of Maya's i-cite.

PALE AND SOFT, the first Penphin sang. AND SCALDING. A moment later, a line crossed out the word "scalding." The more accurate term "warm" took its place as the AIs learned and updated the translation matrix on the fly.

The second, taller Penphin bobbed its snout. STRANGE, STRANGE.

The guards behind Maya drew nearer and firmed their grips on their rifles. She was about to tell them and her accosters to back off when the third visitor whistled, STOP AND RETURN.

The two Penphins retracted their fingers and withdrew.

"I guess that settles who's in charge," Jo said.

After the two subordinates retreated behind the apparent leader, the head Penphin waddled closer to Maya and Jo. It raised both flings and sang, HELLO.

Maya took a slow step toward the Penphin, held her arms out in a likewise gesture, and smiled. "Hello to you as well." When she stopped talking, the speakers on her wristband whistled the translated sentence in the Penphins language.

The leader gave a start while the others flapped their flings.

With her jaw drooping, Maya hoped the translation matrix hadn't malfunctioned. *For all I know, I called them idiots.*

YOU SING OUR LANGUAGE, the leader said. WE EXPECTED TO BUILD COMMUNICATION IN TIME WITH CONCEPTS AND MATH.

Jo, Mendez, and Wallace all chuckled, and Maya relaxed.

"We thought the same things might be necessary," Maya said, "but we deciphered your language from your radio transmissions."

YOU HAVE BIG ABILITIES. THIS IS A BIG MOMENT.

"I agree. Our meeting is an important occasion." She studied their outfits. No writing, patches, or symbols adorned them. "May I ask your name?" she addressed the leader.

WE DO NOT UNDERSTAND.

"What do you call yourself or your people?"

The Penphins looked at one another.

"I'm Maya," she said, pointing at herself. "Maya Davis. At the moment, I'm second in command of this ship." She gestured toward Jo and the others. "This is Jo Ryder, an expert on the history of our civilization. And that's Camila Mendez and Charles Wallace."

The Penphins whistled in pleasing melodies, seeming to understand.

WE HAVE NO SUCH CONCEPTS TO IDENTIFY INDIVIDUAL THINGS, the leader said. HOWEVER, WE HERE ARE THE THINKERS AND EXPLORERS.

"Aristotle and the Astronauts," Jo murmured. "Has a nice ring to it, don't you think?"

Maya tried not to grin. "We, too, are explorers, so we have that in common."

YES, BUT YOU ARE VERY DIFFERENT IN OTHER WAYS.

"You're not like anyone we've ever encountered, either."

WHERE DO YOU COME FROM?

"From outside your solar system. Our sun is a much brighter star. It's white, not orange-red, although it looks yellow from the surface of our blue and green planet."

HOW DIFFERENT. The Penphin opened its mouth, exposing stubby teeth better suited to mashing than tearing anything apart. It had no tongue as far as she could tell. YOU COME FROM FARTHER THAN WE CAN GO. BY WHAT MEANS DID YOU TRAVEL HERE?

"As you noticed, we have big abilities."

YES. YOUR VESSEL IS BIG BUT LESS THAN AT FIRST."

"Less than at first?"

"I think he means damaged," Wallace said.

"Right," Maya said. "We had a run of bad luck when we arrived, but we're doing better now."

The leader tilted its snout and blinked. WE DO NOT UNDERSTAND CERTAIN TONES.

"Tones?"

"I think he means words," Mendez said. "Their language is sound-based—tones, keys, notes, frequencies. Think music."

"Of course. Which tones don't you understand?"

The leader whistled two short notes. No text appeared in her i-cite, but she heard them well enough to discern the equivalent English words. *Human speech sure sounds strange coming from them.* "Better and bad luck. I see. These are positive and negative concepts."

POSITIVE AND NEGATIVE, the leader repeated. LIKE BATTERY TERMINALS OR THE CHARGES OF PARTICLES.

Her team shrugged when Maya shot them a glance. If a human had responded in such manner, she would have assumed they had made a terrible joke.

"No," Maya said. "Something positive is good, like meeting you. We're happy to meet you. Conversely, something negative is bad. We're not happy our ship is damaged."

The Penphin sounded out the words "good," "happy," and "bad." WE STILL DO NOT UNDERSTAND.

"Well, if something you want to happen occurs, it makes you feel good, and if something you don't want to happen takes place, you feel bad."

OH, WANT AND FEEL. WE UNDERSTAND SUCH CONCEPTS. LIKE WHEN WE FELT COMPELLED TO COME HERE TO LEARN WHY A BRIGHT OBJECT HAD APPEARED IN THE SKY.

"Right. The fact you came and we now have the chance to meet is good."

SO GOOD IS MORE KNOWLEDGE AND BAD IS LESS DESIRE SATISFIED.

"Well, sort of, although—"

Jo tapped her on the arm, her face brightening. "I don't think they comprehend value judgments."

"What do you mean?"

"I mean, they don't see things in terms of good and bad or right and wrong. They feel and act on compulsions, but they must not pass judgment on things that happen. Ask them this to test the theory." Jo whispered a question to her.

"What? I'm not going to ask them that."

"Exactly. It's not something you'd bring up to a human you didn't know very well, but I'm betting they won't care."

After mulling over the proposition, Maya addressed the leader. "Please accept my apologies, and feel free to decline answering this question if you find it offensive or uncomfortable. How do you feel when another one of your people dies?"

WE DON'T UNDERSTAND THE TONES "APOLOGIES" OR "OFFENSIVE."

The AI matrices seemed to be improving their ability to translate words not found in the Penphin's language.

WE FEEL LESS WHEN ANOTHER CEASES TO BE. BUT WHEN OTHERS ARE BORN, WE FEEL MORE AGAIN. IS THIS NOT THE SAME FOR YOU?

"Told you," Jo muttered.

"In some ways, yes," Maya said, "although we tend to feel more for people who die who are closer to us."

CLOSER? AS IN PHYSICAL DISTANCE?

"No, closer meaning people we care for more. We develop stronger feelings for people we have greater familiarity with, like family and friends."

WE DO NOT KNOW "FAMILY" OR "FRIENDS," BUT WE THINK WE UNDERSTAND. WE FEEL THE SAME IN CONSTANT FOR ALL.

Maya wondered whether all Penphins were linked in an empathetic manner, which led her to fear her next question. "So how do you feel when you fight?"

WHAT IS FIGHT?

"You know, disagreements, differences in opinion?"

EACH OF US HAS DESIRES WHICH ARE FELT BY THE WHOLE. COLLECTIVE FEELINGS DIRECT ALL COURSES OF

ACTION.

"None of you have ever caused emotional or physical injury to another on purpose?"

WHY WOULD ANY OF US DO THAT?

"Good question." She frowned as she pictured Aunt Brooke blasting a hole through her mother's chest.

The other Penphins waddled up next to their leader and asked to see more of the ship.

"Unfortunately, that isn't possible," Maya said. "We matched this environment to the conditions on your planet, but ours is very different."

WE HAVE PROTECTIVE GEAR IN OUR VESSEL, the leader said.

"I understand, but our ship is 'less' right now. We're in no shape to give a tour. Maybe when the ship is repaired—"

REPAIR, one of the other Penphins whistled. WE CAN BUILD AND FIX.

WE CAME TO HELP, the leader said.

Maya couldn't help but smile. "That's a generous offer, but I'm not sure if that would work. Plus, we have strict rules about who we allow to access our systems."

WHAT ARE RULES?

"No rules?" Jo smirked. "Sign me up."

◆

"Out of the question." Sitting on the edge of a control station in the ECC, Trevor folded his arms across his chest and shook his head.

"It'd be rude of us to refuse their invitation." Jo planted her hands on her hips. "Otherwise, why did we come all this way?"

Maya stiffened her posture. She and Jo seemed to be losing the argument—or more accurately, Trevor had made up his mind long before the conversation had begun. Nevertheless, she still had a few shots left to fire.

"At this point," Maya said, "I think a scouting mission would benefit us, sir. We lost some of our reserves in the collision, and we have no idea how long we're going to be stuck in this system. It makes sense to send a small team to survey their planet, catalog resources, and determine how well it could sustain us."

"I'm not letting you two go on a holiday while we're struggling to keep the lights on here," he said.

Jo stomped a boot. "A holiday? You pompous, short-sighted, Neanderthal-brained—"

Glaring at her, Maya said, "Ensign, you're dismissed."

After flashing Maya a glower, Jo stormed out of the ECC.

"Thank you, Ensign." Trevor said once the hatch slid shut behind her.

"I'm sure that wasn't easy for you."

"You're in command, which means I have to follow your orders," Maya said. "But please give orders in the best interest of everyone aboard ship."

"You're flirting with insubordination, Maya."

"I'm doing my job as first officer. That means informing you when I think you're wrong."

Nodding, he said, "I'll admit there are merits to sending you to the planet, but in my view, it's not necessary at this time. I need all available hands here to coordinate the restoration effort. If the situation gets worse, I'll consider it."

"I agree our chief focus should be to get the ship up and running, but why not work on multiple fronts to give ourselves the best possible chance of survival?"

"I don't plan to survive. We're going home."

"With all due respect, sir, I think you're in denial." She gestured to a display cube showing a visual of the Penphins' home world. "We have no way to send a message or shift back. There's a real possibility we might have to make a home here."

"The fabricators are up and running again. I've got a team working on constructing a transmitter. We can last long enough for help to arrive."

"And how long will that be? After it takes six months for our SOS to reach home, any starship will need six months to get here. That's a minimum of one year, assuming we could send a message this instant—which we can't—and supposing the IEF has a ship ready to leave at a moment's notice. But seven years have passed. We don't have any idea what's going on back home. We should hope for the best but assume the worst." *Which means bracing for an attempt by someone or something to kill the Penphins,* she held back. She hadn't yet told Trevor about Bob or the Vril, and she wasn't feeling very generous at the moment.

"We're nowhere near worst-case yet," he said. "Until then, let's focus our efforts here so things never degrade to that point."

"If nothing else, sending a small team to the planet would boost morale. Everyone wants to know what it's like and how the Penphins live. A few vidsims and stories would lift the crew's spirits."

"I can't justify the allocation of resources on the basis of making people feel better."

Maya growled under her breath. "Not everything is about the bottom line, sir. A good skipper understands there's more to starship operations than the operation of the ship."

"Are you questioning my competency as acting captain?"

"If I may be honest, sir?"

Trevor rested his hands on the control station. "Go ahead."

"I believe you're being unreasonable, unprofessional, and a coward. You're allowing a single-minded desire to get home, your vendetta against me, and a host of other biases to cloud your judgment. We may all die out here because of you."

Swallowing, she braced herself for a severe tongue-lashing. Perhaps he would relieve her of duty or confine her to quarters until she cooled off. Maybe he would throw her in the brig or threaten her with a court-martial, not that any courts existed out here in which to try her.

Instead, Acting Captain Young surprised her, averting his gaze and grunting in exasperation. "Very well. Assemble a small team and get your mission plan to me within the hour." He jabbed a finger toward the hatch. "Now get out of here before I come to my senses."

Eighteen—Sub Rosa
Hyperspace, January 2272 CE

Aboard *The Dragon Lady*, Brooke sat on a bench in an otherwise unoccupied observation lounge. Her legs dangled over the transparent deck plating as the mind-bending latticework of hyperspace rushed past her feet.

This is the first time I've been outside the solar system, she mused while setting her empty cereal bowl aside. *I never pictured it happening this way, but I made it, Dad. Still, I won't feel fulfilled until I reach another star system.*

Behind her, the door to the lounge slid open, and she sighed. *Solitude was nice while it lasted.*

Shin sat down on the opposite end of the bench and leaned forward. Tipping his cap back, he stared down through the deck. "You know, hyperspace has never looked as weird as I'd expect from a higher dimension. I mean, pink? Why pink?"

"All modern drives generate suppression fields that subdue the true nature and effects," she said. "The actual way it looks is beyond human comprehension. If we switched off the field, you'd experience the wildest trip of your life."

"That's right. You're one of the few people who've experienced the real thing. During flight trials of *Viking* and again in the Quasar, right?"

Brooke grunted in apathetic acknowledgment.

"So . . . was everything okay with your quarters?" Shin asked. "Did you get enough to eat?"

"The amenities?" she snapped. "Really? Cut the small talk and tell me what the hell's going on. You said we were going to steal some list. Is it—?"

"What you think it is? Yes. It's a filesim containing the citizen profiles for every member of the Vril, including a detailed history of each agent's involvement."

Brooke blinked. "If we gave that to the ISC, they'd root out every agent and put an end to the Vril."

"That's the idea."

"But the Vril aren't dumb enough to keep a full list like that in one place."

Shin dipped his chin in acknowledgment. "No, they're not."

An icon appeared in her i-cite. When she accessed it, a vidpic popped up showing three small test tubes sitting in a rack. "What are they?"

"Capsules containing the DNA fragments of three senior Vril operatives."

"Great, so we can at least expose them."

"No, if we blew the whistle on a mere three agents, the Vril could cover their tracks. My group spent months setting them up to gather their genetic material for a grander purpose." He sat back. "In the same way the Vril lack a central HQ, the membership information is spread across multiple matrices throughout the solar system. A specific program must be executed to collect the different parts of the list. Then three top-level operatives must consent to a DNA scan to initiate the program. My group managed to get their hands on the program, the three DNA samples, and each piece of the list."

Dipping her brow, Brooke asked, "If you've got it, why haven't you made it public? Why do you need me?"

"The first step was getting the list, but it's jumbled and encrypted. It's like a dismantled puzzle with trillions of pieces, and the picture is scrambled even after you put it together. Step two involves compiling and decrypting the list to make it legible."

"Sounds like overkill of the geekiest variety."

"Welcome to Vril security. You don't keep your organization hidden from the bulk of the human race without the geekiest of precautions." He shrugged. "Besides, your ex-husband implemented similar measures that kept the phase drive out of the Vril's hands for at least a little while."

"I suppose so." She slouched and shoved her thumbs into her jacket pockets. "I assume we're headed somewhere outside the solar system to perform step two. But this cruiser can't reach the nearest star. I doubt it has the antimatter or life support capacity to travel one light year, let alone four—and that's not counting the return trip."

"We're headed to a base a light year from the sun. To make the journey possible, the Vril have increased their cruisers' antimatter supplies and recalibrated their drives for max efficiency, but the trade-off is decreased speed. Throw in the fact that our ships aren't as fast as IEF or ISC Defense spacecraft, and—"

"Wait, I thought the Vril had more advanced tech than everyone else. That's how you built the tri-fighters and pyramid carriers and staged the invasion. Why are your ships slower?"

"The one piece of tech we didn't have until your husband invented it was the phase drive. We had to reverse-engineer it, so our FTL capability is still lagging behind the rest of the human race."

Gazing around the observation lounge, she asked, "So how long am I stuck aboard this thing with you?"

"It should take *The Dragon Lady* a month to reach Psykhe."

"Psykhe?"

"The planetar where the base is located."

"A planetar? You mean, a rogue planet ejected from its star system."

"Right. This stray escaped discovery until the Vril found it a few decades ago. I know it's hard to believe an object as big as a planet could escape detection so close to the solar sys—"

"Not really." Brooke shrugged. "The farther an object is from any star, the less light it reflects, which makes it harder to see. Scientists discovered a handful of dwarf planets in the Kuiper Belt hundreds of years ago, but it wasn't until we got out there that we found thousands of them. It's only a matter of time until somebody spots Psykhe, so I'm curious how the Vril plan to keep it hidden." She thought back to when she had discovered a terraformed Triton. "I know they've got a way to do it."

"The Vril use an advanced form of anti-neudar jamming."

She tapped her fingers on her leg. "So when scanning neutrinos pass through the target, the jamming must somehow show false results."

"Like the planet isn't there. And for good measure, Vril censor AIs intercept the data received by telescopes and probes. If the AIs discover anything hinting at the existence of a planet or human activity, they skew the data."

"Makes sense, I guess." She peered around the lounge. "So what's the plan once we reach this base? Sneak in with the list, decrypt it, and sneak out?"

Shin frowned. "Sort of."

"Sort of how, exactly?"

"Before I tell you, I want you to know how many people have put their lives on the line to make this attempt possible. Also understand that the biggest risks are yet to come."

She wrinkled her nose. "In other words, I'm not going to like step two."

"No, you most definitely won't, but there's no other way. Believe me, we've considered all options. If we're serious about winning the game, we have to go all in and wager everything."

"I'm no stranger to risking my life. If this plan is the only way to fix the ISC and save Maya, I've no choice but to do it."

He lowered his gaze. Fear and worry contorted his expression.

"There's no sneaking into the base on Psykhe," he said after a moment. "It's impossible. There're no holes in the security grid surrounding the planet. A gravimetric distortion field stretches out from it for a radius of a hundred million kilometers, so there's no shifting or teleporting anywhere in the vicinity. And this craft may be a stealth cruiser to the rest of the solar system, but the Vril can detect one of their own ships. They know we're coming."

"Wait, they know we're coming?"

He cringed, anticipating her reaction. "I leaked Zeke's location to them."

"What?" Brooke sprung to her feet, propelled by parental instinct. "They'll kill him."

"No." He held his palms out as she loomed over him. "He's the most stable of all the specimens of his kind ever birthed. It took hundreds of agents to terminate the others, but Zeke has managed to live out a normal life with Xi. The Vril feel the risk of further study is justified as long as they keep him under heavy sedation."

"So you plan to hand him over in exchange for the list? Is that what he is? A sacrificial lab specimen?" She raised a fist.

Shin glared at her. "Do you think they'd hand over a document capable of crushing their organization for one exochild?"

She lowered her arm. "Probably not."

"There'll be no deals. The Vril don't realize our splinter group has commandeered this vessel. As far as they're concerned, it's manned by Vril loyalists. They sent this ship to seize Zeke and bring him to Psykhe."

"Am I supposed to be impressed? You're still giving him to them."

"That's where you come in."

"What do you mean?"

"Have a seat."

Having run out of protests, Brooke parked her butt back on the bench.

"I said they know we're coming. The 'we' in that statement implies two people, Zeke and you."

"Me?"

"They eliminated me by destroying the telescope array, remember? You're the one who's been hiding him. You put up quite a fight when the crew of this ship tried to take him, but they nabbed you along with him—as far as the Vril know, anyway."

Brooke gave a reluctant nod, starting to understand. "You're delivering us as fake prisoners so we can decrypt the list once we're inside."

"Precisely. We'll load the list into a biochip they won't be able to detect and place it on you. Our splinters on the inside will help you decrypt the list and get out with it and Zeke."

"Why not let your people handle everything? I still don't get why you're sending me instead of someone else."

"It's the getting out part that could prove troublesome."

She raised an eyebrow.

"The moment you decrypt the list, they'll know," he said. "You'll need to have Zeke with you beforehand and fight your way out. Our people will do everything they can to protect you both and get you to the fighter bay. I'm confident that once you're in a Pulsar, you'll get him out safe and sound."

Brooke gave a subtle nod, belying the chills coursing through every limb.

♦

Four weeks later, Brooke stood near *The Dragon Lady's* main docking hatch with both hands cuffed in front of her. Zeke lay on a stretcher next to her in the corridor, sedated.

The sight of the helpless kid hastened her heart rate. She took slow breaths, doing her best to suppress any outward sign of discomfort. She had gone over every detail of the plan with Shin multiple times, but the chances of pulling it off seemed slim at best. Too many things had to go right for them to get out alive. *This is the only way*, she kept reminding herself.

Pain stung her forehead as she crinkled her brow. The crew had roughed her up when she had tried to stop them from taking Zeke—or so her cover story went. In actuality, a physician aboard *The Dragon Lady* had grafted superficial wounds into her skin, giving her the appearance of having put up a fight during her incarceration. Cosmetic bruises wouldn't fool the base doctors.

The Vril transport that would ferry her to Psykhe docked at the outer hatch, rocking the ship.

She gazed out the viewport and down past the sleek hull of the short-range transport. The planet looked like a big circle, a shade lighter than surrounding space. The ring system encircling the equator shimmered in random spots where distant starlight struck shards of ice.

An asteroid-sized moon waded within the rings. Its dark surface blended with the planet in the background, so she almost missed it. Magnifying and enhancing it revealed manmade structures and activity. Mining bots had carved out a huge chunk of the moon. It looked as if a gigantic space creature had taken a bite out of it. Scaffolding protruded from the chasm along with the hull of a fierce-looking starship, on the scale of *Horizons*.

The design of the ship resembled the double pyramid carriers that the Vril had used in their play-acted invasion. However, this beast was sleeker and featured a more impressive array of armaments. Double—if not triple—the number of force field projectors pockmarked the hull along with more cannons and launchers than she could count. *She's a destroyer, but what's the target?* Her palms sweated. *Are the Vril planning to stage another invasion, or do they know* Horizons *is still out there?*

The inner hatch in the floor slid open, and three Vril agents climbed aboard. Like the crew of *The Dragon Lady*, the agents wore common street clothing. The choice of casual attire contrasted with the UN uniforms Brooke had seen on Collins's stealth carrier so long ago, but his crew had consisted of handpicked Defense deserters. She supposed the civvies struck her as odd because of her time in the service. The last thing a clandestine organization would do was dress its anonymous members in shiny outfits with nametags and a snazzy logo.

A stout woman instructed the bed to tilt upright and enabled its force field to keep Zeke from falling. Magflux emitters at the foot of the stretcher lifted it a few centimeters off the deck. After floating over the open hatch, the bed lowered into the transport, and the woman followed it down.

The other two agents, a lanky man and a woman sporting a buzz cut, grabbed Brooke's arms and pulled her toward the hatch.

She shrugged them off only to have Buzz Cut jab the muzzle of her handgun between her shoulder blades. Buckling under the pain, Brooke climbed down the ladder through the airlock. The descent proved cumbersome with her hands bound, but she managed.

The interior of the transport reminded her of the cabin in *Viking*, the phase shuttle she had gone post-luminal in for the first time all those years ago. However, this craft seated six and featured modern neurotronic and holotronic control systems.

With a wave of his gun, Lanky nudged her past Zeke and into one of the rear seats.

Brooke plopped down with a defiant scowl and fastened her harness as instructed.

Lanky settled in the chair opposite her and kept his weapon pointed in her direction.

After the other agents had strapped into their chairs, the pilot initiated the departure sequence. The ceiling hatch sealed, the external clamps released, and the transport executed a series of thruster burns. Beyond the influence of *The Dragon Lady's* rotation, the gravity dropped to nothing. Brooke felt her body drift upward, held in place by the harness.

Upon clearing the cruiser, the transport fired its main rockets. Three gees of acceleration pressed her back into her seat.

Halfway to the planet, the engines shut off, and the craft coasted toward reentry.

Her window offered little in the way of a view during the craft's descent through Psykhe's upper atmosphere. All she could discern outside was the glow of molecules scraping against the force field and the dark clouds beyond.

Once the clouds broke, however, the scene transfixed her.

The landscape resembled the primordial Earth from billions of years ago that she had learned about as a kid. Rivers of lava flowed from erupting volcanoes spewing molten rock that exploded on contact with the air. Brilliant flashes of light propagated through the sky for kilometers, reflecting off the cloud cover in shades of jasmine, amber, and mahogany.

Buzz Cut looked back over her shoulder at Brooke. "The atmosphere's mostly hydrogen," she said. "Things get a little explosive, although helium and carbon dioxide keep those flares from burning out of control. We dare not fire rockets within the atmosphere, though." She pointed down at the ground. "All the geothermal activity keeps the surface temperature at a balmy sixty-five degrees Celsius. You can survive out there for a few minutes before your suit and skin start to melt."

To hide her fascination, Brooke donned a blank expression. "Why show or tell me any of this?"

Buzz Cut and Lanky exchanged glances.

Less active terrain rushed past the transport after a hundred kilometers. The angry volcanoes and raging lava streams gave way to rocky hills and plains.

The transport slowed to a hover above a shallow canyon and descended. Unable to use its conventional thrusters in the flammable atmosphere, the craft fired ventral jets that sucked in air and blew it out at high pressure. Meters from the ground, the holographic chasm floor dematerialized, revealing bay doors in the process of opening.

Throughout the two-kilometer drop, the dark chasm brightened.

The transport touched down, and the sound of atmospheric compression within the ship popped her ears.

Hard white light illuminated the hangar bay, forcing her to squint. As her pupils adjusted, the side hatch opened and extended an access ramp. The pilot and the stout woman hopped up and escorted the stretcher with Zeke down the incline.

Buzz Cut and Lanky led Brooke out at gunpoint.

She stopped at the top of the ramp and blinked at the tall technicians working in the hangar. The giants supervised the androids servicing the transport and other spacecraft, including a group of Pulsars.

The Vril's cloned slave race, she mused. *Armin's people.*

Lanky pushed her forward. "Keep moving."

"I thought they all died in the war," Brooke said as they marched toward the entrance to the base.

"We withheld one ship from the attack on Earth and sent it here to establish this outpost." Buzz Cut said. "It took twenty years of pushing their fusion drives past the limit to get here."

Bots, androids, humans, and giants roamed the passageways. Every other person gawked at her, well aware of her identity. She couldn't tell whether they despised or worshiped her. Perhaps they exhibited a little bit of both.

Inside the base, Brooke had expected to find a mature biosphere like the underwater base on Mars, but the Vril had only established the outpost in the last year. Fabricator bots busied themselves with transforming the rocky tunnels into corridors. Bundled cabling of every diameter and color ran the lengths of the floors. The unfinished walls and ceilings supported exposed piping, wiring, and insulation.

Her escorts led her down one level and through a series of unfinished halls not much more than caves.

She slowed her pace when she passed a long window, her mouth hanging open. Dozens of giants at various stages of growth floated in birthing vats, immersed in some type of amniotic fluid. Unlike on Mars, the developing clones were very much alive. Blood and other fluids ran through the tubes connecting the immature clones to their chambers.

What surprised her most was the sight of the other giants attending to the vats. No normal humans worked in the nursery.

"They're growing more of themselves?" Brooke murmured. "Why?"

"Why does any species procreate?" Buzz Cut asked by way of

answer.

"I'll bet that ship in orbit needs a crew, but for what—"

"Enough." Lanky glared at his partner and shoved his prisoner forward. "Keep going."

After descending another level, Brooke stepped into a spacious, high-ceilinged room lacking any furnishings.

The agents shoved Brooke into the center and stepped back. A faint zapping sound signaled the establishment of an unseen force field around her.

"Welcome to your new home," Lanky said as he and Buzz Cut took their leave.

"Where's the head?" Brooke yelled after them as she swung her gaze around the room.

"Ask the AI," Buzz Cut said, pointing at the ceiling, "and it'll extend the force field." She jabbed a thumb over her shoulder at the faint outline of a hidden door.

"What do you expect me to do in between bathroom breaks? Just stand here?"

"Feel free to sit if you like," said the woman who strolled past them into the room. "Or do a headstand for all I care."

Brooke flared her nostrils. "Eve."

The artificial woman stopped at the assumed boundary of the force field and frowned. Her ultra-blonde hair and pale skin showed no signs of Brooke's particle blasts, not that the repaired damage came as any surprise. Years had passed since their confrontation in Shin's sister's home on Ganymede.

Reaching into a small cardboard container, Eve pulled out a French fry, nibbled on it, and moaned in satisfaction. "Do you know how hard it is to get good chips a light year from civilization?" She bit into a second fry, beside herself.

The force field shimmered as Eve stepped through it, unimpeded, while munching on another fry.

Brooke backpedaled as her captor approached, but she could only retreat so far.

When Eve reached arm's length, she lunged forward in a blur and drove a fist into Brooke's stomach.

Gasping in agony, Brooke dropped to her knees and almost keeled over. The muscles in her abdomen tightened, and she gagged. Bile pooled in her throat, but she managed to keep from spitting it up.

After a few seconds, the room stopped spinning, and Brooke peered up at Eve. The woman paced in front of her, finishing the last of her food.

"That was for shooting me," Eve said with her mouth half full.

"Androids may not feel pain, but having my bodily functions and thought processes short out on me wasn't pleasant, either."

Brooke rolled onto her back, feeling the need to ground herself. "Sorry I botched the job of killing you."

"I'll grant you this much. You're honest."

With her stomach cramps subsiding, Brooke sat up to find the android studying her with both arms folded.

"So what now?" Brooke asked.

"Now, you sit here like a good girl while I get the information I need." Eve pointed at the emitters and scanners affixed to the upper portions of the walls.

"What, no medieval torture chair? No agonizing pain while I'm strapped in having the thoughts ripped out of my head?"

"You should indulge in fewer sims." Eve smiled. "Of course, you could save us time and tell me everything I want to know now."

"Not likely."

"I'm going to get it out of you regardless."

"Then I guess we'll do it the hard way."

"So self-righteous." Eve shrugged. After tapping her last fry against her lip, she tossed it into her mouth. "I wonder if torturing that freakish brat would make your more cooperative."

"You can't. You need him to devise a defense against his people. Otherwise, why go to all the trouble to capture him?"

Her captor sighed. "It was worth a try." Her nostrils twitched, and she growled under her breath. "What I wouldn't give to be able to smash that little monster's skull into bloody pieces."

"You've got an awful lot of hate toward one innocent child."

"Innocent?" Eve crushed the empty fry carton in her hand. "Do you have any idea how many people died when we first birthed his kind?" The android shuddered with rage. "An exochild of no more than three years of age forced my mother to stab herself to death with a fork because the vermin didn't like his food. It controlled and killed seven more agents until they finally managed to put it down."

Lowering her gaze, Brooke said, "That's horrendous." She looked up. "But Zeke is no more personally responsible for the death of your mother than I'm to blame for the murders other humans have committed."

"Only because he never had the chance."

"He's not any different from the others you birthed, though, right? Yet he has morals and uses his abilities with restraint. It seems to me his upbringing made all the difference. I can only imagine how those children turned out being raised in a Vril lab."

"What would you have had us do? Send beings capable of

manipulating your every desire and action to homes with normal families?"

"It seemed to work for Zeke."

Eve glowered at her, for once lacking a clever rebuttal.

"Besides," Brooke said, "isn't it just as much the Vril's fault for birthing members of a dangerous exospecies? Perhaps they shouldn't have messed with what they didn't understand."

The android lunged forward. Brooke jerked back and gasped.

Stopping short of trampling her prisoner, Eve glared down at her. "We have to find a way to protect ourselves from them." She held out her arms. "Don't you see, Brooke? By resisting me, you're helping to condemn the human race. Bloody hell. We should be fighting on the same side, not against each other."

Brooke exhaled in relief and narrowed her stare. "I'll concede that we may want the same thing in the long run, but I don't deal with liars and schemers. There's no way I can trust you."

Eve took a step back and adjusted her red jacket. Following a deep breath, the tension escaped the perfect contours of her face. "Well, then." She forced a smile. "After I rip your thoughts, we'll build trust through more modern methods." She stepped outside the force field and toward the exit.

Stopping and turning, she tapped a finger against her temple. "I suggest you think long and hard about how badly you want to remain yourself. Personally, I wouldn't mind a cheerier and more agreeable Brooke Davis."

Brooke scowled at her.

"Have you seen yourself when you do that?" Eve whirled around and strutted out of the room with an inhuman swiftness.

Pressing her palms to her forehead, Brooke fell onto her back and stared at the ceiling.

Nineteen—Coadjuvancy
Fourth Planet, Gliese 581 System, December 2272 CE

A sound like a cricket chirping under water roused Maya from a nightmare, waking her as her aunt shredded her mother's body with particle blasts.

She sprung up on her elbows only to sink down again atop the spongy, makeshift mattress. Adrenaline surged through her veins, filling her with an all-too human fear of the unknown. Throughout the last week, she had reminded herself over and over that predators didn't exist on this benign world, but some instincts were rooted too deeply.

Sucking in oxygen through her breather, she sat up and blinked her itchy, watering eyes. Her meds had thus far failed to counteract everything in the air.

A creature sat perched on the end of the bed. The choomper, as Jo had dubbed it, resembled a cute baby dragon worm out of a weekday afternoon kid's sim. It was the size of an average house cat with a mud-colored tubular body that bobbed up and down. Its egg-shaped eyes, one on either side of its head, fixated on her while it sniffed her bare feet with its bulbous snout.

"Go on, now," Maya said, shooing it away with her hand. "I'm not your caretaker." The Penphins had explained the creature wasn't a pet. They didn't know the term "pet." Rather, it was one of the many planimals—Jo's word for the plethora of indigenous organisms possessing the qualities of both plants and animals—that maintained the planet's symbiotic ecosystem.

The choomper blurped again, seeming somehow disappointed. It bounded down off the bed and slinked out the door-less entrance.

She threw off the heated blanket she had brought and touched her toes to the floor. Like the rest of the domicile, the Penphins had fashioned the floorboards out of their world's closest equivalent to wood. They harvested and refined the strong but bendable substance from a type of seaweed found in their vast oceans. It seemed a little like bamboo but with the hardness and smoothness of seashells. Sort of. This world was so foreign that she often found it difficult to articulate things.

The AM radio on the shelf whistled on low volume.

Goosebumps popped up on her arms. Shivering, she wrapped the blanket around her shoulders. Given that the planet orbited so close to its star—at one tenth of an AU—she had envisioned a much warmer climate before arriving, perhaps tropical or desert-like. However, an air temperature of six degrees Celsius kept her teeth chattering and never varied by more than a degree. With a rotation locked to its primary, the same hemisphere of the planet always faced the sun, so the world experienced little in the way of changing seasons. The Penphins lived on the day side in the temperate zones that began a thousand kilometers north and south of the equator. The trio of satellites *Horizons* had placed in orbit indicated the ocean bubbled like a hot spring at the point closest to the sun.

Dim red rays poured into the dwelling through the oval windows and doorway. At any given point on the planet, the amount of sunlight never changed. Darkness loomed outside the window facing the night side. Through the opposite window, the half-crescent of the sun loomed over the horizon, never rising or setting in the hazy sky. The red dwarf appeared ten times larger than Sol looked from Earth due to how closely the planet orbited to its star. A pink ocean covered by a kind of thick black algae sloshed below.

Despite having spent a week on the planet, she still struggled with how a view so breathtaking could also be so depressing.

She gulped a swig from a water thermos with the *New Horizons* mission logo, thinking back on her last moments aboard. Jo, Councilman Hamilton, archeologist Ensign Camila Mendez, and biologist Ensign Charles Wallace had joined her, each itching for the opportunity despite the circumstances. Much to Erik's dismay, Acting Captain Young had denied his request to accompany the scouting party. Trevor had insisted the ship needed all pilots, but he had at least allowed Erik to fly the transport to the planet and drop them off.

The small landing party had allowed Maya the honor of disembarking first. As the soles of her boots had crunched the hard, mud-colored grass, she had felt a bit dizzy at the notion of her accomplishment. She had become the first human to set foot on a planet in another star system—and one with intelligent life, no less. In retrospect, the lightheadedness might've resulted more because of her need to acclimate to the environment. But still . . .

She had searched deep down for profound words befitting the monumental occasion. After coming up empty, she had simply muttered, "Too fused."

The significance of the moment had waned as the transport had ascended above the thick clouds, leaving her and her team on an alien world for who-knows-how-long. She remembered feeling trapped and abandoned as well as fearful. *What if I hate it here?*

Throwing off the blanket, Maya pulled off her undershirt, knelt down, and rummaged through her bag for a change of clothes.

I don't want to stay here forever, but as a vacation spot, this place is beyond words.

The slapping of Penphin footsteps and the whistling of their language accompanied the text HELLO.

Maya jumped and slammed her head into the low ceiling.

As she drifted back down, she covered her bare chest and turned partway around. "Ari, don't you know how to—?" She stopped herself short of saying "knock." The Penphins didn't construct buildings or rooms with closeable doors. Nor did they understand the concepts of privacy or modesty. She needed to stow her human reactions and respond according to the local culture.

When in Rome, she thought, quoting one of Jo's historical sayings. *Then again, respect for another race's customs should be a two-way street.* "For future reference, humans prefer it when visitors announce themselves and wait for permission before entering another person's enclosed space." Her wristband sang her translated response.

Ari bobbed his snout. WE HAVE ENCOUNTERED THIS CONCEPT WITH HUMANS MULTIPLE TIMES NOW. IT IS STRANGE, BUT WE WILL TRY TO ADHERE IN THE FUTURE. The name Ari was shorthand for Aristotle, the name Jo had given the leader and chief thinker who had visited *Horizons*.

"Thank you."

GRATITUDE, CORRECT?

"You're catching on."

Ari directed an eye toward the floorboards and lifted one of his four feet. WHAT ARE WE CATCHING ON?

Maya stifled a laugh. "Sorry, that was an expression. I meant you're starting to understand human interaction."

SLOWLY. HUMAN INTERRELATIONS INVOLVE GREAT INTRACACIES.

"That's certainly true."

After a moment of standing there, Ari said, WE SHALL WAIT OUTSIDE.

"That would be the most appropriate response in my culture."

He waddled out the entrance.

Maya threw on her uniform and heated jacket and exited the habitat a few minutes later.

Penphins congregated and waddled throughout the grassy plains. They could fly from a young age, so they didn't have much need for streets. A type of vegetable grew on the sharp bushes pockmarking the plains. While safe for humans to ingest, the tart and chalky pepper had given Maya a horrible lemon face when she had tried it.

Citizens flew in and out of the entrances of the higher story dwellings. Huge, redwood-sized vines supported the buildings. Multiple meters in diameter, these tree vines, or vrees, sprouted up everywhere and played a central role in Penphin society. The locals constructed their homes inside and atop them. They nurtured them by pruning and routing aqueducts to their roots. At times, the smaller vines sprouting from the vrees slithered or shuddered, which had startled her on more than one occasion. The Penphins didn't have the concept of religion—a whole other topic for consideration—but they treated the vrees as sacred for a reason that surpassed belief. Maya had learned how biologically inseparable the planimals were when she witnessed an act of cross pollination, although Jo had labeled it with a more straightforward term. That was as far as Maya felt comfortable thinking about it at the moment.

Ari led her to the village commons, flying for short bursts at a time so she could keep up. She jogged after him—or it, more accurately. The Penphins had no gender, and they never seemed to run out of energy. She drew upon every last bit of endurance from her daily gravite injections and the ironman training sessions Trevor had held before the crash.

The government buildings towered above the village up ahead. She had grown even more ashamed of Earth's political system after touring them on the day she arrived. Made possible by the telepathic empathy— or telempathy—that connected the Penphins, the general population appointed officials by feeling out the strongest, smartest, and most nurturing kin. Those selected performed additional iterations of the process, whittling the list down to smaller and smaller groups until no doubt remained about who should lead. Once appointed, the leaders carried out the collective will of the people. There were no lies. Corruption couldn't exist when everyone knew each other's general thoughts and intentions. Maya struggled to wrap her mind around it, and she imagined any human would share in her difficulty.

Upon reaching the central commons, Ari settled down in the grass and spread out like a beanbag chair. The Penphins had little use for seats.

Maya plopped down on the ground next to her escort and accepted a bowl of sweet protein slush that didn't taste anywhere near as bad as it looked. The efficiency and organization of the communal food distribution center impressed her. It functioned as a farmer's market where anyone could show up at any time and eat anything they wanted, free of charge. The Penphins were intrinsically motivated to care for one another, given the telepathy that linked them all. An accident in which two Penphins had collided in mid-air stuck out in her mind. Every Penphin in the area had flinched as if it had happened to each one.

A younger Penphin touched and sniffed her like the two on *Horizons* had during first contact. Ari shooed the child away.

When she had first arrived, the scouting party had endured a period of physical scrutiny that had made her initial groping seem downright indifferent. Maya had felt like a celebrity lab specimen, if such a concept existed. Now that she had spent a few days among them— the Penphins hadn't developed the concept of time until shortly before their space age —the novelty of humans had dwindled.

After breakfast, she followed Ari to the outskirts of the village where an honest-to-goodness airship awaited them. An oblong balloon hovered above an open-air gondola, affixed by a series of tethers. The Penphins had constructed the gondola out of sea wood and metal. Spinning blades, rotors, and fans provided additional lift and control.

The sight buoyed Maya's spirits. "Are we going to the island today?"

YES, Ari said. WE SHALL SHOW YOU OUR LAUNCH COMPLEX.

"That's where you sent your message to us, correct?"

YES.

"Straight out of a steampunk novel written by the residents of Atlantis," a familiar voice yelled from behind her.

Maya turned around to see Jo bounding toward her.

"How was your night?" Maya made air quotes as she spoke her last word.

"Other than a visit by a couple of unexpected roommates," Jo said, her voice muffled by her mask, "fantastic."

"I guess the local shared housing plan has its drawbacks."

Once Hamilton, Mendez, and Wallace joined them, Maya climbed aboard after Ari. A handful of cargo crates along the railing toward the rear of the deck served as seats.

Torches blew and rotors spun, inflating the balloon and lifting the airship with ease, given the dense atmosphere and low gravity. As the ship climbed, it flew toward the night side of the planet. The Penphins had situated their space center at the western intersection of the day and night hemispheres on the equator. *So it's going to get even colder.*

Ari and the other Penphins aboard basked in the frigid air, holding out their flings and soaking in the currents. Maya's thermojacket kept her torso nice and toasty, but the wind stung the skin on her face and hands. After instructing the jacket to produce a stocking cap and gloves, she strapped on the goggles that came standard with the coat. Jo, Mendez, and Wallace did the same.

Below, the grasses, shrubs, and bushes ranged in color from ochre to onyx, so very different from the greens of Earth's flora. Vrees spiraled and sprouted up near patches of saffron flowers on the banks of apricot rivers and lakes. A towering peak that would have dwarfed Mount Everest rose up from a mountain range in the distance.

The airship headed out over the ocean as the sky darkened. Few waves broke the calm of the water. Three small moons circled the planet, lacking the pull to cause tides.

Along the coast, she zoomed in on one of the more fascinating creatures she had seen in her time here. Planimals shaped like miniature hot air balloons glided out from a vree forest on the shore and hovered above a patch of seaweed. Some floated in the water like fishing bobbers. One dove down, submerged, and shot back up like a cannonball.

Wallace labeled them flying pufferfish.

Jo turned from the view and leaned back against the railing in thought.

"What?" Maya asked.

"Something doesn't feel right about this place."

"Just one thing? I don't imagine anything here feels quite right to a human."

"Of course this planet is a total freak show to us, but I'm not talking about aesthetics. This place is almost too perfect. Minus the dark and dreary color scheme, it's a magical fairytale land—and you know what they say about things that seem too good to be true."

Maya massaged her frozen cheeks. "I've had that same feeling."

"It's because evolution is different here," Wallace said.

"What do you mean?" Hamilton stood near the railing. The android wore a short-sleeve shirt and trousers, oblivious to the elements.

Must be nice.

"On Earth," Wallace said, "organisms compete against one another to survive. The better-adapted procreate and the maladjusted die off. Here, there's still a struggle against the environment, but natural selection favors those who help others to survive in an unprecedented form of symbiosis. Carnivores never appeared on this world. With only herbivores, there's far less competition and far more cooperation. I can't begin to speculate on how that arose, but either way, this alternate mechanism may be the greatest biological discovery since evolution."

Maya gave an absent nod as she considered the implications.

"So what does that say about us?" asked Mendez. "Does the lack of conflict make life on this world better?"

"There're multiple angles to that very human question," Wallace said. "The Penphins don't see things in terms of good or bad, so they'd never ask the question in the first place. Of course, it remains to be seen how they'll respond once they understand all sides to our nature."

Jo gave Maya's shoulder a soft punch. "They're lucky Maya Davis isn't Christopher Columbus." Sincerity underlaid her light-hearted jest.

Hamilton nodded. "It'd be too easy for us to exploit these people and their world. Never mind our superior technology. They might do anything we ask—or give us anything we want—because they don't comprehend lies or distrust."

"I don't want to think about what the wrong people could do to them." Mendez stood up from her crate and shook her body out.

"I think we need to give the Penphins a little more credit," Maya said. "Any exospecies that's achieved space travel isn't going to be a bunch of dummies. They're more insightful than you might think. Having said that, it's our job to make sure no one takes advantage of them."

"Is it, though?" Hamilton asked. "I share the sentiment, but I'm thinking about the ethical and practical implications. Is the human race responsible for ensuring the well-being of any less advanced species we encounter?"

"It's not our place to play god. But if we make contact and other humans tarnish that goodwill, then yes. It's absolutely up to the IEF to repair the damage. It's not right for us to make the introduction, walk away, and wash our hands of the situation."

"What if the Greys showed up in the system tomorrow and tried to conquer the planet? Is it our place to defend it?"

Maya flinched at his comment. As far as her team knew, the extrasolar attack still qualified as legitimate history.

Something about Hamilton's stare unnerved her. Whether it was his artificial irises, the fact that he never blinked, or something more, she couldn't say. "That's a complicated question for the ISC Council and IEF Command to answer." She swung her gaze around at the others. "But if I was in charge, you bet I'd protect them."

An hour later, Maya leaned over the railing, gawking at the Penphins's space center as it came into view.

"I wasn't expecting to be impressed," Jo said.

The biggest vrees she had seen yet supported the tall warehouses and factories. Penphins and cargo-carrying airships flew into and out of the structures. An oversized dish antenna shaped like a parallelogram pointed toward the sky. A pair of landing strips—no, not strips, but tracks—thick rails, actually—stretched for kilometers, each rising in height in opposite directions. The two railways, she realized, served as ramps toward the sky.

"You launch your spacecraft using rail guns," Maya said to Ari.

YES. THE DESIGN CONSERVES FUEL.

A covered shell ship rested at the start of railway number one. Rocket booster nozzles protruded from beneath the tarp covering it.

No spacecraft occupied railway two. Maya guessed—and Ari confirmed—the ship he had ridden to *New Horizons* had launched from there. She bit her lip when she remembered his spacecraft. The other two Penphin astronauts—penphinauts; Maya had beaten Jo to that one—had departed *Horizons* at the same time as her scouting party. It had taken the IEF transport shuttle minutes to travel from the hangar bay to the surface of the planet, but the Penphin ship wouldn't return home for another three weeks.

As the airship descended, crew members leapt off the side and flew toward the space center.

Maya and her team disembarked after the ship touched down. Ari led them on a tour of the manufacturing, assembly, testing, and launch control buildings. Penphinauts performed mock repairs and spacewalks in the vacuum chambers of the training facility. Despite their unfamiliarity with concepts like happiness, a jubilant atmosphere filled the place. The whistling of their song-language echoed through the air. The Penphins went about their tasks with dedication and efficiency. The drive to grow and learn permeated the walls, invigorating her.

The last stop on the tour brought her team to the sky watching and communications facility. As she set foot inside the observatory's equatorial room, a frail, wrinkled Penphin turned his snout toward her and away from the eyepiece of a large telescope. The old one rubbed the glass bubbles covering its eyes—the equivalent of glasses—and leaned back, staring.

"Got a name for him?" Maya whispered to Jo.

"The old astronomer and his telescope. Let's call him . . . Hub."

"Hub?"

"Short for Hubble."

At last, Hub sang, YOU RECEIVED OUR TRANSMISSION.

Maya approached and nodded. "We did."

WE DID NOT THINK WE WOULD PERSIST TO THIS BIG MOMENT.

"Well, I'm happy you did."

HAPPY?

I still can't kick the habit. "That means we also think this is a big moment."

The elder Penphin asked a plethora of questions ranging from where she came from to what technology she had used to get here to why her ship was less to why she looked the way she did. Several queries she couldn't understand. Maya did her best to answer without revealing too much. More intuitive than any Penphin she had met outside of Ari, Hub picked up on her reluctance and didn't press her for details.

WOULD YOU LIKE TO SEE? Hub asked, lifting a fling toward the telescope.

"Sure."

She stepped up to it, hunched over, and looked through the eyepiece. Penphin vision must have worked differently than human sight because she saw only a distorted blur.

Initiating the image enhancement program in her i-cite brought the view into focus. The size of a peanut, *Horizons* hung in space at the other end. She could discern the crushed forward section, the citysphere, the defense and engineering modules, and the ring with one remaining antimatter nacelle. The hull glowed, reflecting the vermillion starlight.

Hub led the party to the signal transmission and processing room. Situated in front of control stations, operators worked comm devices resembling telegraphs, flutes, and harps. The musical tones of spoken Penphin reverberated off the walls.

HERE WE COORDINATE COMMUNICATIONS WITHIN THE COMPLEX, MAINTAIN CONTACT WITH OUR SPACECRAFT, AND MONITOR THE SKY, Hub said.

"So this is where it all began," Jo said.

Maya swept her gaze around the room. "This place shows that despite our differences, we both possess an inborn curiosity about whether we're alone and a desire to reach out and . . ." She let her words trail off. The time she had spent on the planet and the conversation from on the airship brought about a realization.

"You're making that face again."

"What face?"

"Your epiphany face, the one where you look like you might scream, drool, or collapse."

Tapping her cheek, Maya said, "Hello. Help."

Jo placed her hands on her hips. "Their initial message." Her face lit up. "Oh."

"It's in their nature to help," Wallace said.

"They weren't asking for help," Maya said with all eyes on her. "They were offering—"

"Ma'am, I think you're going to want to see this," Mendez interrupted.

"What is it?"

A message sent by Mendez appeared in her i-cite. When Maya opened it, a cascade of satellite vidpics of the night side of the planet displayed. Three snow-covered mounds were circled in red on each image.

"Remote sensing has been mapping the surface while we've been here," Mendez said. "*Horizons* alerted me when they found them."

"They look like natural hills to me," Wallace said.

"That's what we thought at first, but look at the last few shots. They've been thermally and spectrally enhanced."

Maya paged until she came to a color-coded map. Hard-edged shapes—rectangles, squares, and so forth—in shades of orange and red resided beneath the blues of the hills. The sensor data accompanying the map indicated the presence of stone and metals.

Using her wristband, she displayed a holographic version of the mounds to Hub and Ari. "Have you seen these hills before?"

Hub and Ari stared at the flickering sim for a moment, mesmerized by the technology.

YES, Ari said. THEY ARE OLD STRUCTURES.

"Your structures?" she asked.

The two Penphins directed their snouts toward one another.

NO, Hub said. WE DIDN'T BUILD THEM.

Twenty—Foment
Gliese 581 System, December 2272 CE

Trevor Young grimaced as he marched inside Star City's main hydroponics farm. "Stop what you're doing right now."

The android workers continued to unload cartons of fruits and vegetables from the transport pallets, oblivious to his orders. *Or someone programmed them to ignore me.*

"Put those back," he yelled. "Every one of those crates goes to the defense and engineering galleys."

When the artificial beings failed to respond, he tried accessing their systems in his i-cite, but the farm AI denied him access. *I'm the damned captain. It shouldn't be able to refuse me.*

He cursed the crew's dependence on the civilian food production facility. Prior to the collision, the forward habitat section had included its own hydroponics farm as well as a state-of-the-art protein synthesis lab. But now, hundreds of hardworking officers found themselves at the mercy of their passengers for nourishment. The arrangement had grated on his nerves from the beginning, and now his fears had materialized.

Flexing his fingers, Trevor swung his gaze around the farm. Row after row of edible plants stretched for hundreds of meters, ascending the curved floor of the innermost level of the citysphere. Sprinklers misted lettuce, carrots, radishes, peppers, cucumbers, celery, and tomatoes in the nearest aisles. Cows grazed in a field while chickens pecked feed in a nearby pen. Overhead, thousands of tiny suns shined through the blue sky, providing life-giving energy.

Out of the corner of his eye, he caught a woman ducking behind the environmental control station within the apple tree orchard.

He jogged over to the station, shouting after her, but the woman pretended to ignore him. She bobbed her head to a song and inspected tree after tree in haste, moving away from him.

As he caught up to her, he grabbed her arm from behind.

The woman spun around and dipped her brow. "Hey, what gives?"

"I know what you're doing." Trevor stabbed a finger at the pallet track leading to the aft section of the ship. "I want those crates reloaded and sent where they belong."

She shrugged out of his grasp. "I'm an agronomist. Distribution isn't my area of expertise."

"How convenient." He folded his arms and glared at her. "I know you have the required access. As the acting captain of this vessel, I order you to reload those cartons at once."

"I'm not one of your soldiers. You can't tell me what to do."

"Then who told you to withhold vital supplies from the men and women who're working to keep you alive?"

Pursing her lips, the farmer buried both gloves in the pockets of her soiled overalls.

"You people refused to cooperate with the crewmen I sent, which forced me to come down here. I'd hoped a malfunction or misunderstanding was holding things up." Trevor blew out a breath. "But you've confirmed this is blatant insubordination. No one in this city has the authority to alter the food distribution quotas without my approval."

The woman's face reddened. "Maybe if those quotas didn't leave us with table scraps—" She cut herself off.

"So this is intentional. Is it your doing—the doing of the agriculture division?"

Turning her attention to the nearest tree, the agronomist rubbed a Granny Smith apple with her thumb, shrugging.

"No," Trevor said, "you couldn't pull this off on your own. You'd need higher-level approval. I bet this came from the top—from Byrne."

The slight flutter of the woman's eyelashes told him he had hit a bullseye. "I'll have a chat with Madam Mayor and get this issue resolved." As he tromped away, he called back over his shoulder, "You and I haven't seen the last of each other."

◆

"I'm sorry, sir," said the android secretary outside the mayor's office.

"Mayor Byrne is unavailable at the moment. Would you like to make an appointment?"

"This can't wait," Trevor spat as he rounded the secretary's desk.

The android stood up and blocked the door. "Sir, please—"

With gentle force, Trevor pushed the artificial woman out of his way and down into her seat. Most basic android models possessed limited reflexes and strength, contrary to popular belief. The robotics necessary to emulate faster and more refined motion or drive greater power than a human didn't come cheap. While Alastair Hamilton might be able to lift a Pulsar, the mayor's secretary could barely pick up her chair. She could do little to impede a fit military man who towered a head over her.

He gave the secretary's chair a shove, sending it and her rolling across the room. Then he interfaced with the door to the mayor's office, overrode the lock, and opened it. *At least something still responds to my access codes.*

Byrne sat behind her desk, her stare locked on the sim above it. With a finger, she directed falling shapes to connect together and cancel out before they struck the desktop and piled up to the ceiling. Her other hand delivered a forkful of salad into her mouth.

Playing games and eating my food? Trevor drew upon all his discipline to keep from turning purple.

"Come in, Ensign Young," she said without looking up. "I'll be with you in a moment."

The acting captain stood rooted in place, jaw and shoulders drooping at her disrespect.

Taking her time, Byrne finished the last bite of her salad and switched off the game. "New high score," the woman said with a condescending smile. "So what can I do for you?"

"You know why I'm here." Trevor marched over to her desk. "Why are you short-changing the crew's food supply?

The mayor reclined in her chair and clasped her hands in her lap. "You're the one who's short-changing us. If you'd adjust your quotas so they didn't result in thousands of starving civilians, you'd arrive at the amount we're sending you."

"Things are tight, but your residents aren't going hungry. Yet you've reduced our allotment by almost a third. One-third. The crew wasn't getting three meals a day before, but now they're down to fewer than two. How do you justify that?"

"A couple weeks ago, when citizens started complaining about not getting their rations, we did an independent analysis. Do you know what we found? It turns out you increased the crew allotment without running it by me. How do you justify that?"

Trevor held back a grumble. "I needed to take immediate action or else the next duty shift would've gone to work on empty stomachs. I probably should've informed you beforehand."

"But you didn't. You thought we wouldn't notice since there are so many more civilians than crewmen. Well, guess what. We did notice, just like we've also noticed a reduction in other supplies and materials. The restoration effort has come to a grinding halt." Byrne threw a hand up in the air. "We're having to ration more than food right now. When something breaks, there's no telling when or if we'll ever see a replacement."

"The factory still isn't running at peak capacity. Fabricators are still broken. As soon as we get one up, another goes down. But the city has its own fabricators."

"Not on the scale of the factory. Right now, we're expending resources like auto-syringes and power cells faster than we can replace them."

"We're working to get things to you as fast as possible. Try to understand that we're all in the same situation when it comes to limited resources."

"Are we, though?" Byrne summoned a display cube, which showed a schematic cross-section of *New Horizons*. Different shades of orange highlighted each subsection of the ship. The bolder the color, the greater number of resources the location was receiving.

The schematic revealed the defense module as by far the boldest section.

"This information is restricted to select personnel," Trevor barked. "Only members of the crew have access. How'd you get ahold of it?"

Byrne folded her arms. "I have my sources."

"Who shared this with you? This is a court-martial offense."

"What I want to know is why, when people are being forced to go without food and medicine, are we stockpiling seekers, fixing particle cannons, and repairing star fighters?"

"Why have past empires allocated resources to military assets during peacetime? Why does Defense even exist given that mankind eliminated war with the formation of the ISC? We need to remain vigilant in case an attack comes."

"An attack?" Byrne flicked her wrist, dismissing his assertion. "I'm no scientist, but it's my understanding space is vast. The odds of another intelligent exospecies pinpointing our location and showing up here at the same time as us are infinitesimal. I've got a better chance of spontaneously growing younger."

Tensing his fingers, Trevor said, "I'll concede the unlikelihood of an attack, but it's my job to make sure the ship's prepared for anything. All the food and medicine in the galaxy will be useless if the Greys show up and we're not battle ready."

"All the guns and missiles will be useless if everyone starves to death."

Trevor entered into a glowering contest with Byrne.

The mayor averted her eyes first. "None of this was an issue while Ensign Davis was heading up the restoration effort."

His chest burned. He knew he never should've let Maya go.

"I don't know how that girl did it," Byrne said, "but she managed to balance things out and keep everyone happy."

"She did her duty." The comment came out sounding unappreciative—Byrne's raised brow told Trevor as much—but he hadn't meant it that way. He commended soldiers who did their duty. To him, there were few higher compliments.

"'Did her duty'? The ship started falling apart the moment she left. Rumor has it you only let her go to get her out of your way."

"What happens between officers aboard this ship is confidential," he said. "As for the scouting party, Ensign Davis made a valid point about needing to survey the planet for potential resources and habitability. I weighed the pros and cons and decided it was worth her going."

"How gracious of you." Byrne sighed. "What I wouldn't give to see what she's seen. The latest report says she's on her way to investigate ancient ruins the indigenous inhabitants might not have constructed."

Shaking his head, Trevor said, "And while she's touring a bunch of crumbled buildings, I'll be busy trying to keep things from falling apart here."

◆

There were too many possibilities to consider, too many permutations—too many ways trillions of rogue algorithms could cause malfunctions and compromise the systems aboard the ship, if not destroy it.

Bob could scarcely keep up.

He spent a full nanosecond—an eternity for an AI—realigning the antimatter containment field for the one remaining fuel pod before it exploded. He sealed micro-fractures in the hull caused by programmed nanites. He prevented seekers from remote-detonating, androids from attacking humans, and the gravity systems from spinning the ship out of control.

What human expression best applied? The ship was a ticking time-bomb.

The most frustrating thing about it all—he had learned the concept of frustration after uploading to *Horizons*—was that he knew his rival AI had no intention of causing any true damage. The pattern and timing of events indicated a 99.9 percent likelihood Bob could fix any issue before it became serious.

Rather, the rogue program created the problems as diversions meant to occupy his processing capacity. As long as Bob remained vigilant, the AI wouldn't succeed in breaking the encryption he had placed on the device. Despite his continued lack of information regarding the device's nature, he knew the Vril hadn't worked it into *Horizons's* original designs for—as an organic being might say—a noble purpose.

The turmoil that the rogue AI had instigated amongst the humans might prove even more troublesome. Bob had discovered too late that his nemesis had affected subtle alterations to the ship's food and resource allocation. Fixing the distribution algorithms would do little good now that the residents of the city and crew had started applying manual changes and squabbling over them. Bob knew of no way to reprogram attitudes or perceptions. He calculated a 72.4 percent chance the AI's provocation of negative human interaction would lead to an outcome he didn't care to process—and he did care, as vulnerable as the feeling left him.

In the picoseconds he had to spare, he hoped reason would convince Maya to listen to him. He enjoyed his interactions with her. She challenged his matrix with subjective queries he couldn't so easily resolve.

Another strange sensation afflicted him: nostalgia. He found himself devoting an increasing amount of available CPU capability to accessing records from years ago. He realized, in vernacular, that he longed for the good old days of supporting the much simpler functioning of a star fighter craft engaged in orbital maneuvers.

Most of all, he missed the one who had helped him achieve his awakening. It might increase his efficiency to interface with her again.

Twenty-one—Extricate
Psykhe, May 2272 CE

"One thousand eight hundred fifty-three, one thousand eight hundred fifty-four, one thousand eight hundred fifty-five . . ." Brooke had lain on the same floor of the same empty room in the same underground base for the last three months. Days ago, she had started counting the grooves in the ceiling. The sobs and self-reproach overwhelmed her unless she occupied her mind.

According to the chronometer in her i-cite, fewer than six months remained until *Horizons* downshifted. She could no longer beat the ship to its destination to prevent the collision—not that she had the means to get out there, anyway.

The fact that Eve hadn't visited her since the day she had arrived frayed her nerves beyond what she could bear. What if the android had gotten what she needed, exposed Shin's group, sent the destroyer after *Horizons*, and left her prisoner to rot without telling her? If so, Brooke congratulated her captor on the irony. As much as Brooke lived for solitude, being left alone in ignorance, powerless to do anything, qualified as the worst brand of torture.

If only she hadn't listened to Shin, she wouldn't have lost years of her life. She had known his plan to infiltrate this place stood little chance of success, so why had she gone along with it? The next time she saw him, she feared she might strangle him to death.

For three months, the highlights of Brooke's day had included meal times and the occasional trip to the lavatory. Sometimes, she went so crazy she asked the AI to use the head just to break up the monotony. Psykhe's one hundred thirty percent gravity brought on fatigue rather quickly during her restroom expeditions. To acclimate, she had started doing pushups, sit-ups, and other exercises to build her strength—and to keep busy. It wasn't like she had anything else to do except count the repeating patterns in the room.

"One thousand eight hundred fifty-six, one thousand eight hundred fifty-seven—" Brooke ceased her mumbling and sat up when she heard the echo of approaching footsteps.

Stepping up to the force field boundary, Eve reached into a bag of chocolates and popped one in her mouth. "It took a little longer than I'd hoped, but I got everything I needed from your scans. I know when *Horizons* will reach the Gliese 581 system and all about Mr. Saito's plan to expose us. Oh, and I had the biochip with the list extracted from beneath your toenail while you slept."

Waves of panic undulated through Brooke's limbs. *Shin's people were supposed to skew the results of my scans. What happened?*

Eve paced along the perimeter of the force field. "Of course, I've known about his group since he formed it. We live in an age where privacy is extinct. Are you aware we have our own police force? We track our members, including our surveillance teams, without their knowledge. No one has ever defected."

"Spying on the spies," Brooke said. "Why am I not shocked?"

"I've allowed Shin to indulge in his mutinous fantasy for my own purposes. I know he faked his death. Requisitioning a stealth cruiser to capture the kid so you could get in here to steal the list was a vintage Vril ploy. In a way, it made me proud."

Forcing her eyes to water in mock reverence, she tossed another chocolate into her mouth. "But it was ultimately self-defeating. I let him execute his plan, sat back, and waited for him to deliver you and the brat into my lap." She flashed her not-quite-human smile. "We seized Mr. Saito and his ship the moment they docked at the shipyard on Eros. Thanks to your scans, we identified and rounded up the treasonous swine who were supposed to help you escape from here."

Brooke's intestines knotted, but she refused to show her concern. She leaned back on her palms and narrowed her gaze at her jailer.

"As for you," Eve said, swallowing, "I've scheduled your cognitive reprogramming for tomorrow. I'm looking forward to working with the new you."

♦

The next day, Lanky and Buzz Cut led Brooke into a lab on the lowermost level of the base for her procedure. The medical facility was cold, white, sterile, and finished, unlike the rest of the base. Operating tables, full-body scanning machines, microscopes, test tubes, beakers, incubators, and cubes showing vital signs and organs filled the room.

A pair of scientists stood near a still-sedated Zeke on the far side of the lab. One drew blood from Zeke's arm. The other marveled at a dozen display cubes showing different brain scans.

She enhanced the gain on her auditory implants.

"We couldn't make sense of this in another hundred years," one of them said.

Brooke averted her gaze. Guilt weighed her down far more than the high gravity. *Sorry I failed you, Zeke, Maya.*

She gasped, forgetting all about her predicament, when she caught sight of the exobeing thrashing around on one of the tables.

Two orderlies held down a living, breathing Grey as it fought against them. The creature made none of the animalistic screeching she had heard in too many sims. Rather, it uttered an electronic clicking sound closer to a data signal than speech.

The shimmering of a contoured body force field shrouded the Grey. As it lost its ability to struggle, a trio of spherical devices floated over and scanned it.

A calm woman of apparent Indian descent supervised the scans. With the forcefulness of an authority figure, she dismissed the orderlies with the wave of her hand.

As they exited the room, the woman stared at Brooke for a moment before resuming her examination.

"What the hell?" Brooke asked her escorts. "You found one of them—alive?" Too many questions jumbled together in her head.

"They still look in on humans from time to time," Buzz said, "but not as much as they once did. They're no more advanced than us now. Their stealth technology no longer fools us, and their ships are slower and less maneuverable than a Pulsar. We set traps, snag 'em, and give 'em a taste of their own experiments. Eventually, we'll figure out—"

"Enough." Lanky raised his gun to help make his point. "She's still the enemy."

"Only for another hour or two. She's not going to remember anything I've said, and we're going to tell the new her everything, anyway. I don't see the issue."

"The Vril don't take chances, no matter how small." Lanky shoved Brooke forward. "Keep moving."

Brooke shuffled toward an operating table being prepped by a pair of doctors in one corner of the lab. At the sight of the many straps and needles on the head restraint apparatus, she cringed.

Trembling, she fought the tears welling up in the corners of her eyes.

A couple meters from the table, Lanky stopped and stood in place. Brooke and Buzz Cut halted and turned around.

"Something wrong?" Buzz asked.

Lanky stared at an antique silver wristwatch and sucked in a breath. "Three . . . two . . . one . . . mark." He lifted his gun and shot Buzz between the eyes.

As the woman's body thudded against the floor, warning klaxons sounded and red emergency lights flashed.

"Attention: code seventy-seven. This is not a drill. Code seventy-seven is in effect." The base AI repeated the message again and again.

Lanky grabbed Brooke's arm and led her toward Zeke.

"What—I don't understand," Brooke stammered.

"Did they start the procedure on you without me noticing?" With a wave of his gun, he ensured the retreating doctors and scientists all fled the room. "This was the plan."

"Eve said she rooted all Shin's people out. She knows the plan."

Lanky snorted. "Our group is the internal police force. We allow her to think she's one step ahead of us so we can stay two steps ahead of her."

"But they scanned me and learned everything."

"You don't think we would've sent you here without thinking of that, do you? Your thoughts told her what we wanted her to know, the names of suckers loyal to her—agents we wanted to eliminate. The only thing she got was the date *Horizons* will arrive, but that couldn't be helped." He came to Zeke's bed and turned to her. "If Shin succeeds in stopping the destroyer, that won't matter."

A sense of renewed vigor quickened Brooke's pulse. "And code seventy-seven?"

Reaching into a drawer in the medical station next to Zeke, Lanky produced an auto-syringe. "Same protocol used to destroy the Mars base."

"So the Vril are burying this place to cover their tracks. But that must mean—"

"Shin leaked Psykhe's location to ISC Defense. The downshifting of their fleet set off the alarms, and they'll reach the planet in a matter of minutes. This place isn't going to be around for them to find, so we need to move." He slapped the syringe into Brooke's palm, transmitted a filesim to her, and headed for the door. "I'll keep watch while you wake up the kid. The button to disable his restraint field is on the control panel at the foot of the bed." Covering the entrance to the lab, he gripped his gun with both hands. "I hope reviving him doesn't backfire," he yelled back. "I know what his kind can do to people."

"He's a good kid." Brooke disabled Zeke's force field and injected him in the arm.

Zeke opened his eyes and looked up at her without any sign of grogginess. Although he never smiled, the tension in his face seemed to relax upon seeing her.

Particle blasts pinged out in the corridor.

"Firefight in the hall," Lanky shouted. "Two allies ambushed four loyalists headed for the lab but weren't able to take them out."

The sound of weapons' fire raged one moment and ceased the next.

Lanky greeted a man and a woman as they rushed into the room. "Philip, Haven, what happened out there?"

"The four of them just collapsed," Haven said, brandishing a rifle with a serrated bayonet.

Zeke sat up and hopped off the bed.

Brooke led him over to the others by the hand, and the party exited the lab.

They reached the matrix farm at the opposite end of the basement level without incident. Zeke knocked out the only agent who stumbled into their path. Most of the base personnel had vacated the lowermost section, Lanky surmised.

Lanky, Haven, and Philip stormed into the data center. While Lanky held the three agents inside at gunpoint, the other two confiscated their weapons.

Brooke stepped inside the frigid room and marveled at the rows of multi-storied AI towers.

She slapped her forehead and cursed. "I don't have the biochip with the list. They took it."

Bending down, Zeke removed his left shoe and sock. He pulled a tiny black dot out from beneath his toenail and held it out to her at the end of his finger.

Brooke wrinkled her nose. "Of course. The real one." She told Zeke to give the dot to Lanky, who set it atop an interface terminal and tried to access it.

The display cubes at the station lit up red. <Access denied,> the base AI said. <Security codes and DNA confirmation from three separate system administrators is required.>

Pointing a heavy handgun at the three hostages, Philip demanded, "Submit to the scans and give us clearance."

The woman in charge folded her arms. "I doubt we're getting out of here alive. If that list gets out, we're dead anyway."

Lanky jabbed his gun into her lower back and pushed her toward the terminal. "Do the scan and enter your code."

"Go to hell."

The rock ceiling and walls rumbled. Dirt rained down on Brooke's head and shoulders.

"The nanites are starting to tear the place apart," Haven said. "We don't have time to coerce all three of them."

Brooke turned to Zeke and gripped his shoulders. "Can you force them?"

He stared at the floor. "Putting people to sleep is one thing, but bending wills isn't right. Xi said there's nothing worse you can do to someone."

"Normally, I'd agree. But we need the list to expose the Vril and stop all the unethical slinking in the shadows." She felt like a hypocrite when she stared into the boy's golden irises. Once upon a time, she had argued for doing the right thing regardless of the consequences. Now, she was asking a child to manipulate three people in order to stop the coercion of forty billion. She was using the same ends-justify-the-means reasoning as the Vril.

Nevertheless, she recalled what she had told Shin when they had first met. In order to take down the Vril, one had to out-con the con artists. She couldn't stick to idealistic principles to win this fight.

Before she could tell Zeke as much, he nodded, reading her thoughts. "I understand."

All three agents walked over to the interface terminal, submitted to scans, and entered their codes. They demonstrated none of the zombie-like motions of drones. Nor did they flush, sweat, or struggle. No veins bulged on their foreheads. They put up none of the fight of free-thinking beings resisting mind control.

Brooke was getting what she wanted without any drama or delay. So why did their anti-climactic compliance send chills rippling through her body?

She shook off the feeling as data filled display cubes throughout the matrix center.

An incoming connection request displayed in her i-cite.

After Lanky verified the request at the terminal, she accepted it. Lines of information scrolled down her mental displays, filling her implanted memory capacity near its limit.

Stopping the stream on a random line, she found not only names and links to ISC citizen profiles but hard evidence, including vidsims of member initiation and daily activities.

"This is it," she murmured. "Everything we need."

Her surroundings shook, forcing her into a wider stance to keep her balance.

As they traversed the corridors and ascended, Lanky took the point. Brooke followed and pulled Zeke along. The three marionette agents trailed while Haven and Philip kept their weapons trained on them from the rear. Despite the protests of Lanky's comrades, Zeke had refused to leave the agents behind to die.

Twice, a cave-in impeded the party's progress, but they managed to find ways around both obstructions. Brooke kept worrying that the Vril would seal them in, but the organization had constructed their passageways with a honeycomb structure for the quickest possible evacuation. The base's interconnected tunnels, lifts, and ladders provided far more routes of egress than anyone could block.

Stepping off the elevator on the uppermost level, Brooke saw light shining through the entrance to the hangar at the far end of the corridor. Her group hadn't encountered another soul on their trek toward the surface. In front of them, Vril agents bolted back and forth between side passages and the hangar, preparing for a hasty departure.

A pair of agents spotted her party and reached for their weapons. Brooke and Lanky blasted them before they could take aim.

The firefight caught the attention of other Vril loyalists, who armed themselves and dove for cover. Brooke pushed her group back into the elevator as the first shots rang out.

She expected to get pinned down—for her entire effort to have been for naught—when the shooting stopped. Multiple thuds reached her ears. When she peered out the door of the elevator, she found the unconscious bodies of over a dozen people sprawled out on the floor.

Zeke walked past her out into the corridor.

"Nice work," she said.

He directed his hawk eyes at her and frowned.

Once Brooke had agreed to let Zeke wake everyone up as soon as the party launched, he put the three agents from the data center to sleep, and the group forged onward.

The weight of Psykhe's higher gravity seemed to lift as Brooke traversed the corridor. *We're almost out.*

Halfway to the exit, Eve stepped into the hallway from the hangar, blocking their escape. She folded her arms. "I'm afraid this is as far as you go."

"Knock her out," Brooke told Zeke as they skidded to a halt.

The boy stood and stared at Eve, who remained upright and conscious.

"He can't." Eve crept closer, like a tiger stalking her prey.

"What's the matter?" Brooke pleaded with him. "She may be an android now, but she was once human."

"Fortunately, what I once was is irrelevant. You see, his people's biotech is so advanced they can control human beings like we can program and direct a bot. It's not mind control. It's total control. They know what makes us—what makes life—tick below the sub-quantum level." She raised her chin. "And why shouldn't they when they created our DNA?"

Brooke struggled to process what she had heard—not that any of it mattered at the moment. Out of parental instinct, she pulled Zeke back behind her.

"This," Eve snarled, indicating her body with a sweep of her arm, "is the only way to stand against them. I'm technology they can't manipulate." She shook her head. "Not that going artificial is any guarantee of salvation. The sum of their scientific knowledge makes us look like we're still in the Stone Age. As I said before, fighting the Vril is counter-productive to the human race's survival."

Despite her best efforts to dismiss the woman's words, Brooke's curiosity sucked her into the discussion. "With all the ability the Vril have developed to manipulate things, why didn't you reveal the truth long ago and goad people into working toward combatting them?"

"That approach would've been far more difficult, unfortunately. People can be selfish, weak-willed, and thick-headed. They do the opposite of what's best for them. Action and consequence, not words of wisdom, are what they understand. That's why the demonstration in the Gliese 581 system is necessary."

"You mean—"

"A shocking preview of what we're up against—as much as the most advanced human tech can manage, at least."

"But the genocide of an entire exospecies?"

"I'll kill off however many civilizations it takes to quell the petty bickering and put us on a path toward rising to the dominant power in the galaxy."

"Dominant power?"

"Give it up, Brooke. You're as good as dead if you try to get past me. But if you join me, I'll spare Maya. Let's work together to prevent our species' extinction."

Brooke gave Eve's words serious thought. She had faced this decision before, and it proved no easier now. Despite their methods, the Vril's goal of saving the human race was difficult to argue against. Morals and ethics were self-indulgent luxuries when faced with the survival of one's people.

But she had learned from experience. "I told you why I'll never join you. Trust. There's no way I can trust anything you say when you've built your foundation on lies and deception. If that's how humans are going to rise to the top, we don't deserve it."

Brooke turned to Lanky, who jumped out in front of her and opened fire. Philip and Haven joined him in blasting Eve.

Their beams pinged off the shimmering green haze that shrouded the android's body.

Swallowing hard, Brooke backpedaled and pulled Zeke along with her.

A maniacal gleam flashed in Eve's eyes, like that of a predator salivating for the kill. She charged forward, swung, and decapitated Philip before he could react.

The man's head struck the floor with a thud muffled by the blood oozing from it.

Haven's eyes widened, and her face paled. Before she could counter, Eve punched a hole through her chest.

Lanky bombarded the artificial woman. As he retreated down a side corridor, he flashed Brooke a determined look and thrust his chin toward the hangar.

The soles of Eve's boots tracked crimson footprints as she dashed after him.

He's drawing her attention, buying us time. Brooke grabbed Zeke's wrist and sprinted toward the hangar.

To her horror, Zeke twisted out of her grasp and ran back toward the lift.

"Zeke!" Brooke cried and started after him.

A guttural scream rang out from the hallway Lanky had fled down.

Eve reemerged into the main corridor. Blood slicked her face and dripped from her fingers.

Gripped by fear and disgust, Brooke retched. Her body trembled at the sight of the maniacal executioner.

With slow, deliberate motion, Eve swung her gaze between Zeke at one end of the passageway and Brooke at the other. "Splitting up. Smart, but it'll only buy you seconds." She took a step toward the lift. "I'm willing to bet you won't leave the brat behind."

Brooke stood rooted in place, torn between her instinct to protect Zeke, self-preservation, and the bigger picture. Her heart bashed against her ribcage, thumping so rapidly that it felt as if it might explode at any moment.

Eve backpedaled toward the door through which Zeke had

disappeared. "Decision time," she said, keeping her focus on Brooke.

Pangs of guilt pierced Brooke's abdomen, but she knew what she had to do.

When Eve reached the door, Brooke whirled and sprinted toward the hangar bay.

"I didn't think you had it in you," Eve yelled after her. "Sacrificing a child for the greater good of your mission? We're not so different after all." She shouted louder as Brooke neared the hangar. "But you're in for disappointment. Every ship's control system requires command code access, so you're not going anywhere. After I dispose of the kid, I'll be along to kill you."

Twenty-two—Termagant
Psykhe, May 2272 CE

Panting, Zeke scuttled around a corner, tripping over a large bundling of power cables. Charlie horses and shin splints sent shooting pain through his legs, courtesy of his teenage body's hyper-growth and his long stay in a laboratory bed. A superhero would never complain, so he gritted his teeth and forged ahead, intent on drawing the primitive mechanical woman—why did she strike him as primitive?—away from the one who had saved his life.

The floor and walls of the subterranean base shifted and rumbled. Fear nipped at him from the back of his mind, but he was able to analyze and regulate it. He chose to accept the biochemicals enhancing alertness and strength but dismissed the other paralyzing emotions. Recently, he had begun to understand why he could control himself and others and see beyond space-time. He perceived a metaphysical information substructure underpinning everything—one capable of imparting anything he wanted to know. He couldn't comprehend most of it yet, but he had gleaned one thing. His people had gained awareness of his existence.

He calculated the seconds until Eve caught up to him while weighing the options for incapacitating her. Although he could do nothing to overpower her raw strength, he figured he stood a reasonable chance of outsmarting her. He couldn't read her thoughts, but like all humans, she possessed an exploitable reasoning capacity derived from a predictable set of emotional impulses.

Looking through the walls, he caught sight of a galley, cataloged the available items there, and formulated a plan.

Zeke dashed inside the kitchen and grabbed the half-full pot out of the coffee maker. After pulling a silver knife out of a drawer, he borrowed a rubber glove from underneath the sink.

An android waitress stood like a statue on standby, staring off into space with her arms dangling at her sides. When he approached her, she came alive and asked if he needed anything.

"Take this," he said, handing her the coffee pot, "and follow me."

As she followed him out the exit at the opposite end of the kitchen, he heard Eve entering the room behind him.

"There you are," she called out.

Zeke told the waitress to stand in the middle of the corridor outside the galley and wait for the approaching person who wanted coffee. "She'll act like she doesn't want it, but she does." After slipping the glove on one hand, he jammed the knife into the wad of power cables just behind the waitress. Sparks flew for a few seconds and then ceased.

Emerging from the galley, Eve raised her fine eyebrows at the waitress standing between her and the boy.

"I believe you requested coffee, ma'am?" the waitress asked, holding out the pot.

"Out of my way." Eve tried to step around her but she blocked her path, pushing the pot towards her.

Snarling, Eve shoved the waitress aside. Zeke observed in slow motion as Eve's forearm shattered the coffee pot and drilled the waitress in the upper torso. The much weaker android's chest caved in. Its stunned expression contorted, although not nearly as much as a human's face would have under the same force. With her arms and legs wafting behind her, the waitress left her feet and began her flight toward the wall.

Her heel struck the protruding knife. At the same time, the coffee doused her, Eve, the knife, and the mass of cables, completing an electrical circuit.

The current jumped between both androids. Crackling electricity consumed them. Terrawatts of power streamed through the cables and into their bodies. Smoke billowed from the waitress, who went limp and thudded to the floor.

With her body gyrating, Eve dropped to her knees, screaming. She toppled over, curled up in a fetal position, and shut down.

As Zeke had seen human teenagers do in moments of triumph, he pumped a fist.

His placement and timing had manipulated the sequence of events into unfolding as he had simulated in his mind. Of all the potential outcomes—of all the possible universes that could have arisen—he had instigated a very unlikely but very fortunate one.

As he stepped around her, Eve blinked and shook her head.

He jumped back.

Pushing off from the ground, Eve rose to her feet. "Clever." She inspected her charred and peeling artificial skin with a frown.

Eve lunged forward, grabbing for him.

Zeke predicted her movements and stepped out of the way. He managed to avoid two further attempts to seize him before she got a fistful of his shirt.

His stomach sank as she lifted him off his feet and threw him against the wall. The impact knocked the wind out of him and shrouded his vision and mind in a thick haze.

After sliding down the wall, he blinked up at his executioner.

"I should never have left you alive in the base." Eve picked him up by the throat and let his feet dangle above the floor. "That's the last time I let compassion dictate my actions."

"How you treat me," Zeke squeaked through his constricted windpipe, "will affect how my people treat humans when they return."

"If the Vril succeed—and we will—your people won't ever develop the ability to threaten us."

"Without us, you cease to exist."

"Not if we beat you to it."

Eve squeezed, and he choked for air.

"Die," she hissed. "Die for my mother and all the people your kind have killed."

"It's you who's dead," he wheezed.

Her eyes widened and jaw dropped as she went flying down the corridor away from him, helpless arms flailing.

Zeke landed hard on his butt and massaged his bruised Adam's apple. Gulping in air, he gazed up at the knight in shining black armor, who had tossed the android clear across the passageway.

It was as he had foreseen.

◆

Clad in her flight armor, Brooke set her particle rifle to rapid fire maximum yield and sighted the android.

Already upright, Eve charged straight at her.

Brooke pulled the trigger, unloading hundreds of pulses per second. The blasts struck Eve's shielding, tinting it orange and red and driving the android backwards.

Eve jumped out of the line of fire before Brooke could overload her force field.

The android skirted the wall and lashed out, knocking the rifle out of Brooke's hands and drilling a punch into her face shield. Its clear nanoplastic rang with the blow but didn't shatter.

As Brooke stumbled to the floor in a daze, Eve kicked her in the stomach.

The reinforced nanotube fibers of Brooke's armor stopped the artificial woman's boots short of penetrating. Brooke sucked in the muscles in her abdomen and exhaled all the air in her lungs, trying to keep from vomiting.

Using the full power of the armor's enhanced musculoskeletal system, Brooke grabbed Eve by one ankle and thrashed her against the wall. The android's head bashed against rocks protruding from an unfinished section of paneling with the force of a jackhammer. Her force field flashed and fizzled out.

Eve's twitching face and body slid down the wall.

Hopping to her feet, Brooke drilled the android's cranium into the rocks a couple more times. Eve fell onto her back, convulsing. The exposed contours of her composite skull showed through patches of missing skin. Fluid the color of burnt umber poured from her mouth as she gurgled. Her eyes shifted back and forth like a possessed doll.

Brooke retrieved her particle rifle and held the muzzle to Eve's neck.

Incomprehensible speech emanated from the android despite her jaw remaining still.

Scowling, Brooke opened fire and severed the android's head from her body.

After catching her breath, Brooke rushed over to Zeke. "Are you okay?"

He gave a weak nod.

She scooped him up and carried him along the quickest route to the uppermost level.

"I heard you," she said. "Somehow, I could feel where you were."

"I know," he rasped.

In the hangar bay, Brooke ordered the maintenance androids who had helped her don the flight armor to suit Zeke up and strap him into the rear seat of a Pulsar. Lanky had included the access codes for the androids and one of the fighters in the filesim he had sent her.

She plopped down into the cockpit. While gravgel rose to immerse her and Zeke, she thought of how many years had passed since she had sat in a pilot's seat. *Not since the telescope array—and that was only a fleeting jaunt.* Her skin tingled as she established a neurotronic interface with the craft's support AI and brought the flight systems to life.

The hangar quaked. Meters away, a boulder dislodged from the ceiling and crushed a Pulsar.

Brooke overrode the safety protocols and forced the inner and outer bay doors to open at once. Yellow-brown atmosphere rushed into the hangar like smoke billowing out of an upside-down chimney. The high pressure currents knocked the androids off their feet.

Firing thrusters, she launched the Pulsar up through the tunnel and rocketed up from the volcanic surface.

Explosions erupted all around and behind her fighter, stressing its force field. Icons warning of a reactor overload flashed in her i-cite. Sweat dripped from her forehead.

The engines shut off, and the Pulsar dropped out of the dark sky like a lead weight, tail-end first.

Zeke's shrieks came out in rasps over the internal comm net.

With her stomach climbing up into her throat, Brooke reached her mind out to the fighter's support AI. *What's happening?*

<Our thrust is reacting with the atmosphere, sir,> the AI responded. *<The atmospheric combustion suppression subsystem must be engaged to negate this effect.>*

Brooke felt her cheeks ripping away from her jaw as she watched a lava pool rise toward her in her rear camera views. *Well, engage it, then!*

<ACS subsystem activated, sir.>

A diagram showing a cross-section of the fighter's reaction control system popped up in her augmented reality. Additional force fields kicked in to protect every nozzle and rerouted engine exhaust clear of sensitive areas. Turbines pumped inert gases and fire suppression nanites into the rocket chamber and forced the mixture out with the exhaust. The blend reduced engine efficiency but extinguished the flames engulfing the Pulsar.

The reactor temperature gauge plummeted, and the engines roared.

Brooke burned the thrusters, pointed the fighter's nose toward the sky, and fired the afterburners. The force of upward acceleration and the high gravity of the planet combined to squeeze her like a trash compactor.

Zeke's grunts ceased. The AI informed her he had lost consciousness.

At fifty meters above the bubbling lava, thrust and gravity cancelled each other out. Brief weightlessness buoyed Brooke's body as she eyed the pool of red-hot death below.

The Pulsar climbed away from Psykhe, leaving a superheated plume in its wake.

She asked the AI for a damage assessment. The fighter seemed to have come through more or less unscathed.

While rising through the dense clouds, Brooke had a few choice words for the AI. *Why didn't that subsystem kick in automatically?*

<The ACS is a nonstandard upgrade requiring command code access and manual activation, sir. I needed verbal authorization to initiate it.>

Another brilliant Vril safeguard . . .

<I'm unfamiliar with the term "Vril," sir.>

Of course you are.

The Pulsar cleared the clouds and stratosphere. Brooke relaxed a little at the calming sight of twinkling stars. Was it her imagination, or did they shine brighter out here than in the solar system?

She tried to contact Shin over the prearranged channel without success. The lack of response didn't surprise her. Eve had claimed she had apprehended him when *The Dragon Lady* docked at the lunar construction facility in orbit. Still, Brooke questioned the validity of the late android's claims. Lanky had said the splinters had stayed two steps ahead of the rest of the Vril, and Shin must have accounted for the possibility of getting caught. For all Brooke knew, Eve had flat-out lied to her, hoping to break her.

The only option she could see was to set course for the moon, Eros, and hope.

After executing a plane change to the equator, she settled the Pulsar into an orbit near the planetary ring system. She had exited the atmosphere on the opposite side of the moon's present location in its orbit, so the Pulsar needed a few minutes to catch up to it.

<Incoming—>

Brooke whipped the fighter clear of a tumbling rock fragment the size of a stratoscraper. Before she could determine its point of origin, she had to dodge out of the way of three other mammoth chunks.

A barrage of micrometeorites and fine dust particles bombarded the Pulsar's shielding.

She scanned the moon only to discover it was no longer there.

When she reached visual range, she magnified the last known location of Eros. The hulking masses of boulders drifted away from where the moon's core had once existed.

Holding her breath, Brooke hoped Shin or ISC Defense had managed to destroy the ship the Vril had constructed to go after *Horizons*.

Further scans dashed any such hope.

She gasped at the broken hulls of a dozen ISC cruisers. Debris from hundreds of Pulsars littered local space.

A million kilometers from the planet, she found the Vril destroyer on course for interstellar space.

<We're being scanned, sir.>

Seconds later, fifty tri-fighters launched from the destroyer toward her position.

Brooke clutched the auxiliary control grips, donned her best scowl, and prepared for battle. *I can take out fifty of them*, she lied to herself. *Hell, I wrote the manual on modern orbital combat.* Despite the truth in the notion, she knew they had her overmatched.

She was in the process of hanging her head when an unsolicited sim stored in the Pulsar's memory filled her i-cite.

"If you're watching this, Brooke," said a translucent upper-body shot of Shin, "I failed to stop the destroyer—but don't worry. I haven't stranded you out here."

He removed his cap and held it in both hands. "Between rigging *The Dragon Lady* to self-destruct and goading ISC Defense into attacking the destroyer, I had hoped we could take it out, but the assault must've failed. That ship's formidable. *Horizons* doesn't have the firepower to take it on." He drew his lips to a thin line. "So now it's up to you."

A schematic of her Pulsar's power systems replaced his image. Three extra antimatter tanks blinked. "We equipped your craft with quadruple the fuel supply and packed enough food and water to sustain two people. Fortunately for you, we get our Pulsars from ISC Defense, so your fighter is faster than any Vril cruiser. You may end up a little stiff and bored along the way, but you can make it back. Once you're home, have your husband release the list so the censors don't block it."

His body shot returned. "The destroyer is the Vril's fastest ship, but it'll still take nine months to reach Gliese 581. That puts it there in late December of next year. You can beat it to *Horizons* if you can get *Nautilus* to launch sooner rather than later."

Nautilus? But construction on it was halted months ago.

"We're counting on you, Brooke. Good luck." Shin signed off.

The sim purged itself from memory.

"Wait, that's it?" Scrunching her nose, she gaped at the approaching fighter wing.

Gathering her resolve, she fired the Pulsar's afterburners and rocketed away from the planet.

The tri-fighters gave up pursuit and returned to their mother ship.

Brooke reached the edge of the suppression field preventing hyperspace travel about the same time as the destroyer reached the opposite end. After watching the ship upshift toward Gliese 581, she sucked in a breath and began her journey back to the solar system.

Twenty-three—Ziggurat
Fourth Planet, Gliese 581 System, December 2272 CE

The snowshoes Maya had fabricated crunched the soft sheet of white beneath her feet as she approached the mammoth hill—or the small mountain, depending on how one looked at it.

Stopping to rest, she sucked in oxygen from inside her helmet and waited for her team to catch up. The walk from the airship hadn't seemed very far when she started out, but tromping through the snow had taxed her muscles, even in the low gravity. Her EVA suit's environmental systems hadn't stopped her glands from drenching her undergarments in sweat. The fact that she was roasting struck her as somewhat ironic given the colder-than-Antarctic temperatures here on the dark side of the planet. Howling winds pelted her with snow.

Still, the view stole her breath as much as the trek across the tundra. Pure white knolls and valleys reflected the light from the stars twinkling overhead. She had little need of her night vision. Massive ice buttes jutted up from the landscape in the distance. Despite the dreariness, she welcomed the change in color scheme, after spending weeks immersed in dim red-orange light.

Up in the sky, an object shone brighter than the stars as it moved toward the largest of the planet's three moons. With *Horizons's* rockets repaired, Trevor had elected to relocate the ship closer to the planet. He had claimed in his last comm that drifting about in open space left the ship too exposed from a tactical standpoint. Plus, the crew could make use of the available lunar resources.

Jo tapped her on the shoulder from behind. "Ready to uncover some history?" she said over the comm.

"Always," Maya said.

"Too bad we don't have more time."

Interfacing with the satellites in orbit, Maya pulled up an animated weather map in her i-cite. The map showed a massive storm front approaching from the north. During the airship ride here, Ari had explained that continent-spanning blizzards often raged across the night side of the planet and could last for days, weeks, or months. The huge white smudge on its way to engulf the area looked like a mean one. "Whatever we do or find, we need to be out of here in eight hours."

Once Hamilton, Mendez, Wallace, Ari, and a group of Penphin scientists joined Maya and Jo, the party traipsed over to the side of the largest hill. A smaller mound protruded from the hill, creating a corner recess that provided welcome shelter from the wind.

Ari's speech-song reached Maya's ears through her helmet's receptors. THIS IS WHERE WE DISCOVERED THE UNDERLYING STRUCTURE. Much more inured to the cold than the humans, the thinker wore a furry, hooded jumpsuit and seemed invigorated by the frigid air.

Penphin excavators had chiseled away ice from the side of the mound, revealing part of a wall constructed from massive stone blocks. Broken scaffolding surrounded the wall and littered the ground in front of it.

Ensign Charlies Wallace folded his arms. "Now what does this remind us of from Earth's past?"

"Let's not jump to conclusions." Jo turned to Ari. "Have you found a way in?"

NO. IT TOOK BIG EFFORT TO EXPOSE THIS SMALL SECTION. THE WEATHER MAKES EXCAVATING THE STRUCTURE IMPRACTICAL. IF AN ENTRANCE EXISTS, WE HAVE NO WAY TO LOCATE IT.

"Luckily, we do." Ensign Camila Mendez's tone indicated she was eager to put her archaeological expertise to the test.

Hamilton pulled a high-resolution neutrino mapping array off his back and plopped the heavy apparatus down in the snow.

Kneeling in front of the scanner, Mendez established an interface. The top cover peeled away, and the emitter projected a sim of the mound.

The projection primarily benefitted the Penphins. Maya viewed the sim in her i-cite.

"Okay," Mendez said. "I've mapped the area, and the AI is extrapolating a full subsurface immersive by merging the ground scans with the sat data from orbit."

The mound in the sim faded away, replaced by a recreation of a crumbling stepped tower.

"It looks like a ziggurat," Jo murmured.

Mendez nodded. "From ancient Mesopotamia."

"But not quite the same."

"Right. The structure is taller and narrower. Also, there aren't any staircases."

"Makes sense. Lower gravity means you can build higher, and what do you need stairs for if you can fly?"

"Good points."

Shorter towers revealed themselves beneath the other, more diminutive mounds.

The most startling manifestations within the sim weren't what the snowy hills had covered but rather that which lay farther down. Ice, snow, and time had buried an entire city eighty meters beneath the ground. Maya noticed how the mounds hid the tops of the tallest buildings, which jutted up from an extensive network of underground ruins.

"Oh, wow." Mendez shivered, more from giddiness than the cold. "This is the biggest find since the mid-twenty-second century."

"When Spencer found those subterranean tunnels beneath ancient structures in Iraq, Egypt, Mexico, and Peru," Jo said, her teeth chattering.

Mendez turned to the group. "I've got good news and bad." She rotated the sim of the tower by ninety degrees and enlarged the apparent front side, which had collapsed. "The bad news is the main entrance, which is the only way in as far as I can tell, is blocked off by meters of rubble. There's no getting to it without blasting half the place to kingdom come. The good news, however . . ." The sim spun by another ninety degrees to the opposite side of the tower. With her fingers, Mendez zoomed the projection in on a thinner section of the exterior. ". . . is that I think we can use our wave guns to melt through the ice to this wall and disassemble it without bringing down the place." She looked at Ari. "Assuming you don't have any objections to us performing an act of desecration."

Ari cocked his snout. WHAT IS DESECRATION?

"Camila is saying that if we create a door," Maya said, "we won't be preserving the structure in its original state. Some humans believe it's important not to alter a piece of history."

After consulting with the other Penphins, Ari whistled, GIVEN THAT WE CANNOT GAIN ENTRY WITHOUT SOME ALTERATION, CREATING A SMALL ENTRANCE SEEMS WORTH THE POTENTIAL GAIN OF ACCESSING THE INTERIOR.

"Man, I love these people," Mendez murmured.

Jo snorted. "Back home, a committee would've squabbled over that decision for months."

"Okay," Maya said, "let's pack up and go around to the other side."

Having reached the designated spot on the opposite side of the tower, Maya stood aiming her wave gun at the snow-covered mound. She enabled the laser sight above the muzzle and moved the red dot per Mendez's instructions.

"Another few centimeters to the left—stop," Mendez said. "Up half a meter and . . . hold it right there. Perfect."

Maya ordered everyone to stand clear and fired. The air between the gun and the mound wavered from scalding heat. Snowflakes that strayed into the energy wave evaporated on contact. A section of the ice sheet on the side of the mound slumped inward and melted away at a rapid pace.

Minutes later, her gun started to overheat, so she let Wallace take a turn. Jo went next, and by the time Mendez had finished, they had reached the wall.

YOU GOT THROUGH IN A FRACTION OF THE TIME IT TOOK US, Ari said.

Maya inclined her head. "Centuries ago, it would've taken us as long as you."

Jo directed a handheld scanning device at the wall. "The edges of each stone are incredibly flat and straight. We're talking millimeter engineering tolerances."

"Just like the blocks and statues of ancient Egypt," Wallace said.

"Each big brick has a mass of thousands of kilograms," Hamilton said. "Even in this low gravity, I don't see how they could've moved and lifted them. I might—might—be able to budge one of them with a running start."

Mendez wagged her finger. "Don't underestimate ancient peoples."

After disintegrating the mortar between a number of stones in the wall, Maya tuned her gun to sonic levitation mode and fired at the topmost loosened block. The stone rattled and dragged toward her with a scraping sound heard above the blowing wind.

Awestruck, the Penphins flapped their flings as her gun pulled the multiple-metric-ton block free of the wall and guided it to the ground.

Jo, Wallace, and Mendez each removed a block, which created an opening of human height obstructed by a deeper wall of stones.

"There's one more wall in the way," Mendez said. "We're halfway there."

Following the removal of four inner stones, Maya stepped through the improvised entrance.

The hair on her neck and limbs stood on end in the pitch blackness. Shivers of fear jumped her heart rate.

Drawing in a prolonged breath, she set her gun to flashlight mode, brightening her way.

The map in her i-cite showed she was in a corridor running along the inside of the exterior wall. She shined her light around, getting her bearings. The builders of the tower had constructed the blocks of the outer wall from off-white limestone, but they had fashioned the interior from mahogany sandstone. She swore she had walked into the largest red brick house ever constructed.

As she stepped further inside, her suit's environmental interface registered the internal temperature as negative ten degrees Centigrade, downright tropical compared to outside. After checking the air quality, she removed her helmet, latched it onto her belt, and fastened her breather over her mouth. She still needed the mask to filter out the high levels of carbon dioxide.

The other scout team members did the same, and the Penphins lowered their hoods.

Jo rushed ahead of Maya and illuminated a series of etchings on the inside wall. Each drawing resembled the kind of squiggly electromagnetic wave one might find on the display of a graphic equalizer. Symbols resembling musical notes were interspersed throughout the waves.

Shuffling over beside her, Ari said, THIS LOOKS LIKE OLD SONG. He whistled the tune.

"Song," Jo repeated. "To you, song is synonymous with language." She laughed and exchanged looks with Maya. "Well, I'll be damned. It's sheet music in cuneiform."

"It's more than that," Mendez said. "This shows the ancient Penphins had advanced knowledge of the full electromagnetic spectrum—and probably a lot more."

"Yet they haven't moved beyond AM radio?" Wallace asked.

"I'd wager they never thought to generate artificial signals until recently," Jo said. "The Penphins are all linked through telempathy. They didn't need to communicate specific bits of information across great distances until their space age." She looked at Ari. "Am I right?"

I ONLY UNDERSTAND PART OF YOUR SONG, Ari said. BUT I THINK YOU ARE CORRECT.

Hamilton stroked his symmetrical chin. "Necessity is the mother of invention."

As the party continued down the corridor and around a bend, Maya posed a question. "There's one thing that's not adding up for me. How was this city constructed on the freezing night side of the planet? The ice and snow and winds would've made it impossible to find the materials for construction much less erect these structures. It'd be difficult with our technology. Why build it here when there's a warm environment on the other side of the planet?"

IT WASN'T ALWAYS THAT WAY, Ari said as he waddled alongside her.

"What do you mean?"

THE DARKNESS AND LIGHT ARE CYCLICAL OVER LONG PERIODS.

Wallace uttered an "Ah-ha" and said, "So the planet isn't tidally locked with its sun."

TIDALLY LOCKED?

"We thought your world didn't spin, and the same hemisphere always faced your sun," Maya said, "but your home must turn at a very slow rate."

Mendez chimed in after a moment. "The sat data confirms the tidal locking isn't perfectly synchronized to the planetary year. The cycle repeats every 400,000 Earth years."

Hamilton whistled. "That would mean this society thrived in sunlight 200,000 years ago, give or take a few millennia."

"That's about as old as the oldest remnants of civilization on Earth," Jo said.

"Ah, crap," Mendez said. "My sat uplink is on the fritz."

Maya stopped the group and checked the satellite data feeds. Sometimes the signals got through to her, and sometimes they didn't. "Same for me." Next she tried contacting *Horizons* without success. Warning icons and error text popped up in her i-cite.

"I can't comm any of you," Jo said.

The other members of the scout party encountered similar issues.

IS THE STRUCTURE BLOCKING YOUR SONG? Ari asked.

"No," Maya said. "Our signals are neutrino-based. Physical objects don't impede them."

NEUTRINOS. WE ARE NOT FAMILIAR WITH THIS TERM.

During her time amongst the Penphins, she had grown adept at ducking such questions. "Someday, you will be." She looked at Jo and Mendez, who had their scanners out. "Anything?"

Jo swung her device all around. "I'm seeing warping of the planet's gravitational field as well as accelerated radioactive decay of a few bizarre isotopes."

"Like the phenomena detected in many of Earth's ancient ruins," Wallace added.

Mendez dipped her brow. "Phenomena not necessarily generated by artificial means."

"At any rate," Jo said. "There's just enough interference to scatter comm neutrinos."

"Makes sense." Maya tapped her cheek. "Our implants send out the lowest energy signals, so we can't contact each other. The sats can sometimes get through because they've got more power. I'd bet the ship can comm us, but we won't be able to respond while we're in here. Is something still generating the interference?"

"I doubt it," Jo said. "Based on the decay rates, I'd say whatever produced these effects happened during the era of this civilization." She holstered her scanner.

"So this society had technology closer to our level."

"Either that, or somebody else visited this place long before us."

The Penphin scientists crooned to one another.

"Do we press on or go back?" Hamilton asked.

"My curiosity is certainly piqued," Mendez said.

Maya weighed the options. "Unless we run into something more threatening, I say we forge ahead. But stay on alert." She checked the time. "We've got five hours left. Let's make them count."

Further down the corridor, the group came across the ancient Penphins's equivalent of a descending staircase. Through a square hole in the floor, a single ledge jutted out from the wall four meters down, halfway to the next level below.

"Only one step," Maya murmured.

Ari descended first. He held out his flings and glided down to the next level, skipping the ledge altogether.

Clearly, this place was made for them. Crouching and getting a grip, Maya lowered her body through the hole and dropped down. She stumbled when her boots contacted the ledge but regained her balance before falling. Repeating the process, she descended from the ledge to floor.

The Penphin scientists followed Ari's lead. Then the human members of her team lowered themselves without incident. Hamilton stepped over the side, plummeted the full eight meters, and landed in a crouch that would have broken organic bones.

Maya's shoulders slumped at the next staircase hole. Given that they had entered near the top of the tower, she foresaw quite a bit of descending in her immediate future, not to mention the daunting prospect of climbing back out again.

"At this rate, we'll have to turn around and head back before we get anywhere," she said.

"Too bad we don't have any thruster packs," Jo said.

Maya placed her hands on her hips. One palm brushed against the wave gun in her holster, and she thought back to when she had saved the mayor's son. "I've got an idea." She pulled out the gun and set it for sonic levitation. Stepping to the edge of the hole, she aimed down at the next ledge below.

"Have you lost your mind?" Wallace asked. "Lifting inanimate objects is one thing. If you don't time things just right . . ."

"Don't worry. I've done this before." She hoped her voice conveyed more confidence than she felt.

Blowing out a breath, she stepped down and fired. Unseen force reduced the rate of her fall. All went according to plan except the aim of her jump had been off. Her right boot landed on the edge of the ledge, but the left missed it. Maya tripped and fell the rest of the way down, face first.

She directed her gun toward the rising floor and fired again. A blast of air slowed her plummet.

Maya's nose grazed the stone floor as she hovered above it. Twisting to the side, she took her finger off the trigger and closed the remaining small distance.

Jo, Mendez, and Wallace learned from her experience and executed more successful attempts. The best—albeit more unnerving—approach involved bypassing the ledge and dropping the full eight meters between levels.

By the time Maya had descended another three stories, she had mastered the float-drop, as Jo had dubbed it.

When she reached a level with a wide corridor and cuneiform covering every square centimeter of the walls, she decided to explore.

The passageway led out onto a setback terrace overlooking a vast open space within the tower.

"This is an archeological dream come true," Mendez shouted. She charged out onto the overhang, taking in the sight. "This puts the largest early structures on Earth to shame."

Maya joined her at the edge of the terrace and looked down, being careful not to stand too close to the rail-less edge. She had to increase magnification and brightness to see through the darkness to the floor fifty meters below. Bits of broken stones had fallen from above. Entrances to various passageways led to other areas of the tower.

As she lifted her gaze, she noticed thousands of small ledges sticking out from the walls. "This room must have been an assembly hall, and the terrace was the stage."

One of the Penphins flew out over the chasm and landed atop one of the ledges.

"Oh, my . . ." Jo gasped.

Maya whirled around and gawked at the statues sitting atop the terrace. Two five-meter-tall stone Penphins rested on a platform against the wall. Steps led up to the platform.

The statues appeared taller, leaner, and more human-like than their modern counterparts. A pair of taller sculpted figures stood between them, each with the head of a bird and the body of a human.

Minutes of silence passed, permeated only by the occasional echo of the structure settling, until Wallace spoke up. "If no one else wants to say it, I will. This is clear evidence of a link between our pasts with extrasolar influence."

WE AGREE, Ari said. YOUR THEORY APPEARS LIKELY.

Jo pulled on her pigtails. "The figures in the center look like Sumerian sages."

Hamilton nodded. Mendez remained tight-lipped.

As Maya studied the statues, she found her thoughts turning to the filesim from Ajunwa. According to claims by her mother and Collins—if Maya was inclined to believe them—the Vril had duped the human race into uniting to prepare it for a larger threat. Did these advanced bird people represent that peril? Was this somehow part of yet another hoax? Or was this something else altogether?

"Hey, what's that?" Mendez rushed over to a pedestal altar positioned in front if the birdmen statues.

As Maya stepped up to the altar, she found a rectangular black box not much bigger than her thumb resting atop it.

"What do you suppose it is?" Jo asked.

WE DO NOT KNOW, Ari said.

"It almost looks like—"

Mendez cut off Wallace and finished his thought. "A technological device." She reached out for it.

Maya swatted the overeager archaeologist's hand away. "Paws off. This is a fragile piece of history—and one that doesn't belong to us."

"I know, I know. I get ahead of myself sometimes." Rounding the altar, Mendez cocked her head every which way at the supposed device. "Amazing. Ryder, get some scans of—"

A priority comm request from *Horizons* appeared in Maya's i-cite but disappeared before she could accept it. Her implants indicated too few data packets had reached her. Maya tried to reestablish the connection but couldn't get through.

"I just got a signal but lost it," Jo said. Mendez and Wallace indicated the same.

Perhaps the growing pit in Maya's stomach was due to the distance underground, the eerie glowers of the bird people's hawk eyes, or the darkness, but she chose to listen to her gut. "We're heading back."

Mendez gawked at her, looking ready to throw a temper tantrum. "But we've got at least another hour to spare."

"We've been out of contact long enough. I need to know what they're trying to tell us."

"I'm sure they're just checking in."

"I'm not due to report in until tonight, and Captain Young is a stickler for protocol."

"But we've barely begun exploring." Mendez pointed at the statues. "The next discovery may explain them." Swinging her finger toward the altar, she added, "Or that."

"I share your curiosity, Camila, but we've got bad weather coming and an unscheduled comm to return. Don't worry. If the Penphins allow it, we can come back after the storm passes." Maya started back the way they had come. "Now let's go. For all we know, the crew's found us a way home."

"What about the device? We can't leave without—"

"It's been buried for thousands of years. It'll be here when you return."

Cursing under her breath, Mendez fell in line behind her with everyone else.

The ascent proved easier than Maya had envisioned. Each team member took turns lifting the others up with their wave guns through the stair holes. The last person someone raised from above. At one point, Maya tried boosting herself up with her gun but soon abandoned the approach. Determining the right angle and amount of force to rise through hole and land without falling back down proved too tricky.

In a corridor halfway back to the outside, Wallace matched Maya's brisk pace alongside of her. "Mendez isn't with us anymore." He jabbed his thumb behind the group.

Maya skidded to a halt and whirled around. Everyone stopped and stared at her—except for Mendez.

"Camila!" Maya's calls echoed throughout the corridor. "Ensign Mendez, get back here right now. That's an order!"

After half a minute, she came to a decision she might regret. "Jo, you're in charge. Lead everyone out and to the airship. I'm going back for Camila."

"What?" Jo shook her head. "No way. We'll all go."

Maya was mulling the prospect when Wallace said, "Part of the comm from *Horizons* got through to me. They say the storm has picked up speed, and we need to get out now."

"Forget it," Maya said to Jo. "I'm not going to risk anyone else's life."

"Why risk your life for hers?" Jo folded her arms. "She's the idiot who decided to disobey orders."

"We don't know that."

"Oh, come on."

"Besides, you know I could never leave anyone behind."

WE COULD LOOK FOR HER, Ari said. WE CAN GO UP AND DOWN FASTER THAN YOU.

Maya considered the offer. "Thanks, but I won't be responsible for anything happening to you."

Jo stomped her boot. "Well, this is dumb—"

"Go!" Maya yelled. She waved her arm in the direction of the exit. "That's an order."

Pouting in protest, Jo led Wallace and the Penphins away.

Hamilton remained.

"I meant for you to go with them," Maya said.

The artificial man flashed his artificial smile. "Fortunately, I don't take orders from you."

Maya hadn't time to argue. She rushed deeper into the tower with the android at her side.

At the first staircase hole, Hamilton said, "To save time, I could jump down with you in my arms."

"No, that won't work," she said. "The force of impact will transfer through you to me when you land. It'd be no different than if I landed by myself."

"Of course. I hadn't considered that."

Maya wasted no more time and jumped. She used her gun to cushion her fall and did the same at subsequent descent holes. When she misjudged her timing, she dropped and rolled before popping up and continuing on without breaking stride. She suffered a few cuts and bumps but nothing major.

"I assume we're heading back to the terrace?" Hamilton asked as they sprinted.

"It's the most logical place for her to go—unless you have any better ideas."

He shook his head.

Minutes later, Maya bolted back out onto the terrace with the statues. She swung her gaze all around until it landed on Mendez's helmet. It sat near the edge of the drop-off next to her EVA suit's oxygen pack.

"Oh, no." Maya rushed over to the headgear and pack. "She didn't fall, did she?" She peered over the side but didn't see anyone below.

The sound of weapons fire echoed throughout the assembly hall.

Maya spun around.

Mendez had emerged from behind one of the statues and was marching toward Hamilton, bombarding him with her wave gun on the particle beam setting. Each rapid shot burned deeper and deeper into the android's chest.

Without breaking stride, Mendez tore Hamilton apart with her blasts. An arm, a leg, and his head exploded away from his body and crashed back down to the terrace.

What remained of Hamilton toppled over and thudded against the stone floor, twitching.

Mendez directed her gun at Maya and drew closer.

Adrenaline surged through Maya's veins. Trembling, she took a step backwards and felt her foot slip over the edge.

Twenty-four—Dissemination
Huygens City, Titan, July 2272 CE

Eight-year-old Elias scampered through the central terrace of Huygens City, chasing his remote-control Pulsar. When he shifted his eyes left, the toy fighter darted in the same direction. When he looked up, the plane rose toward the dome and Saturn overhead. With a jerk of his head, the craft did a barrel roll.

He puckered his lips and blew spitting noises. Blue lights on the front of the Pulsar lit up as it fired its mock particle cannons.

Camera views, battery life, roll, pitch, yaw, and other feedback from his prized possession displayed in his i-cite. The brand new implants embedded in his brain had made neurotronic control of his toy possible. His mom hadn't wanted him to undergo the procedure, but his dad had convinced her. All the kids at school were getting implants, and Elias hadn't wanted to be the only one without them. Dad had understood.

Elias messaged his friend back home on Mars in his i-cite. On his social media feeds, he followed the responses to the vidsim he had posted of his plane doing loop de loops.

"The death-defying ace pilot swoops in for the kill." With gusto, he announced this to no one in particular before directing the plane into a nose dive. "Will our hero live to—?"

With his attention consumed, Elias rammed his nose into the chest of an older boy.

Elias jumped back, more startled than hurt. Error messages indicated he had lost his interface to the fighter. When he craned his neck to see around the bigger kid, he gasped.

After passing through a big news cube, the plane crossed over the railing cordoning off the memorial to the ten thousand murdered colonists and struck the clear case protecting the old space probe.

The teen glowered at him. "Watch where you're going," he said and stomped off.

Elias rushed to the railing. Tears welled in his eyes as the toy drifted down and scraped to a halt along the concrete.

He hung his head as the Pulsar's running lights dimmed.

A gentle hand came to rest on his shoulder.

When he turned, he found his dad standing at his side. Discretely, Dad checked to make sure no one was looking their way.

The pedestrians in the terrace that had noticed the toy crash had since lost interest.

"Cover me," Dad whispered. He hopped over the railing and stayed low between the big plaques listing the names of the deceased colonists. Sneaking around the statues of the surviving children, Dad scooped the plane off the ground and initiated a stealthy return.

Back on the terrace, his dad whacked the fighter a couple times. Elias stopped slouching when the toy's lights blinked to life.

Dad handed the plane to him and rustled his hair. "Its repair systems should fix it up good as new."

"Thanks, Dad."

Elias followed him back to the patio of the restaurant where his mom and big sister sat at a table, relaxing after dinner.

"There's our little runaway." Mom adjusted her stylish sun hat. "Come finish your food. You barely ate anything."

As Elias plopped down, he frowned at the rubbery broccoli, mushy potatoes, and dried up chicken breast on his plate. "I'm not hungry."

"All he wants to do is play with his dumb toy," his sister told his mom before returning to the girl-talk in her i-cite. "She said what? That is so not fused."

"This is a family vacation, Alyssa," Dad said as he settled into his chair. "Tell Starla you'll comm her when we get back to Mars."

"Five minutes." Alyssa hopped up and strolled out onto the terrace.

Mom shook her head at Dad. Sighing, she returned her attention to one of the mammoth display cubes hovering over the terrace.

"Would you care for anything else?" an android waiter interrupted.

"No, we're ready to pay," Dad said.

"Very well. May I interface with your credit profile and withdraw the funds?"

"Yes, I consent."

"Thank you, sir. Your bill has been paid. Have a splendid evening." The waiter left to attend to another table.

Elias's dad leaned toward him. "So what do you want to do tomorrow, son? Hang-gliding through the thick atmosphere? Scuba diving in chilly Lake Cassini? Or how about we rent a buggy and drive across the dunes toward the ice mountains?"

"Those all sound like fun," Elias said.

Dad grinned. "I hear it's supposed to rain tomorrow."

"No way. Bubble rain."

Mom touched Dad's arm. "Are you sure we can afford all this, dear? I mean, the fancy hotel, the excursions, these dinners . . ."

Cupping his hand over hers, Dad said, "I think an ISC councilman should be able to spoil his family every now and then. Don't worry about it."

Elias's face soured as his parents gave each other a peck on the lips. But on the inside, he felt warm and contented.

"Hey, you seeing this?" A classmate pinged him in an i-cite feed.

Four more friends posted similar comments before he had a chance to access his classmate's vidsim reference.

When he played the sim, he saw his dad staring back at him, speaking.

He heard the speech via his implants, and for some reason, all around him.

Looking up, he found his dad's image on every cube floating above the terrace.

"I pledge my unconditional loyalty and life to the cause," Dad's sim said. "I agree to use my position of influence to direct the course of human society toward salvation, no matter the means or cost."

By this time, Mom and Dad had turned to watch the cubes. His dad's face paled. Sweat beaded on his forehead.

The footage switched to showing him sitting behind the desk in his office, engaged in a comm. "I understand. I'll make sure the bill gets voted down. Reinhardt might be a problem. I don't think we'll gain his support without neural restructuring."

"What's this all about?" Mom asked.

Dad didn't respond. His stare remained glued to the cubes.

Elias turned his head and saw four policemen bounding toward the restaurant.

His dad shot to his feet. Mom gripped his wrist, holding him down so he didn't bump his head on the patio awning in Titan's low gravity.

"Councilman Thompson?" the officer in charge asked as he approached the table. "You're under arrest for suspicion of conspiring to manipulate the intrasolar political system. Please come with us."

Dad's expression flushed. "This is absurd." He jabbed his finger toward one of the cubes. "Evidence can be fabricated. These sims prove nothing."

"Clearly, this is some sort of misunderstanding," Mom insisted, now on her feet.

The chief officer showed little emotion. "Please come with us, or we'll have no choice but to apply reasonable force." He puffed out his chest and clasped his hands in front of the belt holstering his stun gun.

"I've been a loyal public servant for fifteen years," Dad hissed. "You've got the wrong man."

"You can state your case at the tribunal." The chief glanced at his men. Two of them approached Elias's dad and grabbed his upper arms.

Dad shrugged them off. "This is ridiculous."

An officer shoved and bent him over the table. Pinning his cheek against his dirty plate, the officer twisted his arm behind his back. Dad grunted.

Trembling, Elias jumped up and dropped his plane.

"Daddy!" Alyssa came lunging over across the terrace.

Another officer bound Dad's wrists with magnetic restraints and pulled him upright.

"Call my lawyer, dear," Dad yelled to Mom. "She'll get this sorted."

Elias watched with his arms drooped at his side as the police escorted the man he loved out of his life.

As they disappeared behind a building, Elias saw another policeman tackling a fleeing woman—a woman whose face now displayed on every cube in the terrace.

◆

"It's the type of mass witch hunt not seen in centuries and a no-win situation for the ISC," Holly reported with stern professionalism. After taking a swig from a coffee mug on her desk, she addressed the dozens of floatcams transmitting the show to billions of viewers. "Good afternoon, and welcome to today's edition of *Point/Counterpoint*. I'm Holly Harper." She faced left. "With me as always is my co-host, the ever-agreeable Dan Gibson."

In her i-cite, she followed the main feed as it panned over to Dan. He sat at the opposite end of the same desk, sporting a stand-up collar suit with no tie that was all the rage this season. The flecks of gray in his hair gave him an aura of journalistic integrity that he had lacked earlier in his career, and every slut in every cocktail lounge from Tallahassee to Triton had taken notice. The bastard kept getting more attractive without trying.

Meanwhile, her appearance had faded in spite of regular rejuvenation treatments. Perhaps she should go full prosthetic, she mused, although a low-level celebrity such as herself could hardly afford it. Life could be so unfair sometimes.

At least on-air she could find satisfaction in sticking it to her co-host like he stuck it to floozies less than half his age.

With a slow shake of his head, Dan projected his trademark high-and-mighty disgust. "Holly, what the hell is Ajunwa doing?"

"The ISC is rounding up the alleged conspirators who staged the extrasolar invasion a quarter century ago, Dan. She's doing what the people have wanted since the truth came out."

"Wait, let me get this straight." Dan held his hands up in a stopping motion. "Tens of thousands of citizens want armed authorities barging into their lives and brutalizing them in front of their friends, families, and coworkers?"

"Brutalizing? I think that's a bit harsh. Reasonable force is being used to restrain suspects when they resist arrest."

"This is a clear violation of civil liberties, and it needs to stop."

"So what would you suggest the ISC do? Issue a polite statement asking these criminals to turn themselves in? Ajunwa has taken tough, decisive action based on the evidence."

"All of a sudden, the proof she needs to pacify her detractors appears out of nowhere, broadcast via every media platform at once? That's far too convenient for me. Where did all this so-called evidence come from, Holly?"

"The source remains a mystery but the evidence itself is what's important." Holly counted on a different finger each time she stated an incriminating item. "Vidsim confessions. Positional data tracking the precise movements and locations of the accused. Surveillance footage showing agents engaged in acts of duplicity. Audit trail logs cataloging the manipulation of information—of human history. Medical records documenting brainwashing procedures—"

"All of which can be manipulated or manufactured."

Holly sighed at her co-host's obtuseness. "If we had only a single piece of evidence damning a single individual, I'd entertain that possibility, but tens of different types of records are implicating a hundred thousand people holding key positions in the public and private sectors. When taken together, what we've seen presents a cohesive and conclusive case that would be near-impossible to forge."

"Irrelevant. All of it."

"Irrelevant? How?"

"It doesn't matter what the ISC broadcasts as long it's enough to justify rounding up everyone who doesn't agree with the status quo." Dan glowered at the cams. "Congratulations, Ajunwa. You've come up with a deliciously vile way to stay in office."

"Oh, Dan. Sometimes I think the only reason I'm still doing this show after twenty-plus years is for your entertaining conspiracy theories."

"I'm glad you're entertained. But do you know what's not amusing? The accused are being tried without due process. These tribunals provide a convenient way for the ISC to circumvent the legal system. Ajunwa is sweeping these purported war criminals, as they've been classified, under the rug quickly and quietly."

"What's the alternative? Put a hundred thousand people through the full process with appeals and all? The trials would last for decades."

"All I know is that Ajunwa needs to back off before her selfish actions lead to war."

The main feed centered on Holly, and a map of the solar system appeared next to her head. "That's the issue. The ISC is in a precarious position. They can't allow the accused to walk the streets unpunished, but they can't arrest, try, and sentence them without causing political friction, either." The map highlighted select countries and colonies throughout the solar system. "Yesterday, the Chinese Solar Republic, African Union, and East Martian Coalition passed laws to try and convict suspects within their territories and began rounding them up. When Ajunwa sent ISC Defense to collect alleged criminals from Marius on Ganymede, local authorities refused the transfer, and a standoff ensued. One officer was shot but suffered no critical injuries, fortunately, before Ajunwa recalled her forces."

Dan sat back in his chair and crossed his arms. "With most major-nations states having pulled out, the ISC is a dying club of has-been Ajunwa loyalists. No one recognizes the ISC's authority anymore. The only reason we continue to humor our lame duck chancellor is because she commands a formidable arsenal. But we won't be bullied. If war is what she wants—"

The cubes in the studio fuzzed. A warning scrolled across the bottom of the main feed.

TECHNICAL DIFFICULTIES. PLEASE STAND BY.

When the cubes returned to functioning, a new vidsim had usurped every display. The individual that the sim implicated left Holly paralyzed and Dan with the widest, most self-satisfied grin in the history of grins.

◆

Howling in defiance, Xiaoqing whipped a stone at a riot control officer. The rock ricocheted off the officer's bioshield without him noticing, much to her chagrin.

Other protestors hurled objects and obscenities at the soldiers holding them back. Like the waters of a parted sea, the mob threatened to rush into the path the authorities had cleared for the chancellor's egress from ISC Headquarters in New York.

Xi had Zeke to thank for restoring her personality. As she had raised him over the years, he had somehow exhumed the memories and convictions the Vril had suppressed. His running off again with her brother—the traitor responsible for the theft of her identity—had ripped a hole in her heart, so this event gave her the chance to release her frustration.

Most everyone, including Xi, had turned out to cheer on the stepping down of the treasonous shrew. Other demonstrators supported Ajunwa and clamored for greater scrutiny of the lies against her. The two sides' opposing viewpoints had thrown the courtyard into heated pandemonium. Full-scale riots loomed a single act of police brutality away from erupting. Xi could smell the sweet scent of insurgency in the air.

With a firm belief in each individual controlling his or her own fate, she had opposed Ajunwa's policies since the days of the old UN. Extremists called for the chancellor's execution, the ISC's abolishment of the death penalty notwithstanding. A nation-state that had declared its independence could make it happen, they cried. Xi thought them too soft. Death would let off the old hag who had destroyed human civilization, far too easily.

The masses quieted when the front entrance peeled away.

A group of soldiers escorted Ajunwa and her lawyer outside. They had cuffed the chancellor's hands in front of her body. Otherwise, she walked on her own without restraint. A slight shimmering shrouded her, indicating the presence of shielding, a wise precaution. Surprise—and disappointment—might come over Xi if no one took a shot at her.

At the sight of Ajunwa's head held high, the mob resumed its outcries. Protestors pushed past the riot troopers. Soldiers incapacitated them with stun guns before they got anywhere near the chancellor.

The police held the throngs of activists back, clearing her route toward the armored prison rover. A spacecraft could have flown the chancellor straight from the roof of the stratoscraper to the detainment camps the ISC council had set up on Mars. But in an effort to save face, the council had agreed not to use taxpayer credit to give her special treatment. Plus, certain powerful detractors reveled in seeing her shamed.

As Ajunwa neared the rover, she passed the group of reporters in the crowd. Spherecams stayed far away from the chancellor. The council had promised snipers would shoot down any cam that violated the restraining distance. As much as the media conglomerates salivated over getting close-ups of the juicy scandal, they valued the expensive devices too much to defy the law.

Reporters shouted at Ajunwa using voice-amplification implants.

"How many of your elections were rigged, Madam Chancellor?"

"Your involvement supports the theory that the old UN and ISC were behind the workings of the organization that staged the invasion."

"How do you respond to these allegations?"

Halting mid-stride, Ajunwa turned her dark, penetrating gaze on the media. "I'd like to issue a statement."

Her escorts allowed her to approach to within a meter of an ISN reporter, who directed three spherecams to hover the minimum distance away from her. According to the ISC Charter, a suspect had a right to speak on his or her own behalf during the arrest process.

Xi had exercised the clause on more than one occasion.

To her surprise, the mob quieted enough to hear the chancellor speak.

"Citizens," Ajunwa's powerful voice boomed. "Fellow human beings. It's been a privilege and an honor to serve you all these years. During that time, I've labored to improve the quality of life for everyone. Despite a few rough patches, I think we succeeded. Together.

"Today, I stand here accused of conspiring against you. I won't cry innocent, for that is the hallmark of the guilty. However, I implore you to consider how much sense this makes. Dig deep down and ask yourselves whether a public servant who has promoted human unification her entire career—one who has stuck to her stance in the face of attempts against her life—would wheel and deal behind your backs." She glared at the closest spherecam. "Consider long and hard whether I've committed such deception, or whether this ruse to remove me is another part of that elaborate deception."

Protestors scoffed and cursed at her words. Supporters applauded.

"During my final months in office," Ajunwa said, "I devoted myself to building the ability to defend and save that which we hold most important—that which may seem far away but is now within reach. I can only hope I was able to do enough. In time, I hope you will understand me."

Turning from the crowd, the chancellor marched into the prison rover.

The angst of the mob reached a crescendo as the subject of their intense hatred made her getaway. Demonstrators bull-rushed the riot police, overpowered them, and chased after the rover as it zoomed off down the street.

Charged by adrenaline-fueled disgust, Xiaoqing threw her shoulder into the midsection of a riot officer and knocked him off his feet.

Electricity coursed through every cell in her body as the pulse from a stun gun struck her in the back. Shooting pain ran up her spine and branched out into every limb and digit. Unable to stay on her feet, she face-planted onto the concrete walkway, convulsing.

♦

With guilt-induced knots twisting her intestines into tight spirals, Brooke gawked at the scene in front of ISC headquarters. She hadn't seen Xi in any of the feeds in her i-cite, but Brooke knew Shin's sister had gone there to protest. *I hope she's okay.*

Brooke hung in a fetal ball within the living room of the habitat she and Zeke had called home since returning from Psykhe. Kevin had arranged for Dr. Walter Bell, a trusted colleague, to hide them in his private residence. The dwelling doubled as a research facility on Ida, a modest-sized asteroid in the main belt. Using ISC Defense grid data Shin had preloaded into the Pulsar, Brooke had avoided detection during her return flight.

As much as she enjoyed the peace and quiet of this wayward outpost, she couldn't stand lying low while society self-destructed all around her.

How can this be happening? she mused as Dactyl, a moon tinier than *New Horizons*, rose from right to left over Ida's cratered horizon. *Releasing the list was supposed to purge the Vril and fix everything, but it's only made things worse.*

To prevent Vril censor matrices from erasing the data before it disseminated, Kevin had instructed his AIs to time-release the information from millions of different access points. He had also ensured copies multiplied faster than anything could delete them. Tapping into the ISC solar positioning system, he had synced the citizen profiles with each Vril agent's current location. This had resulted in each agent's personal evidence displaying on the devices in their vicinity. At the time, the feat had seemed like a stroke of genius.

I may've loathed Ajunwa, but I respected her. Was she really working for the Vril all along, or was there something to what she said before they took her away?

Zeke floated into the room, sipping from a water packet. She swore he had grown by four or five centimeters since they had traveled to Psykhe—not that a person's height mattered much in microgravity.

"She's all right." He fixed his eagle-like stare on her. "The turmoil isn't your fault."

"I know," she mumbled.

"You can lie to others, but I know what you're thinking. You feel responsible, and it's gnawing away at you from the inside out."

"So what? I don't have anything better to do at the moment, and wallowing keeps my mind occupied." She kicked her legs and rotated upside down relative to the asteroid. "We risked our lives for what? To make everything worse?" As she spun upright, she growled in frustration. "To top it off, I'm no closer to saving Maya."

With his foot anchored in one of the handles on the floor, Zeke grabbed her wrist.

All her inhibitions fell away, and she lost control. Her stomach churned, every muscle in her body cramped, and she began choking on sobs. Visions of her father's ion flyer exploding over the Rockies flashed through her mind. The moment she found her mother's limp body sprawled out on the bed haunted her. Images of her sister bleeding out and the times Brooke had almost punched Maya for her youthful defiance brought on one convulsion after another. Every mistake she had ever made—everything she could possibly feel guilty about—bombarded her, leaving her wanting—no, needing—to rip her skin from her body.

Zeke released his grip. The memories and feelings faded, although not quickly enough.

Gasping for breath now that she could breathe again, Brooke wrapped her arms around her trembling torso. "What the hell did you do to me?"

"Only what you've been doing to yourself for years."

"I don't—" She let her words trail off at Zeke's raised brow. "I do torture myself, but not like that."

"But you do. I only turned off the sectors of your brain that assert self-control—like a few too many shots of alcohol. You took care of the rest."

Brooke wiped the sweat from her forehead and cheeks. With her strength returning, she scowled at him. "What the hell for?"

"To show you how stupid it is for you to continue on like this. Stop beating yourself up."

"Stop trying to play superhero. There are certain things people don't want you to save them from."

"How true. You've grown so used to tormenting yourself that your personality unraveled when I released you from it."

"Next time, try saying something instead."

He gave a pitying shake of his head. "Really? You would've listened to me and all of a sudden chosen to become a happier and healthier person?"

She averted her gaze.

"No," he said. "Of course not. Humans respond to actions and feelings. Words are so ineffective it's a small wonder you developed language at all. You needed that experience to understand."

"I'll be the judge of what I do and don't need."

He shrugged. "You've closed yourself off again. I guess it's pointless to tell you that deep down, you want to change. You wanted the experience. Otherwise, I wouldn't have allowed you to have it."

"Just stay out of my head unless I ask for it out loud, okay?"

"Whatever you say." After finishing the last of his water packet, he reshaped it into a shiny hat and placed it on her head. "This should protect you from my powers."

She lowered her eyelids. "Very funny."

"I know you want to laugh harder than that. Happiness is within your reach, Brooke."

A realization congealed at the forefront of her mind. "Within my reach . . ." She grabbed Zeke's shoulders and smiled. "Was she talking to me?"

Zeke studied her face, reading her mind. "I think she was."

After downloading Ajunwa's statement, Brooke replayed the last part of it on the cubes in the room.

"During my final months in office," the sim of Ajunwa repeated, "I devoted myself to building the ability to defend and save that which we hold most important—that which may seem far away but is now within reach. I can only hope that I was able to do enough. In time, I hope you understand me."

"Building the ability to bring what's important within reach," Brooke paraphrased. "I'll understand in time, as in the future where *Horizons* will end up. She was talking to me about *Nautilus*. But construction was halted, funding was lost."

"Actually, that's only what the chancellor led the public to believe."

Brooke swung her body to face Dr. Bell, who hovered in the hatchway leading to the rest of the facility. A spring-green lab coat flowed around the Irishman's body.

"Sorry, I didn't mean to eavesdrop," he said through a thick red beard.

"Don't worry about it," she said. "What did you mean?"

"It's true *Nautilus*'s budget was cancelled, but Ajunwa re-appropriated funding under the table to complete it. Despite using every diplomatic strategy to try to avoid war, the woman was a staunch realist, not to mention stubborn. She intended to use the ship in the fight against seceding nation-states if it came to it. I've been performing hush-hush work on its weapons systems, and let me tell you, she's got some serious teeth."

"That's why Shin told me to get to *Nautilus*," Brooke muttered. "Somehow he knew Ajunwa never gave up on it." She drifted closer to the doctor, feeling lighter than weightless in the low gravity. "How soon until it's ready to go?"

"Its shakedown flight is in two months."

"But with Ajunwa removed from power . . ."

"I don't imagine the council will let you borrow it."

"Well, then," Brooke said. "I've no choice but to sneak aboard and alter the flight plan."

Twenty-five—Taphephobia
Gliese 581 System, December 2272 CE

As the main hatch to the ECC slid open, Trevor rose from the central duty station. He flexed his fingers behind his back and frowned, hiding the trepidation keeping him up at night.

Mayor Byrne stepped inside the room and swung her gaze around, clearly paranoid that he might have set a trap.

Two members of her new civilian militia accompanied her. Defense-issue particle rifles hung from the straps slung around their shoulders. Byrne had procured weapons from ship's stores through her sources—sources that Trevor had thus far failed to root out. *At least they haven't gotten their hands on the wave guns.*

"Care to explain why you've reduced the city's rotation and lighting?" she asked.

"As I said over the comm," Trevor said, "we're working to fix the problems."

"I'm sure you are." Byrne snorted. "You know that gravity and illumination affect crop yield and animal growth, right? You're not just punishing us. You're compromising everyone's food supply."

"I told you, the malfunctions aren't intentional. That said, if you would remove your militia from the hydroponics farm and adhere to the food quotas I defined, it might motivate me to speed along the repairs."

"Those quotas leave the city without much more than one meal a day. If we comply, we starve."

"If you don't, we may all starve."

Byrne's fingers stiffened, ready to clench into fists. "We can't go on like this."

"You're right. The last time I sent my officers to the farm, one of your people got trigger happy and a firefight almost broke out. If your militia destroys food production, we'll have a mess on our hands."

"Oh, so the damage would be our fault despite the involvement of both sides?"

Resisting the urge to pull at his crew cut, Trevor said, "My soldiers are trained. Yours aren't. The existence of your unauthorized army is a danger to us all."

"You're worried." Byrne narrowed her gaze, studying him. "We outnumber you and—"

"Sir," Ensign Sadi Pérez, the officer assigned to the neudar scanning station, interrupted.

"Not now, Ensign," Trevor barked. To the mayor, he said, "Worried? About noncombatants? You need to stop biting the hand that feeds you."

"We're the ones feeding you, you idiot," Byrne stammered.

"I didn't mean 'feed' in the literal sense, Madam Mayor."

Now on her feet, Ensign Pérez tapped Trevor on the shoulder. "Sir, you need to see this now."

Trevor pulled his nose away from near-contact with Byrne's face. "What is it, Sadi?"

Pérez led him back to her station. Byrne followed right behind him.

The stars within Pérez's main display cube wavered. Stretching away from a central point, space-time churned. "There's a sizeable distortion forming ten-thousand kilometers from our initial entry point into the system," she said. "A wormhole is about to open, sir."

"A ship." Chills coursed through Trevor's every appendage.

"Is it friend or foe?" the mayor asked.

"We'll know shortly," Pérez said. "Whoever it is, the predicted max diameter of the wormhole means something the size of *Horizons* is coming through."

Everyone in engineering command gathered around the neudar station.

A reflective sphere bulged out from the center of the churning event horizon. From within the three-dimensional wormhole, the incomprehensible nature of hyperspace gave birth to a mammoth spacecraft with recognizable design features. The ship had the shape of two pyramids connected at their bases. The four sides of each pyramid stretched much longer than the base was wide, giving the vessel the look of a double-ended spearhead. Huge rocket nozzles, antimatter nacelles, and thousands of particle cannons protruded from each end of the beast.

Trevor knew a ship built for combat when he saw one.

The wormhole shrank and disappeared behind the destroyer.

"It's the Greys." He spun and bellowed at the crowd behind him. "All hands, general quarters!"

The crew bolted to their stations and sounded the alarm.

"Tactical," he ordered, "arm all weapons and begin neutrino jamming."

"Aye, sir," Ensign Tokala Sigo said. "The scattering field won't hide us for long, but it'll buy us time. With the planet's innermost moon between us and them, it should take them awhile to pinpoint our location."

Glancing at a cube showing *Horizons's* position behind the moon, Trevor nodded. "Thank you, Tokala. Sadi, what do your scans show in terms of armaments?"

Pérez cringed. "They're armed to the teeth, sir. Hundreds of particle cannons, lasers, and launch racks. Eight wide-beam, high-yield plasma ejectors, one on each hull surface—those were in the research and development stages when we launched seven years ago. They've also got triple our shield power. We'd be at a significant disadvantage even in tip-top shape."

Trevor couldn't help but swallow.

When Byrne stepped over next to him, he said, "Still upset I devoted all those resources to the defense systems?"

"You don't intend to fight that thing, do you?" she asked.

"We'll have to eventually."

"Like hell. There's no shame in a strategic retreat."

"Without the phase drive, running would only delay the inevitable."

"I don't know about you, but I'd rather die later than sooner."

"There's no choice."

"You heard her." Byrne waved her hand, indicating Pérez. "We're outgunned. There's no hope of beating that monstrosity."

"Not with a direct assault. But with the proper strategy—"

"Run. Do not try to fight that thing."

He knew he should remain respectful, but he had grown tired of this obstinate woman's meddling. "Did I miss the ceremony where they swore you in as captain?"

Byrne's face flushed with anger, and her eyes wavered in fear. Whirling, she waved for her guards to follow her and headed for the hatch.

Before she exited, she yelled, "I suggest you heed my advice, or you won't be captain for much longer."

♦

With the heel of her boot hovering over the edge of the tower's terrace, Maya threw her arms out to regain her balance. She teetered backwards, heart thumping, for what seemed like forever. But at last, perhaps through sheer willpower, she forced her body upright and stumbled forward.

Panting in relief, she dropped down on one knee.

When she lifted her chin, she found the barrel of Ensign Camila Mendez's wave gun aimed between her eyes.

"Sorry, Maya," Mendez said. "This is nothing personal."

"How is threatening to kill a friend not personal?" Maya asked as her breathing evened.

Staring at the ceiling high above, Mendez snorted. "The fact you don't yet know why we're doing this is a testament to the complexities of time and existence."

"We? As in the Vril?"

"I wasn't sure if you knew we existed yet."

"So it's true. But what does that have to do with me?"

Mendez motioned for her to stand.

With slow, gradual movements, Maya rose to her feet. "I don't know what's going on, but right now I'm more concerned about you. We've been friends for years. As IEF, we're supposed to represent the better qualities humans have to offer. How can you be a part of an organization based on lies and deceit?"

"You wouldn't ask that if you knew who built this place, its original purpose, and what we're up against."

"What we're up against?" Maya thrust her chin out at the tall, bird-headed statues behind Mendez. "You mean these exobeings who seem to have influenced the Penphins' development?"

"Influenced their development? That's like saying the Big Bang had a slight influence on our universe."

"So what're you implying? That the beings portrayed in those statues created the Penphins? And given the similarities between this place and ancient structures on Earth, they may've done the same with us?"

"The truth is more complicated than you could ever imagine." Keeping her gun pointed at Maya with one hand, Mendez held out her other fist. "The collision killed every agent except for me, so the mission of infiltrating this place became my responsibility. And that mission included a simple directive." She opened her palm, revealing the black box within it. "If this device was here, you had to die."

Maya's eyes widened, mouth hung open, and brow lifted. A million questions gridlocked her brain, and she forgot to breathe. "How could anyone know what we'd find down here? Why would it have anything to do with me?"

"Unfortunately, I'm not privy to that. All I know is you can't be allowed to find out."

Maya locked stares with her one-time friend and felt the sincerity she radiated. In that moment, Maya knew the misguided double agent would kill her.

Gripping her gun tighter, Mendez brushed her finger along the trigger.

Before Maya could second guess herself, she jumped backwards off the edge of the balcony.

Mendez adjusted her aim and fired.

The particle blast struck Maya in the upper chest, near her right shoulder. Scalding pain undulated through her body as she fell.

She had done some quick math in her i-cite before jumping. A fifty-meter freefall separated her from the bottom. On Earth, she would have gone splat by the count of three. But in the twenty percent gravity of this world, she had about fourteen seconds until she impacted the ground, giving her a chance at survival.

Fighting against the seething agony, and with her stomach pressing against her larynx, she fumbled for the wave gun in her hip holster. She needed to cushion her fall.

Mendez leaned over the edge and took aim at her.

Maya thought her gun to molecular destabilization mode, flung her arm up in the air, and fired.

The overhang vibrated, cracked, and crumbled. Shards of stone and soot broke away a split second before chunks of the terrace dislodged and dropped.

Thrown off balance, Mendez got off a pair of wild shots that missed her target.

She retreated back toward the statues to avoid falling.

Twisting around, Maya toggled her wave gun to sonic levitation mode, pointed it down, and shrieked as the stone floor flew up to greet her. She depressed the trigger a second before slamming into the ground.

The cushion of air produced by the gun slowed her descent. As she landed, her forehead banged against the floor, shooting needle-like pain through her brain. The gun jabbed her in the abdomen.

She lay there, fading in and out, woozy and retching.

A gut feeling compelled her to roll toward and beneath what remained of the terrace. Each time she flipped over, her shoulder throbbed, her neck ached, and she almost passed out.

Stones big and small thudded against the floor space she had vacated. Particle beams rained down, blasting the stones into thousands of tiny pieces.

Too terrified to scream, Maya flung her arms up as debris buried her.

◆

Kneeling at the edge the broken terrace, Camila kept blasting away.

She stopped after a minute and gazed down at the dust cloud her fire had kicked up.

Putting on her helmet, she engaged her suit's thermal imaging system and detected no heat signs. She also ran a neudar scan, but the distortions were still skewing the results.

Satisfied she had accomplished her objective, Camila stood and cursed the damage she had caused to an archaeological treasure. Her chest grew heavy, weighed down by the guilt of defiling the place—and of killing a friend.

She shook off the remorse. Maya had always been too self-righteous for her own good. The human race needed people in charge willing to ensure its survival no matter the cost. She didn't relish the thought of eliminating this exospecies, but when weighed against the alternatives, she knew the Vril had chosen the right course of action.

At least this beautiful structure will remain intact, she reassured herself.

She shoved the device into her pocket and pushed Hamilton's remains over the edge of the balcony. After taking one last look at the statues— what she wouldn't give for more time to study them and rest of the ruins—she made haste back to the surface.

◆

"Forget it," Jo snapped at Wallace via her helmet comm. "We're not leaving without our team members." This she said while staring down the approaching storm from the sheltered recess near the mound. Over the mountains in the distance, a towering sheet of darkness rolled toward them, blocking the stars to the north.

Fierce gusts whipped snow everywhere. The occasional chunk of ice pelted her suit. Soon, the wind speeds would grow powerful enough to pin them down.

"We need to go," Wallace said. "That's what Maya ordered us to do." He pointed back at the blizzard about to swallow the area. "If we don't get the hell out of here within the next few minutes, we won't ever leave."

He grabbed her wrist, trying to lead her to the airship. The Penphins had flown back to it and maneuvered it closer to the mound for them.

Jo yanked her arm away. "We give them until the last possible second."

"If it were just you and me, I'd face the prospect of a noble death." He jabbed a thumb over his shoulder at the ship. "But we're putting our hosts in jeopardy, too. We need to go now."

"You're a coward. You only want to save yourself."

"You're risking all our lives because you don't want to leave your best friend behind."

"I'm the ranking officer here." She poked his face shield with her index finger. "You're way out of—" She cut herself short upon seeing Mendez stumble out of the exit and collapse.

With Wallace right behind her, Jo tromped through the snow and bent down next to the archeologist. "Are you okay?"

Mendez nodded her flushed and tensed face behind her helmet visor.

"What happened?" Jo asked. "Where are Ensign Davis and Mr. Hamilton?"

"They . . . they saved me," Mendez whimpered, on the verge of tears. "I went back to capture better sims of the statues and device. I was standing on the terrace when Maya showed up and it started to collapse."

Shock paralyzed Jo. She could muster no breath with which to gasp.

"She pushed me away in time but couldn't get clear," Mendez said. "When Hamilton tried to save her, they both fell and hit the ground. Heavy stones dropped from the terrace and buried them. They're both dead." She pounded the snow with a gloved fist. "It's my fault. I was so selfish and stupid. I never should've gone back."

Jo shook off her dread. "You're right about that. You disobeyed orders, but we'll deal with that later. How do you know they were killed?"

"I ran a thermal scan but didn't find any heat signatures. I also tried a neutrino sweep for life signs but came up empty."

Wallace helped her up. "Falling fifty meters in point two gees wouldn't have damaged an android of Hamilton's caliber."

"I wouldn't have thought so, either." Mendez sniffled and exhaled. "A stone must've crushed his head. Even in low gravity, those things have a lot of mass."

Springing to her feet, Jo headed toward the entrance, head and chest burning with determination.

Wallace grabbed her arm again. "Where do you think you're going?"

"I haven't heard anything conclusive," she said. "They could still be alive."

"Even if they survived, there's no time. The storm will be on top of us any minute."

"But—"

Mendez clutched her other arm. "He's right, Ensign Ryder. It took me fifteen minutes to get back here."

"I'm sorry, ma'am," Wallace said, "but we don't have a half hour to spare. C'mon."

Forcing herself to accept the inevitable, Jo let them pull her toward the airship.

◆

Maya couldn't keep still or hold her breath any longer. Despite not having heard a sound for minutes, she couldn't know for certain whether Mendez was still around. But it didn't matter. The irritation in her throat and lungs forced her to gag and cough up the dirt she had inhaled. A bout of sneezing followed from the dust the blasts and falling rocks had kicked up into the air.

No particle beams came raining down upon her as she choked on gulps of carbon dioxide. Groping around for her breathing mask, she found it still hanging around her neck. *Thank the stars.* She pulled it up over her mouth and sucked in filtered oxygen.

As her coughing and sniffles subsided, she looked around but couldn't see a thing. Darkness shrouded her. Earlier when her team had scouted the tower's interior, the group had lit up the place with multiple light sources. When she had gone back for and confronted Mendez, she hadn't had time to dwell on her fear.

Now she lay all alone in pitch blackness, eighty meters below the ground on the freezing night side of a strange planet.

Her heart pounded against her ribcage. Panic washed over her, and she hyperventilated her throat hoarse.

Fumbling for her wave gun, she set it to maximum brightness. The eerie shadows cast by broken chunks of terrace played tricks on her mind, but the gun lit up the area enough to calm her.

She switched off the force field the gun was still projecting. Reconfiguring the shield to fool a thermal scan and protect her from the falling debris had proven tricky, but it had worked well enough to keep her alive.

When Maya pushed herself up on her forearms, she cried out and fell back. The sensation of searing needles pierced her chest, and her head spun. A health scan indicated she had second and third degree burns along with a concussion. She had also suffered hairline fractures in the ulna of her left arm and fibula of her right leg. Two ribs had broken when she had landed on her gun.

Reaching down with her good arm, she searched for the med pack on the belt of her suit but couldn't find it. *I must've lost in the fall.* She realized her helmet had also gone missing. *They must be around here somewhere.*

She ran her hands over the ground, finding nothing but stones of all shapes and sizes. *Crap, no. Is the med kit buried?* Further blind searches failed to uncover it.

Injuries be damned, she rolled onto her side and pushed up with her good limbs.

Agony set off every nerve ending, and she collapsed on her broken arm. Pain shot through it as she scraped her skin against jagged debris.

A wave of helplessness washed over her. Frustration gave way to seething anger, which made her dizzier than ever.

Her chronometer indicated the storm would engulf the tower in a couple minutes. Her team was undoubtedly aboard the airship and long gone, which offered some peace of mind. Mendez had undoubtedly joined them and contrived a plausible excuse for what had happened. No one would know Maya's one-time friend had stranded her here, killing her. There was no denying it. She would starve to death long before another living soul visited this place again.

Despair overwhelmed her.

Her lower lip trembled and her eyes watered. She didn't want to cry or feel sorry for herself, but she couldn't force back the tears. A part of her insisted she had a right to feel the way she did, so she gave into it.

The sobs brought on another bought of nausea, and she lapsed in and out of consciousness.

In a daze, she felt her body lift up off the ground. *Am I dying? Leaving my body?* Yet she swore multiple pairs of cold, thin fingers gripped her appendages.

A stinging blast of frigid air perked her up. Her helmet rested atop her head but wasn't affixed to her suit. Darkness loomed beyond the visor, which was off center from her nose. The strange hands still clutched her as she floated in nothingness, squirming to no avail.

As panic threatened to consume her, the darkness dropped away.

Stars twinkled all around her. Below her dangling feet, the rumbling clouds of the storm raged. Four Penphins held her in their grasp as they flapped their flings toward the airship.

She hissed in pain as they set her down on the upper deck.

Jo climbed up through the hole leading to the lower deck, took a long look at Maya, and exhaled in relief.

Furrowing her brow, she swung her gaze back and forth between Maya and the hole. Rage contorted her face, and she drew her wave gun.

As Mendez emerged from the hole, Jo pressed the gun to her forehead.

"What are you doing?" Mendez asked, widening her doe eyes.

"Give it up," Jo snapped. "I know you tried to kill her."

The archaeologist shifted her gaze to Maya and then back to Jo. "It wasn't me. It must've been Hamilton."

"Changing your story, now, are we? If he was trying to save Maya from falling, how did she get shot?"

"I don't know. Maybe he shot her after they fell."

Jo raised her eyebrows and tightened her grasp on her weapon. "You said you saw stones bury them."

"I did. I swear." With reddening eyes on the verge of tears, Mendez shook her head. "Maybe Hamilton survived, dug his way out, and shot her. Maybe that was his plan all along. I don't know." She trembled. "I fled like a coward, okay? I don't know what happened after they fell."

Leaning back on her elbows, Maya tried to interject the truth, but her throat only rasped.

Jo turned partway around to look back at her friend.

Mendez whipped out her gun, pointed it at Jo, and began to depress the trigger.

Maya gasped.

A particle beam tore through the back of Mendez's skull and shot forth from her forehead. Blood sprayed Jo in the face. The beam missed her left pigtail by a centimeter.

Mendez's eyes glazed over, and she went limp. As she fell, her chin caught on the upper deck, snapping her neck.

Her lifeless body dropped and thudded against the floor below.

Jo stared down the hole with her mouth agape, face whiter than the ice far below the airship.

Wallace climbed to the upper deck, wave gun in hand.

◆

Maya bent down and closed Ensign Camila Mendez's eyelids. Jo and Wallace had helped her move the young woman's corpse to a far corner on the lower deck. Blood trickled down her cheek from the mouth.

After covering Mendez with a seaweed tarp, Maya stared at the device in her palm that the archaeologist had taken from the tower. The Vril had sent Maya's one-time friend to kill her over it. They had known it existed on a planet twenty light years away and two hundred thousand years ago. She couldn't begin to wrap her mind around the implications.

Two other thoughts bubbled to the surface that didn't strike her as coincidence. One, her aunt—the woman who had shredded her mother to pieces—had once associated with this organization. And two, *Horizons* had somehow skipped seven years during its hyperspace shift here.

A million questions weighed on her mind, but with Mendez dead,

Maya knew she wouldn't be answering them any time soon.

Despite the medite injections that had mostly healed her physical ailments, her abdominal pangs showed no signs of subsiding.

She shoved the device into her pocket and stood up.

"How're you feeling?" Jo asked as she came up behind her.

Maya rotated her arm in a tight circle and nodded. "Still a little sore but better, thanks. And you?"

"I'm fine—still a little rattled, but fine." Jo looked down at the tarp. "I still can't believe that two-timing bitch tried to kill you."

"You seemed to know she was guilty as soon as you saw the Penphins with me."

Jo shrugged. "I first suspected something was off when she said she'd used her neudar to look for you. Camila knew the space-time distortions were interfering with neutrino signals. If the comm had been working, we could've contacted each other and avoided the whole situation. At the time, I assumed she hadn't been thinking straight. She'd been through a traumatic experience, after all."

After shaking out her body, Jo patted Maya's jacket in the location where Mendez had shot her, forcing her to wince.

"But when I saw that big ole scorch mark on the front of your suit," Jo said, "her comment came back to mind."

"Nice catch," Maya said. "Too bad Hamilton wasn't as lucky as me."

"I feel bad saying this, but between Camila and him, I would've placed my bets on the creepy android being the baddie."

"I know what you mean. Let this be a lesson to refrain from judging while still keeping our eyes open."

"Gee," Jo said. "I guess near-death experiences turn a girl into a wise old sensei."

Maya gave her friend a light shove. "You're not the only one who gets to utter fused sayings."

Wallace walked up behind them. "So why did she try to kill you?" he asked.

Before Maya could decide whether to tell them everything, she received a comm from Trevor. "Ensign Davis here, sir."

"Maya." His baggy eyes appeared in her i-cite while his voice echoed throughout her head. "We've detected another ship in the system."

"Another ship? Have you identified it?"

"Yes. It belongs to the Greys."

Another mind-screen appeared, showing a vidsim of the heavily-armed destroyer.

A surge of near-panic shot through her at the prospect of the inevitable conflict. *As if enough hasn't gone wrong today.* The question of whether the behemoth of a ship belonged to a real exospecies or the Vril popped into her head, although the answer might not matter. "I've got unfortunate news as well, sir."

"Oh?"

"Mendez and Hamilton were killed while exploring the ruins. I'll send you a full report once I've comprised it."

Trevor took his time responding. "It's a tragic loss, but under the circumstances, we'll deal with it later."

"Understood, sir. Do you want us to return to the ship?"

"No. Sending a transport for you would give away our position. I waited to contact you until the moon we're hiding behind moved over your position."

"Jamming will only hide the ship for so long, sir."

"I'm aware of that, Ensign, which is why we're preparing a preemptive strike."

"That ship looks formidable, and *Horizons* is damaged, so you're hoping to even the score with a surprise offensive." Maya mulled it over. "I'm not in love with the idea, but I don't see too many other options, either."

"My thinking exactly." He shook his head and grumbled. "The odds aren't great, but they'd be better if I didn't have to wage battles on two fronts."

"What do you mean?"

"Mayor Byrne has been fighting me on everything since you left. She's formed a citizen's militia and threatened to take the ship if I don't turn tail and run, which will only delay the inevitable."

Maya stewed over the news. "You have to come get me, sir. Let me manage things with her."

"I'd love to, but I won't risk my only advantage. I can handle her."

Her shoulders drooped despite a weight lifting off her chest. One part of her wanted to go back while her more selfish side felt safer on the planet. Given the Vril's plan to somehow eradicate the Penphins, though, she questioned the latter assumption. Bob had said there was a rogue AI on board working against him to launch a doomsday device.

A certainty welled up inside of her. She had to get up to the ship somehow. "Sir, we need to figure out a way to—"

The comm channel terminated. She tried to reestablish it without success.

"I think something's blocking the signal," Jo said.

"That could mean the destroyer's found *Horizons*." Maya growled under her breath. "It's so frustrating being down here and not being able to do anything."

"I know what you mean."

Overcome by restlessness, Maya climbed to the upper deck and stormed over to one side of the ship. After putting on her gloves, she gripped the railing and stared up into the sky. Something she hadn't seen in a while—sunlight—peeked up above the horizon as the airship approached the day side.

HAVE YOU RECOVERED FROM YOUR INJURIES?

Maya flinched as Ari came to stand alongside her.

"Mostly," her wristband sang. "Thank you for sending your people to save me. I'm very grateful."

WE BELIEVE THE APPROPRIATE RESPONSE IS "YOU'RE WELCOME."

"Yes, you learn quickly."

She stared out at the reddening landscape for a couple minutes before Ari spoke again.

PLEASE HELP ME UNDERSTAND WHAT TRANSPIRED BETWEEN YOU AND THE HUMAN NAMED MENDEZ. HOW COULD ONE BEING HARM ANOTHER WITHOUT BRINGING HARM TO ALL?

"I wish we asked that question of ourselves more often," Maya mumbled.

I COULD NOT HEAR YOUR SONG.

"Sorry," she said, raising her voice. "My people's feelings aren't connected like yours. Internalized empathy keeps most of us from harming one another, but some people don't pay attention to those feelings."

THIS CONCEPT OF SEPARATED FEELINGS IS DIFFICULT TO COMPREHEND.

"I hope you never have to comprehend it, although I fear you'll be forced to sooner or later." She looked around the upper deck and noted the other Penphins going about their duties. Not one of them had approached any of the humans since Wallace had shot Mendez. "I don't blame your people for staying away from us. I don't want to be near myself right now."

WE DON'T UNDERSTAND HOW A BEING COULD NOT BE NEAR ITSELF, BUT WE HAVE FELT IT PRUDENT TO OBSERVE YOU FROM A GREATER DISTANCE.

"Prudent indeed. You may need to learn to protect yourselves from us."

WE DO NOT OBSERVE TO PROTECT OURSELVES. WE OBSERVE WITH THE INTENTION TO HELP.

Maya swiveled her head and stared at Ari. Coming from a human, the statement would have sounded like boasting. But a Penphin didn't know such things. A Penphin only thought of helping.

Smiling, she said, "You've taken on a large task, but I'll appreciate any insight you can provide." Her smile faded, and she slapped the railing with both hands. "Right now, what I need is help getting back to my ship."

Ari placed his fling on her shoulder. THEN WE SHALL TAKE YOU.

Twenty-six—Expropriate
Jupiter Trojans (Greek Camp), September 2272 CE

Brooke snuck up behind a rotating cargo carrier in her Pulsar, flying within the sensor blind spots Kevin had uploaded into her support AI. She maneuvered in close to the dormant aft nozzles while avoiding external cameras and view ports. The stealth fighter she had commandeered on Psykhe jammed neudar, but at this distance, she worried about someone spotting her by direct visual observation.

Her heart hadn't stopped thumping since she had downshifted out amongst the Trojan asteroids. Foreknowledge of the cargo ship's itinerary had allowed her to time her reentry into normal space to coincide with the ship's emergence. As Kevin had predicted, the space-time distortions of the ship's bigger wormhole had masked the disturbances produced by her fighter's smaller vortex. No one had noticed her so far. Still, she remained fearful that the IEF base might detect her and foil her plan to divert *Nautilus*, before she had a chance to try.

If the cargo ship or base had spotted her months ago, they would have issued a warning. But now, they had orders to shoot on sight. With Ajunwa removed from office, the intrasolar government infrastructure had grown dysfunctional. Repeated appeals by the new Martian Coalition demanding the ISC find another site for its Vril holding camps had fallen on deaf ears. As a result, the coalition had fired the first salvos of a potential war when they had attacked an ISC Defense carrier transporting the alleged conspirators to Mars. Then, in an incident that had flashed Brooke back to a quarter century ago, fighting had broken out between splinter groups from Ganymede and Callisto over ownership of the aerostat particle collectors in Jupiter's atmosphere. Revolutions aimed at purging the ISC consumed almost every nation-state and colony.

She sighed in a futile attempt to release her tension.

"Something comforting," Zeke said from the rear seat.

Brooke sat up straight. "Huh?"

"You were wishing your father or sister were still alive so they could say something comforting to you."

"Remember how we talked about getting other people's consent before reading their thoughts?"

"Sorry, but it's hard to ignore your thoughts when they're shouting."

She stuck out her lip. "Is it too late for me to bring you back to Ida?"

"You can't succeed without my help."

"True, but that doesn't mean I have to like it."

"But you do like it. You won't admit it, but you're glad to have me along."

Grumbling, Brooke lamented her interactions with the teen. His mind-reading faculties meant she rarely got to be right.

"You mean I won't allow you to convince me of something you don't believe," he disputed her thought.

"Fine, but this mission is dangerous. I'd never forgive myself if anything happened to you."

"That I know you mean, but your plan won't work without my presence."

Brooke wrinkled her nose and conceded the argument. The plan, even with an assist from Zeke's powers, would require a hefty dose of luck to succeed. She needed to sneak aboard, make her way to engineering command, upload the program Kevin had written, and avoid discovery until *Nautilus* embarked on its shakedown flight. When the ship upshifted to hyperspace, the program would lock the phase drive on course for Gliese 581 and refuse input until downshift.

A warning blinked in her augmented reality, indicating that Agamemnon had come into range of the naked eye. The brownish-red smudge hung amongst the stars, one of millions of Trojan asteroids sharing the orbit of Jupiter around the sun. A tiny speck of a moon circled the smudge.

She magnified Agamemnon until the 167-kilometer-diameter asteroid enlarged to fill her i-cite. The domes and other structures on the base covered multiple square kilometers of the cratered surface. Mining bots and automated rovers roamed the landscape.

As the asteroid rotated, the construction facility that the IEF had bored into the side of the rock face spun into view. Eight-legged fabrication bots crawled throughout the web of scaffolding.

Goosebumps popped up on Brooke's arms after another quarter turn of the asteroid.

Nautilus hung in the center of the scaffolding with its mighty bow protruding outward. Lacking a city sphere, the revolving starship measured one and a half kilometers in length, twenty-five percent shorter than *New Horizons*. In the early construction phases, Ajunwa had ordered the biosphere removed. She had repurposed the exploratory spacecraft as a battleship, and the end product reflected her vision.

With the sphere gone and the forward and aft sections connected, *Nautilus* appeared sleeker and more maneuverable than its predecessor. The ring supporting the half-dozen antimatter nacelles hugged the rear section, leaving the ship's fuel supply less vulnerable. Particle and laser cannons, seeker launch tubes, and plasma ejectors protruded from every square meter of the reinforced hull.

Brooke waited until the cargo ship reached its closest point to the construction facility on its way to the base. Burning thrusters, she weaved the Pulsar through the scaffolding, descending deeper into the asteroid.

Having traveled far enough inside the asteroid to reach the engine block of the ship, Brooke maneuvered her fighter to an airlock. There she turned over control of the Pulsar to the support AI, instructing it to sync the craft with the ship's rotation and situate the cockpit below the hatch. Nearly one gee of force pressed her down into her seat.

"Ready?" she asked Zeke as the cockpit drained of gravgel.

"Yes," he said without a jitter in his voice.

She opened the canopy and ordered her AI to input the access code Dr. Bell had given her. The code belonged to a member of the doctor's staff who had recently passed away. Bell had promised to apply enough red tape to ensure the late woman's code remained active long enough for Brooke to use it.

The outer airlock hatch slid open and extended a ladder. Brooke grabbed the first rung, pulled herself out of the cockpit, and climbed.

After Brooke and Zeke had ascended into the airlock, she sealed the outer hatch and used her flight armor's thermal imaging system to check for anyone in the vicinity. As she had hoped, no one occupied the out of the way maintenance corridor on the other side of the inner hatch.

She pressurized the airlock. Pulling off her helmet, she armed her particle rifle.

"You shouldn't need that with me along," Zeke said.

The rifle pinged as it reached full charge.

"Let's hope you're right," she said.

Brooke opened the inner door and stepped out, brandishing her weapon. Zeke followed behind her.

Four bends, three hallways, and two levels later, a pair of heat icons appeared in her i-cite, heading her way around a corner. By the time she thought to ask Zeke to do something about them, the crew members had turned and headed off in the opposite direction.

"As far as they know," he whispered, "they decided the electrical junction they were on their way to fix could wait until after lunch."

Zeke averted five close encounters of a similar nature as they worked their way to the engineering command center.

Outside the hatch to the ECC, Brooke glanced at Zeke, indicating he should work his magic.

He nodded and held his palm out toward the door.

Despite the confidence she had in his abilities, she hesitated before entering. Redirecting a couple of people away from them was one thing. Taking control of a major nerve center within an interstellar starship—a room manned by tens of officers—seemed like it might require something more.

"Don't worry," he said, reading her concern. "They won't notice us."

Sucking in a deep breath, Brooke stepped close enough to the entry hatch for it to sense her movement and slide open.

As she crept through the doorway, sighting her rifle, most of the room's occupants lay sprawled out on the floor or hunched over their duty stations. Conscious crew members went about their business, oblivious to their fallen comrades or the presence of trespassers.

She jumped out of the path of a man who marched right past her. He exited the ECC without having noticed the near collision.

"Why didn't you knock them all out?" Brooke asked.

"If someone elsewhere in the ship comms engineering and no one answers," Zeke said, "it might raise suspicion."

"Good thinking. But why not keep them all awake, then?"

"My abilities have limits. Otherwise, I'd take control of all forty billion of you and fix everything."

"Wouldn't that be swell." She slung her rifle over her shoulder and searched for the interface terminal to the phase drive.

An officer sat at the drive control station, monitoring its status in various display cubes. The patch on the front of the man's uniform read Lieutenant O. Fofana.

Brooke produced the data chip containing the override program from a compartment in her suit and conveyed her desire to Zeke.

Lieutenant Fofana swiveled his chair toward Brooke and held out his hand. After accepting the chip in his palm, he placed it on his station and accessed it. Indecipherable text filled three of the display cubes. Kevin had told Brooke that scrolling data indicated the program was in the process of rewriting the destination protocols.

So far, so good.

Red lights flashed. Alarms screeched.

Flinching, Brooke reached for her rifle and cursed her luck. *Kevin's program should've bypassed all the security safeguards. What the hell went wrong?* Her forehead and palms grew clammy.

A female voice with a thick Aussie accent thundered from the drive control station. "What've you done to my engines, Lieutenant?"

Brooke shot Zeke a glance.

"I'm not sure, Captain," he forced Fofana to respond. "I'm investigating now."

"I can't seem to comm you directly, Obi," the captain said. "Something wrong with your implants?"

"I'm sorry, ma'am. I started having issues with them yesterday, but I haven't had time to visit the infirmary."

Zeke whispered to Brooke, explaining that while he could control someone's use of embedded biotechnology, he couldn't directly operate the tech.

"Is that so?" the captain asked. "It seems like others in engineering are having bigger problems than you. The biometric monitoring systems show twenty-three unconscious crew members and two unidentified individuals."

"I don't know what's going on, Captain," Fofana had no choice but to say. "I've got all I can do to make sure the drive doesn't blow us apart."

"I'm sending Commander Yermakov along with security and medical teams."

"Understood, ma'am."

Zeke directed his attention toward the main hatch. "I should be able to keep them all away."

"Yeah, but that's only going to delay the inevitable." Brooke ran a hand through her sweat-soaked hair. While considering a very limited set of options, she kept trying to place the familiar voice of the captain. "Regardless of what happens to us, our top priority is to alter the drive's destination."

"I could make Fofana change it."

She leaned in front of the Lieutenant and swiped her fingers through a cube. The interfaces sufficiently resembled those found in a Pulsar that she could gauge the current status. "It looks like recent security upgrades to the drive OS rejected the program's access attempt. Everything's locked down and senior-level authority is required to get back in."

"Could the commander who's on his way here do it?"

"Yes, he's the first officer." She stomped her boot. "But it's pointless. The destination will show up on every navigation display if the commander updates it. Someone will notice it's Gliese 581 long before upshift. We needed the program to report a false endpoint."

"How about—?"

Lieutenant Fofana went limp and fell out of his chair. Everyone else in the room collapsed along with him.

"What happened?" Brooke asked. "Did you knock them out?"

Nodding, Zeke said, "I couldn't keep controlling the people in here and put everyone outside in the hall to sleep." Lines creased the teenager's forehead. "I'm starting to get a little overwhelmed."

Staring at the hatch, she considered retreating back to the Pulsar. All signs pointed to her coup as having failed. Zeke could ensure a safe return to the fighter. Using the Pulsar's stealth capabilities, they could slip away from the asteroid and disappear into hyperspace.

I'll have to live to fight another day. She decided to withdraw. The last thing she wanted was the all-but-defunct ISC getting their hands on an exochild and his incredible powers.

Zeke's expression told her he understood and agreed.

Brooke took a step toward the hatch but froze at the sound of the captain's voice.

"To the would-be saboteurs who're mucking with my ship," she said. "I've located and confiscated your getaway vehicle, so don't bother trying to escape."

Panic-induced tremors undulated through Brooke's body.

"This two-way channel is open," the captain said. "Tell me what you want and what you hope to accomplish."

Brooke looked at Zeke, unsure of how to respond.

The skipper's voice exuded confidence. "Whatever you tried, you failed miserably. If you give yourselves up without a fight, I promise you'll receive due process. Test me, and you won't like the outcome."

The thought of heading for the closest hangar bay and stealing a Pulsar crossed Brooke's mind. But even if she made it there, the fighter's control systems would be encrypted. Nor was there anything to stop *Nautilus* from detecting and destroying one of its own spacecraft before she could get far enough away from the asteroid to upshift.

Gripping her rifle in desperation, Brooke was thinking about blasting everything in the command center when Zeke started coughing.

Her lungs and throat started to itch. The room spun, and her knees wobbled.

"Knockout gas," Brooke rasped, coughing. "Put on your helmet."

As she finished reattaching her headgear to her armor, the hatch slid open. Three floating spheres flew into the ECC.

She pulled Zeke down behind a control station as the attack spheres unleashed a series of energy pulses.

Her instruments identified the beams as stun pulses that would have difficulty penetrating her flight armor. But if a pulse struck Zeke, she would lose the only thing preventing the crew from mounting a full assault against her.

Zeke lay on the floor, retching.

Popping up behind the console, she sighted her rifle on one of the spheres, fired, and blew it apart. Then she pivoted and blasted the second sphere.

A pair of hands grabbed her arm as she scanned the air for the pesky third sphere. Turning, she found an android technician assailing her.

At least six androids had somehow snuck into the room unnoticed. Perhaps they had entered while she had been focused on dispatching the first two spheres.

The enhanced strength provided by her flight armor allowed her to shrug off the first android like a small child.

Another set of hands groped the base of her helmet, feeling for the release button.

A third android got a grip on her rifle. It wouldn't let go, so she aimed and blasted it in the chest.

From the ceiling high above, the last remaining sphere shot and stunned Zeke.

Brooke gasped as an android pried off her helmet.

Her first breath brought on a fit of coughing. Her eyes stung and watered. She couldn't see anything.

Another android yanked her rifle away from her.

She clawed at her throat, unable to breathe. Nebulous thoughts jumbled together in her fading mind.

Stumbling, she keeled over and passed out.

Twenty-seven—Ambuscade
Gliese 581 System, January 2273 CE

"The last of the charges and thrusters are in place, sir."

"Nice work, Erik," Trevor said, praising Second Lieutenant Maxwell in his i-cite. "Now get back to the ship on the double."

"Understood, sir."

Trevor closed the channel.

Standing with his arms folded, he studied a series of display cubes in engineering command, watching the beginnings of his plan unfold.

In one cube, Maxwell's Pulsar, his wing mate's fighter, and a transport lifted off from the fourth planet's outermost moon, an oblong rock with a six-kilometer diameter. Each spacecraft maneuvered using minimal thruster burns. Their main reactors remained dormant to restrict power emissions and lower detectability.

The rear camera views from the transport appeared on another display, showing the holes that the mining bots had drilled into strategic locations on the lunar surface. The bots had buried antimatter explosives and reaction control systems as a surprise for the destroyer.

Trevor prided himself on his knowledge of military history. He had studied the war against the Greys in detail. During the Battle of Themisto in 2248, General Frederick Douglas had led mankind's unified forces to victory using a brilliant strategy. Trevor hoped the same tactics would work again.

Centered in another cube, the destroyer followed a slow, cautious course. It would reach *Horizons* in fewer than two Earth days.

His skin tingled at the prospect of engaging in what Defense had trained him to do. At the same time, the fact the enemy had him outgunned left him perspiring more than usual.

"Jenelle, prepare to get underway as soon as Maxwell and his team are back on board," he ordered his nav officer.

"Yes, sir," Ensign Williams responded.

"Tokala, prepare to bring all weapons to ready status."

His tactical officer, Ensign Tokala Sigo, turned from his duty station. "Aye, skipper."

He settled into the seat behind the centermost duty station in the ECC. He had adopted the seat as his makeshift captain's chair.

While checking the status of the ship's systems, a comm request from Byrne appeared in his i-cite.

He didn't want to take the time to answer her, but he accepted her comm, anyway. Somehow, he needed to put a stop to the cold war that had broken out between the civilians and crew.

The mayor wasted zero thought-speech on pleasantries. "Are you still planning to carry out your surprise attack?"

"Yes, the operation is about to commence."

Byrne softened her mental tone. "Trevor, I'm begging you. Please reconsider."

"I'm sorry, but a preemptive strike gives us the best chance for survival."

"There must be an alternative. Can't we hide behind the larger planets in the system or the star itself?"

"For a while, maybe, but in the end, we'd be forced to engage them anyway."

Her tone hardened. "I'm giving you one last chance to call off the attack."

He considered her words. *A good skipper takes the time to consider all options*, he told himself. By staying close to the planets and their gravitational fields, he could make it difficult for the destroyer to shift near *Horizons*. One slight miscalculation and the enemy ship would end up plummeting through the atmosphere or stuck halfway in a mountain. Now that he thought about it, he could keep such a cat and mouse game going for some time.

However, running would drain the ship's precious resources. When they ran out, the ship would have no way to defend itself. It made more sense to mount an assault now while they still could do it.

"The attack proceeds as planned," he said. "I recommend you get everyone in the city to the designated shelter areas and secure the biosphere."

"Very well," Byrne said. "I refuse to stand by and let you lead us to the slaughter." She closed the channel.

Trevor tried to get her back, but she refused to respond. "Damn it." He resisted the urge to slap his console.

The officers in the ECC looked back over their shoulders from their duty stations.

Silence permeated the room—the kind observed during a funeral.

"Sir," Ensign Williams said. "Maxwell has returned and is ready to relaunch with the main fighter wing."

Rising to his feet, Trevor straightened his uniform. "Double the security personnel in the engineering and defense sections, and set course for the third moon."

◆

Maya hopped out of the airship that had flown her from the Penphins' space complex to the staging platform for launch railway two. Wedging her helmet under her arm, she gazed at the shell craft perched atop the rails.

Jumping out of the airship after her, Jo asked, "You're serious about going through with this?" Her breathing mask muffled her words but not her feelings.

Jo disabled her wristband to prevent Ari and the Penphins prepping the craft for take-off from overhearing her. "I appreciate history more than anyone, but I can't get behind you entrusting your life to this antiquated piece of . . ." Placing her hands on her hips, she gawked at the vehicle. "I'd feel more comfortable riding a unicycle on a busy expressway."

"I feel the same way, but my mind's made up." Maya rested her hand on Jo's shoulder, comforting herself as much as her friend. Thoughts of every possible thing that could go wrong had gnawed at her since Ari had first offered. "I have to get back to the ship and help in any way that I can."

"And if you don't survive the ride there?"

"Let's give our hosts a little more credit. They flew their ship all the way out to *Horizons*." Maya's chest deflated as she made her next point. "Ari says their liftoffs have achieved a better-than ninety-five percent reliability rate."

"Great. One in twenty odds of exploding in midair—like the firecracker launches of three centuries ago. Somehow, that doesn't fit my definition of reliable."

"I'm sure the launch will go smoothly."

"Still, this is a bad idea. That wildebeest of a mother ship is bearing down on *Horizons*. You could get caught in the crossfire without any means of defense."

"The destroyer won't reach the planet for two days. The Penphins can get me to the ship in half that time. I should be safe and sound before the first shots are fired." Maya bit her lip. "That doesn't leave much time to resolve the turmoil aboard, but I'd rather try than do nothing."

"Call me selfish, but I'm not thrilled about staying here."

"Unfortunately, their craft only seats three: the pilot, Ari, and me. But at least you won't be the only human here." Pointing above the vrees in the distance, Maya said, "Join Ensign Wallace at their space center after I leave. I'm sure he's willing to serenade you with all the Darwinist theory your little heart desires."

"The man knows what a woman wants," Jo droned.

Maya wrapped her arm around her friend's back. "A Penphin scientist promised to take him on an expedition. Go and learn all you can about this planet's history. That's why you came out here."

"That doesn't sound so bad, actually." Jo slouched. "But I don't think I could take much joy in it knowing the ship might be blown to smithereens at any moment, killing you and stranding me here."

"There's nothing you can do about it, so you might as well make the best of things here."

The two friends entered into a goodbye embrace and squeezed each other tight.

"Be careful," Jo said as she pulled away.

Maya forced a grin. "Aren't I always?"

Her friend raised an eyebrow.

After Maya donned her helmet, two Penphins lifted her into the air and carried her away.

The launch vehicle lay horizontal on the railway. As she flew toward it, she got a good look at the huge rocket nozzles protruding from the rear of the bulky first stage. Ari had explained that stage one would kick in the moment the craft left the railway. A narrower second stage for upper atmospheric lift and orbital ejection comprised the middle module. At the front of the craft, a conical payload fairing protected the shell-shaped crew and cylindrical service module.

The spacecraft reminded her of the Saturn 1B rockets she had seen in museums on Earth. The similarities struck her as uncanny—almost too coincidental, even—until she reminded herself that the same laws of physics applied everywhere in this universe. Despite her knowledge of the realities of spaceflight, she still struggled with why the simple act of exiting an atmosphere required such elaborate measures. Twenty-third-century human technology had spoiled her.

After the Penphins stuffed her through the crew module's side hatch, Maya crawled through the narrow airlock and into the main cabin. At present, the fairing covered the ovular portholes, darkening the cockpit. A handful of blinking, egg-shaped filament bulbs of varying shades of red provided dim illumination.

As her pulse started to race, she enabled her night vision. Doing so quelled her anxiety and saved her from banging her head and knees.

Her breather failed to filter out the rotten algae smell of the cramped cabin, which brought on a trio of sneezes. She inhaled and exhaled slow, deep breaths through her nose until her nostrils acclimated.

She settled into an acceleration chair next to Ari. Possessing more flexible skeletal structures than humans, the thinker and pilot remolded their bodies to fill out their cup-shaped seats. Maya had no choice but to sink her posterior all the way back into her cup and bend forward with her chest almost touching her knees.

While Ari and the pilot strapped her in with a sinewy seatbelt, her suit's audio inputs registered the clank of the inner airlock hatch closing and latching.

Her suit also picked up the AM radio signals in the cabin. Song-speech originated from mission control and provided subsystem status updates.

The controls were tangible. The Penphins favored manipulating tiny joysticks over pushing buttons with their squishy, vine-like fingers. Needles wrote sine waves to paper like polygraphs. The closest equivalents to digital controls in the cabin were on-off switches.

HOW DO YOU FEEL? Ari whistled.

"A little uncomfortable," she said. "And claustrophobic. But I'll manage."

THIS SMALL SPACE IS RESTRICTIVE. IS THIS AN INSTANCE IN WHICH WE SHOULD APOLOGIZE?

"No. I appreciate you taking me to my ship. Quite frankly, I wouldn't blame you if you didn't want to expend the resources of your space program to be my personal shuttle service."

Ari directed one quizzical eye bulb toward her. THIS IS WHAT THE SPACECRAFT IS FOR.

"For helping," Maya whispered, smiling. "Don't worry about me. I'll deal with the cramped accommodations."

As if sensing Maya's unrest, Jo commed her and transmitted a live visual feed. The feed showed Maya what her friend saw. Being able to see what was happening outside went a long way toward relieving

Maya's anxiety.

A back-breaking hour later, mission control sang the all-clear, and Ari confirmed their ready status.

No countdown commenced. One moment, Maya sat wedged into her seat. The next, multiple gees of force slammed her back into her chair as the railgun fired the launch vehicle forward along the tracks. Vibrations shook the cabin and chattered her teeth.

Rotating upright, the vehicle threw her onto her back and leapt way from the incline. The first stage engines fired, further shaking the fragile craft despite the decrease in g-force.

After a few minutes, the shuddering ceased, signaling the shutoff of the main rockets. Jarring force rattled her as the first stage fell away.

With far less dramatic flair, the second stage engines ignited.

The planet's gravity released its hold on her body, and she grew lighter.

A slight lurch indicated the second stage shutoff and release.

Orange-red sunlight assaulted her dilated pupils as the payload fairing blew away from the craft.

Unencumbered, the spacecraft soared toward its rendezvous.

Maya scooted to the edge of her seat and gaped at the view outside the porthole. *Horizons* should've been on the other side of the black and pink globe, headed for the third moon. Instead, the ship encircled this side of the planet. Fireworks erupted all around *Horizons* as the destroyer pursued it into a lower orbit.

◆

In the ECC, Trevor ran a palm down his face in a futile attempt to wipe away his miscalculation. He had expected the destroyer to alter course to intercept *Horizons* near the third moon via conventional propulsion, giving him time to blow the natural satellite apart and hurl fragments of it at the enemy ship.

But the destroyer had shifted inside the orbit of the third moon. This bold risk within the gravity well of a planet had landed the predators almost on top of their prey.

Trevor's preemptive strike had gone out the airlock. Left with no other choice, he had scrambled his fighters in defense and fled toward the planet for cover. In a best-case scenario, he could keep the destroyer at the edge of weapons range for a few hours, perhaps a day at best.

He tried not to dwell on how Byrne had been right. Still, his turning tail hadn't stopped her militia from starting firefights in the corridors connecting the biosphere with the defense block. His soldiers had kept them confined to the city, but the civilians had the numerical advantage. If they kept pressing with a willingness to risk their lives, they would break through into the defense and engineering modules at some point.

Leaning back in his seat, he listened to his subordinates' panicked reports and responded without allowing emotion to creep into his voice. Outwardly, he needed to give the impression he had control of the situation until the bitter end. But in reality, all he could do was watch the battle unfold and hope along with everyone else.

♦

All around Erik's Pulsar, the more advanced enemy spacecraft reduced his squad mates to bits of shrapnel.

He downshifted his Pulsar, emerging from hyperspace on the tail of a tri-fighter the moment it reappeared in normal space. Bracketing the bandit in his mental sights, he unleashed a spread of seekers. His support AI predicted at least two should hit the mark with over ninety percent certainty.

The tri-fighter executed an immediate upshift to hyperspace, disappearing off his scope. Meanwhile, eight of ten seconds remained until his fighter's phase drive recharged.

"These bastards don't play fair," Bastet yelled over the comm net, grunting her way through a maneuver.

"I know." Erik scanned for his opponent's point of egress. "No drive charge times. Instantaneous shifts. They've got a definite edge, but at least we're facing even numbers."

"But for how long? They're blanking us three to—"

Bastet's signal cut out as her craft exploded in an all-too-brief flash.

He had a fraction of a second to mourn before his support AI intruded upon his thoughts. It warned him of a tri-fighter popping out of a wormhole behind his Pulsar.

The bandit unleashed a barrage of projectiles.

Erik spun his fighter while zigzagging it in an evasive pattern. Every seeker missed or detonated against another except one, which struck his Pulsar's dorsal shielding. The impact distorted his force field, drove his shoulders up into his seat harness, and sent his craft tumbling.

After stabilizing his fighter's attitude, his AI matrix offered a damage assessment that could have been a hell of a lot worse. The seeker had struck his shielding at an angle rather than head-on, leaving only superficial denting and scorching on the underside of the fuselage.

The course of the dogfight brought him closer to the planet. For some reason, the tri-fighter that had attacked him was rocketing toward it rather than continuing the fight.

His AI mapped the bandit's trajectory. Two other tri-fighters followed paths with the intention to rendezvous with it. A slow-moving object rising up out of the atmosphere presented a likely target.

His AI identified the object as a shell craft. Bioscans revealed two Penphins and one human aboard.

Twenty-eight—Rescussor
Jupiter Trojans (Greek Camp), September 2272 CE

The inordinate amount of time Brooke had spent in confinement hadn't inured her to captivity. *Nautilus's* brig may have provided the solitude she so often craved, but being held against one's will sucked all the introspective bliss out of alone-time.

Sulking, she leaned back against the headrest of the twin bed and hugged her knees atop the comforter. The lavish room looked more like a featureless hotel suite than a holding cell, complete with a separated washroom. The ship's fabricators had fashioned her prison jumpsuit from a material silkier than anything she owned.

The solid wall beyond the foot of the bed reminded her of the room's true nature. Through the one-way partition, the guards on the other side could see her but she couldn't see them.

When she wasn't berating herself for failing to divert the ship, she worried about Zeke. She assumed the captain had figured out he had been responsible for knocking the crew out and was keeping him under sedation. The skipper had probably ordered him taken to the infirmary where the medical staff had uncovered the differences in his physiology. If they had allowed him to wake up, he would have taken control of the people around him and busted Brooke out of her cell by now.

She lauded the captain's quick assessment of the situation and the tactics she had employed to stop her. Having realized the intruders could somehow sedate and manipulate humans, she had flooded the room with knockout gas and sent in technology Zeke couldn't control. Clever.

Try as she might, Brooke still couldn't place the captain's voice. Her thick Aussie inflections had struck Brooke as familiar, but perhaps her unrefined hearing couldn't distinguish one accent from the next. Maybe when she had gone to see Ajunwa in Melbourne, she had heard someone similar. The guard who had brought her last meal had stated Captain Gibbons would be along to interrogate her, but the name hadn't triggered any recollection.

Tipping her head back, Brooke closed her eyes. She kept picturing *New Horizons* slamming into the centaur and exploding, killing Maya in the process. *Even if I hadn't botched the only chance I had to get out there, she might still be dead.* She punched the mattress.

A faint whooshing—the sound of the wall fading from opaque to transparent—reached her ears.

The intercom buzzed.

When she heard the captain's accent, she directed her gaze forward.

"Well, I'll be damned." Behind the transparent wall, a familiar face that had aged with time studied her with amusement.

Brooke blinked to make sure her vision wasn't playing tricks on her. "Ruby?"

Captain Gibbons placed a hand on her hip. "No one's used my call sign in twenty years." Smirking, she asked, "So what in bloody hell were you trying to do to my ship, Angel?"

Feeling the weight lift from her shoulders, Brooke said, "That's going to take some explaining, but I promise you I had a good reason."

"I look forward to hearing it." Gibbons ordered the guards to escort Brooke to her command cabin and marched off.

Thirty minutes later, Brooke sat facing Gibbons across her desk in the plush office adjacent to the main command center.

"Dismissed," Gibbons told the man and woman who had led Brooke there.

Hesitating, the officers' glances danced between their skipper and the prisoner.

"We'll be fine." Gibbons shooed them away with a flick of the wrist. "Angel here is an honorable woman—a questionable decision-maker, but honorable." Resting her elbows on the desk, she intertwined her fingers, set her chin atop them, and winked at her guest. "If it turns out she isn't, I'm confident I can take her."

The officers looked at one another in resignation and exited the room.

Unable to manifest a smile at the jibe, Brooke studied her former subordinate. The Amazonian woman had at least a head on her, height-wise. From the definition in the muscles beneath her Defense uniform, she frequented the calisthenics facilities aboard ship. Her overall look and attitude did little to dispel the stereotype of tough women from the Australian outback.

Such observations made Brooke a little self-conscious. While she had stayed in reasonable shape over the years, her figure wasn't quite as chiseled as it had been in her twenties. "You've still got that beguiling confidence, but you've changed, too, Ruby—I mean, Captain Gibbons. Of course, we only knew each other for a few months."

"Call me by my first name, Tess." Gibbons stood. Opening a cabinet, she pulled out a bottle of scotch. "I've had to do a lot of growing up to get where I am. After Huygens, I flew against the Greys when they attacked Earth and nearly tuned out half a dozen times. Afterwards, I decided I didn't want to die in a cockpit." She set two short glasses down on the desk and popped the crystalline bottle open. "Most of us lack your raw talent behind the stick. Drink?"

Brooke shook her head. "No thank you, Tess. Alcohol's never agreed with me." She refrained from mentioning the convulsions that might result because of her condition. Years ago, she had tried drinking in hopes of soothing the nerve damage brought about by her spark use, but the experiment had backfired. Alcohol suppressed the inhibitions that kept her symptoms subdued, leaving her more vulnerable to muscle spasms.

"Suit yourself." Gibbons poured a glass for herself. "Can I get you anything else?"

"Water, please."

The captain retreated to the sink in her private kitchenette. After filling the other glass, she handed it to her guest. "Cheers."

Brooke clinked glasses with her host and asked, "What happened to my friend?"

"Your accomplice is sleeping comfortably in the medical bay. I've got more than a few questions about him, but they can wait until we've reminisced." Gibbons gulped down half her drink and topped it off.

While sipping her water, Brooke looked around the command cabin. A sofa and lounge chair rested against the wall next to the kitchenette behind Gibbons's desk. Stars scrolled past the two long, narrow viewports running the length of the deck. Medals, plaques, and vidpics paying tribute to the life of Tess Gibbons adorned the walls. One cataloged a safari she had undertaken in the Australian bush with friends. Another showed her shaking an admiral's hand while accepting her promotion to captain.

Brooke hid a frown behind her glass. The footage of the ceremony conjured up buried dreams of what she might've accomplished in another lifetime. If she hadn't defied Ajunwa and gone to rescue Maya, she might be the one occupying this room.

Then again, raising her niece had been the most rewarding experience of her life. As she perused the small museum's worth of memorabilia, she didn't see any evidence of a significant other or children. *Success seems to have its price.*

She gave a start when she noticed the vidpic her fighter squadron had captured while stranded on Titan in 2247. The footage featured her team, Ruby, the surviving children, and herself posing in a group.

"Takes me back every time I look at it." Swirling her scotch, Gibbons swiveled her chair toward the vidpic. "You kept us together in an impossible situation. I owe you my life."

Dipping her brow, Brooke said, "We worked together to get out of there."

"That we did. Then we both moved on to bigger things. You went down in history as the first to go post-luminal." The captain took another swig and refaced her visitor. "I've followed you ever since. Your life has taken some, shall we say, perplexing turns. You quit the service and went into teaching, a move that never seemed quite right to me. Then you did time for stealing a Pulsar near Pluto. And now I find you aboard my ship, trying to sabotage it. So what gives?"

With both hands, Brooke cupped the glass in her lap and stared down at it, mulling over how best to respond. Gibbons was asking for the motivations behind her life story. Brooke had never much liked talking about herself. Plus, the answers required knowledge of things few people knew, even now with the Vril exposed.

"My sister was killed in the war," she began, "so I left to raise my niece. If I'd died in combat, Maya would have been left all alone." Brooke finished her water. "The destruction of the telescope array and my being here were botched attempts to save her."

Gibbons furrowed her brow as she put away the scotch and refilled her guest's drink. "But your niece and *Horizons* were declared lost."

"Declared, yes, but they're still out there."

"How do you know?"

How? Brooke almost laughed. *Based on a crazy theory about sentient AIs committing acts of sabotage with time travel and an exokid's sixth sense, that's how.* The story sounded ridiculous, and she didn't have a single shred of hard evidence to back it up.

The captain plopped back down into her seat. "With all due respect, don't tell me you're not willing to let your niece go."

Brooke's mouth hung partway open as she came to a decision. Despite a blunder that should've extinguished her last hope to reach Maya, good fortune had placed a former comrade in prime position to assist her. In order to gain Gibbons's trust and cooperation, Brooke needed to tell her the full truth without holding back.

"Maya means everything to me," she said. "I'd pursue the slimmest chance of her still being alive to an early grave. But it's not just me. There're so many things that've led up to this, and it's all because of the Vril."

The lines in Gibbons's forehead creased. "I don't think I'll ever get over how we fought a fake war. Thousands of people died for nothing. Bloody conspirators." She directed a suspicious glare at Brooke. "What do you have to do with them?"

"That depends. How long do we have?"

The captain summoned a display cube and swiped a finger through it. "Engineering's finished purging the program you uploaded to the drive OS. The crew's performing final system checks prior to launch. We're scheduled to depart in about an hour." She waved the cube away. "But we leave whenever I say we leave, so you've got as long as it takes."

Brooke drew in a breath and began her tale, starting with the destruction of the water treatment plant on Europa in 2247. She explained how UN Security President Collins had manipulated her and her career, how she had cheated her way into the history books by sparking, how stealing the phase fighter prototype to rescue Maya had resulted in Ajunwa booting her from the military, and how the Vril had worked behind the scenes to hold the ISC together out of fear of the real extrasolar threat.

For seventeen years, she had wondered whether she had seen the last of the Vril. Then a defecting agent had showed up in her bedroom one morning, throwing her life into turmoil all over again. After learning the organization planned to exterminate the Penphins and sacrifice *Horizons* to shock mankind into good behavior, she had uncovered an exochild with mind-control abilities, found out *Horizons* had skipped seven years in hyperspace, allowed the telescope array to be destroyed in a failed attempt to contact Maya, and been responsible for releasing the evidence the ISC was using to round-up the Vril.

She ended with, "I'm not proud of all of the things I did. But each seemed necessary at the time."

Throughout the monologue, Gibbons had nodded here and there, pursed her lips, and raised the occasional eyebrow. Now, she sat running her fingers around the rim of her empty glass. "So you were hoping to rig my ship for a detour." She chuckled. "I can't say I would've done any differently in your place."

"I know I'm not deserving of any favors, but I still have to ask."

The captain pushed to her feet and performed an up-close inspection of the vidpic taken on Titan, sighing. "I sympathize with your story, Angel. I knew there had to be more behind the decisions you've made, assuming it's all true." She shook her head. "But I'm afraid I can't help you. I can't justify violating orders and taking a ship the ISC has spent the better part of the last decade constructing on an unauthorized year-long rescue mission. Not with full-scale war imminent. I'm sorry."

"If we don't go, that destroyer will kill everyone aboard *Horizons* and eradicate one of the few intelligent species known to exist. Surely, that trumps the latest homeland squabble."

"I don't disagree, but it's not that simple." Gibbons whirled to face her. "I swore an oath when I took this command—nay, when I joined Defense. My word means something to me."

"I respect that, but doesn't this qualify as one of those rare exceptions? Duty shouldn't mean blind obedience."

"If that were the only consideration, maybe, but the larger concern is the war."

"You keep talking about all-out war like it's a foregone conclusion. I see a lot of political unrest, but there's no guarantee everybody's going to start blasting everybody else. If anything, the fall of the ISC should give everyone the independence they want."

"Despite the story the media's spinning, talk of the ISC falling is premature. The council and those in power aren't going to stand by and let every nation-state go on their merry way. This ship is a testament to that." Gibbons sat on the side of her desk and lowered her voice. "The public knows every major government entity has been stockpiling arms for years, but what's not as well-known is the extent of the buildup. Everyone's been constructing a fleet to protect their own interests, and many more skirmishes have broken out than the one involving the Vril transport to Mars."

The captain leaned over to her desk and called up a tactical display cube showing a map of the solar system. Using her thumb and forefinger, she expanded the volume of space in the vicinity of Uranus. Red highlighting colored one of the planet's moons. "I assume you've heard about the 'accident' that happened on Oberon?"

"The news feeds said the phase port's antimatter reactor lost containment and exploded, taking out half the colony."

"That's the official story. In actuality, the new Kuiper Belt Alliance bombed the phase port, cutting Eris and Makemake off from the rest of the solar system. The attack was the KBA's declaration of independence." She leaned in closer to her visitor. "*Nautilus's* shakedown actually took place a week ago. We're here in space dock repairing minor damage from being ambushed during the flight. When we launch again, we'll be heading out to Eris to 'disband' this new alliance."

"So the war's already begun," Brooke mumbled in a daze. "It's madness."

Gibbons shrugged. "Maybe, but orders are orders. And I, for one, believe in not letting what I've fought for all my life fall—" She cut herself off as her eyes shifted back and forth, reviewing something in her i-cite. "Speak of the devil."

The captain bolted past her and out the door. Hopping up, Brooke followed her onto the bridge.

Nautilus's primary command center resembled its counterpart aboard *New Horizons*. Brooke had never visited the latter ship, but Maya had showed her so many sims of it that she felt as if she had been there. The captain's chair rested atop a raised circular platform in the center of the room. Occupied by Commander Yermakov, the first officer's seat was situated to the right of the big chair and behind the remote sensing, navigation, and tactical stations. Manned control stations lined the edges of the bridge. Holocubes littered the air, floating like clouds. Mammoth display screens adorned every wall, acting like viewports. They showed a full 360-degree view outside the ship despite the room's location at the center of the command module.

As Gibbons stepped atop the platform, she barked, "Report."

A security officer stopped Brooke at the railing surrounding the platform.

"Eight wormhole exit points confirmed," Yermakov said in gruff baritone. His thick Russian accent grated against Brooke's eardrums. "Spacecraft carriers hailing from the Confederacy of Texan Colonies, African Star Union, and East Martian Coalition."

"So they're hoping to catch us with our trousers 'round our ankles," the captain mused.

"Even eight's a suicide mission against the ISC flagship."

"All hands: general quarters."

At their duty stations, officers hastily prepared the ship for battle.

A cube bigger than Brooke's habitat on Makemake materialized at the front of the bridge. The display showed eight pinpoints of light brighter than the surrounding stars. Magnification increased until the hulls of the approaching carriers filled the cube.

Gibbons turned to her guest. "Now you see why we can't leave."

Brooke tried to push past the guard, but he blocked her path.

The captain instructed the man to stand aside.

Gripping the railing, Brooke looked up at her former teammate. An angst-riddled sense of urgency surged through her. "This is why you have to listen to me. What good will fighting this battle or future battles do?"

"It'll make them think twice about seceding," Yermakov said.

"Will it, though?"

"Once we paste their *zhopas*, they won't dare oppose us."

"So the ISC's brilliant plan is to beat the rest of the solar system into submission? Don't you see what's happening here?"

Gibbons lowered her posterior into her seat. "We're becoming a dictatorship."

Brooke ran around the railing and stepped up onto the platform. "Exactly. What will the ISC do if it wins? Rule with an iron fist?"

"But if we give in, the solar system descends into anarchy."

"Either way, it's a no-win situation."

The officer at the remote sensing station swiveled his chair to face them. "Weapons range in ten minutes."

"Arm all weapons and prepare to disembark." Pursing her lips at her visitor, Gibbons said, "So your alternative is to run away? This flagship was built to dictate the outcome of the war. Any action I take has to fall in line with that objective." She drew out her last sentence as if she wanted convincing.

Brooke sensed the opening. "Then consider the political climate when *Horizons* first shipped out. People were captivated by humankind's first-ever flight of fancy from the solar system. Forty billion hopes and dreams soared when that beloved ship left and plunged when it was lost."

"Point being?"

"If you stay here and fight, you'll be making a bad situation worse. But if we go and bring *Horizons* back, it may be enough to affect a ceasefire."

"Let's say we succeed," Gibbons said. "Do you honestly think news of the ship's return would persuade everyone to set aside their differences and get along?"

"Maybe, maybe not. At the very least, it would be the first positive news in years. It's a better plan than trying to beat everyone into submission."

"Seven minutes," the remote sensing officer said.

After gripping her armrests in thought, Gibbons rose to her feet. "Unfortunately, I can't see any way around engaging the ships coming this way."

Brooke's arms drooped. "But . . ." She let her words trail off at the sight of the captain's smirk.

"You don't think they'll let us shift out of the system without a fight, now, do you?" The captain stepped closer to navigation. "Prepare calculations for a shift to the Gliese 581 system." She stared up at the main display cube before turning back to Brooke. "We'll affect some shock and awe by blanking these drongos before we take our leave. Call it a compromise."

"I can live with that." Shaking off the giddiness induced by her triumph, Brooke asked, "How quickly can we get there?"

"*Nautilus* is faster than *Horizons*. Astrodynamics is determining the exact timespan, but the trip should take somewhere between four and five months."

"We need to get there in four. It's September now, and that destroyer will downshift in January." Brooke sent Gibbons the estimated date and time Shin had given her.

The captain blew out a sigh. "Four might be pushing it, but I'll see what the whiz kids in Astro can come up with." She folded her arms. "One more thing. Since I'm doing you a favor, it's only fair you return it."

"Of course. Anything."

"I can't have a prisoner loitering on my bridge during a battle."

"I understand." Brooke gave a slow, resigned nod. "Do you want me to go back to my cell?"

Gibbons gawped at her and laughed through her nose. "Ensign," she yelled, flagging down a young man hurrying past the platform. "Find the Colonel here a proper uniform and flight gear. Have the hangar prep her ride."

"Yes, ma'am." The ensign saluted and rushed off.

Brooke blinked at her. Chills and hot flashes coursed up and down her spine.

"What's with the stupid look?" Gibbons slapped her on the shoulder. "You do remember how to pilot a star fighter, right?"

Untying her tongue, Brooke stammered, "Of course, but—"

"And you're still Brooke Davis, right? The greatest pilot of them all?"

"I don't know if I'd go that far—"

"All my flyboys and girls are raw. My fighter wing commander was in diapers when you and I last flew together. Assume his position. He'll be your dash-two."

"Okay, but—"

"Now get down to the launch bay and order the handling officer to familiarize you with things."

"Right."

"Right?" Gibbons mocked her. "Colonel, how is it we address a superior officer?"

A smile crept its way onto Brooke's face, and she saluted. "Yes, ma'am."

♦

By way of sonic tube, Brooke arrived at *Nautilus's* main hangar with under three minutes to scramble. A spacecraft handling officer, Lieutenant Kealoha, jogged alongside her from the entrance, explaining the most important launch and flight protocols while leading her toward her fighter.

As they rounded a row of Pulsars, she slowed her pace at the sight of her ride, a new type of fighter craft she had never seen. Kealoha identified it as the YPF-17 Blazar. Only the prototype had come off the assembly line before funding had been lost, he said.

Bulkier than a PF-5C Pulsar, the next gen fighter didn't perform as well in atmosphere but surpassed its predecessor in every other way. Antimatter reactors had rendered fusion engines obsolete. The craft could manufacture relativistic seekers as fast is it could launch them. It still possessed backup particle cannons, but relativistic beaming emitters had replaced them as the primary guns. Similar to the stellar phenomenon of the craft's namesake, the emitters extruded jets of plasma at speeds near that of light.

She did a double-take when the lieutenant revealed that the designers of its phase drive had done away with charge times. The Blazar could shift in and out of hyperspace on a whim, the number of times limited only by its antimatter supply.

After two androids helped her don her flight armor and helmet, she shook hands with her wing mate and climbed into the cockpit.

The canopy grew out of the fuselage of the craft and congealed to seal her inside. When she settled into her seat, its cushioning conformed to her contours, holding her in place snugly but not uncomfortably. A restraint field shimmered around her body, taking the place of a physical seat harness. She found that she could make slow, gradual movements, but sudden motions of her torso or legs met with great resistance.

She interfaced with her craft's support AI. Gravgel rushed in to immerse her as the Blazar's launch platform dropped through the deck and flipped. The bay doors opened, and her fighter emerged atop the platform, latched to the hull.

Detaching her craft, she thrusted away from the ship and fell in behind the 480 Pulsars under her command.

The ensuing skirmish flashed her back to her brief tour as Jovian wing commander. It took a great deal more self-discipline to hang back and coordinate the logistics from afar than to charge headlong into the thick of things.

Ironically, her years as a flight instructor aided her as much as her firsthand combat experience. Both served her well, but she found herself employing the same strategies and correcting the same mistakes in this real fight as she had in her simulated classes. She directed traffic, coordinated with the flight controller aboard the bridge, and barked orders, trying her best to remain diplomatic in light of the rookie blunders that she witnessed.

The enemy fielded older model Pulsars with pilots lacking ISC Defense training, giving her forces a distinct advantage. Captain Gibbons's offensive strategy reflected an understanding of the superiority her vessel possessed over any other. With unbridled ruthlessness, she charged *Nautilus* straight at the approaching ships, forcing them to veer off course. From its launch tubes, the ISC flagship fired warheads the size of antique Gemini rockets that blasted through the carriers' force fields and ripped apart their hulls.

In one maneuver, Gibbons plunged her ship straight at a Texan carrier, unloading its plasma ejectors at point-blank range. The carrier's midsection buckled, and it tore apart, leaving two halves of a broken ship.

With five carriers adrift or destroyed, the remaining three recalled their fighter units and retreated. Brooke recalled her forces, of which she had lost twenty-three units.

Only when her Blazar rested in its launch struts back on *Nautilus's* hull did she allow her muscles to relax. She may have regained her commission in unofficial and illegitimate capacity, but she refused to let that sour what she had accomplished.

"Nice work, Colonel."

Brooke nodded at Gibbons's image in her i-cite.

"By the way," the captain said, "the kids in Astro have calculated the absolute fastest shift we can manage without bleeding our fuel reserves dry."

Nautilus's estimated time of arrival in the Gliese 581 system popped up in front of Brooke's eyes. The date was two days after the destroyer would downshift.

"Let's hope *Horizons* can manage until we get there," Gibbons said.

"Let's hope," Brooke echoed. A comingling of trepidation and anticipation heightened her breathing.

The captain signed off.

As the bay doors slid closed above Brooke's descending fighter, she watched the rush of hyperspace replace the stars above her head.

Now, she thought, her real mission could begin.

Twenty-nine—Confluence
Gliese 581 System, January 2273 CE

Her back aching, Maya sat wedged within the uncomfortable acceleration chair aboard the Penphin shell craft.

YOUR SHIP HAS DEVIATED FROM ITS EXPECTED COURSE, Ari said.

Increasing magnification, Maya watched *Horizons* and the destroyer disappear over the horizon of the Penphins's home world. *The destroyer must've risked shifting closer to the planet, which would've thrown off Trevor's entire plan.*

A speaker in the cabin sang. HIGH LIGHT AND ENERGY EMISSIONS ARE TAKING PLACE NEAR THE TWO VESSELS, whistled a mission controller from the surface. THESE DISCHARGES SERVE NO DISCERNABLE PURPOSE, YET THEY COULD LESSEN BOTH SHIPS. WE ARE SCANNING TO FIND THE REASON.

WHAT IS HAPPENING? Ari asked.

Maya slouched even more so than the chair forced her to do. "They're fighting."

FIGHTING. WE HAVE HEARD YOU USE THIS TERM BUT WE STILL STRUGGLE WITH ITS MEANING.

"Let's hope you always do."

After a moment, Ari sang, WE COULD INCREASE SPEED AND

CHANGE INCLINATION TO ALLOW YOUR SHIP TO CATCH UP TO US.

"No," she said. "As much as I want to go back, we can't risk going anywhere near those energy emissions, or we'll be blown to pieces."

WHAT WOULD YOU LIKE US TO DO?

She was mulling her options when Erik commed her.

"Maya!" his image yelled in her i-cite. The volume of his voice and his heavy breathing conveyed uncharacteristic fear. "Perform evasive maneuvers!"

"Maneuvers?" she asked, hoping against all reason he wasn't warning her about what she thought. "Why?"

"Three enemy fighters are headed your way. They'll enter weapons range in under two minutes."

A chilling twinge of panic shot through her.

She checked the altitude dials and looked down at the fluffy pink clouds below her. The fragile craft couldn't possibly reenter the atmosphere—much less land—in two minutes.

♦

Downshifting his Pulsar on the tail of one of the three tri-fighters, Erik stole a brief moment to praise his good fortune. The bandits could have shifted straight to Maya's position and destroyed the Penphins's spacecraft in a second or two, but they had opted to approach it using conventional propulsion. Perhaps their curiosity had gotten the better of them. Maybe they hadn't realized who or what they were going after, so they had decided to creep up on it. Either way, it didn't matter. Their dallying had allowed him to catch up.

He unleashed a barrage of seekers at the closest tri-fighter. The bandit jettisoned countermeasures, taking out half his projectiles, and upshifted before the rest struck it.

The other two triangles disappeared into hyperspace.

With his pulse throbbing, he kept his mind on the trigger, waiting for the bandits to reemerge. He cursed his charge timer, which still had five seconds to go, as well as his limited antimatter supply. His Pulsar couldn't remain in hyperspace for long without sucking his reserves dry.

All three tri-fighters appeared at once, surrounding him with a pincer attack. They fired their particle cannons at his Pulsar but refrained from launching missiles, wary of a stray hitting an ally at such close range.

Erik spun and stair-stepped his fighter while returning fire. His support AI's guidance allowed him to dodge over ninety-percent of the rapid blasts but a number of them still struck his craft's shielding. He clenched his stomach muscles as the impact jarred the cockpit. His Pulsar's force field shimmered orange.

He darted toward the nearest of the three bandits, hoping the other two would hold their fire in fear of hitting their comrade. If it worked, he would gain a small window of time in which he would only have to deal with the closest enemy.

Instead, the tri-fighter he was racing toward shifted away. The others launched a volley of crisscrossing seekers at him.

His charge timer hit zero, and he upshifted before the projectiles got him. From hyperspace, his instruments showed the seekers detonating at the location he had vacated.

He considered shifting to the Penphins's craft to defend it, but that would draw the bandits closer to Maya. He dismissed the idea.

After locating one of the three tri-fighters in normal space—the other two must have upshifted—he emerged facing the underside of the first triangle's fuselage and unleashed everything he had at it. Strangely, the bandit pulled few avoidance maneuvers. His beams and one of the seekers hit home, almost knocking out its force field.

The other two triangles appeared on opposite sides of his craft and flung more missiles his way. Launching countermeasures, he rolled his Pulsar out from in between them and toward the planet.

Before his charge timer hit zero, two of the warheads pelted his fighter. The first overloaded his force field. The second drove his helmet back against his headrest. Pain drilled into his skull. Dizziness muddled his thinking and vision.

His support AI informed him he had suffered a concussion.

Shaking off his disorientation, he found that the AI had righted the Pulsar's attitude, reduced speed, and set an orbit for atmosphere entry. His canopy had cracked, allowing gravgel to leak out into space. Warning icons flashed in his augmented reality. His fighter had lost main power.

Without the ability to withstand significant g-force, he knew the tri-fighters could finish him off if they wanted. He couldn't shift out of danger without power. Thrusters still functioned, so his only option was to set down on the planet, as his AI had deduced.

Neudar showed the three tri-fighters had resumed course for the shell craft.

He slapped the armrest in frustration—an act which lacked much force within the gravgel—and contacted Maya.

◆

"I couldn't stop them," Erik told her. "I'm sorry, I . . ."

Maya felt his disgust. "You did what you could. All you can do now is concentrate on getting down in one piece."

"I can at least keep tabs on the approaching bogeys. You've got less than a minute until they're on top of you."

"Okay, thanks." She forced her dry throat to swallow. "Don't worry. Everything will work out."

While living in that lie, she wished for someone to comfort her. She also fantasized that, maybe, the Vril wanted to seize the craft and capture her.

She turned to Ari. "In all likelihood, we're about to become less, as you might say."

Ari bobbed his snout. SUCH IS THE WAY OF LIFE. WE HAVE LEARNED AND BECOME MUCH MORE SINCE YOU ARRIVED. IT HAS BEEN A POSITIVE EXPERIENCE, IF I HAVE YOUR SONG CORRECT.

One corner of her mouth curled at the Penphin's viewpoint, but the smile faded. "I'm sorry we brought all this turmoil upon you." She hung her head. "As wonderful as it's been getting to know you, we never should've come here." Snorting, she added, "Maybe Trevor and my father were right. Maybe we should've stayed in our own solar system."

CONTACT HAD TO OCCUR WITH ANOTHER SPECIES AT SOME POINT IN TIME. WE FEEL OTHERS BESIDES YOU MIGHT HAVE BEEN LESS.

"You mean, you think contact with humans was best? Some of my people intend to eradicate yours, so I can't say I agree."

NO, YOU MISUNDERSTAND. WE ARE NOT ACCUSTOMED TO THINKING IN INDIVIDUAL TERMS, BUT WE MEAN CONTACT WITH THE SINGLE YOU.

"Me?"

YES. WE CANNOT FEEL YOU DIRECTLY, BUT WE CAN SENSE YOUR HELPFUL INTENTIONS.

Emotion overwhelmed her. She drew in a prolonged breath, blew it out, and wiped a tear from the corner of her eye. "I appreciate that. I only wish I was going to be around to repay the help you've given me."

"Ten seconds to weapons range, Maya," Erik reported.

"I understand. Take care of yourself, Erik." She could sense he wanted to say something more but couldn't find the words.

Finally, he managed to say, "You too."

Maya reached out and held Ari's sinewy, eight-fingered hand. "This is what my people do to show affection."

THIS I UNDERSTAND.

Gazing out the side viewport, she searched for her executioners. At full zoom, she caught three specs of light approaching from a higher orbit.

"They've fired seekers, Maya!" Erik shouted. "Six total. Four seconds to impact."

She resisted the urge to clamp her eyes shut. *Goodbye Aunt Brooke, Uncle Kevin, Jo, and everyone else. At least I had the opportunity to experience this adventure.*

Six deadly twinkles rapidly grew and brightened.

"Holy . . ." Erik gasped.

Space-time warped and distorted kilometers from the shell craft. Concentric waves rippled outward from the central wormhole. An object appeared and disappeared in the center, moving away from the craft quicker than Maya could follow.

All six seekers exploded against the distortion waves, throwing off the spacecraft's attitude. The pilot fired thrusters and re-oriented it.

◆

Unwilling to abandon his friend until the bitter end, Erik had delayed re-entering the atmosphere and remained in a low orbit. Now, he sprang forward in his seat, unable to believe his displays.

A type of star fighter his AI couldn't identify had re-entered normal space for a millisecond. The pilot had disabled the fighter's wake limiter on emergence, stayed ahead of the gravimetric turbulence to avoid obliteration, and upshifted again. The distortions from the wake had acted as a shield and destroyed the seekers, protecting the fragile spacecraft behind it.

His support AI insisted the calculations necessary to pull off such a maneuver remained beyond the AI's capabilities. No matter how great the technical feat, Erik knew the stunt had required a ridiculous degree of human skill and daring.

He tracked the three tri-fighters. One exploded the instant the new fighter appeared again. A second blew apart before it could upshift.

The last triangle shifted to hyperspace, and the newcomer did the same.

◆

Above the curvature of the planet in the distance, two flashbulb explosions caught Maya's attention. As the lights were flickering out, a tri-fighter downshifted outside the porthole, darting right at the shell craft.

She didn't have time to gasp.

Bright purple beams sliced through the tri-fighter's force field, tinting it to dark orange. The ensuing explosion whited out everything.

Clamping her eyes shut, she whipped her face away from the porthole and threw her arm up to shield her head.

The light dimmed as quickly as it had blinded her.

When she opened her eyes and refaced the window, Maya saw a squarer version of a Pulsar with heavier armaments. The more advanced fighter floated between the remnants of the explosion and the shell craft, shielding it. Shards of debris struck the new fighter's force field, which glistened a darker shade of blue.

Ari and the pilot removed their flings from their eyes.

She accepted a comm request from the fighter.

"Maya, please tell me you're okay."

"Aunt Brooke . . ."

"Thank the stars."

Only now did the magnitude of Maya's near-death experience hit her. "Oh, Auntie, is that really you?" She trembled and whimpered.

"Yes, squirt, yes it is."

Another voice came over the channel.

<I'm pleased to hear you remain living, Maya.>

"Bob?"

A THIRD VESSEL IS APPROACHING THE PLANET, mission control sang.

♦

When *Nautilus* had first downshifted after four months in hyperspace, its sensors had found debris near *Horizons's* arrival point and the centaur, now farther along in its orbit.

Brooke had dropped to her knees on the deck of *Nautilus's* bridge in anguish. She had shown up too late, she had assumed.

But remote sensing hadn't discovered enough wreckage for the impact to have destroyed the ship.

Seconds later, sensing had detected the Vril destroyer approaching the Penphins' home world and what remained of *New Horizons* in orbit. Gibbons had wasted little time calling for general quarters and shifted the ship closer to the planet.

Brooke had ordered the fighter wing to scramble and rushed to the hangar bay.

Before she had issued the mental command to catapult the Blazar away from the hull, a secure uplink request had appeared in her i-cite. The transmission had requested she overwrite her fighter's AI matrix, so she had almost dismissed it as Vril subterfuge. But upon validating the sender, she had donned a warm smile and accepted the uplink. Her neurotronic display interfaces had flickered, gone offline for a few seconds, and flashed back to life. That was when she had heard the voice of a dear old friend.

There had been no time to reminisce. Bob had been tracking Maya since she had gone down to the planet via the surveillance satellites *Horizons* had placed in orbit. The Penphins had launched her from the planetary surface in one of their spacecraft, and three tri-fighters had targeted it. The moment Brooke had learned of her niece's peril, she had disembarked from *Nautilus* and shifted to the rescue.

Now, with the three immediate threats dispatched and Maya alive and well, Brooke allowed herself a brief moment to indulge in the fulfillment of her dream. *I finally made it, Dad,* she thought while reveling in her surroundings. The rays of the red dwarf star tinted her cockpit to shades of amber and scarlet. Meanwhile, the odd beauty of the planet's coffee-colored continents, amaranth oceans, and pink clouds filled her with an unfamiliar sense of tranquility. *I'm here in another star system.*

◆

"I'm retreating like you wanted," Trevor insisted. He mind-spoke to Byrne over an audio-only channel via his implants. She refused to provide a visual feed.

Shooting to his feet in the ECC, he did his best to keep his tone level.

His attention darted between cubes showing tri-fighters blanking his fighter wing all around the ship and the destroyer closing the gap between them. The Greys' vessel should've been hitting *Horizons* with long-range weaponry by now but had thus far held back. The fact his enemy hadn't seized an obvious tactical advantage unsettled his stomach far more so than if the ship was taking heavy fire—not that he was complaining.

What he did have cause to gripe about was how the mayor and her militia were taking over the ship.

"Stop this mutiny and return control of the armory to me—please," he said. "I can't defend the ship without weapons."

"You had your chance to concede," Byrne snapped.

"Is there no reasoning with you?" Trevor pleaded. "I'm doing what you asked."

"Yes, but only after the Greys foiled your plan. If we'd fled rather than staging an attack, we'd have a larger buffer between us and them."

"Until they shifted closer to us again."

Byrne snorted, scoffing at the notion. "This ship needs a leader who makes decisions in the best interest of all those aboard."

"You don't have any military or starship operations training."

"I know how to lead. I'll put that up against your desire to charge to your death any day of the week."

Clenching his fingers, Trevor glowered around the ECC. The chatter of battle-speak filled the room. Sweat beaded off of foreheads creased in concentration. Ensign Jenelle Williams applied continual adjustments to the ship's orbit to keep the destroyer at bay as long as possible. Ensign Tokala Sigo coordinated the AIs controlling the ship's guns, launch tubes, and defensive systems, working to keep tri-fighters from going on strafing runs along *Horizons's* hull.

Williams and Sigo were loyal officers as, far as he knew. Somehow, Byrne had gotten to some of his people and turned them. She couldn't have taken the armory otherwise. The munitions storage facility was one of the most heavily guarded locations on the ship. All his orders to flood the sections she occupied with knockout gas had gone unfulfilled. What had she done or said to them, he wondered? Promised three meals a day? Lied about how she had a way to get them home? Convinced them a politician was better qualified to command a starship than the top-ranking graduate from the ISC Defense Academy? Try as he might, he couldn't fathom the infidelity she had sowed among the crew.

With traitors in key positions on her side and a growing number of supporters—including a civilian population outnumbering the crew—it was a matter of time until she showed up on his doorstep, calling for his head.

"Respectfully, I'll ask you one last time," he said. "Please release control of the armory."

"Please release control of this ship," came her curt reply.

Growling under his breath, Trevor closed the channel and came to a decision. He had shown Byrne every courtesy. He had given her every opportunity to stand down. He had been far more diplomatic than most famous commanders in Earth's history.

He waved over his acting chief security officer.

"Sir?" Ensign Rashard Knight jogged over and saluted.

"I want Byrne stopped," Trevor ordered.

Knight shifted in his stance. "My teams are working on it, sir."

"Civilized tactics aren't getting the job done. We're facing a life or death situation."

"What are you saying, sir?"

Trevor held the man's gaze. "I'm saying we're done treating her as a compatriot with rights and privileges. Assemble a team of officers you can trust, locate her exact whereabouts, and drag her here by the hair."

"Yes, sir."

As Knight turned to leave, Trevor grabbed his arm. "Ensign, if she refuses to come . . ."

Peering back over his shoulder, Knight hesitated for a moment before nodding. "Understood, sir."

An impact jostled the ship. Trevor stumbled forward and almost fell.

"What the hell was that?" he barked.

Ensign Sadi Pérez shouted at him from her remote sensing station. "A group of tri-fighters have punched through the shielding on a section of the engine block and breached the hull." She waved her hands in front of her interface cubes, gaping. "A spacecraft has downshifted near the breach and is docking."

"In other words, we're being boarded."

"It looks that way, sir."

As if we don't have enough problems, Trevor ruminated, but something didn't seem right about the enemy's actions. Up until now, he had believed the Greys had wanted to eliminate *Horizons*—get the humans out of the way so they didn't interfere with the eradication of the Penphins. Under that assumption, the exobeings had little reason to board the ship. However, their present actions explained why the destroyer hadn't fired at *Horizons*.

So why the house call? he wondered. Why not destroy them and be done with it? What did *Horizons* have that they wanted? Its phase drive? The damaged-beyond-repair EMG? Human prisoners? None of it seemed enticing enough.

Trevor turned to Knight and ordered him to deal with the boarders. The conflict with Byrne would have to wait.

"Sir," Pérez said, "the destroyer's thrusted into an escape orbit."

"They're leaving?" He rushed over to her station. "Right when they had us where they wanted us?"

Her face lit up. "There's a third vessel emerging from the far side of the planet."

Williams bounced up and down in her seat like a child. "The ship's transponder signal indicates it's an ISC Defense warship, but I've never seen anything like it." She put its image up on the main display cube.

"It looks like *Horizons* except no biosphere and heavier armaments," Sigo said.

"The ISC doesn't have warships." Trevor folded his arms. "I guess things have changed back home in seven-plus years."

The cube tracked the warship as it pursued the destroyer out of orbit.

"We're receiving a comm request from the warship, sir," the comm officer said.

He nodded, doing his best to contain his enthusiasm. "Let's hear it."

"This is Captain Gibbons of *Nautilus*," a woman with a thick Australian accent said. "Sit tight while we chase these buggers away. Then we'll see about getting everybody home."

Cheers erupted throughout the ECC.

Trevor contacted Byrne and informed her of the news. When she agreed to a truce, he collapsed in his chair and almost slid off the edge in relief.

◆

The elation Maya had felt at hearing the voice of the beloved aunt who had raised her had given way to abhorrence toward the woman who had murdered her mother.

"Maya, can you still hear me?" Aunt Brooke asked from the Blazar. "Bob, I'm not getting through to the exocraft. Did the channel go dead? Are we being jammed?"

<Negative, ma'am. I cannot reach *New Horizons* or *Nautilus*—most likely due to their proximity to the destroyer—but short-range channels are open.>

"I'm here," Maya replied.

"Thank goodness. Don't scare me like that."

"Sorry, I wouldn't want to withhold anything that might upset you."

Static crackled over the comm before Brooke responded. "Tri-fighters could show up at any moment. We need to get out of here."

"My friends have set course to land on the planet. You can accompany us down—"

"That'll take too long. It'll leave you exposed, and I need to join the fight."

"Then what do you suggest?"

<We should be able to perform a spacecraft-to-spacecraft personnel transfer in approximately one minute.>

"You mean dock ships?" Maya bit her lower lip. "But they're not compatible. I'd need to exit the airlock hatch, you'd need to open your canopy, and I'd have to drift across."

"I don't like it, either." Brooke said. "But the sooner we start, the sooner we'll finish."

Maya turned to Ari within the cramped cabin of the shell craft. "I don't want to abandon you," her wristband whistled.

IS THIS NOT WHY WE BROUGHT YOU? Ari put to her.

Smiling at the creature's ever-straightforward helpfulness, she sucked in a breath. "Okay, let's give it a try."

"My gravgel's draining, and I've given Bob thruster control," Brooke said. "By the time you get out here, we'll be in position."

"Thank you," Maya said to Ari as she worked her way out of her seat and floated into the airlock. "For everything."

YOU ARE WELCOME. Before she swung the inner hatch closed, Ari added, WE WOULD LIKE TO SEE YOUR PLANET IN THE FUTURE.

"I'll return someday and take you back with me. I promise." She shut and locked the inner hatch. After double-checking her suit's life support systems, she pulled the lever to depressurize the airlock.

Popping open the outer hatch, she found her aunt standing in the open cockpit and staring back at her through her helmet visor. The fighter held position a couple meters away.

Leaning over the side of the cockpit, Aunt Brooke extended her hand. "Grab hold."

Maya pushed partway out of the airlock and reached toward her. The tips of their gloved fingers touched.

<I'm detecting a space-time distortion. The appearance of an enemy fighter craft is imminent.>

Brooke pulled her hand back. "Damn it. Abort and prepare to—"

<Please continue with the transfer, ma'am.> As Bob spoke, the Blazar launched a spread of seekers from its dorsal tubes, teetering the fighter. Its thrusters fired, stabilizing it.

Fighting to keep her balance, Brooke stretched out her hand again. Maya pushed all the way out of the airlock and grabbed ahold of her aunt's wrist.

Past the Blazar, Maya watched the projectiles strike a tri-fighter at the same instant it appeared. She ripped her gaze away from the blinding fireworks, losing her grip in the process.

Shrapnel from the explosion struck the fighter's ventral shielding, which Bob must have enabled. Again, the Blazar shifted orientation, and again, its thrusters righted it.

She felt her aunt catch her arm and yank her closer before she drifted away.

Brooke pulled her into the rear seat.

Maya grabbed the backrest of the forward seat and guided herself the rest of the way inside the cockpit.

As she and her aunt settled into their seats, the canopy congealed overhead. A restraining field locked her in place while gravgel rushed in to immerse her.

<Another bandit is about to appear, ma'am.>

The moment the cockpit finished filling, Aunt Brooke spun the Blazar away from the shell craft. Maya's head spun as they upshifted to hyperspace. The strange, mind-bending distortions of a higher dimension surrounded her. A split second later, the fighter returned to the stars, blasting the tri-fighter in front of it. Unable to react in time, the bandit exploded.

Brooke situated the Blazar between the blast and shell craft, protecting it.

At Maya's insistence, they escorted the Penphins into the atmosphere. When the crew module ejected its service module, and the former began to glow a bright orange, Brooke pulled the Blazar up and away from the planet.

"I need to get back to *Horizons*," Maya said over her suit's comm link.

"*Nautilus* has engaged the destroyer." Brooke fired the afterburners and rocketed toward the other side of the planet, driving Maya back into her seat. "I need to join the battle."

<I'm detecting the enemy vessel on an escape trajectory with *Nautilus* in pursuit.>

"Where's *Horizons*?" Maya asked.

<If we follow our present course and perform a seventeen-degree plane change, we'll catch up with it in eight minutes—I'm receiving a comm request from *Nautilus*.>

"Patch it through," Brooke said.

"Colonel," Gibbons said. "We've got 'em on the run, but they're heading further into the system, not out of it. I'd wager they'll turn and punch at some point. I need you back in charge of the fighter wing."

"Understood, Captain." Brooke lifted the Blazar away from the planet.

Maya tapped her cheek in thought. "Wait, where's the destroyer headed?"

"Is that the infamous Ensign Davis I've heard so much about?" Gibbons asked.

"Yes, ma'am."

"They've set course for the second planet, Gliese 581 b."

"Why would they go there?"

"Your guess is as good as mine, Ensign."

Thinking back on what she had learned from the filesim, Bob, and Mendez, Maya said, "It doesn't make sense. The Penphins's home world and *Horizons* should be their target." Her gut tightened. "What if they're trying to lure us away for some reason?"

"They might very well be," Gibbons said, "but we can't let them hang out in the system. They either leave, we destroy them, or they destroy us."

"What about the device you said is aboard *Horizons*, Bob?"

"What device?" Brooke and Captain Gibbons asked at the same time.

<My attempts to learn the function and purpose of the device the Vril hid within the engine block have been unsuccessful. However, the copy of me aboard the ship continues to block the rogue AI from accessing the device.>

"Rogue AI?" Brooke asked.

Puckering her lips, Maya said, "There's more going on here."

"Let's take it one problem at a time," Gibbons said. "The destroyer is the main threat. Once we make sure it can't threaten *Horizons*, we'll deal with these other issues."

"I agree," Brooke said.

Brooke maneuvered the Blazar into formation with the hundreds of other Pulsars flanking *Nautilus*. "I've little doubt the Vril have a few surprises left for us, but like the skipper said, we can't sit around and wait."

Blowing out a long-winded sigh, Maya acquiesced to the wisdom of her elders. "I hope you're right."

Thirty—Feint
Gliese 581 System, January 2273 CE

"And as we left the solar system," Brooke said, finishing her recap of the last seven and a half years, "war was breaking out."

Faint static hissed over the comm, broken up only by the bleeps of her mental displays.

After setting the Blazar on course for orbital insertion around the second planet, she summoned a camera view of the rear seat. Maya sat with her arms at her side, staring out the canopy at the Neptune-sized hot giant designated as Gliese 581 b. Brooke could see enough of her niece's face through her helmet visor to discern a troubled frown. Despite Maya's tense expression, she appeared not to have aged since Brooke had last seen her. Only two months had passed for the girl since Brooke had arrived, but the reality of it still unnerved the parental figure in her.

At last, Maya droned, "Sounds like we were better off stuck out here."

Brooke wrinkled her nose at the response. Their family reunion hadn't manifested quite as blissfully as she had envisioned. Disappointment and irritation commingled in her chest, pressing down on it.

She stiffened her spine and tried again. "I've told you what happened with me while we were apart. I'd like to know what you went through."

"Oh, not much," Maya said. "I survived a crash that killed a third of the crew and all the senior officers. Then a former friend shot and tried to bury me alive."

"And don't forget narrowly escaping the jaws of death when your aunt showed up in the nick of time." Despite Brooke's upbeat tone—or perhaps because of it—her words came out sounding trite and condescending.

"Right . . ."

"Okay, what's up with you? You act like you couldn't care less to see me."

"I care. I just . . ."

"Just what?"

When Maya didn't answer, the turmoil mixing within Brooke's chest gave way to rumbling. "Listen, I went through hell to rescue you." Family or not, she had grown tired of her niece's attitude. "I don't expect heartfelt gratitude, but I do deserve to know why you're upset with me."

"Oh, I see. You're deserving of full disclosure but not me."

"Full disclosure?" Brooke needed a moment to connect the comment to their old argument. "You're still upset about not knowing how your mom died?"

"Actually, I know now—no thanks to you."

Brooke fought the urge to slide down and out of her seat. Perspiration slicked her forehead and palms, so much so she decreased the temperature within her flight armor.

She flinched as Maya snarled, "How could you kill her?"

With her breathing and pulse quickening, Brooke's muscles tensed. She turned over control of the Blazar to Bob, hung her head, and clamped her eyes shut to keep the remorse from overwhelming her. "Maya, I—"

"I can't believe I was raised by the woman who executed my mother. No wonder you refused to tell me."

The horror of Marie's death replayed in Brooke's mind. Tears welled in her eyes, clouding her vision. "I . . ." Her throat tightened. How could she possibly explain?

"Did you feel bad at all when you killed your sister?"

"I loved Marie." Sobs muffled Brooke's words. "She was my best friend. Without her, I wouldn't be alive." A familiar self-loathing consumed her as she blamed herself for her sibling's and parents' deaths all over again. "I didn't mean to—"

"Oh, I'm sure you didn't mean to, but you did what suited your purposes. Tell me, are you still working for the Vril? Was the plan to kill her, kidnap me, and raise a helpless child for your own purposes?"

"Maya, no. I've never worked for the Vril, and I certainly never planned on anything happening to Marie. Everything I've done has been to protect you and stop them."

"'Everything you've done'—like stealing, getting decommissioned, doing time, offing your sister, and missing my speech. Once a felon, always a felon, I suppose."

A seething tremor coursed through Brooke's every appendage. "How dare you? Do you know what I've given up for you? What I went through to get out here?"

Maya sighed. "It makes me wonder if I'm any different—if, deep down, human beings aren't all monsters. Spending time amongst the Penphins has made me wonder." She sniffled. "I used to be such a naïve optimist, but if the heroine I've looked up to my whole life can murder, I could be capable of—"

<Pardon the interruption, Maya,> Bob interjected, <but I believe your negative perceptions are based on skewed data.>

"Skewed data?" Maya folded her arms. "What do you mean—?"

"Colonel." Captain Gibbons's forceful tone usurped the comm net. "The destroyer's dropped into a low orbit on the other side of the planet and will swing around in five minutes. I believe they'll strike at that time, so I need all units in position for a counter offensive."

Blinking the tears out of her eyes, Brooke inhaled and collected herself. "Understood."

Gibbons signed off.

"We'll have to table this discussion for later, squirt," Brooke said.

"Don't call me that," Maya hissed. "I've always hated it."

"Then why haven't you ever said anything before?" Brooke called up the fighter wing deployment charts and began doling out orders.

Maya didn't answer the question, but after a couple minutes, she asked, "So what am I supposed to do? Sit back and enjoy the ride?"

"You'll be anything but bored very shortly."

"I'm not worried about boredom. I need to get back to *Horizons*."

"I'll take you once the destroyer's no longer a threat. In the meantime, be happy you're still alive."

"How long will that last in a star fighter headed into combat?"

"I thought you wanted to be a pilot?"

"'C' students don't get to be fighter jocks, remember?"

Brooke grumbled. *The girl never lets anything go.* "We're a command craft," she said, steering the conversation in another direction. "We should avoid the thick of the battle."

"One stray shot and the Davis family line ends."

"Listen to me closely, Maya. I didn't come all this way to die. I won't let anything happen to you. I promise."

To Brooke's relief, her niece's tone softened. "I'm going to hold you to that."

♦

All Maya could do was stress over everything while playing the passive passenger. She grappled with her aunt's misdeeds, news from back home, the situation here, and her personal demons until her brain went numb.

She studied the second planet. It looked like a cross between Venus and Neptune. Mahogany, vermillion, and tangerine cloud bands wrapped around the globe. Given the world's proximity to its sun, the temperature of the gasses ranged somewhere in the neighborhood of several hundred degrees Celsius—hence, its designation as a hot giant. An ocean rested below the clouds containing more water than found within the Sol system. The planet's high gravity placed the ocean under extreme pressure, compacting it into an exotic form of ice despite the heat. The exotic ice surrounded a rocky core many times bigger than the Earth.

It's so fused, but at the end of the day it's just another human battle ground.

Dismissing such thoughts, she scolded herself for her cynicism and behavior. The moment she had reunited with the closest thing she had to a living parent, she had lashed out in spite. Had she been too hard on her aunt? Brooke had clawed and scraped her way out here, risking everything to save her life. People who murdered loved ones didn't perform such selfless acts—or did they?

Nevertheless, the woman had killed her mother. Maya didn't know how one moved past such a transgression.

Her eyes widened when all the Pulsars in front of the Blazar scattered or shifted away. Multiple wormholes flashed into existence. The next thing she knew, extreme g-force was forcing her internal organs into places they didn't belong as her aunt engaged a tri-fighter.

It took her a moment to figure out she needed to breathe through her nose or in short grunts. Her eyes struggled to uncross and focus on her twisting and turning surroundings. The stars and planet whipped past the canopy again and again, never seen from the same angle. Now, she knew what it felt like inside a centrifuge.

She found it easiest to concentrate on the displays in her i-cite. Bob had granted her implants read-access to the Blazar's augmented reality, which allowed her to follow the action.

The fighter zigzagged, rolled, and spun like a gyroscope. It burned thrusters, afterburners, and retroburners, sometimes all at once. Hundreds of seekers leapt from its launch tubes while its plasma ejectors sputtered like flame-throwing machine guns. The Blazar upshifted and downshifted at will, interchanging normal space-time and hyperspace as effortlessly as the flicking of a switch. Explosions flashed and dimmed all around her.

Throughout it all, she gained a first-hand appreciation for her aunt's abilities and the level of skill a great pilot required. Brooke pulled acrobatic stunts and pushed the fighter in ways Maya wouldn't have thought possible. But what impressed her most was how quickly and seamlessly her aunt did everything. The veteran didn't need time to think. One split-second reaction followed the next and the next and the next. Maya swore her aunt and the Blazar were one in the same. Brooke didn't fly like a person inside a vehicle. She functioned as the brain of a body.

For the first time, Maya accepted that she didn't belong in a cockpit. The specific sentiment that crossed her mind was *Get me the hell out of here*.

Brooke steadied the fighter's orientation.

Maya's i-cite showed her aunt had blanked five tri-fighters. The dogfight seemed as if it had lasted minutes, but only seven seconds had elapsed since the wormholes had manifested.

The battle had brought the Blazar so close to the planet that its atmosphere blocked out the stars. Unless Maya turned her head all the way around, the red and orange clouds provided the sole backdrop.

Ahead, Pulsars and tri-fighters engaged in combat near *Nautilus* and the destroyer. The two ships raced around the planet, bombarding each other across the kilometers separating them with every brand of ordinance at their disposal. The ISC warship followed a slightly higher orbit as it pursued the destroyer further down toward the hot giant.

"Why's the destroyer dropping further into the atmosphere?" Maya asked.

"*Nautilus* has been pounding it," Brooke said. "It must intend to use the clouds as cover."

"There are plenty of less treacherous places in the system to hide. This planet alone has rings and moons. If I wanted to escape, I'd shift out of the system, not fly into the atmosphere of a big old . . ." Maya let her words trail off as her abdomen constricted.

"What're you saying—yes!" Brooke shook a fist at the massive explosions detonating around the destroyer's aft rockets. "Their engines are out."

The enemy vessel coasted toward the hot giant, and its weapons went silent. *Nautilus* descended after it, closing the distance while hammering away. The force fields of both ships began to glow as particles of hydrogen and helium scraped them.

"A big old planet," Maya mumbled, finishing her sentence. "High gravity—inescapable if you drop too low." She lurched forward in her seat. "Tell the captain to pull out now."

"What?" Brooke balked at the suggestion. "We've got them—"

The pyramidal destroyer fired its forward and ventral rockets. Slowing and reversing its plunge in a matter of seconds, it climbed and accelerated toward *Nautilus*.

Gibbons's ship fired maneuvering thrusters but not in time to avoid the collision. With the sharp end of its aft pyramid, the destroyer rammed the underside of ISC warship where the bottom two antimatter nacelles connected to the ship. Then the Vril burned their vessel's supposedly-damaged rear rockets.

The impacted nacelles exploded in a brilliant flash, ripping apart the rear half of *Nautilus* and annihilating most of the destroyer.

Crippled, both ships plummeted toward the mighty planet.

As *Nautilus* went down, it jettisoned two of its remaining four antimatter pods into a higher orbit. Aunt Brooke had the presence of mind to order the remaining units of the fighter wing to defend the precious fuel.

"They were never retreating," Maya muttered, sinking in her seat. "They were luring our only ride home to its demise."

Thirty-one—Bereaved
Gliese 581 System, January 2273 CE

"Fab me a flux generator," Crewman Malik Abrams asked his colleague while opening a maintenance panel on one of *Horizons's* fusion reactors.

"Coming right up." Behind him, repair technician Aida Santini asked her tool fabricator bot to produce the requested device. Atop the surface of the cubical bot, a dozen mechanical arms extruded composite materials from nozzles laced with nanites toward a point in the center. As the arms danced, an object took shape at a rapid pace.

A minute after she had issued her request, Aida grabbed the finished generator from atop the fabricator and handed it to her coworker with a smile.

Turning toward her, Malik accepted the tool and melted inside at the sight of her expression. He often found it hard to concentrate on his job when she directed those dimples at him. Despite her self-effacing claims to the contrary, the smudges of grease on her cheeks and forehead added to her cuteness. Her raven hair, when put up in a bun, gave her an elegant appearance far too regal for repair work.

He had been working up the nerve to ask her to dinner ever since the task of rebuilding the ship had attached them at the hip. The fact they worked so closely together every day had provided him with a convenient excuse to delay. If she didn't feel the same way, they would end up mired in excruciating awkwardness for who knew how long. But now that *Nautilus* had shown up, they would be going home soon. Not only would the uneasiness between them be brief if she said no, but who knew where they would each end up once they got back.

Now's the time. No more excuses.

"Hey, um, Aida," he stammered through a bout of cotton mouth. "There's something I've been meaning to ask you."

"I see." Leaning toward him, her smile morphed into a playful grin. "I think I can guess where this is going."

Her directness took him off guard, and he gave a start. "You do?"

Her grin drooped. "Oh, um. I thought I did. What were you going to ask?"

"What did you think I was going to ask?"

"I'm not sure anymore."

"Neither am I." He resisted the urge to slap his forehead. This was not going at all how he had envisioned it. *Just spit it out!* "Actually, I am sure. I wanted to know if, maybe sometime after work, you'd like to—"

"Attention all hands." Acting Captain Young's words boomed throughout the reactor hold and scrolled across the bottom of Malik's i-cite. "Code thirty-four is in effect. Enact emergency procedures immediately. This is not a drill.

"I repeat, code thirty-four is in effect . . ."

Twinges of panic numbed Malik to the repeated announcements. "Code thirty-four. That means—"

"The ship's been boarded." Aida turned to the fabricator bot. "Particle handgun."

"Nope," the bot said. "I don't do weapons."

Malik glowered at it. "A flux generator is as dangerous as any gun."

"You don't need a gun to do your job, smartass."

"Smartass? Who's the smartass?"

"Stop being a wuss and ask the girl out."

Aida's face flushed redder than the nearby star.

He placed his hands on his hips and stared at her. "What the hell?"

"Sorry, I don't know where it got that idea." With a curse, she kicked the side of the fab bot and told it, "Override the security lockout based on my authorization."

The bot sighed in exasperation. "Fine, I'll make your stupid gun."

As the machine's arms weaved the weapon into existence, Malik made up his mind. "I do want to ask you out."

The smile returned to Aida's face. "It's about—" Her eyes widened as a flash of light struck her from behind.

"Aida!" Malik caught her as the blast drove her toward him.

Her blood splattered him in the face. When he wrapped his arms around her back, her charred and mauled flesh singed his hands.

He lowered her to the ground and shook her, calling out her name.

Her eyes stared straight ahead. He felt for a pulse but found none.

The pounding of heavy footsteps shook the deck. When he looked up, he counted at least ten tall, lanky troops wearing white environmental suits rushing toward him. They trained their rifles in his direction.

One of them fired, blasting him in the neck. Searing pain tore through him, and he collapsed on his side. The urge to clutch the wound compelled him, but his arms refused to move. Tears filled his eyes, both from the agony and Aida's death.

As the intruders crowded around him, a shorter individual strutted out from behind them.

The blonde-haired woman pursed her lips at the bloody mess. After taking a bite out of an apple, she marched past him across the reactor hold.

When she reached the far wall, she stood staring at it. A hatch he had never known existed corkscrewed open with a hiss. Deep clanking signaled the release of latches. To the best of his fading knowledge, only the internal workings of the main rocket engines resided behind the wall.

The last thing he saw before an intruder shot him in the head was the woman climbing inside the hidden passageway.

◆

Ignoring her niece's protests, Brooke dove her fighter into the hot giant's atmosphere after *Nautilus*. She kept trying to comm Gibbons without success.

"That kamikaze run supports what I've been saying," Maya yelled. "If we don't get back to *Horizons*, something worse could happen."

"I'm not going to abandon these people," Brooke said. "I convinced them to come out here. This is my fault."

"What do you plan to do, though? One fighter can't evacuate the crew of a starship."

"I won't give up on the captain until she's beyond help, and Zeke is still aboard."

"Zeke? You mean the exokid you rescued?"

"Yes. He's probably still sedated, oblivious to the fact he might die." Deep crimson clouds swirled around the canopy, growing darker and darker as she descended. "How much farther, Bob?"

<Less than sixty seconds to intercept, ma'am. However, if the ship continues its descent, fewer than twenty minutes will remain until we can no longer escape the gravity well.>

"Assuming we don't slam into the hot-ice layer or get crushed first," Maya said.

Brooke increased speed. "I guess we'd better be quick."

The white noise of a comm signal trying to get through pierced her eardrums.

"All hands, proceed to escape craft," came Gibbons's broken-up orders. "Avoid the aft sections of the habitat module."

"Ruby," Brooke shouted. "Tess, can you hear me?"

"Angel, is that you? It's good to hear your voice."

"What's your situation?"

"My situation?" She laughed. "Plummeting to my death."

"You know what I mean."

Gibbons evened her tone. "You know how it is. I don't leave until everyone else is away. The evacuation is one-third complete so far."

The Blazar's sensors registered transports, fighters, and escape vehicles ascending from the ship.

"Do you know if Zeke's okay?" Brooke asked.

"The medical bay is on the edge of the damaged areas," the captain said. "It's still pressurized, so there's a good chance he's still alive, but it's sealed off. There's no getting to him. I'm sorry."

Brooke fought the urge to hang her helmet.

The clouds in front of the Blazar parted, bringing the warship into view. The vessel plunged nose-first with the mangled aft section of the crew habitat module pointed up at an angle. The jagged ends of deck plating and walls that had once comprised the concentric levels of the ship jutted out behind it. Force fields and emergency bulkheads sealed off some sections but not all.

"When you say there's no getting to him, you mean from the inside, right?" Maya asked what Brooke was already thinking.

"Yes, but . . ." Gibbons used her "aha" tone. "I see what you're getting at."

"Bob," Brooke said, "scan for the closest place to the infirmary where we can dock. Any breach we can enter through will work."

<I've located a suitable disembarkation point, ma'am. Getting there will proceed more quickly if I take control.>

"Go for it."

Bob brought the Blazar in behind what remained of *Nautilus*. Once the fighter drew near enough, the ship shielded it from the air flow and turbulence decreased.

Burning thrusters, Bob synced the craft's orientation with the still-spinning warship and brought them closer still. Around the edges of the hull, the thrusters fired at max output in an attempt to stabilize the rotational gravity.

Brooke fell down into her seat. *Feels like the gravity's wavering between twenty and thirty percent, maybe?*

Bob positioned the Blazar's nose a meter from an exposed corridor.

After draining the cockpit of gravgel, Brooke told the canopy to peel away and stood atop her seat. She held her arms out to maintain her balance as the fighter wobbled. "I don't think we can make it across, Bob. Can't you get any closer?"

<There are numerous variables in flux, ma'am. My margin for error will increase exponentially if I reposition the spacecraft nearer. If any part of the fuselage strikes the ship, the force may throw you clear of the cockpit.>

"I can get us over there," Maya said.

"How?" Brooke asked, peering down at her.

Standing up, her niece unclipped a handgun with a dish-shaped muzzle from the waist of her suit. "Crawl down and trust me."

"Seriously?"

"Clock's ticking."

Grumbling, Brooke hopped back into the rear seat.

Maya wrapped her arm around her aunt's waist and pointed her weapon away from *Nautilus*. "Hold on."

As Brooke grabbed hold of her niece, the girl jumped up from the back of her seat and fired the gun. A wall of force pressed against them, pushing them across the gap and into the corridor.

When Brooke's boots contacted the deck, she let go of her niece, tucked, and rolled.

Maya landed on her feet and kept her balance.

Extending a hand, the girl helped her up.

Brooke rushed deeper inside the corridor with Maya at her side. Emergency plasma strips flickered, providing dim light. Her suit's audio receptors picked up no sounds in the decompressed hallway.

"Tell me where to go, Bob," Brooke said.

The AI displayed the fastest route to the medical bay in her i-cite.

Upon reaching an intersection, she followed Bob's instructions and turned right, but her niece pulled her to the left.

"No, the medical bay is this way," Brooke insisted.

Maya nodded. "I know, but if this ship is laid out anything like *Horizons*, we need to go this way first."

"Why?"

"Because . . ." Maya pulled her aunt to a storage closet. "Zeke's coming with us, right?" She pressed the buttons on the control panel next to the door.

As the entrance slid open, Maya rushed inside and returned with a spacesuit.

"Of course," Brooke relented.

The two women lunged around bends, ascended one level toward the outer hull, dashed down another corridor, and came to an abrupt halt at an emergency bulkhead blocking their path.

Her niece wasted little time whipping out her gun and taking aim.

<Twelve minutes remain,> Bob reported.

"It's going to take a lot longer than that to blast through," Brooke said.

"Good thing I don't plan on blasting through." Maya pressed the trigger. Innumerable tiny cracks propagated throughout the thick metal partition. Seconds later, it shattered like glass.

"Remind me to try out that gun sometime," Brooke said as she forged ahead.

Staying with her, Maya shook her head. "Sorry, but I'm not sure how comfortable I'd feel handing it over to you."

"Why? You think I'd use it on you? I've done a lot of things I'm not proud of, Maya, but shooting someone I care about isn't one of them."

Her niece skidded to a halt. Brooke did the same.

"Don't lie to me," Maya growled.

"We need to keep moving." When the girl folded her arms, Brooke said, "I've never lied to you—withheld things, yes, but never lied."

"I watched you shoot Mom in cold blood."

Brooke gaped at her. "I did no such thing."

"Liar. I saw it happen."

"What? How?"

<Nine minutes.>

Brooke cursed. "We need to move or we'll end up killing each other." She sprinted toward the infirmary. To her relief, Maya followed.

Upon reaching an open door, Brooke rushed inside and bumped into the desk within the center of the small room. "Hey, it's a dead end."

<This is the chief physician's office. It has entrances to both the hallway and infirmary.>

"I see." Maya stepped into the room. "We can use it like an airlock so we don't decompress the medical bay."

<Affirmative.>

The door slid shut behind Brooke. After the office filled with air, the opposite door to the infirmary parted.

Inside, she found Zeke alone and unconscious. The teen lay face down on the deck next to the bed from which he had fallen.

"They just left him like this?" She couldn't believe it.

"When the destroyer collided with the ship," her niece said, "I'm sure the staff did all they could do to save themselves."

Brooke lifted Zeke by his armpits while Maya grabbed his legs. Together, they hoisted him onto the bed.

While Maya suited him up, Brooke whipped open cabinet drawers until she found an auto-syringe loaded with a nano-stimulant.

As she stabbed Zeke in the arm, a cube materialized in the air near the bed, showing Gibbons's disheveled expression. Control stations sparked behind her on the otherwise dark and abandoned bridge.

"I'm glad to see you found him," she said.

Zeke stirred.

"Is everyone away?" Brooke asked the captain. "You ready to get the hell out of here?"

Gibbons stared at the deck and drew her lips to a thin line. "The evacuation is as complete as it's going to get."

"What does that mean?"

"There aren't any working escape craft left."

Brooke's arms dangled at her sides. "We'll come get you."

<Five minutes, ma'ams.>

"There's no time." Gibbons forced a smile. "Besides, four's a crowd in a star fighter."

"Tess . . ." Brooke's throat grew so dry she couldn't swallow.

"If it wasn't for you, Angel, I would've died a long time ago. I'm happy I was able to return the favor."

"But—"

"Go. Leave before you waste my heroic sacrifice by dying." Gibbons saluted. "Find a way to get everyone home."

Brooke nodded, slowly, and returned the gesture.

The cube shrank and disappeared.

When she turned toward the bed, she found Zeke opening his eyes.

He studied her face and sprang to a sitting position, "I understand. Let's go."

As Brooke glanced at Maya, Zeke followed her gaze. He flinched and blinked when he noticed her.

The ship whined. Bulkheads warped and dented, buckling under the atmospheric pressure.

Zeke donned his helmet, and the three of them sprinted out of the medical bay.

<Two minutes,> Bob reported as Brooke reached the Blazar at the end of the breached corridor.

The meter-wide gap still separated the fighter from the ship.

"Move in closer, Bob," she said. "There's no time to worry about the consequences."

<Understood, ma'am.> Bob maneuvered the open canopy to within safe jumping distance.

Brooke sent Zeke first. The teen hopped over into the rear seat and sat down.

She waved Maya toward the fighter. "You next."

"It's going to be a tight squeeze."

"This is no time to be shy."

As her niece bounded over, one of the Blazar's aft rocket nozzles struck a protruding beam. Maya fell into Zeke's lap, and the fighter drifted farther away from the ship.

With a running start, Brooke leapt out of the corridor. Vertigo seized her as conflicting forces acted on her body. One moment, she felt ten times heavier. The next, she was weightless. Then she was falling. Or was she spinning?

She landed on the side of the cockpit but not quite in it, holding on for dear life.

Bob backed the Blazar away from the ship and stopped the fighter from rotating with it.

Now weightless, Brooke managed to pull herself inside.

As she oriented her body in her seat, gravgel doused her.

<Our time has expired. We can no longer achieve sufficient velocity to escape the planet's gravity.>

"Let's hope there's margin for error in your calculations." While pointing the Blazar's nose toward the stars, Brooke checked on her passengers. The rear seat possessed enough width for Zeke and Maya to sit huddled side by side. "I'll try to avoid any crazy maneuvers. Ready?"

They both nodded.

The instant the immersion cycle completed, she maxed out the afterburners. Bone-crushing force stressed the gel and tested the limits of her endurance. Grunts from the back seat reached her ears as the fighter strained upward against the mighty world's grasp.

The struggle between machine and nature raged on for minutes and kilometers.

<We lack sufficient velocity.>

"Then we upshift now," Brooke squeaked out her constricted windpipe.

<If we execute a phase shift under the influence of this pressure and gravity, the spacecraft will be torn apart with an 88.2 percent certainty.>

"There's no—" Her instruments registered a massive detonation. The last two antimatter nacelles affixed to *Nautilus* ignited as the ship struck the hot-ice below.

Her stomach grew lighter as the Blazar accelerated in its climb.
<The force of the blast has increased our velocity, ma'am.>
"It's giving us a push," she said through clenched teeth.
Aided by the explosion's pressure wake, the fighter shot upward.
The cloud cover thinned.
<Shock wave approaching. Impact in five seconds.>

Thirty-two—Sundered
Gliese 581 System, January 2273 CE

Particle beams crisscrossed throughout the corridors leading to the reactor hold in *Horizons's* aft engine block. Having set aside their differences, the civilian militia and ISC Defense soldiers worked together to pin the boarding party down in the hold. The tall trespassers stopped and held their positions at the entryways, no longer falling back.

Trevor observed the firefight from the ECC, forgetting to breathe at times. Somehow, the intruders had managed to disable the cam feeds in the hold, so he had no idea what was going on inside it. His first inclination had been to seal off the hold and decompress it, but the enemy had blocked all remote access to the systems there. For all he knew, the Greys might be planting charges, overloading one of the reactors, or cutting the power to the environmental systems. The ship could blow at any moment, and that would be it for all aboard. Thirteen brave men and women had perished in defense of the ship so far. He doubted they would be the last.

How had exobeings gained the knowledge necessary to override control systems aboard a human vessel, he wondered? Were they that much smarter and more advanced? Or had someone on the inside helped them? The situation reminded him of how the Greys had hidden from and manipulated human tech back in the war.

Trevor was mulling over what to do when the lights in the ECC flickered and failed. Every display cube and control station blacked out, shrouding the room in darkness. The auxiliary plasma strips failed to activate.

Muttering and heavy breathing echoed off the bulkheads.

Something rocked the ship.

He shifted his weight to keep from falling. Shudders reverberated through the deck.

Before he could order everyone to remain calm, everything flashed back to life.

"What happened?" he demanded.

"Every power system went offline, sir," Ensign Sigo said after consulting a technician. "Primary, secondary, and tertiary, all at once."

"That shouldn't be possible."

"I know. I can't explain it."

"What about that tremor?"

Sitting at her sensing station, Ensign Williams swiveled her chair toward him. "The enemy transport that brought the boarding party exploded while docked. Considering that section was already breached, the damage isn't too much more extensive."

"What destroyed it? One of our fighters?"

"Actually, it was one of theirs, sir."

Trevor furrowed his brow while approaching her. "They blanked their own craft?"

She refaced her station. "It appears so. One of the tri-fighters turned on it, fired a spread of seekers at it, and shifted away. Two of our pilots saw it happen. With the transport destroyed, all the remaining enemy forces retreated."

"The external comm system is also down," another officer reported. "It doesn't appear to be damaged, but I can't bring it back online."

An internal comm request from his head of security appeared in his i-cite. Trevor routed it to one of the main cubes for a wider view.

"Sir," the headshot of Ensign Knight said. "The boarding party has stopped shooting and thrown down their weapons."

The cube showed one entrance to the reactor hold and zoomed in on the deck. The tall, gangly intruders in the doorway lay still on the floor with their rifles strewn across the floor.

Knight entered the picture with four other soldiers backing him up. Approaching one of the fallen trespassers with caution, he poked and prodded the being with the muzzle of his rifle. The individual didn't budge. Setting aside his weapon, Knight knelt and ripped the intruder's helmet off.

The human male possessed pale, anemic skin. His eyes and mouth remained locked open with his head turned to the side.

Finding humans as part of the Greys's attack force didn't faze Trevor. They had used abductees back in the war as well.

"It looks like they activated a suicide device, sir," Knight said. "Personnel stationed at the other entryways have confirmed the entire boarding party is dead."

Trevor was halfway through a sigh of relief when Williams cupped her hand over her mouth and cried out through her fingers.

"What is it, Jenelle?"

She pulled her hand away from her face. "I've detected a huge release of energy in orbit of the second planet. *Nautilus* and the enemy destroyer collided, resulting in an explosion that tore them apart. Both vessels descended into the atmosphere." She swallowed. "There's no way *Nautilus* is capable of ascent."

Each and every crew member's face went blank. The shock in the ECC was palpable.

Acting Captain Young's legs wobbled. Had he stood within his quarters, alone, he would have dropped to his knees in front of his bed and buried his head in his arms.

But in front of his crew, he straightened his posture and expression. "Rashard, assign a team to figure out what the intruders were doing in the reactor hold."

"Understood, sir," Knight said.

The cameras in the hold came back online. The main cube showed a security team and a group of techs entering. He gulped when he saw Ensigns Malik Abrams and Aida Santini's lifeless bodies lying in the middle of the deck.

Flexing his fingers, Trevor doled out additional orders to everyone. Then he plopped down in his command seat, trying not to focus on the implications of *Nautilus's* destruction.

"Sir," Williams shouted. "I'm showing another explosion, this time deep within the atmosphere of the second planet."

◆

Mayor Abigail Byrne settled into the chair behind the desk in her office in city hall. Closing her eyes, she moaned in satisfaction. It felt good to be home. She had spent the last few weeks lying low with her son in various hideaways, fearing the moment when Acting Captain Young would get serious. Had he sent a strike team with orders to shoot her if she didn't surrender, she would probably be in the brig or dead.

She had taken great pride in out-maneuvering the raw ensign—hell, the young man didn't have all that many years on her teenage son. With strength in numbers on her side, the promise of full bellies for all, and expert politicking, she had convinced civilian family members and friends to sway beloved crew members in key positions. With the loyalty of the right people secured, spreading out to control the majority of the ship had required nothing more than timing, stealth, and the bopping of a few heads. A handful of shots had been fired, resulting in a few minor injuries—nothing simple medite injections couldn't remedy. Otherwise, her takeover had proceeded with the type of non-violent action that gained a leader support from the populace.

When Trevor had informed her of *Nautilus's* arrival, she had told her militia to hold their positions and cancelled her raid on the ECC. She hadn't wanted to give up what she had taken in case the situation took a turn for the worse, but she had seen little purpose in continuing the coup with the prospect of returning home a reality. She had even assigned members of her militia to help defend the ship against the boarding party. Assuming they could put a stop to the intruders and *Nautilus* took care of the destroyer, the Sol system was but a short hyperspace shift away.

Opening her eyes and leaning forward, Byrne popped open the salad container sitting on her desk and prepared to feast. She was squeezing raspberry vinaigrette dressing out of a packet when one of her aides barged into her office.

"Madam Mayor," the smart-suited young man stammered in haste. "I've good news and bad. Which would you like to hear—"

"Skip the drama and spit it out already," she said.

"Right. The boarding party has been stopped. Apparently, they all killed themselves. We're not sure what they were up to yet, but an investigation is under way."

"And the bad news?"

The aide stood in place, tight-lipped and pale.

"Well?" Byrne asked while stuffing a bite of salad into her mouth.

"*Nautilus* and the enemy ship destroyed one another," he said.

She dropped her fork. Bits of carrot and lettuce fell from her mouth.

"You know what this means," the aide said. "We're stranded here all over again."

Byrne sat back, resisting the urge to spit up the little she had managed to eat.

Tuning out the world beyond her head, she stayed her self-pity and considered her next move. Even with the threat of attack eliminated, the fact remained Young was an inexperienced and incompetent leader. She saw no other alternative. If they were stuck in the system for a while longer—perhaps a lot longer—she needed to remove him from command before he made another decision that jeopardized them all.

The coup was back on, she decided.

"Thank you," she said. "You're dismissed."

Again, the aide didn't budge and struggled to speak.

She lifted her brow. "Something else?"

"Um, yes—" The aide leapt out of the way as Ensign Knight and four armed soldiers barged past him into the office.

♦

<Contact imminent.>

In a rear camera display, Maya watched the blazing clouds of fire behind the Blazar balloon toward it. She leaned closer to Zeke and cringed, expecting the blast wave to incinerate them

Aunt Brooke engaged the phase drive. A wormhole formed in front of the fighter, shrouded by the atmospheric gasses. The cockpit shook and rattled like a tuning fork as the spacecraft, pressure, gravity, and space-time distortions fought against one another.

All the forces quieted as the craft slipped into hyperspace.

When the Blazar downshifted out amongst the stars, Maya slid down in her half of the back seat and relaxed.

"Everyone all right?" Brooke asked.

"Yes," Zeke responded without a hint of stress in his voice.

Maya sat up. "Still alive. I think."

"Glad to hear it," Brooke said.

<Ma'am, I'm detecting friendly forces on the other side of the planet.>

"Adjust trajectory to rendezvous."

Bob maneuvered the fighter into a higher orbit over the course of the next few minutes.

Maya spied a collection of bright specs and increased magnification. Hundreds of Pulsars and tens of transport vessels gathered around the pair of antimatter nacelles *Nautilus* had jettisoned before plunging to its demise. What remained of the destroyer's tri-fighter wing littered local space.

Her aunt tried an unbefitting cheery tone. "Those should contain more than enough antimatter to get *Horizons* home."

"True." Maya frowned. "Unfortunately, the ship's exotic matter generator was damaged beyond repair in the crash. Without the EMG, the ship can't enlarge and sustain a wormhole big enough to upshift. All the antimatter in the universe won't do us any good without that part."

"The EMG can't be repaired? Or replaced?"

"No. It's too complex and sensitive an instrument to fix or fabricate out here."

"What about—"

Angst and exhaustion crept into Maya's bones. "Face it. We're stranded here until another ship arrives."

Brooke's tone grew sullen. "They haven't even begun constructing another ship like *Horizons* or *Nautilus*. We may be out here for years."

The reality of their plight weighed Maya down far more than any gravitational pull. She had fought so hard to make the best of the situation and to avoid being killed by all varieties of threats. She had put everything she had into restoring the ship, helping its occupants pick themselves up, and maintaining a positive outlook. But now all that hope was gone. Thoughts of the device Bob had mentioned and how it might still activate came to her, but she didn't care anymore. She gave up shouldering the burden.

A plan involving her going down to the Penphins's planet formed in her head, although she wasn't in the mood for any of their help. Rather, she envisioned herself traipsing across the frozen tundra of the night hemisphere until she keeled over and face-planted in the snow. In her present state of mind, the idea seemed like sweet release.

She sounded like her aunt, she realized, which knotted her insides that much tighter.

"The survivors are headed to *Horizons* and bringing the antimatter in tow," Brooke said. "Shall we join them?"

Maya turned away from Zeke. Facing her side of the cockpit, she curled up as much as she had room to do. "Whatever."

A minute passed, but the Blazar remained in its current orbit.

"Did you mean what you said before?" Brooke asked. "Am I the heroine you've always looked up to for inspiration?"

The obvious attempt to brighten the mood led Maya to groan. "Up until I learned you blew a hole through my mom's chest at point-blank range."

Her aunt's voice grew earnest. "I never shot Marie."

"The evidence says otherwise."

<No, it does not.>

"Stay out of this, Bob," Maya snapped.

<In the majority of other cases, I would comply with your request. In this instance, however, I feel I must, as they say, set the record straight. Your aunt did not discharge a weapon at your mother.>

Maya sat up straighter. "The filesim showed her doing it."

<That imagery, like everything else the Vril have concocted, lacks accuracy.>

"The Vril? But Chancellor Ajunwa gave the information to me."

"Ajunwa?" Brooke said. "The council forced her to resign after being exposed as an agent. I knew it."

<I lack the knowledge of whether the former chancellor altered the footage from that day or whether the Vril manipulated the data without her awareness. In either scenario, the most probable objective was to turn the two of you against one another.>

"Those conniving—"

"But why?" Maya asked, interrupting. "What would they gain by going to all the trouble? I mean, we're hardly that important. I'm certainly not. I've risen to second in command aboard *Horizons*, but that was because of what you did, Bob. They couldn't have known the crash would happen . . ." She let her words trail off as she recalled what Mendez had told her. Her one-time friend had insisted Maya needed to die.

Reaching down, she ran a hand over the tiny black box in her pants pocket beneath her suit.

<I cannot answer such questions, but the fact remains the record provided to you was falsified. I can assert this because I was present.>

Maya bit her lower lip, dreading the next logical question. "So how did it happen?"

Her aunt blew out an uneven breath. "On Collins's orders, Ajunwa's guards turned on her and us. They were the ones who went to shoot Marie. I didn't know what else to do, so I instructed Bob to fly the phase fighter prototype outside the room and blast the guards through the windows. I pulled your mom down to the floor before Bob fired, but . . ." Her voice wavered and cracked. "Debris struck her." She started bawling. "I tried to save her, but in doing so I killed her. It was my fault, Maya. I'm responsible, but I didn't shoot her."

<I can confirm the accuracy of this recollection of events. Your aunt and I are both indirectly accountable for your mother's death.>

Maya sat in silence, not knowing what to feel.

Brooke sniveled. "I never told you because I didn't want you to hate me—and to protect you from the Vril's lies. I didn't want you to lose your optimism. You inherited that from your mom." She cleared her throat. "I love you like my own daughter, Maya. You mean everything to me. When they declared *Horizons* lost, I didn't know how to cope—"

Springing forward, Maya gasped. "What did you say?" She whacked Zeke with her arm in the process and apologized.

"I said, I didn't know how to deal with your death after they gave up the search."

"The search." The mental gears spun in Maya's head, snapping her out of her funk. "Of course. The IEF would've sent a . . . and we skipped seven years, so . . ." She bounced up and down in her seat like a hyperactive toddler. "It's been here the whole time. Do you know what that means?"

"Not a clue," Brooke said.

Zeke shook his helmet.

"Bob, I need you to help me locate something." Maya gripped the teen's arm, overcome by shudders of elation. "We're going home."

Thirty-three—Dybbuk
Interstellar Space, January 2273 CE

Brooke shifted the Blazar out of hyperspace beyond the edge of the Gliese 581 system. A thousand kilometers ahead of the fighter, the interstellar probe the IEF had sent to search for signs of *New Horizons* coasted along. It followed an orbit that would return it to the Sol system in a million years, give or take a few millennia.

In many ways, the probe resembled a miniaturized version of the ship it had traveled here to find. From the pointed nose to the aft engine block, its cylindrical hull stretched for one-hundred meters. Three smaller antimatter nacelles affixed to a ring encircled the main cylinder. Unmanned, the probe lacked a city sphere but rotated as a means of attitude control.

"I'm still not clear what it's doing out here," Brooke wondered aloud.

"After the probe transmitted its findings and gave up the search," Maya explained from the cramped rear seat she shared with Zeke, "IEF cultural contamination and planetary protection protocols required it to shift outside the system and go into standby mode."

"The IEF didn't want the Penphins to find it," Zeke said.

"Right. Not only do we not want to leave our trash in someone else's backyard, but the technology could have grave consequences in the wrong hands."

"So why not shift it home?" Brooke asked.

"It doesn't have enough fuel left. Plus, the IEF wanted to leave it nearby in case *Horizons* showed up and needed it after all. The comm system, small remaining quantity of antimatter, and of course, the EMG could be life-savers."

"If that's the protocol, why didn't you think of tracking this thing down sooner?"

Maya sighed. "I should've, but I think the time slip muddled my thinking. I've been here for two months, but over seven years have passed back home. The paradoxical idea that a probe arrived and gave up the search for us before we got here took a while to click."

"I suppose I can understand that. The probe's EMG is compatible with *Horizons* even though the ones in the Pulsars aren't?"

"Yes, star fighter EMGs are much smaller and have a different shape. The interstellar probe uses a type more similar to *Horizons*. It's half the size, but it can be adapted to work with a few modifications."

As Brooke burned the Blazar's thrusters toward the probe, Maya said, "Bob, transmit the access codes."

<Transmitting now. Codes have been accepted.>

The probe's running lights blinked to life, and its spin rate increased.

<Internal atmosphere and gravity should reach nominal levels in five minutes.>

Brooke had praise for her non-corporeal friend on the tip of her tongue but he cut her off.

<I'm detecting—>

"I see it." She fired the Blazar's retrorockets and slowed their approach. "Damn."

"Why are you—" Maya swallowed her question as the tri-fighter docked with the probe rotated into view.

"Looks like somebody had the same idea as you, squirt."

"Guess so."

"Zeke, can you take control of whoever's on board?"

"As far as I can tell," he said, "there's no one over there."

<I'm detecting no biological heat sources anywhere within the probe. However, the power output of its reactors could obscure life signs in the aft sections of the ship.>

"To be on the safe side," Brooke said, "we'll operate under the assumption that someone's aboard."

"I don't blame you," Zeke said.

"I agree," Maya said. "Still, we need to get over there as soon as possible. For all we know, the Vril have sabotaged the EMG."

Brooke grumbled. "Don't even suggest that."

With her pulse throbbing, she took her time bringing them in closer, ready to upshift to safety at the first sign of trouble. The probe hadn't armed its weapons, but she refused to discount the possibility of it firing on them, especially with the tri-fighter present.

Contact jarred the Blazar as it latched onto an exterior hatch.

After draining the cockpit of gravgel—an act that left Brooke feeling too vulnerable—she stood and retrieved her particle rifle from the front compartment. Turning around, her seat's backrest morphed and flattened, allowing her to crawl over it.

"Lift up your feet," she instructed her passengers, who complied without protest.

The hatch in the floor between the front and rear seats slid open.

"Follow me." Brooke charged her rifle and dropped down into the airlock.

Once everyone had vacated the Blazar, she shut the outer hatch.

Pressurizing the airlock, she opened the inner door and led them into the outermost of the probe's three concentric levels. The lit corridor she stepped into was only one-and-a-half-meters tall, which forced her to crouch, especially in her flight armor.

"Where to?" she asked.

Maya pulled off her helmet and tapped her cheek in thought. Brooke almost told her to put the headgear back on, thinking they should stay prepared for decompression or a chemical attack. But after a moment, she removed her own helmet, deciding direct use of her senses might alert her more quickly to danger. Her armor's readouts displayed in her i-cite.

Following their lead, Zeke drew in a gulp of the stale, metallic-smelling air.

Her niece headed toward the rear of the probe. "We need to uncouple the EMG, which we can do from the control center forward of the engine block."

An important consideration struck Brooke as she kept pace. "How big is the EMG? Will we even be able to transport it?"

"Don't worry. I can hold it in the back seat."

"To think our ability to cross twenty light years depends on a device small enough to sit in your lap."

"People who worked with vacuum-tube computers centuries ago had similar thoughts about the microprocessor."

Brooke insisted on taking point. She led them through hallways and down to the innermost level.

Outside the engine control room, she and Maya took up positions on opposite sides of the hatch with their weapons drawn. Brooke told Zeke to stand behind her, checked to make sure her niece was ready, and issued the open command. When the door slid aside and no shots came flying at them, she poked her rifle through the entrance, followed by her head.

The control consoles within the room blinked and beeped. Cubes floated above the main console on the wall across from the hatch, showing astrometric measurements and system status information. The interior was a bit too dim for Brooke's liking. Too many shadows loomed around the edges of the room. "Can you turn up the lights?"

"The environmental controls won't respond," Maya said, wide-eyed and flinching at any minor clank or hum. Her niece had never conquered her fear of the dark.

A figure emerged from the pitch blackness shrouding one side of the room.

Gasping, Maya jumped.

Brooke whipped her rifle toward the figure and started to depress the trigger.

The android technician stopped and cocked its head at her. "Welcome aboard. Do you require my assistance?"

Brooke pulled her finger off the kill-switch and exhaled. "Not at the moment."

"Very well. Do let me know if you need anything." The android stepped over to the main control station and stood facing it, motionless.

"He recognizes our access codes," Maya said from behind her, "so he shouldn't pose a problem."

As Brooke crept into the room, she swung her rifle back and forth. She waved Maya and Zeke inside when she reached the center of the room.

"Hurry up and do what you need to do," Brooke said.

Maya holstered her wave gun and rushed over to the main console. After ordering the android to stand clear, she placed two fingers on the neural interface pad. Zeke joined her as Brooke stood guard with her back to them, distrusting the rest of the room.

Her niece jerked back from the console.

"What?" Brooke asked.

Maya turned toward her, her face tensed. "The EMG is still in its cradle, but the decoupling sequence has already been initiated."

"Meaning we interrupted the thief before he could make off with it." Brooke gripped her rifle tighter.

"A thief who's still here."

"Caught in act." A female voice echoed throughout the room.

The silhouette of a woman moved in the shadows.

Maya drew her wave gun. Zeke stood stiff as a bulkhead.

As the figure stepped into the light, Brooke scowled. "You," she snarled. "I killed you."

"Really, Brooke? I'm disappointed." The android lifted her thin brow. "You used to catch on so much faster in my candidacy training classes." She straightened the top half of her sleek red flight armor, reached into a pouch affixed to her hip, and tossed a few crunchy, orange puffs into her mouth. "If I must spell it out for you," she said, chomping away, "I'm the next incarnation of my predecessor." With a wave of her hand, Eve Two added, "New and improved."

"You hitched a ride aboard the destroyer."

"I guess if captains 'hitch rides' aboard their own ships." Eve Two stuffed another puff into her pale, symmetrical mug. "After you killed the first me on Psykhe, my loyal crew had plenty of time to construct and enhance yours truly during the transit. The great thing about maintaining neural backups of one's self is the immortality. I can create an unlimited number of me."

"I can't think of anything more revolting."

"You never did have much of an imagination." Eve Two took a step closer.

Brooke raised her rifle. Sighting it, she rubbed the trigger with her finger.

The android held up her palms. "Careful, now. I don't want to hurt any of you."

With a cursory glance, Brooke failed to identify a weapon in the artificial woman's possession. *She must have one integrated into her body.*

"We've been through this, old friend." Drawing nearer, Eve Two shook her head, disappointed. "Do you think I'd let you beat me the same way again? My armor and shielding is more powerful than yours. I'm stronger and faster than the old me. By the time you land enough shots— if you can even hit me—I'll have killed the lot of you." She glowered at Zeke. "I'm particularly looking forward to ripping you limb from limb."

"You're bluffing."

"I could be, but are you willing to risk the kiddies' lives to find out?"

Scrunching her nose, Brooke tried to contact Bob. Connection errors popped up in her i-cite, indicating the presence of neudar jamming. Even if she had been able to get through, though, the engine control center was located too deep inside the probe. The Blazar would have to blast through the hull to get to them, killing friend and foe in the process. She also couldn't think of anything he could remote control to help, given everyone's close proximity.

She cursed under her breath and lowered her rifle. "Put down your gun," she told Maya.

"Maybe against a particle rifle she's got the advantage," Maya said, "but not against this thing." She took more careful aim. "I know of no defense against being destabilized at the subatomic level."

"Oh, is that one of those new wave guns?" Eve Two ogled the device like a geek at a technology convention. "I've been wanting to try one out, but the IEF made them so very difficult to get ahold of." In a blur, she lurched forward and pried the gun away from the girl before she could squeeze the trigger.

The mild hum of the wave gun went silent. Its glowing parts dimmed.

With her heart bashing against her rib cage, Brooke re-sighted her rifle on the android.

Eve Two backed off and inspected the gun, pointing it toward the deck.

Brooke relaxed and held her fire.

"There was no point in taking it." Maya clutched her sprained wrist and winced. "It only responds to me."

The artificial woman stuck out her lower lip. "What a shame." She stared down at the gun in her hand, and her eyes wobbled.

The device hummed to life once again.

Maya flinched in surprise. Zeke backpedaled.

"What, you thought I didn't know how it worked?" Eve Two gripped the weapon tighter, getting a feel for it. "DNA and brainwave profiles are easy to come by. I collected yours long before you understood such things, Maya Davis."

"What does that mean?" Maya asked.

"I don't suppose you'd remember. I made sure of it before I let your aunt rescue you."

Brooke swore her pulse stopped for a moment.

Eve Two shot her a glance. "That's right, Brooke. I never cared about the phase fighter prototype. Reverse-engineering the less complex capsule turned out to be a quicker and easier way for the Vril to achieve FTL capability. No, I wanted your niece."

"Why?" the girl asked.

Brooke jabbed her rifle in Eve Two's direction. "What did you do to her?"

"There you go again," the artificial woman said. "Always assuming I have some nefarious agenda. I didn't take Maya to harm her or as a hostage. I took her to test her, to see if we'd succeeded with what we'd tried to create."

Maya leaned forward. "What you'd tried to create?"

"The sole purpose—the singular driving motivation—behind

everything that the Vril do is to prepare the human race to defend itself against his kind." Eve Two thrust her chin at Zeke. "Of the many things we've tried, I'm one example, an artificial being with a human mind they can't control. Maya's another, a biological being they can't manipulate. He knows it, but from your reactions I'll assume he hasn't told you."

"What's she talking about?" Brooke asked him.

Zeke stared at the deck. "I haven't been able to read Maya since I met her."

"When were you planning to mention—?"

Maya interrupted. "What am I? I don't have Zeke's abilities or feel special in any way."

"I remember the aptitude you showed in the games we played together all those years ago," Eve Two reminisced. "You don't have super powers like in comic sims, but your understanding of things at age five was uncanny. You figured out how to solve a centuries-old puzzle called a Rubik's Cube all by yourself and beat my junior officers at strategy sims."

"Maya's always been good at stuff like that," Brooke said. "All it proves is she's a human being with above-average intelligence."

"Don't take my word for it. Ask the boy."

All heads again turned to Zeke.

"My people fear and revere her," he said. "I can sense it from them."

Brooke did a double-take. "You're in contact with them?"

"It's hard to put into words, but there's an information substructure permeating everything. Distance has no meaning to my people anymore."

"Some type of network based on quantum entanglement, maybe," Maya mused while tapping a finger against her cheek.

"As my awareness has increased, I've realized they've been reaching out to me."

"So where are they?"

"I don't know exactly."

"The Vril know their home world once existed somewhere in this galaxy," Eve Two said. "Two hundred thousand years ago, they weren't any more advanced than we are now. But today, at their rate of progress, who's to say where they've gone."

With her gaze directed up at the ceiling, Maya bit her lip in thought. "I gathered as much, but I wasn't wondering where they live. I mean, why aren't they here, on Earth, and everywhere around us? If they're so powerful, why're we still alive and free to have this conversation?"

"That's a good question. Care to share, boy?"

"My people are split into different factions," Zeke said. "Like humans, they've struggled to unite in culture and ideals. They—or rather we, I guess—have a complicated set of ethics that makes human behaviors and moralities seem very straightforward."

"In other words," Maya said, "certain members of your race would just as soon control or exterminate us, but others are holding them back."

"In simplified terms, yes."

"No matter how far a people advance," Eve Two said, "stability never lasts forever. Sooner or later, we'll have to face them. When that happens, the Vril won't sit back and let them decide whether the human race gets to keep on existing—or gets to exist in the first place."

In the first display of anger Brooke had seen from Zeke, the teen clenched a fist. "But the Vril's goals aren't all noble. My people would be far more likely to leave humans alone if you'd stop what you were doing back in the lab on Psykhe."

"Like typical overlords, your people fear others rising to their level of power. What we're doing is necessary to learn, grow, and survive. If your people have such high ethics, answer this question. How is it fair or just to place a cap on another species' evolution?"

"So if this machine humans use as a tool of convenience," Zeke said, pointing to the android technician standing near Brooke and Maya, "became self-aware, demanded equality, and started building starships and weapons, you'd be fine with it?" He narrowed his hawk-like stare. "Or would you simply deactivate and dispose of it before it turned on you?"

Eve Two aimed the wave gun at the primitive android and fired. The device buzzed but no visible beam projected from the tiny dish at the end of it.

From jaw to foot, one side of the tech's body cracked and crumbled. Its one remaining eye dimmed, and it went limp.

Brooke jumped out of the way as it flopped down onto the deck.

"Your people don't have exclusive rights to the secrets of existence," Eve Two spat at Zeke. She let the arm holding the wave gun dangle at her side. "The phase drive I helped invent gives us the ability to challenge your dominion over space and time."

The mention of time in conjunction with the phase drive resonated with Brooke.

Zeke appeared unfazed. "My people aren't constrained to the linear passage of time or to this universe," he elaborated, having heard the screams coming from her mind. "We've solved the greater mysteries of the multiverse."

"If they hadn't," Eve Two said, "none of this—none of anything— would exist."

"You're saying they're gods?" Brooke asked.

"Not in the traditional religious sense. Their level of technology makes them god-like to us, but they're fallible. We have a chance against them." The artificial woman raised the wave gun and pointed it at Maya. "A chance we once thought you gave us."

Pangs of fear seized Brooke. Sighting her rifle, she prepared to fire.

With her chest heaving, her niece whipped her hand up. "Stop. You'll only get us killed."

Glancing back and forth between them, Brooke complied, although the pangs intensified.

"Smart girl," Eve Two said to Maya. "Too smart, perhaps. We birthed you to be our salvation, the only one of your kind that panned out. Your protection was once mandated by the very top, but the timeline predilections have shifted. If I let you walk out of here with the EMG, you're likely to betray and destroy us all."

"You're talking about a hypothetical something I may or may not do like I've already done it," Maya said.

"But you have, and you will. In a gesture befitting the paradoxical nature of existence, it's my job to make sure you never get the chance to do what you've done."

Sensing that Eve Two was about to squeeze the trigger, Brooke leapt in front of Maya. "You'll have to kill me first." She dropped her rifle and held out both arms.

"Get out of the way," Maya yelled.

The android woman fired.

At first, Brooke felt nothing. Then the inside of the flight armor covering the right side of her body heated up and scalded her.

She stared down at her shoulder, watching as the armor glowed orange and caught fire. Parts of the molten composite popped and splattered. Bits struck her neck and cheek, burning it.

Shrieking in agony, she keeled over as the liquefied material seared her flesh.

She rolled around on the deck and flailed her extremities.

Through eyes flooded by tears, Brooke saw her niece standing over her.

"You shouldn't have done that," Maya fumed.

The girl's anger seemed directed at her, although Brooke struggled to concentrate on her distant-sounding voice.

"That was a lesser setting, Brooke," Eve Two said, "although I doubt you're thanking me about now. Consider the pain payback for ripping away my chance to head up the phase fighter project and for sending me plunging to my death in Neptune's atmosphere." She shook her head. "Listen to me. Sometimes, I don't know who I am with two neural patterns jumbled together in my head."

Brooke tried to curse and tell her where she could go. All she managed to push out of her throat was a whimper.

Through watering eyes, she watched the maniacal woman direct the wave gun toward her.

"Go ahead," Maya said.

The comment stabbed Brooke deeper than any physical torment.

No blast came as Eve pulled back her weapon, sounding intrigued. "So you've learned of your aunt's true nature."

"She killed my mother—her own sister—and my grandparents, so maybe she's getting what she deserves."

"What she deserves is far worse than she'll ever get."

"I'm kind of irritated, actually."

"Only irritated?"

"I mean at you, not her. You've never bothered to ask me what I want or where my loyalties lie. You've assumed I'm the harbinger of death, but for all you know, I'm willing to join up and let you use my abilities however you see fit."

Brooke's body continued to shudder. The extreme torture subsided as shock crept in on her.

Eve Two stood silent for what felt like ages.

She snorted. "Nice try. For a brief moment, you almost had me fooled. You've got far too much silly idealism and compassion swimming around in your head to join the Vril. No matter how badly your dear old aunt has wronged you, I can't believe you'd side with me over her."

"Maybe, maybe not," Maya said.

The android aimed her weapon at the girl. "I don't appreciate having my intelligence insulted." She lowered her voice to a rumbling hiss. "Truth be told, I was always going to kill you last, Brooke. The suffering you're enduring now is nothing compared to the anguish you'll experience when your niece's lifeless body collapses on top of yours."

Writhing on the deck, Brooke tried to cry out—tried to plead, beg, or do anything else that might spare Maya. But Brooke had all she could do to rasp for breath and stay conscious.

The shrill buzz of the wave gun sounded off.

Thirty-four—Prominence
Interstellar Space, January 2273 CE

Standing in the middle of the engine control room aboard the probe, Eve Two fired the commandeered wave gun at Maya. Brooke lay on the deck at her niece's feet, skin singed and body paralyzed by anguish, unable to protect her.

The whirring of the gun increased in intensity.

From her straight blonde hair to her scarlet boots, the artificial woman's body gyrated. She lost control of her motor reflexes and her grip on the gun, which fell from her grasp.

Eve Two shrieked in higher and higher pitch until her skull exploded in an echoing pop.

As tiny bits of shattered android rained down on Brooke, she felt the prick of an auto-syringe in the side of her neck.

She blinked the blood out of her eyes to find her niece crouching at her side.

"I never thought I'd be thanking Trevor for pulling a prank on me," Maya murmured, looking down at her.

Brooke struggled to focus on—let alone understand—the comment.

"Zeke," Maya called out, "get her out of her gear while I grab the EMG. Then let's get the hell out of here."

The latches and pneumatics sealing Brooke's armor clicked and hissed. The modular pieces loosened their grip, falling away from her burnt body.

"Oh, and Auntie," Maya said, standing up. "It may take me some time to forgive what you did, but I still love you."

That was all Brooke needed to hear to allow her waking mind to drift away.

♦

Trevor Young pushed up from his seat as Ensign Knight and his team escorted Byrne into the ECC. Recent events had mired him in a fatalistic fatigue. After enduring the loss of life, the second stranding of the ship, and everything else that had gone wrong, he was happy something— anything at all—had worked out.

When he had learned of *Nautilus's* destruction, he had stowed his grief and planned ahead. He had known Byrne wouldn't honor the truce. Thus, he had sent his head of security to apprehend her before she could go back into hiding and order her militia to continue to fight.

Stopping a meter away from him, Byrne adjusted her wrists in the magnetic cuffs binding them. "Release me at once," she snarled.

The officers and crewmen manning their stations shifted in their seats. Everyone looked up or over their shoulders.

"Once you order your people to end the mutiny," Trevor said.

"Do you honestly think apprehending me will put a stop to it? Or solve anything?"

"I do. We can work together to figure out the food rationing and get things back to normal. With one comm, you can end this madness."

"That one comm, as you say, would place this ship under the rule of a military dictatorship."

"This is a Defense vessel. I'm the captain. I should be the one in charge."

"First of all, this is a colony and scientific ship, not a military one. Second, you're the acting captain by default. You were never meant to be in command."

"Like it or not, I'm the most qualified candidate based on the chain of command. These protocols have withstood the test of time. We'd be better off if you abided by them."

"If I'd abided by them, thousands of civilians would've starved to death."

"I think you're exaggerating."

"Hardly. If I hadn't done what I did, there would've been riots. The people would've turned on me. We would've had anarchy instead of a civilized conflict."

Trevor held back a sigh. After all that had happened, they were still rehashing the same old argument. "I guess we'll have to agree to disagree. Now, the conflict's over. You've lost, so you're going to have to try things my way."

With her shoulders drooping, Byrne hung her head. "Very well. If we must do things the militant way . . ." She lifted her head and glared at him. "So be it."

Knight and his three security officers raised their rifles. Fanning out, they sighted Trevor and most everyone else on the bridge.

Ensigns Jenelle Williams and Sadi Pérez, along with several other officers, jumped up from their stations. Whipping out their particle handguns, they took aim at their captain.

Byrne shed her restraints and produced a small laser pistol from behind her back.

Panic seized Trevor's nervous system as he drew his wave gun. He had expected such treachery, but the reality of it still hit him like an antimatter bomb.

The service had schooled him on every conceivable scenario, though. He had planned for this situation.

At his insistence, every officer and crewmember wore a piece at all times. Now, those loyal to him hopped to their feet, drew their handguns, and pointed them at the traitors.

His tactical officer, Ensign Tokala Sigo, brandished his weapon and showed his support with a nod.

The two secondary hatches leading into the ECC slid open. Armed soldiers charged inside and directed their heavy rifles at the conspirators.

Rather than balking, Byrne's eyes shifted to the sides of the room. Android technicians turned from their duties, yanked tiny firearms out of ankle holsters, and targeted the soldiers.

Trevor assessed the situation, clenching his fingers around his gun. He found himself facing an old-fashioned standoff. Each side had about the same number of weapons trained on the other. No one had the edge. He had seen this situation too many times in sims. If one person flinched or grew trigger happy, a bloodbath would ensue.

No one could risk firing, yet no one dared yield, either.

One person acted before everyone locked their elbows and sighted their targets. As Byrne whipped the pistol out in front of her, she shot him in the abdomen.

Trevor grimaced as pain like searing needles tore apart his belly flesh. In the act of clutching the wound, he dropped his gun and fell to the floor, landing on his butt with a thud.

Amidst the agony, he knew what would happen next.

Gritting his teeth, he held out a blood-stained palm. "No one shoot."

He dropped his hand to the floor to keep from keeling over backwards and winced, preparing to die.

Friend and foe shifted in their stances. Panting echoed throughout the room. Weapons jostled in shaky hands, but no one fired.

Reapplying pressure to his injury, Trevor cursed, both in relief and pain. "I need a medic," he groaned.

"You're lucky you don't need a coffin," Byrne said. "I was aiming for your head."

As he glowered at her, bleeding out, the standoff continued.

◆

As Maya downshifted the Blazar into orbit around the Penphins' home world, she swore she had never seen a more beautiful sight—at least, not since she had first set eyes on *Horizons* in the sky above Triton months—no, years—ago. The vermillion rays of the red dwarf glinted off the spinning biosphere and aft modules of the starship. Despite the missing front third of the ship, it still moved her. Repair bots worked to affix the two antimatter pods recovered from *Nautilus* to the ring, giving the ship a triple set of nacelles containing enough fuel to get home.

In her lap, she held the critical component that would enable the return journey.

<I'm still not receiving any response from the starship,> Bob told her. <The communications systems don't appear to be active.>

"I guess we'll find out what's going on once we're aboard," Maya said.

Bob synced the fighter's velocity and orientation with the rotation of the ship. With his help, she set the craft down on one of the landing platforms located on the hull of the defense module. She may not have possessed her aunt's combat skills, but she knew more than enough to get from point A to point B and dock.

As the platform descended and flipped around, she peered back over her shoulder. "Not too shabby for a 'C' student, eh?"

Crammed into the rear seat with Zeke, Brooke hissed in pain. "I suppose I should expect something like 'beloved aunt and unfair grader' on my tombstone."

"The second part, at least." Maya grinned.

"I guess I'll always live to regret that. But at least we're still alive, not that I understand how or why."

"Every wave gun has a neural interface. When the android swiped the gun from me, I began working to reprogram it via the same backdoor a crewmate of mine used to make me lose my shirt—literally." Maya tapped her cheek. "I refused to believe the prank was an accident, so in my spare time, I figured out how he did it.

"On the probe, I needed to alter the firing mode without Eve noticing. I bought time with all the talk of me not caring whether you died. The Vril concocted the false filesim to turn us against each other, so I figured she might believe me for a little while if I acted like they'd succeeded. I hope you know I didn't mean any of it."

"I do now."

"Impressive," Zeke said. "I couldn't have orchestrated the outcome any better."

The Blazar came to rest in the main hangar bay. Maya hopped out, set the EMG down, and helped Zeke lower Brooke onto a stretcher a pair of androids had floated over.

"You're alive," a familiar voice shouted. "Hey Erik, she's alive!"

Turning, Maya saw Jo jogging toward her across the hangar.

The two friends locked into a firm embrace.

Once Jo released Maya, Erik took his turn.

Stepping back from the hug, he said, "I saw that fighter from *Nautilus* take out three tri-fighters." He pointed at the Blazar. "But I had to set down and wasn't sure what happened afterwards."

"Long story short, my aunt showed up and saved me." Maya glanced at Aunt Brooke sprawled out on the stretcher.

Her aunt dipped her chin in her direction, and Maya returned the gesture.

The androids directed the stretcher out of the hangar and to the infirmary.

Erik folded his arms across his flight suit. "We just got back, too. Neither of us have set foot outside the bay."

"After Erik joined me on the planet," Jo said, "a couple of Pulsars showed up and brought Charles, Erik, and me back—plus one additional passenger."

Maya followed Jo's gaze to a cart an android was pushing toward them. A squishy cushion filled with gravgel rested on top of the cart. Atop the cushion sat Ari. The Penphin thinker wore a pair of big, dark goggles and a breathing apparatus on his snout. The breather connected to a large air tank on his back.

"What're you doing here?" Maya asked. "I mean, I'm happy to see you, but our environment isn't right for you."

SINGIFICANT EFFORT IS REQUIRED FOR US TO MOVE. Ari's breather muffled his song. WE ARE TIRED, BUT IN TIME WE BELIEVE WE WILL ADAPT.

"Ari insisted on coming," Jo said. "He said something about you promising to show him our home world. I told him we might be able to take him with us, but that was before *Nautilus* was destroyed."

The mood in the hangar grew somber.

"Well, he's in luck." Maya bent down and picked up the EMG. "We are, in fact, going home."

Jo's jaw dropped. Erik's eyes widened.

"Is that what I think it is?" he asked.

Placing her hands on her hips, Jo said, "I don't believe it. Where'd you find it?"

Maya recapped everything that had happened to her since launching from the Penphins' planet. She also introduced Zeke to her friends but refrained from mentioning his origins or abilities.

"You're beyond fused, girl," Jo said.

Addressing Ari, Maya asked, "Are you sure this is what you want? I don't know when we'll be back."

TO REPEAT WHAT THE JO INDIVIDUAL SAID ABOUT VISITING OUR WORLD, THIS IS THE OPPORTUNITY OF A LIFETIME. THE RISKS ARE ACCEPTABLE IN ORDER TO BECOME MORE.

Maya smiled. "Then more it is. I guess we'll need to find you quarters and—"

A spacecraft-handling officer came sprinting over to them from across the hangar. "Ensign Davis," she said, chest heaving. "Thank the stars you're here."

The officer told her about the mutiny and standoff in the ECC.

After sending Jo and Erik to the reactor room with the EMG, Maya sprinted out of the hangar.

Outside the main hatch to the ECC, Zeke caught up to her.

"I know what's going on in there," he said. "If you'd like, I can knock everyone out or force them all to get along."

"That'd make everything a lot easier, wouldn't it?" Maya placed her hand on his shoulder. "But if we're going to make it home—or make it as a species in general—manipulating people isn't the answer."

He nodded.

"Here." She pulled her arm away. Pulling out her wave gun, she placed it in his hand. "Hold on to it for me."

"But—"

"Now go. Keep Aunt Brooke company while she recovers. If she says she wants to be alone, she's lying."

"Isn't that the truth, but will you be okay unarmed?"

"I don't know." He hesitated, so she added, "One more weapon will do more harm than good in there."

After Zeke disappeared down the corridor, Maya sucked in a deep breath and stepped into engineering command.

The barrels of several dozen handguns and rifles greeted her.

She threw her hands up in surrender. Every hair on her arms and neck straightened. She swore they might all pull away from her body.

"Ensign Davis," more than one crew member exclaimed.

Byrne looked over her shoulder, keeping her pistol trained on Trevor. "Maya . . ."

Acting Captain Young sat hunched over on the deck, holding his midsection. Blood coated his uniform and hands. Sweat slicked his paled face.

"Are you all right, sir?" Maya asked.

"I've been better," he squeaked.

"He needs medical attention."

A crewwoman holding a bioscanner in one hand and a handgun in the other said, "The blast struck a kidney and his intestines but missed anything more major. He'll live for now."

"Everyone put down your weapons." Maya dropped her arms. As she stepped further into the room, the door slid shut behind her. "Now, before anyone else gets hurt."

"Tell the mutineers to do it first," Ensign Sigo said. "We can't let them take control of the ship."

Ensign Pérez shouted, "With the mayor in charge, I'll finally get a decent meal. Hell, maybe I'll even get to spend fewer than twenty hours a day in the ECC. Tell Acting Captain Young and his people to stand down."

"I'm glad you're back safe and sound," Byrne said, "but I'm not sure your presence changes anything, not as long as we're stranded out here."

"What if we're not?" Maya said.

The mayor blinked at her. "What do you mean?"

Maya swung her gaze around the room. "Two words, people. Search probe." She locked stares with Trevor, whose eyelids had grown heavy. "What's the protocol?"

The expressions on everyone's faces contorted as they grappled with the hint.

Just when she thought she would have to spell it out, Trevor perked up. "Oh my . . . it's been here all along."

Pérez caught on next. "The IEF would've sent a probe here to search for us."

"But because we ended up skipping seven years," Williams said, "the one they sent years ago would've given up the search before we arrived."

"Which means it's been hanging out at the edge of the system with a perfectly good EMG all this time," Sigo finished.

"I'm glad all this feuding hasn't clouded everyone's thinking," Maya said.

Byrne looked like she wanted to hop up and down. "Well, let's go get it, then."

"I already did. It's being installed as we speak."

"Seriously?" Williams asked.

As if on cue, the cubes at Pérez's navigation station blinked and beeped. Turning, she dropped the arm holding her gun and interfaced. "The phase drive," she said, shaking with joy. "It's back online."

Everyone in the ECC stood in silent astonishment.

Maya approached Byrne, placed a hand on her arm, and lowered it. "Shall we go home?"

One by one, each person—and android—lowered and disarmed their weapons.

"Crewman," Maya ordered the woman who had assessed Trevor, "see to it that Ensign Young gets treated."

"Yes, ma'am." The woman rushed over to a panel next to a console, grabbed an auto-syringe from a med kit, and gave Trevor a shot.

Through the tear in his uniform, his skin congealed, and he sighed in relief.

"Now," Maya said, rubbing her palms together, "let's prepare for depart—"

Bob's voice boomed from the audio system. <Maya, the device—>

An earthquake-like tremor shook the ship. All the lights and cubes flickered. A couple of people lost their footing and hit the deck. Trevor hugged the floor while Maya and everyone else bent at the knees to stay upright.

"Bob?" Maya yelled when the tremor subsided.

As Trevor sat up, he asked, "Who's Bob?"

"A friend. What happened?"

<The initiation of the EMG activated and launched the device from a hidden bay between the aft rocket nozzles.>

Dread seized her. "Launched where? At the planet?"

<Negative. Toward the star.>

"The system's sun? But why . . ." She let the question trail off, having more or less figured it out. There were only so many possibilities.

<I've collected enough information to deduce the device's function. It's a CME initiator.>

"CME?" Byrne furrowed her brow.

"The acronym stands for coronal mass ejection," Maya said. "The device will cause a prominence—essentially, a solar flare—to form on the surface of the Penphins' sun. Solar particles ejected by the prominence will irradiate the day side of the planet."

"Meaning most of the life on the planet will contract radiation poisoning and die," Jo said as she rushed into the ECC, followed by Erik.

"It's what they intended all along."

"What who intended?" Trevor asked.

Maya pressed her palms to her temples, trying to figure out what she could do. "Tokala, can we destroy the probe before it reaches the star?"

Ensign Sigo studied his tactical cubes and shook his head. "It went relativistic and is already inside the corona. Even if we went after it with lasers, we couldn't get it before it enters the chromosphere."

"Jenelle, how long do we have?"

Working her station, Ensign Williams pulled up a cam angle of the red dwarf on the main cube and dimmed it to make the star visible. A large, black sunspot was forming on the raging surface.

"It's hard to say precisely," she said, "but the AIs predict a window of four to five minutes for the prominence to form and eject material. Then it'll take another two minutes for the mass of particles to strike the planet."

<I can refine the overall projection to six minutes and thirty-eight seconds.>

"Less than seven minutes until we kill the people we came here to meet," Maya said. "Think, think. What can we do?"

"Can we shoot the particles with our weapons?" Byrne suggested. "Maybe disperse them?"

"Not likely." Sigo pointed at the growing sunspot. "Think about how big a star is. While smaller than our sun, this one's still the size of two hundred thousand Earths. The area and volume of space taken up by the ejected particles will envelope the planet. We could spend a lifetime blasting away and not affect enough of it."

"I don't see how we could thrust an asteroid into the path of the ejection mass that's big enough to block it," Williams thought out loud.

Trevor stood, apparently feeling better. "Neither can the ship extend its force field widely enough to block the solar material. If we had a few years to build some type of shield wall closer to the sunspot, maybe, but we don't have the time or resources." He glanced at Maya. "I don't see what we could do."

Maya opened her mouth, trying to force out an idea. Something about Jenelle and Trevor's unworkable plans resonated with her, but she couldn't figure out what.

Hanging her head, she said, "I don't know, either."

<I've run simulations of the suggested options, all unsuccessful. I'm afraid my ability to improvise is still evolving.>

Everyone else in the room wore horrified expressions in silence.

"Forgive me for my selfishness," Byrne said, "but there's no reason for us to die. We should shift home."

A phase shift, Maya considered, raising her gaze. *What about it?*

As the solution hung just beyond the grasp of her conscious mind, the main entrance to the ECC slid open. Aunt Brooke hobbled into the room, propped up by Zeke.

"I heard what happened," Brooke said.

Maya stared at her aunt's healing but still-disfigured face, thinking of how the woman had rescued the shell craft.

Like a rush of blood to the head, the answer flooded Maya's brain. "Auntie, you're a lifesaver." She stood up straight. "Bob, can *Horizons's* wake limiter be disabled like a phase fighter's?"

<Technically, yes, but the resulting space-time distortions could have devastating effects on anything in the vicinity—oh, I comprehend now. Very clever, Maya.>

Brooke's eyes lit up. "It just might work—if the distortions spread out far enough."

"Well, let's think about it," Maya said. "Back in the war, you destroyed large pyramid carriers with a much smaller fighter craft. *Horizons* is the size of those pyramids, so the effect should scale up." She tapped her cheek. "Even still, we'll need to get close."

"Close enough to the star to redirect the clump of solar material before it expands too much," Trevor added.

"The AIs confirm we'd need to enter the corona," Williams said. "But determining the orbit, coordinates, and timing without running detailed sims is beyond them."

< I can handle the mathematics.>

Maya tapped her palm with one finger, using the hand to represent the star and her fingernail to denote the ship. "We don't have time to fly all the way into the corona under conventional thrust. The heat would fry the ship, anyway. We'll need to shift twice like you did to protect the shell craft, Auntie.

"At the right moment, we'll shift near the prominence for a fraction of a second, which won't be long enough to get toasted, and shift away again. To make sure we retain enough antimatter to get home, we stay at hyperspace after the second shift and head straight for the Sol system. All that, plus accounting for the star's gravity, will take some serious calculations, Bob."

<Understood.>

"Now hold on a second," Byrne said. "What's the likelihood that this plan succeeds? The idea of hurling ourselves into the fire to save the locals may seem noble, but if there's a significant chance we won't succeed, we should stop and consider what's in the best interest of the people aboard this ship."

Maya nodded. "It's scary. Believe me, I don't want to die any more than you do. But risking the lives of a few thousand people to save millions—not to mention preserving a precious planetary ecosystem—seems acceptable to me regardless of the odds." As Byrne twisted her expression, grappling with the proposition, Maya added, "Could we live with letting these people die, knowing we had the means to save them?"

The mayor shook her head.

Everyone in the ECC agreed with the sentiment.

"Okay, then," Maya said. "Sadi, take us out of orbit and toward the star. Bob, prepare the double-upshift itinerary."

"Now breaking orbit," Pérez announced.

The main display cube showed the planet drifting out of the picture.

<Program complete and ready. First shift is set to commence in thirteen seconds.>

"All right, everyone, brace yourselves," Maya said. "If this doesn't work, it's been an honor."

The crew played a game of musical chairs for seats. Whoever got to them first strapped in tight. People who missed out found a spot along the edges of the room or near a console where they could grip a handhold.

Trevor blocked everyone from sitting in his makeshift command chair. After offering it to Maya, he took a seat on the deck.

Nodding in thanks, she settled into the chair and gripped the armrests.

Aunt Brooke crouched at her side and held her hand.

<Three, two, one, zero. Upshifting.>

One moment, stars filled the main cube. The next, the display showed a sheet of flaming marigold, tangerine orange, and ruby red.

Thirty-five—Extol
Neptunian System, July 2273 AD

With hands clasped behind his back, Captain Henrik Westerberg paced the bridge of the ISC star cruiser *Kingston*, listening to a report from his first officer.

"American, Brazilian, Chinese, Russian, and Martian forces have downshifted well inside the orbit of Nereid," Commander Gabriela Zavala said from her post. "They should reach Triton in fifteen minutes. ISC Defense is moving to engage."

The main cube displayed hundreds of enemy carriers deploying thousands of Pulsars. Another display showed the ISC's outnumbered and outgunned forces orbiting Triton in formation with the *Kingston*.

Westerberg ordered his fleet to scramble all fighter craft in defense of the moon.

His frown hid any outward display of the trepidation gnawing at his innards. Most of the nation-states of Earth and all of Mars had purged the ISC from their soil. Gassendi Colony on Mercury, Landis in Venus's atmosphere, Mars, and Huygens City on Titan had all declared their independence along with the Kuiper Belt Alliance. With Russian and Chinese forces from Ganymede occupying Callisto and Europa, the last remaining ISC loyalists had fallen back to Triton and taken refuge in its defunct IEF bases and colonies.

When Westerberg thought about it, he failed to identify a sensible reason for the continued hostilities. Everyone had achieved the independence they had demanded. This latest war felt like an out-of-control machine. It seemed as if someone had broken the power switch, leaving no way to turn it off.

The destruction of the Vril holding camps had only fanned the flames. According to the media feeds, a prisoner had somehow gotten hold of an antimatter charge. The suicidal madwoman had told the guards she would rather die than endure captivity or let them execute her. When she had detonated the explosive, she had taken the other one hundred thousand inmates with her, including former ISC Chancellor Danuwa Ajunwa. Their deaths had rid the solar system of an inconvenient problem, but the massacre had also led to vehement finger-pointing by the quarreling factions of mankind.

Fear and resentment motivated this assault, Westerberg surmised. The rest of the solar system refused to allow retreating members of a corrupt dictatorship, as the public saw the ISC, to put down roots, lick their wounds, and pose a threat in the future. They had come to finish the job. Thus, it fell on his shoulders to defend the last remnants of a fallen empire.

For the briefest of moments, he considered surrendering, but setting down arms would only reduce the coming battle to a massacre.

At the end of the day, though, such musings were nothing more than an indulgence for a duty-bound officer. Westerberg had his orders.

"Five minutes until engagement," Commander Zavala reported.

Following a heavy sigh, he hardened his demeanor and began to dictate combat strategies to his officers.

"Sir," the remote sensing officer shouted. "I'm detecting gravimetric fluctuations outside the combat zone. A wormhole is forming, and a big one at that."

Westerberg tensed. Was the enemy trying to outflank him? Did other territories intend to join the fight? That massacre might take place if the entire solar system ganged up on him.

"Order wings four and five to defend against a possible second front," he said.

"Sir," the sensing officer said, "a massive ship's exiting the wormhole."

The main cube showed the churning vortex as it expanded. After disgorging the damaged vessel, it shrank and disappeared. Flaming wisps shrouded the ship but dissipated on contact with the near-vacuum of cold space.

Westerberg blinked. At first, he misidentified the ship as *Nautilus*.

According to official reports he had struggled to accept, solar forces had attacked and destroyed the warship during its shakedown flight. But this vessel featured a spinning biosphere and had lost the forward command and habitat modules.

"I don't believe it," Zavala said, shaking her head. "The transponder signal registers as IEF-01." She swiveled in her chair toward him. "Sir, it's *New Horizons*."

"After all these years, she was still out there." He curled one side of his mouth upward.

His faint smile faded as *Horizons* headed straight for the center of the combat zone.

"Order all units hold their fire and fall back," he barked. "Contact the other fleet commanders."

"Do you think . . . ?" Zavala asked.

"I don't see how anyone could mount an effective assault with that ship in the way." For the gruff Westerberg, the statement qualified as an exuberant outburst.

◆

Lieutenant Commander Maya Davis stood on stage with her shipmates in the former ISC Council hall in Red Rock City on Mars. Filled with a mix of anticipation and foreboding, she awaited the start of the hastily-assembled homecoming ceremony for *New Horizons*. Representatives from every nation and colony in the solar system filed into the auditorium, yet the spherecams outnumbered the people.

Given the attendance of mankind's leaders, peace talks would follow the ceremony. *Horizons* had averted a major skirmish when it had gotten in the way of the battle for Triton, but the lull in the fighting would prove brief if the proceedings fell apart.

As conversations echoed throughout the auditorium, Jo gave her a light punch in the arm. "Why so glum, Lieutenant Commander?" She over-enunciated her friend's new rank, ribbing her as she so often did.

"I'm not glum, Lieutenant Ryder," Maya retorted, "just contemplative."

"We defied the odds," First Lieutenant Erik Maxwell said, "and made it back in one piece."

Lieutenant Trevor Young folded his arms and gave a reluctant nod.

"Believe me, I'm glad to be home. It's just that . . ." Maya's mind wrestled with everything that had happened. Certain things still didn't make sense. Once she put the puzzle together, she would confide in her friends.

Giving her the once-over, Jo said, "You're restless. Despite all we went through, you can't get back out there soon enough."

Maya bit her lip and forced a smile. "Maybe."

Faculty from the Solar Science Society ascended to the opposite side of the stage and took their seats, cueing Maya and her shipmates to settle into their chairs. As one of the few remaining intrasolar institutions still enjoying a semblance of public approval, S-cubed had elected to coordinate and host the event at the request of the squabbling territories.

When the society director, Professor Kevin Sommerfield, stepped up to the podium, the audience quieted.

Maya had yet to process Uncle Kevin's separation from Aunt Brooke. What had seemed like a happy marriage when Maya had left had dissolved in some part because of her reported loss. The former spouses had embraced and even kissed after the ship had returned, but things had felt different between them. Regardless of their relationship status, Uncle Kevin had assured his niece-in-law he would always be there for her.

Her uncle introduced the returnees and welcomed them home. After the applause died down, he jumped into a concise summary of the ship's journey, from disembarking eight years ago to rebuilding after the collision to *Nautilus's* sacrifice to salvaging the EMG from the probe and saving the Penphins from the CME.

Cubes projected throughout the assembly hall, showing footage of the averted disaster. Satellites in orbit of the Penphins' planet had recorded and transmitted the vidsim to the solar system via the interstellar probe's comm array. A column of crimson flame spewed forth from the surface of the star. Concentric ripples propagated through space from a point in front of the raging solar prominence. When the superheated plasma struck the distortion field, particles ricocheted off it at angles directed away from the planet. The satellites noted trace amounts of radiation penetrating the field, meaning the indigenous population would suffer aftereffects like higher cancer rates. But the Penphins would survive.

They had Maya to thank for their salvation, Uncle Kevin declared, his face beaming.

The recognition warmed her heart, but what mattered most was the unveiling of the full truth, replete with the uncomfortable realities. He didn't hold back the Vril's manipulation of everything or the existence of a more advanced exospecies lurking somewhere out there.

He did, however, tweak his story to account for two omissions. First, he kept Zeke out of it, granting the teen the chance to live a life without scrutiny among humans. Second, he withheld the true capabilities of the phase drive.

Invoking mind-numbing technical terminology, he blamed *Horizons's* skipping seven years on a fluke malfunction involving time dilation and promised that the society would take steps to ensure it didn't happen again. Time passing more quickly for those aboard the ship was not the same thing as traveling to the future, he clarified.

Withholding parts of the truth didn't feel right to Maya, but she accepted the reasoning. If the unstable political climate of the solar system provided any indicator, the human race wasn't ready for time travel.

When Uncle Kevin spoke of the destruction of the Vril holding camps, he suggested mankind now had the opportunity to start anew, provided they chose to seize the moment. At long last, the solar system had shed the scheming from the shadows.

The defunct organization served as the perfect scapegoat, freeing everyone from guilt and providing a rallying point around which to move forward. The overwhelmed expressions worn by the influential people in the crowd indicated the Vril might've succeeded with their shock-and-awe agenda. Despite their neat and tidy bowing out, something told her she hadn't seen the last of them.

Her uncle's introduction ended by observing a moment of silence for the people lost during the mission, including Captains Reed and Gibbons.

Representatives appointed by the former residents of Star City took their turn at the podium next. A man mourned his wife and son who had perished in the collision. Families stood huddled together, telling of their fight against hunger.

Mayor Abigail Byrne spoke last in the civilian segment. Ever the politician, she massaged her words, making her mutiny sound like a gallant effort to provide the acting captain with much-needed assistance. The ordeal she had helped everyone through served as her platform to campaign for a position in whatever emerged from the ashes of the current conflict.

One by one, members of the crew told their tale. Williams, Pérez, Sigo, and Knight recapped their struggle to keep the ship up and running. Charles Wallace painted a verbal picture of the beauty and driving forces of the Penphins' ecosystem. Erik recapped his fierce dogfights against the tri-fighters, Jo talked about the impressive ruins, and Trevor downplayed the turmoil aboard ship.

Without exception, each and every one of them bestowed more praise upon Maya than she felt she deserved. To hear her friends tell it, she had single-handedly saved the day.

As Trevor shuffled back to his seat and her turn to speak came up, she found her body free of the tension that had paralyzed her prior to the speech she had given at the launch ceremony. Facing a room full of a few thousand people didn't seem so bad after all she had endured.

Her only jitters came when Jo whispered, "You're up, soda stain."

Maya approached the podium to deafening applause. When the noise died down, she recapped her personal highlights and gave credit to people she felt deserved it, especially to her reclusive aunt, who had bowed out of the ceremony.

She concluded her speech with what she hoped would help to bring about the future she envisioned. "I'm privileged to have spent time with the Penphins, so I'd like to give you the opportunity to meet one of them." Holding out her hand, she beckoned to Ari off stage.

The thinker waddled out from behind her shipmates, moving well in Martian gravity a little higher than found on his planet. Murmurs, side talk, and a few outbursts broke out.

For effect, she asked him to flap his flings, although he couldn't fly in Mars' thinner atmosphere. She also engaged him in brief conversation. As his musical tones echoed throughout the auditorium, an AI translated them and projected a human-sounding voice on a delay.

"Believing everything happens for a reason seems too narcissistic to me," she again addressed the attendees, "but I don't think we met the Penphins by accident. They're a mirror for us. They're all linked by telempathy, meaning they can feel each other's thoughts. Even now, with twenty light years separating him from his people, Ari can feel them as if he were still on his world. He knows they're okay, and they can feel he's safe with us. None of them have ever hurt another of their kind on purpose because harm done to an individual is felt by all."

She gripped the sides of the podium. "To us, the concept of zero conflict sounds far-fetched, and perhaps rightfully so. Our two peoples have very different natures, which is why I believe the dream of human unity has to die."

Even in a room permeated by anti-ISC sentiment, the comment elicited dipped brows, wide eyes, and whispers. Uncle Kevin cringed like a wounded animal.

"All my life," Maya said, "I believed in the ideal of one united mankind. In my naïve optimism, I didn't understand why everyone couldn't get along. But after visiting the Penphins, I understand why that can never be for us.

"Think of things this way. What would happen if we designated their planet as a human territory and forced them to live by human laws and customs? It wouldn't work. They're too different, and so too are different groups of humans. This is why separate human institutions must exist to allow people to pursue health and happiness in different ways.

"Now, I'm not saying we should all split up and go our separate ways. That would be an extreme step in the wrong direction. I'm no politician. I don't claim to have all the answers. But what I foresee is an institution that protects the autonomy of different nations but provides a framework for collaboration and cooperation. We have the ability to settle other star systems and meet other peoples, so we need to start thinking beyond ourselves. Whatever mutually beneficial alliances we create should steer clear of terms like 'intrasolar' and instead embrace the interstellar distances that our future will span.

"Call me biased, but organizations such as the IEF and S-cubed embody these ideals. They can serve as a foundation. Let's get out there and settle new exoworlds. There's more than enough space and resources for everyone to live the way they want without infringing upon others' freedoms, and there's so much more to learn. We must also work together to prepare for threats we don't yet possess the capacity to defend against today."

Taking a breath, she concluded her speech. "And so I'll leave the details to people more experienced in these areas than I am. But in your talks, I implore you to keep the Penphins in mind. Every time you're tempted to squabble over something petty or sell someone short for your own benefit, look up into the sky toward their star. Think about the world out there where selfishness and deceit and aggression are foreign concepts. If that place exists, we can at least learn to stop shooting at one another."

◆

Leaning against the wall at the back of the auditorium, Brooke soaked in her niece's speech. The parental figure in her swelled with pride despite her efforts to appear nonchalant. If she didn't know better, she might swear Maya had gained the wisdom of the years she had skipped.

A pair of senior officers from the Japanese Aerospace Wing stood up from their seats in the back row and headed for the exit. As they passed Brooke, they addressed her as "General."

She nodded in acknowledgment and then sighed at the irony. After almost three decades of pining, she had regained her commission with the rank of major general. The only problem? The rank was honorary, granted by S-cubed, a non-military outfit, for PR purposes. No unified aerospace defense force existed anymore, and she didn't subscribe to the politics of any nation or colony enough to sign on with their armed forces. For all practical purposes, her career was right back where it had been before *Horizons* had departed.

Perhaps the best reward for her return had been Kevin allowing her to stay off the stage. If she had known she would have to endure the excruciating adulation of this mob, she might've stayed in the Gliese 581 system.

She straightened her leather jacket. *Maybe I should go back to teaching?* Shoving a thumb in one jean pocket, she played with the press pass dangling around her neck, mulling the prospect.

As the crowd showered Maya with an ovation, an individual rested their back against the wall next to Brooke, bumping shoulders with her.

"Care for one?" the hatted woman asked, extending a bag of licorice sticks toward her.

"No. Thanks." Wrinkling her nose at the violation of personal space, Brooke glared at the perpetrator and jerked away from her.

Eve Three pushed her stocking cap up out of her eyes. "Really? Must we go through the whole 'shocked to see you' routine again?" This she said while nibbling.

Brooke stood gaping at her, unsure whether to run, scream, or alert security.

Against every instinct, Brooke grabbed a licorice stick and leaned back against the wall. What else could she do, really?

"It's so inspiring, isn't it?" Eve Three said. "The triumphant return home, a new day dawns for humanity, and all that."

"If you say so," Brooke droned.

"It reminds me of a different time—of another lifetime. Sometimes, I miss the spotlight, but my current line of work has its advantages."

"How can that work continue with your minions euthanized?"

Raising a thin eyebrow, Eve Three pulled a soda bottle out of her heavy coat and took a swig. "I've been an android for over eight years, and I'm still basking in every delight. I can eat and drink whatever I want with no guilt or consequence, unlike a human being." She twisted the cap back on the soft drink and shoved it into the pocket of her long coat.

As Kevin issued concluding remarks, the artificial woman held her hand out toward the audience. "Give people what they want—what feels good—and they'll gobble it up despite knowing the harmful truth."

"Somehow," Brooke said, "this was all part of the latest ruse by you con artists."

"I consider myself a social architect. When a civilization grows dysfunctional, it's time to tear it down and build anew."

Brooke blinked in realization. "You never intended to shock the ISC into greater unity, did you? That always struck me as a rather vague goal."

"The ISC wasn't working, so we did what needed to be done."

"The splinter group. Letting a bunch of college kids detect the Mars base. Allowing me to steal and release the list—" Brooke let the hand holding her licorice dangle as pangs of nausea cramped her abdomen. "By the stars, the list. Tell me you didn't send all those innocents to their deaths."

"Innocents? I'd hardly use that term to describe human roadblocks to the future."

"You butcher. You killed one hundred thousand people to get them out of the way."

"And replaced them with agents of change," Eve Three said. "Now that we no longer exist, we're free to begin the next phase of building a better tomorrow—or rather, a better yesterday."

Clenching a fist, Brooke resisted the urge to grab the android by her coat lapels. She knew any assault wouldn't end well for her. "At least the filesim you concocted failed to turn Maya against me, although I'm still not sure why."

Finishing off another piece of licorice, Eve said, "Let's just say in order to help Maya fulfill her role, you may have to stand against her." Pocketing the licorice, she turned to leave.

Brooke grabbed her by the shoulder. "You said help Maya, but I thought you wanted her dead? Will you try to kill her again? If so, I won't rest until I purge every last copy of you."

The android directed her feral stare back toward her. "Your hollow threats are heartwarming but unnecessary."

"Then you don't intend to harm her?" Brooke pulled her hand back.

"I couldn't before, and I dare not try now, even if I wanted."

"What does that mean?"

"Why don't you ask her?" Eve Three strolled toward the exit. "I trust the girl's put it together by now."

Thirty-six—Immemorial
Mars, July 2273 CE

Hours after the ceremony, Brooke sat at a picnic table in the courtyard of the former ISC headquarters, awaiting her niece in a melancholy state of mind. She propped her chin up on one palm and rested her elbow on the table, gazing out over the deep canyons of Valles Marineris. The evening sun tinted the horizon above the rocky landscape to shades of scarlet and tangerine. Lakes and rivers shimmered, reflecting the sunlight.

Her right hand shook. With her left palm, she gripped her other wrist to hold it still. The meds had kept her deteriorating nervous system in check throughout her ordeal to rescue Maya. But ever since Brooke had departed Gliese 581, the suppressants had grown less effective. She supposed that on some subconscious level, her body knew it could let go.

The arthritis-like symptoms weren't a serious concern at the moment. Increasing her dosage quelled her trembling, but she wondered how much time would pass until she finally paid the price for her spark use.

Kevin sat down next to her, stealing her from her thoughts, and stared off into the distance. "How're you feeling?"

Hiding her hands in her lap, she shrugged. "Selfish. Since Marie died, my sole purpose in life has been to raise and protect Maya. But now that she's all grown up, I no longer have a purpose."

"Ah. Thinking about what's next, eh?" He folded his arms and rested them on the table. "Well, I only sat in on part of the armistice proceedings, but it sounds like everyone may settle on a form of Maya's suggestion. Someone threw out the name Interstellar Alliance, which seemed to catch on favorably. Zeke's people were a popular topic. It's a near certainty the IEF will not only be reinstated but expanded to absorb ISC Defense. We're going to be building many more starships like *Horizons*, which will need experienced pilots and leaders."

"I guess that might not be so bad." Fondly, she studied his graying whiskers. "But I've been thinking about other things, too." She swallowed. "I know I can be difficult to deal with sometimes. I can understand if you're adamant about moving on without looking back, but . . ." She let her words trail off, unsure of how to convey what she wanted to say.

After a moment, he said, "One fact will always remain, Brooke. There are things you care about more than me."

She gripped the bench with both hands to keep herself from keeling over. "I know."

"Having said that, life's not without risk and sacrifice. As I watched what you did for Maya and waited, not knowing whether I'd ever see you again, I realized something. If I were placed in a similar position, I'd do the same for you." He placed his hand on top of hers.

Gazing into his eyes, she donned a goofy smile and melted.

An android groundskeeper approached the picnic table, interrupting the moment. "I'm afraid there's no loitering in the courtyard after hours," he said.

Glaring at the artificial man, Brooke snarled, "Get out of here before I rip your—"

"Calm down." Her husband restrained her.

The android took a seat on the opposite bench. "Professor, did my attempt at humorous deceit have the desired effect?"

"Oh yes." Kevin grinned.

Brooke blinked at the android. "Bob?"

"Hello, ma'am."

"Wow, I've never seen you in a body before. It suits you."

"Thank you. Observing you through actual eyes is a positive experience for me as well."

She had much on her mind to say to her old friend, but she held back when she saw Zeke leading the Penphin visitor across the courtyard toward them. Unused to walking any significant distance, the four-legged creature paused his waddling to rest every few seconds.

"I thought we agreed that you'd keep a low profile," Brooke said as

Zeke stepped up to the table.

"So far, I've been unable to decide on a proper disguise," Zeke joked. "The reporter alter ego has been done too many times."

"You know what I mean. You were supposed to wait for us at the professor's lab."

"You didn't want me to do that. Besides, Ari and I sensed one another and had to meet."

Shaking her head at Kevin, she sighed. "How do you discipline a kid who can read your mind and alter your thoughts and actions?"

"I guess he disciplines you as much as you do him," Kevin said.

Ari sang in higher and lower pitches to everyone at the table. The melody sounded almost as if an audio synthesizer had produced it.

"That means hello," Zeke said. "He also likes the redness of Mars. It reminds him of home." Before Brooke could pose her next question, he added, "Yes, I can understand him. The sounds he makes are music, and music is simple math."

Brooke looked over her shoulder and saw Maya standing in front of ISC headquarters, shaking hands with a man wearing an IEF uniform.

Parting ways with the officer, Maya cut across the grass lawn toward the group and waved. As Maya passed by a row of chrysanthemums, she stopped to sneeze.

She bent down to hug her aunt and uncle when she reached the table.

Plopping down next to the android on the opposite bench, Maya said, "Hi, Bob."

The AI dipped the chin of the commandeered groundskeeper. "Hello, Maya."

"How'd you know it was him?" Brooke asked.

"Why else would a random android be sitting here with you?" Maya directed a finger back and forth between Bob and herself. "We've done this before."

"I see." Brooke leaned over the table. Lowering her voice, she told her niece about her chat with Eve Three. "She claimed you'd know why the Vril no longer want to kill you."

Maya tapped her fingers against the table. "They never wanted to kill me—well, they both did and didn't. They had to try, at least."

"Please clarify this supposition," Bob said.

"Let me ask this. Did the CME initiator need the EMG to operate or launch in any way?"

"Negative. They are independent subsystems."

Kevin stroked his chin stubble. "But your report and the story I told the solar system claimed the activation of the EMG is what triggered the doomsday device."

"The EMG triggered the initiator only because the Vril rigged it to do so," Maya said. "The initiator didn't launch when we first arrived in the system because Bob caused the collision and kept the rogue AI from activating it."

"What AI?"

"The Vril uploaded a semi-sentient program into the starship's systems prior to its disembarkation," Bob explained. "The program's main function was to make sure the initiator launched, but I managed to block its access. Later when I uploaded to the Blazar, I left a copy of myself aboard the ship to, as they say, continue the fight."

"Then how was the initiator able to launch? Did the rogue AI somehow best your copy?"

The groundskeeper cocked his head. "That is an outstanding question. After we returned to *New Horizons* from the probe, I found that both my copy and the rival program had been wiped from the ship's memory. All change log entries were erased, so no record exists of who launched the device or how it was done."

"According to Trevor," Maya said, "the Vril boarded *Horizons*. He told me the ship lost every power system all at once, which should never happen. " She sat back and tapped her cheek. "This is all guesswork, but I think Eve Two came aboard, executed a complete system shutdown and restore to wipe Bob's copy, and rigged the device to launch once a new EMG was installed."

"I can count the number of people on one hand—both living and deceased—with the expertise to pull that off." Kevin ran a hand through his hair. "If this android had the neural structure of my former colleague in her head, she'd be one of the capable few." He shivered at the notion.

Brooke slapped both palms down. "What are you saying, squirt? That Eve could've launched the device while she was aboard? But that would mean she never needed to leave *Horizons* and get the EMG from the probe."

"Exactly," Maya said. "So why did she bother?"

"Well, with her starship destroyed, she didn't want to end up stranded in the system. Her plan might've been to bring the EMG back to *Horizons*, launch the initiator, and shift home with everyone else."

"That's one potential answer, but she sacrificed the destroyer and its crew. I think she was more than willing to part with a single copy of herself. Returning home would've been nothing more than a bonus."

"Now you've lost even me," Zeke said.

Everyone leaned in closer to Maya as she continued. "The Vril know the drive is capable of time travel. They have knowledge of the involvement of Zeke's people in our past, and somehow, I factor into all of that. This is going to sound very egocentric, but what if the entire mission was all about me?"

"You're right," Brooke said. "You're the center of my world, and that theory still sounds conceited."

"I agree, but maybe everything was a kind of test, one which the Vril hoped I'd pass."

Kevin directed a doubtful stare in the girl's direction. "As a scientist, I can't accept that anyone could predict and manipulate events precisely enough to cause events to play out exactly as they did—not even with foreknowledge of things to come. The multiverse is too stochastic, and there're too many variables out of our control."

"That's why I said they hoped I'd pass. I didn't say they knew I'd pass. They had contingency plans for each potential outcome." Maya began counting on her fingers. "If the ship never crashes, the device launches, kills the Penphins, and the Vril get their shock and awe. If Eve Two kills me on the probe, she takes the EMG back to *Horizons*, the genocide results, and shock and awe. If I stop her and save Penphins— which I believe was the primary desired outcome—the result is still more or less the same. And now time travel is possible. Don't you see? They're manipulating events and—"

"Experimenting with alternate timelines—universes—for the day when they can literally do it." Kevin cupped a hand over his mouth.

"Exactly. Aunt Brooke, think about when we faced Eve Two on the probe. If you're an agent serious about completing your mission, you don't stand around and reveal your plans to the opposition like a cliché evildoer in a bad sim. You shoot first and ask questions later."

"It's like she was challenging you to blow her head off," Brooke muttered.

"Either way, the Vril get a favorable outcome, " Maya said, "only things turn out most favorably if I best her—or so I'd like to believe."

Shaking his head, Kevin said, "Still, all this seems beyond even the Vril."

"Beyond the Vril, or beyond humans?"

All eyes turned on Zeke.

◆

Eve Three strolled into a conference room on the top floor of the former Martian ISC headquarters building. Removing her hat and coat, she settled into a chair at the long table and accepted a cup of coffee from an android servant.

"Bring me a triple-fudge brownie," she told it. "No, wait. I'll have a slice of New York cheesecake with extra cherries."

As the android left to fulfill the order, Danuwa Ajunwa frowned at her from across the table. "Still obsessed with food, I see."

"Neural transplants often magnify old habits," Eve said, "so don't be so quick to judge. Something similar may happen to you once you're in your new body."

Eve Three's dessert arrived.

"With any luck, I'll become obsessed with perfecting my serve," Ajunwa said. "How are the peace talks going?"

After savoring a forkful of cheesecake, the android said, "Our operatives are hard at work making sure the alliance forms and the IEF becomes a force to be reckoned with."

"It's a pity I'm no longer involved, but it was time for me to step aside."

"Conditioning your successor hasn't gone as smoothly as I'd hoped. Mr. Saito is being quite stubborn. The cognitive reprogramming only partially took."

The door swished open, and Shin Saito trudged inside the room. Two armed agents accompanied him.

"Speaking of your replacement," Eve Three said.

Shin settled into a seat next to the artificial woman. Sweat slicked the tense brow beneath his flat cap. He took his time placing his hands on the table and stared down at them.

The two agents stood behind him.

"How are you feeling today, Shin?" Eve Three asked.

"I'm, um, I'm not sure," he said. "A little queasy maybe."

"Do you remember what you have to do?"

His forehead wrinkled as he struggled for the answer. "Rise to a position of prominence within the new alliance," he answered at last.

"That's right," Eve Three said, lifting another forkful toward her mouth.

"Eve," the man standing at the windows said. "A word, please."

Eve Three set her utensil down. Springing to her feet, she hurried over to speak to the mastermind behind all that she had accomplished.

As she came to the windows, she looked down in the same direction as the leader of the Vril. The Penphin, Director Sommerfield, Zeke, Brooke, and the leader's daughter all sat together in the courtyard far below.

"Yes, Mr. Katayama?" she asked.

Takashi Katayama sipped from a water bottle without averting his gaze from the view. "It pains me to see Shin in such condition."

"I'm sorry, sir. I've scheduled another procedure, and I'll see to it the doctors perform detailed neural mapping sims before proceeding. We'll get it right the second time."

Sighing, Katayama said, "I shouldn't pity him. My son chose to turn against us. He brought this on himself."

Eve Three remained tight-lipped.

"How are the experiments progressing?" he asked.

"Slowly," she said. "There's no forcing the breakthrough of all breakthroughs. The scientists think it could still take decades, but that's all conjecture."

"The sooner we achieve it, the sooner we can place the human race on an even footing with them. Until then, we'll be at their mercy should they decide to come." He took another swig and thrust his chin toward the picnic table below. "It's in her possession?"

"Mendez almost screwed it up, but yes, your daughter ended up with it. Maya's still carrying the device and hasn't yet told anyone about it."

"Very well." Katayama turned from the window. "Now it becomes a matter of time."

♦

The chirping of birds and crickets filled the eerie silence that had fallen over the table in the courtyard. A blood-red sunset served to thicken the collective anxiety level.

Seeking to lighten the mood, Brooke asked her niece, "So what was your conversation about with that officer before you came over here?"

"Oh, you mean with Captain Hayes?" The girl wiggled her eyebrows. "He was talking about correcting a huge oversight."

Kevin folded his arms. "What oversight?"

"Can you believe we've traveled twenty light years to another planetary system, yet we've never made the four-light-year hike to the nearest star?"

"Alpha Centauri, huh?"

"That's right. The skipper's planning on augmenting a star cruiser and increasing the antimatter supply. It should take a month to get there. He asked me to join his crew. I said yes."

"So soon?" Brooke almost had a conniption. "But we just got back. We've barely spent any time together, and—"

"Don't worry, Auntie. They won't be ready to go for weeks. I promise we'll get plenty of quality time before then."

The Penphin whistled and flapped his flings.

Maya stood. "Speaking of quality time, I promised Ari I'd take him to see Earth. How about we head to the beach near my old place in Auckland, grab some fruity drinks, and relax for once?"

Nodding, Brooke said, "Sounds good."

"Great. I'll catch up with you there."

"Where are you going?"

"I have an errand to run first." Maya rounded the table and kissed her aunt on the head. "See you all soon." She rushed off across the courtyard.

Kevin rose from his seat and joined Zeke and Ari. "Shall we go?" He started leading them toward the phase port. "We'll need to take a few precautions to avoid reactions to Ari."

"I can make people not notice him if you want," Zeke said.

Rising to her feet, Brooke took in her surroundings.

A bird—a long-billed starthroat—landed on the picnic table. After cocking its head at her, it spread its wings and flew away.

As she watched it soar, an unfamiliar sense of calm and certainty filled her. Deep down, she knew it was only a matter of time until she, too, took flight again.

◆

With a present tucked underneath each arm, Maya strolled up to the front door of a private habitat in New Gallilei's residential district.

She interfaced with the door panel. After ringing the buzzer, she gazed up at Jupiter while she waited. In the eight years since she had last set foot on Callisto, trying to reach Triton in record time, terraforming had progressed to the point she no longer needed a breather. She inhaled a deep breath, drawing the fresh air—or more accurately, the recycled and purified atmosphere—into her lungs. The air still seemed thinner than on Triton or Mars, but it wouldn't be long until every planet and major moon in the solar system came to resemble Earth.

When the door slid aside, the young man who answered stared at her with a blank expression.

"Caden Fisher?" Maya asked.

It took Caden a moment to work up the nerve to speak. "It's you."

A toddler came scampering down the hall behind him and clamped onto his leg. "Who is it, Daddy?"

"It's the lady from the news, Joey, the one who brought the ship back home."

Maya shrugged. "That's me."

The boy hopped up and down, chanting, "Too fused, too fused."

"Go back inside and play, please," Caden told his son.

After the boy disappeared inside the house, Caden said, "I saw the welcome home feed, but it's still hard to believe. You've barely aged in eight years."

"I know I'm a little late," Maya said, "but I keep my promises." She held out the presents.

Caden accepted the first gift, a heavy rectangular box. Opening it, he found a pair of shiny new magblades inside. "I haven't bladed in years," he said, shaking his head and smiling. "Thanks."

He took and pulled apart the second box. Smaller than the first, it contained a pebble Jo had collected from the Penphins' home world, Maya explained.

As he held the tiny rock in his hand, marveling at it, he said, "This came from their planet?"

"That's right."

"I don't know what to say."

"Say we're even." Maya winked at him.

Caden's eyes reddened. He blinked, forcing back the tears, and hugged her.

Patting him on the back, she said, "Glad I could make your day."

"Joey's mother passed away right after he was born."

"I'm sorry to hear that," she whispered.

"Things have been hard. Your visit means a lot."

As he pulled away, an object fell out of his pocket and landed on the front step.

Perplexed, Maya stared down at what looked like the thumb-sized device she had found in the ancient tower on Ari's planet. Her confusion grew when she reached into her pocket and found the device still there.

Pointing a trembling finger at the object, she asked, "What's that?"

"The metatoy?" Bending down, Caden tapped the top of the device, powering it up. "Car."

Flabbergasted, Maya watched as the metatoy morphed into a toy race car and drove around in circles. "Where'd you get it?"

His brow dipped. "You can buy it anywhere. Check this out." He picked up the car. "Sword."

The vehicle transformed into a laser sword. Grinning, Caden gripped the handle and whipped the humming blade back and forth. When he slashed her with it, it passed through her chest without causing harm.

"Too fused." She tapped her cheek, trying to figure out how it worked. "Nanite fabrication? Holographics?"

"A little bit of everything, I'd imagine." He raised an eyebrow. "I wouldn't think the acting captain of a starship would find it all that fascinating."

"You wouldn't believe how fascinating I find it."

"Huh." To the sword in his hand, he said, "Off." The play weapon shrank back into its thumb-sized inactive form. "Metatoys were all the rage this past holiday season. The thing cost me a small fortune, but my son begged me for it." He stuck out his lower lip in guilt. "But I won't deny playing with it on occasion."

Maya gave a slow, absent nod.

Pulling her metatoy out of her pocket, she held it out to Caden in her open palm.

"Looks broken." With a chuckle, he asked, "Have you been playing rough with it? It only came onto the market a few months ago, but it looks years old."

"Or older," she mumbled.

"Older?"

"Can I see yours for a second?"

"Sure." He handed her his metatoy.

Holding one device in each hand, she compared them. Caden's toy had a smooth black finish with the text "MetaToy by NanoFun Industries" in big white lettering. In contrast, the exterior of Maya's felt rough, and all the lettering had worn off.

She handed Caden's metatoy back to him, but he refused to take it.

"Keep it," he said, shaking his head. "Yours is busted, and you gave me something—two things, actually. It's the least I can do to repay you."

"Won't your son be upset?"

"Don't worry about him. He plays with the packaging more than the actual toy."

After hesitating for a moment, Maya stuffed both metatoys into her coat pocket. "Thank you. I hope the blades and pebble bring greater joy into your life." She turned to leave.

"Hey, um," Caden said. "It's been a while since I've asked anyone out, but it'd be a shame if we never saw each other again."

Looking back, she messaged him the personal address she had activated upon returning.

"Thanks," he said. "Coffee next week?"

She smiled. "I'd like that."

After saying goodbye three more times, he retreated inside and closed the door.

Maya wandered down the path from the habitat and stopped at the sidewalk leading out of the neighborhood. There she pulled the toys out of her pocket and scrutinized them.

Flipping over the one Caden had given her, she noticed tiny characters depressed into a groove on the back. The letters and numbers looked like a continuous line to the unaided eye. When she magnified them, they turned out to be a unique serial number identifying the unit.

Dirt filled the groove on the back of the metatoy she had found in the Gliese 581 system. Gently, she rubbed the dirt away with her thumb.

The numbers on both units were identical.

Throwing her head back, she stared up at the stars, wondering where—and when—this discovery would take her.

To be continued . . .

The story continues in *Beyond Yesterday*, the third book in Greg Spry's Beyond Saga.

In the decade since returning from the Gliese 581 system, Commander Maya Davis has risen through the ranks while pushing the boundaries of deep space exploration.

When Director Sommerfield finally manages to access the device she found in the ruins on the Penphins' home world, the Interstellar Expeditionary Force grants Maya command of the *Yesterday*, humankind's first space-time vessel.

The fulfillment of a lifelong dream leaves Maya overjoyed. But her elation is crushed when she learns her first command is a suicide mission from which she can never return.

Based on the astounding information revealed by the device, Maya time-shifts the *Yesterday* 200,000 years into the past to confront Zeke's people, beings who wield the ability to control humans like pieces of technology.

Uncovering the truth behind this powerful exospecies' visit to Earth presents her with a no-win paradox. If she thwarts their agenda, the human race she knows might never come to exist. But if she does nothing, she may condemn mankind to a fate worse than extinction.

The first two chapters of *Beyond Yesterday* follow this preview as an extra bonus. Thanks for reading and enjoy!

About the Author

Greg Spry was cloned in the year between the releases of *Star Wars Episode IV: A New Hope* and *Star Trek: The Motion Picture*. Coincidence? He majored in industrial engineering at the University of Wisconsin—Madison before earning a graduate degree in space systems from the Florida Institute of Technology. When he's not writing the next epic sci-fi adventure, he enjoys sampling tasty microbrews, eating hot wings, and cheering on the Wisconsin Badgers and Green Bay Packers. Visit his personal website at www.gregspry.com.

One—Terra Incognita
Aryana, Fomalhaut Trinary System, September 2283 CE

The pitch-black horizon brightened to a deep sapphire, announcing the alien dawn. As Aryana's sun crested the mountains in the distance, the sky exploded into a kaleidoscope of color no artist could hope to capture.

Sitting on the edge of a steep cliff, Commander Maya Davis squinted until her corneal implants, or i-cite, dimmed the blinding glare. The tension in her muscles lessened as the breaking day banished the night. Despite her passion for space exploration, Maya had never quite conquered her fear of the dark.

Maya bit her lip to subdue any lingering fright and leaned back on her forearms. A vast ocean surrounded her, pockmarked by more island chains than she could count. New Jodhpur, the colony the starship *Serendipity* had traveled twenty-five light years from Sol to establish, rested on the largest landmass in sight.

She had teleported out from the colony to this island with its spectacular view, wanting one last glimpse of the breathtaking scenery before shipping out to the next star system.

Goosebumps of elation popped up on her skin. This moment—right here, right now—was why she had joined the Interstellar Expeditionary Force.

Patches of vibrant algae, mold, and bacteria thrived atop every island.

The tough organisms grew in exotic shades of indigo, scarlet, and tangerine, a result of the blue-white light absorbed from the blazing sun.

No grass, bushes, or trees sprouted up from the dirt compacted by this super-Earth's high gravity. The flora and fauna that grew on the terraformed planets and moons of the Sol system could never have survived the radiation here.

The planet's strong gravity had also shaped the low mountains to the west. No snow capped their flat peaks. Instead, the slopes looked as if a painter had dotted them using a rainbow of acrylics.

Aryana's landscape reminded Maya of a simulation she had played as a kid. In the sim, she had skipped among giant gumdrops, candy canes, and lollypops growing straight out of the ground. She had driven mini candy cars along roads of jelly beans and gummy bears. After arriving at a ginger bread house, she had taken a bite out of the car's licorice steering wheel.

Her stomach gurgled. In her rush to beat the sunrise, she had skipped breakfast.

Maya reached out and touched a clump of shiny fuchsia lichen. It felt hard and smooth, as if glazed in a kiln. Nothing here was sweet or edible, of course. Someday, perhaps, the IEF would discover a candy planet. The chances were slim, but it was fun to imagine.

Behind her a soft whirring noise stole her attention.

Looking back over her shoulder, she watched a wormhole three meters in diameter appear above the ground. A shiny black boot emerged from the reflective sphere.

Once the rest of Ensign Nicolaus Kepler had exited the phase portal, it shrank and disappeared behind him.

"There you are, Commander," Kepler said, his speech muffled by the breathing mask he wore over his nose and mouth. The breather filtered the excess carbon dioxide from the air.

After hustling over to her, Kepler stopped and bent forward, panting. Once his breathing evened, he stood up straight and saluted. "Ma'am, I'd like to request a moment of your time."

Maya raised her voice to ensure he heard her clearly through her own breather. "My duty shift doesn't start for another hour, Ensign."

"I apologize, ma'am, but there's a matter that requires your attention."

Maya chuckled at his intrusion. The real reason she had ported out here was to have a moment alone. Even when off duty, colonists and subordinates continued to hound her about construction bot breakdowns, hydroponics malfunctions, climate control glitches, work shift schedules, food ration disputes—the list had no end.

"Very well, Ensign," she said. "At ease."

"Thank you, ma'am." As Kepler relaxed his body, he almost keeled over in exhaustion. "I don't think I'll ever get used to the gravity here, even with the daily gravite injections."

"One-point-three gees are tough on the human body. So what did you want to discuss with me, Ensign?"

Clearing his throat, Kepler spoke in a business-like tone. "The flow rates have decreased in the underground water pipes to the colony's fusion generators."

"How much has the power output dropped?"

"Seven percent at last report, ma'am."

"That's within tolerance, but if it gets any worse, we'll have a problem." Maya tapped her cheek in contemplation. "The AIs might've miscalculated the pressure ratios. I'll take a look at it first thing after breakfast."

Counting on his fingers, Kepler listed off other issues requiring her attention. After reporting the last one, he said, "The city engineers are begging the skipper to leave you behind, Commander."

"They'll manage just fine once we're gone."

"I'm sure they will, ma'am." The view caught Kepler's eye. He shuffled over to the edge of the cliff and stepped out onto a short ledge.

His jaw dropped as he stared out over the ocean. "Too fused . . ." he whispered, conveying his awe with popular slang.

Maya smiled, recalling her own doe-eyed optimism after graduating from the IEF academy. Kepler held the position of operations liaison aboard *Serendipity*. Maya had filled the same posting on *New Horizons* to begin her career. With their shared histories and the ensign's eagerness to take on the multiverse, she had developed a soft spot for him.

She held her palm up to block the overpowering sunlight. Her fingers split the rays of electric blue, creating a lens flare effect.

As Fomalhaut A climbed higher, its warmth turned to scorching heat.

A radiation alert popped up in Maya's i-cite. "The UV dosage is approaching safety limits, Ensign. Enable your bioshield."

Kepler nodded. "Yes, ma'am." The space around his body flickered as emitters woven into his uniform shrouded him in a force field. A fraction of a second later, the distortions disappeared, and the field became invisible.

In her i-cite, Maya activated her shield as well. Her skin cooled.

"I'm amazed the radiation doesn't fry every living thing, ma'am," Kepler said.

"The organisms here thrive on UV light," Maya said. "They absorb it as their main source of energy."

"I guess they never go hungry."

"Scientists used to think that a young, hot star like this one couldn't sustain life. But life has a way of defying expectations."

"Look what the sun's doing to New Jodhpur, ma'am." Kepler pointed at the settlement. "It's like the colony's putting on a lightshow."

The electromagnetic dome that protected the colony glowed a shade of deep violet. The secondary solar panels encircling the perimeter shone like big blue spotlights.

As Maya increased her i-cite zoom, she saw thousands of colonists and bots working to erect habitats, pave roads, and build greenhouses beneath the dome. Children scampered down streets and played in the new park.

"The colony does look like a big festive beacon," Maya said.

Kepler weaved a hand back and forth through the air. "Whoa . . ."

A slight shimmering—like the heat haze above asphalt in the desert—trailed his hand. The glare of the sunlight enhanced the prismatic distortion.

"It's the hypofield that prevents unwelcome guests from downshifting from hyperspace unannounced," Maya said. "The emitters were the first things we installed when we established the colony, along with the teleporter to make supply transport easier."

"Yes, ma'am." Kepler poked his index finger into the shimmering effect twice. "It's so fused." Drawing the bottom half of a semi-circle beneath the two dots, he completed a smiley face.

Maya's smile muscles fought against her frown.

"Also, Commander," Kepler said, "you got a couple messages in the latest transmission."

A mail icon popped up in Maya's i-cite. "You could've pinged me with this info, Ensign."

"Yes, ma'am." Kepler stared up at the sky and shrugged. "But then I wouldn't have had an excuse to come out here."

Maya shook her head.

"Oh, and Commander?" he asked.

"Yes, Ensign?" she responded, deadpan.

Kepler's grin stretched out his thin beard and cheeks. "Happy birthday."

"Thank you, Ensign." Maya opened the mail viewer in her i-cite.

The first message was from her aunt, Vice Admiral Brooke Davis-Sommerfield, who opened by wagging a finger. "Don't expect any singing." With her well-practical scowl, Brooke did her damnedest to project stoicism—it was part of her charm—but Maya knew that deep down her aunt cared more than anyone.

"Happy birthday, Squirt." Brooke referred to Maya by the nickname she had used the first time they met. Maya had been four years old at the time. After living in the Jovian system for six years, Brooke had returned to Earth. Brooke hadn't spoken to her sister, Marie—Maya's mother—since leaving, so Brooke hadn't known about Maya. Brooke had never been fond of children, but after spending time with Maya, the two had developed a bond. When Marie died, Brooke adopted Maya.

"I hope you're doing well out there on the frontier," Brooke continued. "Planning the defense scheme for the first interstellar phase gate is taking up most of my time these days. Well . . . I won't keep you. Be safe, and know that I love you." The vidsim ended.

Short and to the point as always, Maya noted to herself.

The next message originated from her uncle-in-law, Kevin Sommerfield, the director of the Scientific Society of the Interstellar Alliance. Kevin had earned the nickname "Modern Einstein" when he invented the FTL phase drive. Maya thought that if she were to look up the term "introverted scientist" in an encyclopedia, she would find Uncle Kevin's vidpic there. Kevin wore his archetypal lab coat like a second skin, and preferred tinkering in obscurity to the spotlight his invention had cast upon him.

Kevin had always shown her great warmth and understanding—far more than Brooke ever had, even though her aunt loved Maya like a daughter. Maya looked upon Kevin as her father. Her real father cared more about building his financial empire than playing any role in her life. Maya tensed at the thought of her father.

"Maya!" Kevin's virtual headshot shouted so loudly she flinched. "I did it. I got it working."

Maya sat up so quickly that she grew woozy in the high gravity. As she gripped the edge of the high cliff, her heart pounded in anticipation.

During the *New Horizons* mission ten years ago, she had led a team into the ruins on the Penphins' home planet. In a chamber within a tower that had remained undisturbed for 200,000 years, Maya had found a toy that a Mars-based company had invented in the twenty-third century.

"It took ten years," Kevin said, "but I finally managed to piece the metatoy back together." When he had first attempted to activate the toy, its brittle nanostructure had crumbled like a burnt log turning to ash.

He ran his hand through shaggy hair that had turned mostly gray. The stubble on his chin and the bags under his eyes suggested the project had been keeping him up at night. "The metatoy's too fragile to transform anymore, but I was able to transfer its data into the newer toy Caden gave you."

The mention of Caden flashed Maya back to the time she had visited him, after she had returned from the *Horizons* mission. When he had given her the newer toy, she had compared it to the one that was 200,000 years old. The serial numbers had matched.

Maya and Caden had enjoyed a brief romance, one of the few she had experienced in her life. Things had been magical until she received new deployment orders. Caden had wanted her to remain in the Sol system, but Maya wasn't willing to give up exploring interstellar space. They hadn't spoken since she had shipped out.

Thoughts of Caden weighed heavily on her. She knew she had made the right choice. However, she couldn't help but wonder if she would always struggle with romantic relationships, given the demands of her career.

"The newer toy's interface is active," Kevin said, "but I still can't access it."

Maya's shoulders slumped.

"But that's because it's showing a mind-blowing authentication prompt," he said. "Nothing I've tried has worked so far, but I have reason to believe you'll have better luck."

Me? Maya hung on her uncle's next words.

Kevin's thin, bearded face paled. "The prompt keeps flashing the same four-letter word. It's your name, Maya."

She dragged a hand down her face. As incredible as the notion seemed, she had suspected the toy somehow related to her personally. What were the odds of her finding it on a distant planet, then having the present-day version of the toy handed to her only months later?

For a decade she had stewed over the toy's origins. The mystery teased her curiosity like an itch she couldn't scratch. She wanted—no, she needed—to resolve the paradox of the toy's existence. Now, at long last, perhaps—

"Incoming war—"

That was all Maya heard over her neural comm before it cut out.

"Say again, *Serendipity*?" She tried pinging the ship without success.

Bright light whited out her surroundings.

Maya threw her arm up to shield her face. Whipping her head to the side, she clamped her eyes shut.

A concussive blast boomed in the distance, followed by a tremor that jarred the cliff. The ground beneath her shook so violently that she feared the tall, narrow island might collapse.

Her butt slid halfway off the cliff. Gripping the edge, she twisted her body and rolled back, avoiding a fatal plunge.

Maya sensed that the light had faded and cracked open her eyelids. Then the ledge beneath Kepler collapsed.

Flailing his arms in terror, the ensign plummeted. He turned, reached out, and sank his fingers into nearby stable ground. But his digits tore and slipped, lacking the strength to support his weight. In the time it took Maya to lunge a step toward him, he dropped out of sight.

Maya wracked her brain for how to save him. In one-point-three gees, and given the drag from the thick air, he would strike the crashing waves in a few seconds.

Interfacing with the colony's phase teleporter—she pinged the network three times before getting a response—she locked onto the ensign's position and opened a portal below him. Then she whipped her wave gun out of her hip holster. Setting the gun for sonic levitation, she gripped it with both hands, fell backwards, and pointed it up at the sky.

High overhead, the opposite end of the portal burst open. Kepler dropped out of it, limbs flailing.

Maya fired straight up at him. The acoustic levitation effect created by the gun slowed his rate of descent, reducing his momentum.

Kepler came crashing down on top of her before she could roll clear. Their bioshields repelled one another like magnets. Kepler tumbled away in one direction. Maya slid along the dirt in the other. She hissed through gritted teeth as sharp moss poked her in the back.

Her neurosensory implants numbed her pain.

According to her health monitoring sim, the impact hadn't broken or cracked any of her bones. Nor had it crushed or punctured any internal organs.

Kepler howled in pain. His bloodied hands trembled. When clawing to break his fall, he had scraped skin from his fingers and bent back his nails.

Holstering her gun, Maya rushed over and knelt beside him. "Take deep breaths, Ensign." She retrieved an auto-syringe from her belt and jabbed it into his neck. "You're going to be fine."

His shaking and howling ceased as the injected medical nanites took effect. In an hour, the medites would heal his fingertips, making them as good as new.

Maya pushed to her feet. "*Serendipity*, please respond," she mind-spoke. "New Jodhpur, are you receiving me?" The diagnostics in her i-cite detected interference due to neutrino jamming. "We must be under attack."

"The Greys?" Kepler asked as he lay on his back, taking deep breaths. Sweat drenched his pale face.

"Most likely."

"Like the attack near Epsilon Eridani."

Maya shivered at the memory of the horrific incident she had barely survived. "Let's hope not." Hurrying to the edge of the cliff, she stared out over the ocean and magnified her surroundings via her i-cite. Towering waves beat against the shorelines of every island.

She caught sight of a science bot that had landed on a small island nearby. Oblivious to what had happened, it went about its business collecting soil and lifeform samples.

"Did a Hyperflare blank a saucer, ma'am?" Kepler asked.

"I don't think so," Maya said. "Based on the garbled comm, I'd wager one of our 'flares intercepted a warhead meant for the colony." The shield dome surrounding the settlement flickered.

Maya rapped her finger against her cheek and thought out loud. "With the hypofield in place, the Greys couldn't have shifted anywhere near the planet. They must've fired the warhead from long distance—but they also had to have known one of our fighters would shoot it down. The warhead detonated too far away to threaten the colony, which suggests New Jodhpur wasn't the target."

She snapped her fingers in realization. "The piping."

With the color returning to his face, Kepler forced himself to sit up. "What about the piping, Commander?"

Maya turned to him. "The fusion generators supply power to the rad shield, but you said the water flow had slowed."

"Yes, ma'am."

"The Greys must've snuck onto the planet and plugged up the plumbing. Then they force us to blow up their warhead to divert our attention." *But divert us from what?*

"If the water levels drop too low, the generators will shut down. The rad shield will go offline."

"Which will force us to evacuate the colony. They know we couldn't get people off the surface quickly enough. With the comm down, it would take hours to get everyone into the underground shelters."

"Plus the civilians don't have bioshields, ma'am."

"People are going to die." Maya stomped her boot. "Every time we establish a new colony this far out, they try to drive us back."

Holding his tender hands close to his body, Kepler asked, "The IEF doesn't know why, Commander?"

"For a while, we thought we might be straying into their territory. But attacks against ships and settlements in different directions from Sol have cast doubt on that theory."

The ensign gave an absent nod.

Maya folded her arms. "The Greys lurked behind the scenes throughout our history, never destroying or conquering primitive humans. Then, three years ago, they gave up centuries of hiding and attacked the research outpost near Epsilon Eridani. We still don't know why."

With a series of pixelated flashes, the colony's rad shield tinted to a lighter shade of lavender.

"The shield's failing." Maya's muscles tensed. "If I were the Greys, I'd send in a team to finish the job. I need to get back."

"How, Commander?" Kepler asked.

Staring down at the turbulent ocean, Maya considered using her wave gun to levitate all the way to the colony. She had used the gun to slow her fall or cross short distances on plenty of occasions, but New Jodhpur rested a kilometer away. Theoretically, firing a burst every few seconds at the right angles would allow her to hop all the way there. But a slight miscalculation on any shot could send her plummeting to her death. She decided it wouldn't work in practice.

"I can't ping the ship or the colony teleporter because of the jamming," Maya said. "I was lucky to get a signal through to save you before losing all contact."

Biting her lip, she whipped her head around, searching for something that could help her.

The breeze picked up, flinging spores into her face. Maya's breather protected her nose and mouth, keeping her from sneezing, but her eyes itched and swelled. *Not now.*

With a thought Maya instructed her bio-implants to release antihistamine into her bloodstream. *You'd think modern medicine would've come up with a cure for allergies by now.* As the irritation in her eyes faded, she spotted the science bot.

The bot was taking off from the island. She tried to ping it, but the jamming blocked her attempts.

Pulling out her wave gun, Maya toggled it to sonic tractor mode, aimed at the airborne bot, and fired.

The bot slowed in its flight toward the colony until it stopped in midair. Shaking, its hyper-conducting magnets fought the unseen push-pull.

"Come on, come on." Maya gripped the handle with both hands.

Unable to resist the high-low pressure stream created by the gun, the bot slid through the air toward her.

A minute later, she had yanked the bot close enough to get a signal through to it. Interface menus popped up in her i-cite, giving her control of the bot as it flew to her.

When the bot reached the island, she instructed it to jettison the samples it had collected, lightening its load.

It wasn't until the bot was hovering over her head that her pulse quickened.

Kepler rubbed his neck—gently, given his tender fingers. "Ma'am, you don't really plan to. . . ."

Maya shrugged to hide her trepidation. "It's rated for up to a hundred kilos of return samples." Stuffing her gun into her holster, she stared at the bot. "Then again, that's per standard gravity. In one-point-three gees—"

"You might be close to maxing it out, ma'am."

Narrowing her eyes at him, Maya said, "Young ensigns would be wise not to comment on the weight of superiors."

Kepler winced.

Maya rubbed her palms together, then sucked in a deep breath and instructed the bot to descend to within arm's length. "Sit tight and heal up. Your bioshield and hydro-protein pills should keep you going. I'll be back for you—hopefully."

The ensign frowned.

Maya grasped the manipulator arms on either side of the bot and told it to rise. Increasing power to its levitator magnets, the bot lifted her off her feet. She could feel the force of the bot's magnetic resistance pushing against and through her. As Maya's feet flew over the edge of the cliff, she gulped and tightened her grip.

"Good luck," Kepler yelled from behind her.

Despite the angry sea below her dangling boots, Maya ordered the bot to descend toward the water's surface. A hundred meters out from the colony, she had dropped to only twice her height above the water. Her sore arms, weakening fingers, and sweaty palms strained to keep their hold on the bot's manipulators.

Feeling her left hand slipping, she adjusted it to get a better grip. She lost her grasp, and her left hand slipped free. With her heartbeat on rapid fire mode, she squeezed with her right hand to keep from falling.

The uneven weight caused the bot to teeter and flip on its side. With its magnetic emitters no longer pointed toward the planet, it dropped straight down.

Her face smacked the water first. As she completed the belly flop, the surface tension pummeled her stomach like a roundhouse punch. Stinging pain coursed throughout Maya's body as she plunged into the frigid ocean.

Two—Moribund
New Mars, Alpha Centauri System, November 2283 CE

Two officers saluted Vice Admiral Brooke Davis-Sommerfield as they passed her in the corridor.

Returning the gesture, Brooke bounded toward Base MAVEN's command center in the half-standard gravity of New Mars.

She stopped in front of a window that ran the length of the corridor. Alpha Centauri B, the star New Mars orbited, descended toward the cratered surface, setting the horizon ablaze in shades of amber and marigold. High overhead, Alpha Centauri A shined brighter than a full moon in Earth's sky.

The rocky landscape of New Mars filled Brooke with a longing for simpler times, before the Interstellar Alliance had terraformed every major planet and moon in the Sol system. Brand new habitat domes, each larger than a sporting arena, comprised Hues colony. The curvature of the shiny domes reflected the sunlight from the binary stars.

When none of Brooke's obnoxious, eager-to-please aides came rushing after her, she allowed her shoulders to relax. The higher she had risen in the ranks over the decades, the more difficult it had become to find time alone—and she lived for her solitude.

Absently, she ran her fingers over the three stars affixed above the left breast of her IEF uniform. Her rank as a vice admiral, duties as commander-in-chief of IEF Aerospace, and recent posting to MAVEN had kept her out of a cockpit for far too long.

"Your life's too valuable to risk out in the field," IEF High Admiral Westerberg told her before she left Sol. "We need you coordinating fleet maneuvers and planning defense strategies behind the lines, and the phase gate is top priority." Normally, an officer with the rank of commander would oversee the base, but Westerberg had placed her in charge due to the recent attacks by the Greys.

At first Brooke had seethed with anger over the assignment. She perceived it as a blatant attempt by Westerberg to keep her grounded. But after cooling down, she had seen the logic in his decision.

Pangs of nostalgia washed over her as she recalled her days as a combat pilot. Had it been ten years since she last flew a star fighter as part of any meaningful sortie? *Not since Gliese 581.* She scrunched her nose in disgust.

As if being relegated to a desk job hadn't been bad enough, her doctor and her husband had sided with Westerberg because of her health.

Shooting pain pierced her left arm and leg. She shook out her limbs until it subsided.

She focused her attention on the mountainous dome that dwarfed all the others. The Momma Dome, as the residents of Hues colony had nicknamed it, housed the classified energy source that powered the interstellar gate connecting Mars and New Mars across four light years. Despite being married to the man who had invented the gate, Brooke didn't know what resided beneath the dome.

But such details didn't affect her duty. She had taken command of MAVEN to protect the phase gate during its shakedown tests. Soon, she would be out of here and searching for ways back into a cockpit.

Brooke's mind grew heavy, and her muscles tensed. Drawing in a breath, she shook off the dizziness and nausea.

A flashing icon in her i-cite indicated an incoming message from her husband, Kevin. With a mental click, she played the vidsim. Kevin had recorded it hours before driving through the Mars end of the gate in the Sol system.

Kevin's headshot appeared in her i-cite. "Hey, Brooke." Sitting in the passenger seat of a rover, he ran a hand through shaggy gray hair. "I've informed Base MAVEN and Hues colony of our departure through official channels, but I wanted to send you a personal note before we leave. I know you think I should let someone else be the first to traverse the gate, but I couldn't pass up the opportunity."

He folded his arms and grinned. "It was never very fair that you got to experience hyperspace before me, using the drive I invented. So I'm stealing the spotlight this time."

A hint of a smile crossed Brooke's face. As much as she hated to see him risk his life, she would be the galaxy's worst hypocrite if she faulted him for it.

The vidsim switched to his view, ahead of the rover. Across a plain covered by rust-red dirt and patches of olive green grass rested the Mars end of the gate. The top half of a wormhole with a twenty-meter radius towered above the ground like a sun that refused to set. Around the circumference of the wormhole churned the salmon-pink hue of hyperspace. Brooke couldn't see the generator or nacelles, though. The machinery that maintained the gate resided kilometers away and in orbit, far out of sight.

Pointing at the gate, Kevin said, "We can't see New Mars, of course. That would be the equivalent of seeing a day-and-a-half into the future, which hasn't happened yet. Once Hues opens the gate on the exit end, the people there should be able to see us driving toward them."

Brooke glanced at the time in the bottom corner of her i-cite. Kevin had entered the gate over a day ago. Five hours remained until he emerged.

"Due to the time dilation effect," Kevin said, "the trip will be as quick as stepping through a door for me. But you'll have to wait thirty-seven hours to see my bright, smiling face. Once we finish this trial run, we'll be able to start sending colonists through to fill those domes."

The view switched back to Kevin. "Well, I need to get going. Try not to stress about my safety. I'll be there before you know it. Love—"

Before the vidsim ended, her right arm spasmed. She gripped her wrist to hold it still and sucked in deep, even breaths.

Just as the shakes appeared to have subsided, her body convulsed.

She lost all sensation below her waist and then fell.

As her shoulder thumped against the cold floor, she shuddered from head to toe.

Her vision and mind blurred, and she blacked out.

When Brooke awoke, she was lying on the floor where she had fallen. The health monitoring sim in her i-cite confirmed she had suffered another seizure due to the degeneration of motor neurons. Her implants had pumped meds into her bloodstream to subdue the seizure and relieve the pain, but they could do nothing to reverse the damage.

"There is no cure." The words of her physician echoed in her head.

The physician had given Brooke the bad news during her last visit. "Your nervous system has degraded due to the, shall we say, 'recreational activities' you engaged in in your youth," the pompous shrew had informed her. The physician hadn't really been a pompous shrew, but

Brooke sometimes had a tendency to blame the messenger.

Sitting on the edge of the exam table, Brooke snorted at the physician's euphemism. "Just say it, Doc. I was a drug addict, and now I'm paying the price for my spark use."

Kevin had only made things worse by saying, "You're sixty now. Few fighter pilots are still flying at your age."

"There might not be very many, but there are some," Brooke had countered. "Besides, sixty is the new twenty."

"But you're not a healthy sixty-year-old."

"There's no reason why a few faint wrinkles and gray hairs should keep me grounded."

"You're not facing the reality of your condition."

Brooke had scoffed in disgust. "I feel just fine."

Damn it all. She tensed in frustration as she remained lying on the floor in the corridor.

Once she regained feeling in her lower body, she felt warm and wet in the groin area. *Really?* She told her uniform to self-clean.

A young officer came bounding down the hallway as she was sitting up. When he noticed her, he rushed right over. "Are you okay, Admiral?" He bent down to help her stand.

"I'm fine, Lieutenant." Brooke waved him away.

"You look awfully pale, ma'am," the lieutenant said. "I'll comm for a medic."

"Cancel that comm." Brooke hopped to her feet. Piercing pain shot through her skull. She kept her mouth closed and gritted her teeth, suppressing any outward sign of the pain. "I sat down to rest for a moment. Something I ate must not have agreed with me. I've flushed my system and feel better."

"Are you sure, ma'am?" The lieutenant tilted his head, looking less than convinced.

"Quite sure." She glowered up at him, donning her best scowl. Despite standing over a head taller than her, he shrank back. After hesitating, he turned and continued back in the direction he had been heading.

"And, Lieutenant," she called after him.

The officer stopped and turned. "Yes, Admiral?"

Swallowing the guilt and embarrassment, she ordered, "Keep this to yourself."

"Understood, ma'am." He walked off.

◆

Brooke sat cross-legged at the situation table in MAVEN's command center. Thirty minutes remained until Kevin would emerge from the gate.

Lieutenant Emilia Tereshkova approached her. The young woman of no more than twenty-five had arrived on base as Brooke's chief aide the week before.

Tereshkova was a pilot with a specialty in starship helm operations. She had graduated first in her class from the academy three years ago, with commendations from both the Aerospace and Fleet divisions. Brooke had approved the posting, but she had yet to understand why an officer with such impressive credentials had requested such a role.

Tereshkova carried a tray from the officer's mess. "Your lunch, Admiral," she stated with a grating Russian accent. "Today, I wanted to bring it to you personally."

The sight of the travel box of Fruity Planets atop the tray dismissed Brooke's concerns, at least for the moment.

With a rare smile, she accepted the tray. "I can't remember the last time I . . . wherever did you find it?"

"The *Magellan* had a few boxes in stock, ma'am," Tereshkova said. "Before the starship deployed, I had them sent down."

When Brooke tapped the box with a finger, it morphed into a bowl. Planet-shaped marshmallows floated in the milk that filled it. "How did you know this was my favorite food?"

Very matter-of-factly, Tereshkova stated, "It's in the public record, ma'am." Black bangs dangled above her penetrating eyes. Brooke approved of her no-nonsense frown.

"You must've done some digging." Grabbing the spoon extruded by the box during its transformation, Brooke scooped up her first morsel and inserted it into her mouth. As the sugary cereal touched her tongue, she closed her eyes and basked in the sweetness. Her skin tingled in delight.

"No, ma'am. I've known since I was a kid."

Brooke blinked. "I'm curious, Lieutenant," she said after swallowing. Setting the spoon down on the tray, she asked, "Why would an accomplished pilot ask to serve on my staff?"

Tereshkova nodded. Apparently, she had been expecting the question. "I put in for this posting to shadow the greatest pilot of them all. I've got the rest of my life left for flying."

Brooke didn't know what to say. She had never excelled at showing gratitude, affection, or any other positive emotion.

Tereshkova stood at attention, staring at her.

"Thank you, Lieutenant," Brooke said. "You're dismissed."

Tereshkova saluted, turned, and exited the command center.

As Brooke finished her cereal, the chatter in the command center increased. Base personnel had begun implementing the gate defense strategy.

"Now deactivating the hypofield," the defense systems officer reported from a nearby control station. "All satellite and surface emitters have been disabled. The field is down."

The liaison to the phase port said, "Hues is now initializing this side of the gateway."

"If an attack's going to come, it'll be any moment," Brooke spoke up. "Stay alert."

Every officer in the room sounded off, "Yes, Admiral."

"No blips or gravity distortions detected," the remote sensing officer confirmed. "The threat board remains clear."

Brooke tapped her fingernails on the edge of the situation table. With each passing moment, her heart pumped more rapidly.

From the opposite end of the sit-table, the flight controller said, "The *Spitzer*, *Chandra*, and *Magellan* are now deploying fighter groups Epsilon, Zeta, Omicron."

Three-dimensional renderings of the starships in orbit appeared above the table. Thousands of miniature PF-77 Hyperflares swarmed from the ships. The phase fighters flashed, disappeared into hyperspace, and blinked back into reality, scattering into their assigned orbits.

To display the tangible renderings, or rends, emitters built into the table created tiny projection wormholes. The wormholes delivered nanites into the air that morphed into tangible shapes that a person could manipulate on a whim.

Brooke summoned a rend of the gateway promenade in the Hues colony phase port. With a shift of her irises, she rotated the rend, studying it from different angles.

The mini-promenade resembled an antique model train set she had once seen in a museum. Enlarging the rend, she observed a handful of technicians, officers, and civilian officials standing near the semi-circular gate. A crowd of several hundred people, the current populace of the colony, had gathered beyond the cordoned-off arrival area.

A rend of New Mars the size of a beach ball replaced the promenade above the sit-table. Ice covered the poles of the maroon world. An intricate latticework encircled the planet, representing the network of satellites and platforms. If an unidentified object violated the grid, the AIs would alert the fighters in orbit, which could shift on location in under a second.

However, space was vast. No defense grid yet conceived could guarantee the immediate neutralization of a threat, given the immense volume of space around a planet.

"This strategy still makes me nervous, Brooke," Admiral Westerberg had told her during the final defense planning session at IEF Command on Triton. "With the hypofield offline, a hundred times as many ships still wouldn't be enough. An enemy fighter could downshift anywhere and strike the colony before our units can react."

Brooke had given a slow nod. "I wish there was a better way, sir. All we can do is deploy our surface assets near the colony and base. With our orbital units, we cover the maximum volume of space without spreading them too thin. Then we cross our fingers and hope that no attack comes during the few minutes the hypofield is down."

Westerberg had interlocked his fingers and banged them against the conference table. "If only we didn't need to take the field offline."

"Our fighters and starships can shift in the presence of the field," another admiral had said. "Any spacecraft with the algorithm can circumvent it. Why can't the gate?"

"Unfortunately, even the slightest gravimetric fluctuation can collapse the gate," Brooke had replied, paraphrasing her husband's long-winded explanation. "The precision and power required to traverse the four-light-year distance are too great."

Shifting in her seat in MAVEN's command center, Brooke studied the rends. Her right hand shook until she dispersed meds into her system. For a moment, she feared the onset of another seizure, but the episode passed.

"Hues indicates one minute to arrival," the port liaison announced.

Sitting up straighter, Brooke switched to the rend of the promenade and magnified it.

The liaison said, "Arrival imminent."

The wormhole in the phase port wavered and rippled.

A hover rover emerged. Its boxy chassis flew out onto the promenade as if it had exited a garage.

As the rover settled down onto the pavement, two others joined it.

Kevin stepped out of the first vehicle. The lanky scientist's shaggy hair and lab coat blew in the artificial breeze. He waved to the crowd and all around, knowing Brooke was watching.

"Hues has begun gateway shutdown procedures," the liaison said.

"Reinitializing the hypofield," the defense systems officer announced.

Blowing out a prolonged breath in relief, Brooke sank back in her chair.

The rend of the promenade shrank away, replaced by a sector of space above the planet. Five of the hypofield generator satellites exploded in brief flashes of light.

Brooke jumped out of her seat.

Toggling to an overhead view of the cratered surface, the threat table showed three other generators exploding. Emergency klaxons howled throughout the base.

"Eight of the field generators have been destroyed," the defense officer yelled. "The losses have created a gap in the field near Hues colony."

The remote sensing officer shouted, "I'm detecting hundreds—no, thousands—of wormhole signatures in high orbit."

"Confirmed. Approximately two thousand dish-shaped fighter craft have appeared along with five motherships."

A rend of the enemy fleet popped up above the sit-table.

"The Greys," Brooke muttered. "Order the fleet to fire at will."

"All orbital units, fire at will," the weapons officer repeated over the comm.

Relativistic beaming emitters, heavy particle cannons, and lasers fired toward the Greys' fleet from the starships and platforms in orbit.

Without the hypofield to constrain the enemy saucers to conventional propulsion, they blinked away in rapid succession, upshifting to hyperspace. All friendly fire passed through the empty space they had vacated.

The saucers downshifted everywhere around the colony, littering the sky.

"All fighter groups and surface units," Brooke ordered, "engage the enemy."

Damn it, she thought with a scowl. The Greys had waited until right before the hypofield reinitiated to destroy the generators, which were most vulnerable during their power-up cycles.

Leaning over the sit-table, Brooke observed the battle on dozens of rends. Hyperflares materialized on the tails of saucers, making strafing runs on the colony. Spacecraft fired relativistic particles, streams of plasma, and zigzagging seekers at each other as they blinked in and out of reality. More often than not, friendly fighters blanked bandits before the latter did any harm. But every now and then, a projectile or beam pelted the shield dome protecting the colony, tinting the dome crimson.

Brooke kept watch on the promenade in her i-cite. Kevin and his welcoming committee lay on the ground, covering their heads with their arms.

As she studied the combat zone, a pit formed in her stomach. Her fighters were only achieving a two-to-one kill ratio. Also, the Greys seemed to be concentrating their assault on the west and north sides of the colony even though the phase port and generator dome were located at the south end.

Two explanations for the puzzling strategy struck her. Either the Greys had determined—incorrectly—that the colony's defenses were weakest farthest from the phase port, or—

"Second wave downshifting in low orbit," the remote sensing officer reported. "Two-thousand additional saucers on approach from the east."

The first wave was a diversion.

Brooke redeployed her forces to account for the latest enemy wave. As the battle continued to unfold, she squeezed her seat's armrests. Her units had outnumbered the first wave. However, the second wave had doubled the number of enemy forces. Considering the low kill ratio, the IEF stood a significant chance of losing.

To be precise, the tactical AIs predicted a thirty-seven percent possibility of defeat. That was much too high for her liking, so she issued additional orders.

All throughout the combat zones, Hyperflares struggled to blank saucers. Dogfights dragged on for seconds. Given the speed at which orbital hyper-combat took place, seconds might as well have been eons.

A tremor rocked the base. Then, on the east side of the colony, an intense flash signaled a massive explosion.

"Enemy forces have scored a direct hit," the defense officer shouted. "The colony's force field is failing in sections."

The sight of her husband cowering on the ground pushed Brooke to a decision.

She shot to her feet. In her i-cite, she ordered the hangar bay to prep her ride.

As she bounded away from the table, everyone in the command center stared at her.

Brooke stopped. "I'm going out there." Pointing at the next highest ranking officer, she ordered, "Commander, take charge until I return."

The commander gave a reluctant nod. "Yes . . . yes, ma'am."

"You'll do fine," she said, softening her tone. "You'll all do fine. Just focus and do your jobs." Brooke bolted out of the command center before she or anyone else had a chance to question her decision.

Halfway to the hangar bay, Lieutenant Tereshkova caught up to Brooke, matching her brisk pace through the corridor.

"I take it you plan to deploy, Admiral?" Tereshkova asked in her even tone.

"Word travels fast, I see," Brooke said without breaking stride.

"It's my job to know what're up to and attend to your needs, ma'am."

Brooke skidded to a halt. As her subordinate did the same, Brooke whirled on her. "You mean someone ordered you to keep an eye on me. Who? Westerberg?"

For once, Tereshkova hesitated. "Um, yes, ma'am. The high admiral said that in an event such as this one, I should respectfully request that you reconsider coordinating our defenses from your assigned post."

Throwing her arms up into the air, Brooke growled under her breath. *I haven't been grounded by a flight surgeon. Westerberg wouldn't order me to stay out of a cockpit without medical justification, so he's assigned me a damned babysitter.*

"Request denied." Brooke broke into a near-sprint toward the fighter bay. "We're getting pasted out there. Our forces need a competent field commander or else we might lose this one."

"I understand ma'am," Tereshova said, chasing after her. "May I ask if you've chosen a dash-two?"

"A wing mate will only slow me down."

"Ma'am, the regs prohibit solo deployments. All fighter teams must operate in pairs."

"I know the regulations, Lieutenant."

"Of course, ma'am. What I'm saying is that I'd be honored to fly with you, if you'll have me."

Brooke and Tereshkova stepped into a lift.

As it ascended, Brooke said, "I was blanking bandits long before you were born, kid. I'm afraid trying to keep up with me will only get you killed."

"I know I'm young, Admiral, but I'm an accomplished pilot. I flew against the Greys near Procyon—"

"And received a special commendation for it," Brooke said, folding her arms.

"Yes, ma'am."

After staring at the insistent officer for a moment, Brooke sighed in resignation. "I can't very well ignore regulations, can I?"

Within seconds after launching from MAVEN in a Hyperflare, Brooke had torched two saucers, and Tereshkova had blanked a third.

The fear and uncertainty that had gripped Brooke had given way to shudders of exhilaration. Between the feel of the gravgel pressing in on her and the tightening of her muscles during a high-gee turn, she knew she was back where she belonged.

MAVEN's flight controller, all starships in orbit, every fighter, and the planetary tactical network each synced telemetry to Brooke's Hyperflare. The suite of AIs that operated her fighter's subsystems processed, prioritized, and fed the data into her subconscious so that she didn't have to think. "Omicron, alter course to sector two-oh-nine and deploy in a battle spread formation," she shouted after identifying a weak spot in the second wave's formation.

"Epsilon group," Brooke barked over the comm net, "stop engaging in solo combat and work with your wing mates." Teamwork had become a lost art, given the frequent blinking in and out of reality by modern pilots.

Tereshkova shifted her Hyperflare kilometers behind Brooke's fighter and dispatched a saucer that had been heading in their direction. Brooke realized she had been wrong to try to head out alone.

"New target coordinates, Ensign," Brooke said.

"Received, ma'am," Tereshkova said. "Lead the way."

Brooke upshifted her craft to hyperspace, tracking four saucers harassing a pair of rookies in low orbit.

The moment her fighter emerged in normal space, her neurotronics read her intentions and fed them to her tactical AI. Targeting brackets auto-locked onto each of the bandits. Her Hyperflare unleashed volleys of seekers at each saucer before the thought to launch them entered her conscious mind.

Propelled by three-dimensional thruster arrays, the seekers darted up, down, left, right, backwards, and forwards through the vacuum of space faster than any spacecraft could maneuver.

A seeker struck one of the saucers before it could upshift. The explosive impact threw the saucer into a violent spin. Smoke trailed the craft as it shot off, helplessly, on a trajectory away from the planet.

The other three saucers blinked away into hyperspace before the seekers reached them. Having missed their targets, each seeker disarmed and followed paths away from friendly forces.

Prompted by tactical data and compelled by instinct, Brooke yawed her fighter one-hundred-and-eighty degrees and flew backwards.

As one of the three remaining saucers appeared in front of her craft's nose, she fired her particle cannons, scoring multiple direct hits. The bandit's shielding glowed bright red, and the craft exploded. Then bogey number three re-entered normal space above Brooke's fighter, diving straight at her.

Tereshkova's Hyperflare swooped into reality on Brooke's port side and forced the saucer to dart away. With a barrage of seekers, the ensign blew the bogey to pieces.

With the fighter wing under Brooke's direct command, the kill ratio increased. The Greys' numbers had thinned, and they were scattering more than attacking. The tide was turning in the IEF's favor.

"I recommend we fall back to base, Admiral," Tereshkova suggested. At low thrust, their Hyperflares flew a few kilometers above the surface on the outskirts of the colony and combat zone.

Brooke opened her mouth, intending to agree.

A warhead struck the ventral fuselage of her fighter before she could speak the words. With her energy harness clamping her into her seat, the impact drove her stomach up into her throat. Her brain pressed up into her skull, threatening to burst. Hit off center, the Hyperflare spun like a gyroscope with little air resistance to slow its somersaults.

"Admiral!" Tereshkova shouted over the comm net.

Brooke reached out to the fighter's AIs with her mind, but the warhead had knocked them offline.

As the Hyperflare tumbled, she stretched her hands out for the auxiliary control grips, hoping to manually fire her stabilizing thrusters.

She convulsed as she lost all motor control. Every muscle in her body felt like it was extending past the limit and snapping back again and again. Knifing pain pierced every part of her body.

Brooke howled in agony and vomited, spraying her helmet face shield as her fighter slammed into the planet's surface.